Advisory

This dark tale is for mature readers (age 18+).

It explores sensitive subject matter, including scenes of graphic violence, sexual situations, and disturbing imagery, language, and concepts that readers may find unsettling. Themes of misogyny, domestic abuse, and sexual assault may be triggering for some readers. <u>Proceed with caution.</u>

All people, places, cultures, histories, traditions, and religious practices in this book are fictional.

ISBN: 978-1-7356769-2-0

First Print Edition – October 31st, 2020

Cover Art and Illustrations by:

Micah Chaim Thomas

Printed By:

Lost Boys Press

www.lostboyspress.com

Dedicated to Chad, 16, who dreamed of one day writing a book about monsters.

So long as the Grim Seed spoils the earth, you, too, shall carry its burdens.

— Sister Dirt

God is dead and no one cares
If there is a hell, I'll see you there

— Trent Reznor

It is when we notice the dirt that God is most present in us; it is the very sign of His presence.

— C.S. Lewis

I
Orphan Rock

1978

1.

Chipped dishes in the sink. Red, frothy mold floated on top of half-scrubbed pans. Fat maggots squirmed around the forgotten edges of the basin. Cigarette butts formed clumpy islands in cups of muddy water. Horseflies tapped on the windowsill. A baby mewled from the nursery at the back of the old stone-stacked house nestled at the base of Orphan Rock.

"Coming, Little Snake!" Esther rubbed her bloodshot eyes.

The teenager hunched over a propane stove. A bottle of milk warmed in a battered pot. Her greasy blonde hair stuck to her dirty cheeks in clumps. She squeezed her knees together when a drip of water trickled down her bruised inner thigh beneath her only nightgown. "No, goddammit! Not now."

She leaned against the old icebox and stole a breath. With her hand resting on her pregnant belly, her blue eyes tracked a bark scorpion skittering across the far wall.

He put a pig in you.

You make pig babies, don't you?

Just breathe, pigfucker.

She closed her eyes.

Minister's sun-chiseled face appeared in the warmth

behind her eyelids. Tan skin, chestnut eyes, shaggy hair that curled at the ends. That Burt Reynolds smile.

I'm going to run away with you someday.

Two pinkies entwined through a rusty cage.

The air chilled when a hidden door—one of many—to The Dark tore open. A screaming rip in the shadows that two bloody hands pulled open.

Snarl, the watchful boy wrapped in barbed wire, slithered through the obsidian portal. The blood that crusted the edges of his thousand cuts was deep purple, and his one working eye was black and golden like fire on oil. His tattered Sunday best rotted away years ago, leaving a walking wound of a boy wearing only scabs and rags to hide his shameful parts.

"What's the matter? *You feeling down?*"

"The baby's *fucking* coming!"

Snarl didn't blink. "You sure about that, Coyote?"

She pointed at the puddle of water around her black-bottomed feet.

"Well, if it ain't my favorite Injun come to celebrate my most sacred of birthdays!"

Minister's drunken grin stretched for miles. He opened his arms and gave Wallace "Macho" Machado a brotherly hug, and it was no minor feat. The Ghost River man stood over six feet tall with a stout chest. Unlike Minister, who wore the same pair of jeans every day of the week and a soiled mechanic's shirt with his name embroidered over the breast pocket in the best lettering Esther could sew, Officer Machado patrolled Ghost River in a crisp tribal police uniform.

"Budweiser, Macho?"

"Sure, Mona. Draft."

"You off duty? I fucking hope so."

"Am now." Macho unclipped the badge from his brown

button-up and set it on the bar. Mona delivered his beer.

"Thank Christ. I thought you came on official business."

"Beer first with the birthday boy." Macho winked.

"Fuck, yes. I will accept your plan of action, deputy."

They toasted.

"How old are you now? Twenty-three?"

The skinny man shrugged. "Sounds about right. You'd think I'd fucking know, considerin' every birthday I celebrate in Ghost River is a goddamn miracle with no guarantee of another."

Macho laughed into his glass. "You're telling me."

Despite seeing double already, Minister lit a cigarette and pointed at a picture framed across the bar. A group of Ghost River men in military fatigues posed in front of a combat chopper. He squinted to make out the young, familiar face of his best friend sitting in the open cockpit. "Look at that handsome devil hero right there," he said, smoke billowing out of his nostrils. "Soaring like a fucking eagle. *Over all them green jungles!*" He knocked the ashtray over, didn't care. "I ain't ever flown before. Don't think I'd have the stomach for it anyway." The holy man from Orphan Rock withered for a few seconds, but a sip of whiskey perked him right back up. "What kind of chopper is that again? I know you've told me before, but I don't listen to redskins…"

"Bell UH-1. The Huey."

"The Huey! The Booey! You flew that fucking whirlybird, didn't ya? Who cares what it's called? Names don't mean shit." Minister laughed, his contention cutting. The years Macho left for 'Nam were lonely ones in Ghost River, and it still stung like a scorpion prick when he dwelled on them dark days. "I bet you blew them funny rice hats right off their heads."

Officer Machado rolled his eyes. "You're drunk as shit."

"Fair assessment." Minister clicked his tongue and pointed at Macho's nose.

"Frankly, I'm surprised she's letting you out tonight. I didn't think you'd be here. But where else would you be?"

Minister tapped his cigarette into the spilled ashtray.

"Which *she* we talking about here?"

"How about Esther? The only decent woman in your life."

"Esther!" Minister rubbed his brow in weariness. "Well, she's about as fun as a heart attack these days. Pregnant. *Very pregnant.* Probably watching television. Ever since we got that new antennae, we're picking up the local channels in Phoenix. Can't get her off the couch without begging. All day long…game shows and soap operas. Never a football game on."

"I don't know how you do it." Macho's voice barely loud enough to cut through the jukebox noise. "Leaving her alone out there. Markus too. That land. *That goddamn land…*" He caught himself. "Sorry, I'm still in *serve and protect* mode."

"It's all right. We don't choose who we are, but we got to be those people anyway." Minister pointed at his empty whiskey glass. Mona lifted her eyebrow.

"Didn't I cut you off?"

Wallace chuckled. "If not, you should."

"Come on now!" Minister slapped the bar top. "Ain't no harm in having a few drinks on your birthday! It's almost the last call anyway!" He adopted a strange accent and swung his bent elbows with drunken swagger. "*I'm desertfolk, and I shall have my fucking whiskey or suffer ye!*"

Mona's expression begged Officer Machado for help.

"I wouldn't if I were you."

She smiled nervously. "Sorry, Minister—"

"One more shot ain't going to hurt nobody, 'specially me! I was never gonna live long anyway." The holy man's eyes sparkled in the smoky bar. Two golden coins flashed in the black ripple of a wishing well. Mona cocked her head a little to better see the angels in his snakeshine.

"Sure thing," she said. "One more for the road."

Macho slapped the bar and let out a laugh. "*Jesus, man!* If it weren't your birthday, I'd arrest you."

Armed with a fresh pour in his glass, Minister toasted the Wagon Wheel's bartender with a sly wink. "I don't care what Macho says about you, Mona. You're good people." He swallowed the liquor. "Hard to find in Ghost River."

"Well, you've had enough now, *Birthday Boy*." Macho signaled Mona for the tab. "I don't plan on putting this badge back on tonight to pull your ass out of a ditch."

Minister's gaze drifted across the room to an attractive Ghost River woman shooting pool by her lonesome. Her brown eyes settled on the nine-ball, lining up the perfect shot. A chalked cue pumped between the tight loop of her finger. In. Out. In. Out.

Crack!

"The tribal council needs a favor."

Minister perked up. "It pay? I need the money."

"Consider it rent. Maybe a little on top."

"Let's hear it."

Officer Machado looked over both shoulders, scanning the smoky bar for open ears. When the coast cleared, he began, "The Commissioner of the Bureau of Indian Affairs is planning a visit to Ghost River next week. After what happened at Pine Ridge, the feds are in a major titty-twist about tribes stockpiling weapons, building militias, misappropriating funds…the list goes on. It's a real concern right now in DC. They want a peek in our books, and that's just not a workable scenario."

Minister smiled darkly. "I bet not."

"Resources and contingencies matter to the council. We've spent a long time gathering our rainy-day fund." Macho retrieved two twenties and a five-dollar bill from his faux leather wallet. "They want to discuss a way forward. One that benefits all of us, *even her*. Meeting's tomorrow, er…*today*. Are you going to be able to pull yourself together by then?"

"*Yes, sir!* Just tell me where I gotta be and when."

The pool shark dropped the nine-ball into the corner pocket. Her raven hair framed a sexy, desertborn smile carved from the sandy basin of Ghost River just for him.

Silver moonlight spilled into the sanctuary of the Chapel on the Mound. Potato Sack, the biggest of the Broken Kids, hauled Esther over his blubbering shoulder past dusty pews toward the rickety pulpit. The coarse burlap of his mask and gown burned her skin and smelled like moist cobwebs. The eyeholes were empty—flesh cold. The fevered snort of a desperate pig warmed the hole of her ear. She was a little girl again with grimy knees, running through the cactus patches while the wild boars chased her. *Feed. Fuck. Fury. Feed. Fuck. Fury. Feed—*

The Crooked Woman stood at the spider-webbed podium. Her back arched like a bent buzzard's neck, and her sharp fingers scratched symbols into the rotted wood of the dais. She wore a yellowed dress, stained with age. A tattered veil covered her pallid, scarred visage and black-eyed stare. Snarl stood at her side, grinning like an obedient dog. "Dirt on your knees, Coyote."

Esther spilled on the floor. She swung her shins over and sat up on her knees in the powdered sand. She lifted her gaze toward the cloudy rose window and clasped her hands together in prayer. Behind the Crooked Woman stood the Dead Tree, gnarled roots growing from the sacred dirt hill called the Mound. Windchimes and effigies dangled from spidery branches, jingling in the desert breeze. Luminarchs, souldust butterflies, circled above the sacred dirt with glowing, blue wings that pulsated like bottled fireflies in the everdark church.

"*Shit!*" Another contraction.

Esther squeezed Minister's hand when Markus was born. He sang Waylon Jennings to her when they hung her in the Dead Tree to birth her first child. *Was she seventeen?* Might have been. *Was he maybe twenty-one?* Had those wild eyes that she loved and that short holy boy beard she liked to scratch. "It'll be OK," he told her, weaving his pinkie around hers. "*I promise.*"

And it was OK. Markus was born without a hitch. Afterward, they cut her down from the gnarled branches, and the Crooked Woman was pleased enough to let her rest awhile. She took the baby away, of course, and left the orphans behind in the chapel. Esther recovered on a blanket stretched across the dirt. She bled a lot, but Minister was there to wipe fresh water on her skin, tell her she was brave, and spin make-believe stories of faraway lands that they'd run away to one day.

"I had a dream last night," Esther had told him, smiling broadly before diminishing into a blush. "Never mind, it's fucking stupid. You'll just laugh."

"Tell me!" Minister sat up, lighting her cigarette.

Esther shook off the embarrassment and laughed. "OK. In the dream, we took a *vacation* to California. We saw the ocean. Disneyland. With the big *fucking* castle."

"And them Mickey Mouse ears?"

"Yes! You had a pair!"

"Wouldn't that be a sight?" Minister twisted the bloody water from the rag into a dented pail. He was gentle, took pride in making sure she was cared for. "The Northamms at Disneyland. Can you imagine? They'd toss us out within the hour."

After they laughed, he looked a little down.

"What's wrong?"

"Nothing. It sounds like a nice dream is all."

Esther crossed her arms. "I know it'll never happen. It's just fun to dream."

"Dreaming is fucking dangerous." He rested his back against the Mound. "Every time I dream, my heart dies a little bit. I think I might need a new one someday."

"*Hurry, Coyote!* Say the Dirt Prayer, and let's get you roped up!" Snarl's shrill order tore her away from daydreaming. The boy wrapped in barbed wire squeezed the back of her neck. Barbs scratched her skin. "The boonchild is coming."

Esther nodded, feeling the baby in her belly kick.

"What comes from dirt,
must be cleansed.
Give my life to make amends.
Bleed this heart,
Escape damnation.
On my knees,
Suffering is salvation."

Music to her old ears, the Crooked Woman floated down to Esther. She offered a haggard claw. With a resilient nod, the girl accepted her chilly fingers and followed her to the Mound. There, thousands of ancient eyes peered out of porous tunnels dug deep into the spoiled earth that kept all the Grim Seed's putrid miracles hidden below the crust of things. The boy wrapped in barbed wire laid out a dirty blanket, and Esther dropped to her knees. She opened her mouth like a robot.

The Crooked Woman filled her throat with dirt.

Minister fucked her inside of the Dodge Retriever's cab. Her smooth, brown legs snaked around his lean torso. He stood outside of his beat-up tow truck, jeans at his ankles, and an unlit cigarette dangled from his dusty lips. She moaned a little when he rubbed her vagina with his fingers, felt his dick sliding inside of her. All the motions, moistures, skin folds, and ridges created perfect birthday bliss for a man who never felt his wife when they made love. Doomed that way since the day they ate the dirt, and he became the vessel for The Pig.

All that we do, we do for Delora.

A warm breeze picked up.

Minister looked over his shoulder.

Even though he was miles away from that stone-stacked house he called home; he could still feel the shadow watching at the window, knocking on the glass to come inside. Pigs never had their fill, and neither did Minister these days. Weren't enough whisky to drink or barflies to nail, and there weren't no way to keep that fucking shadow from his marital bed. *All snakes are born with a hole in their heart. That hole is a door.*

The riverfolk woman sighed softly, while he clung to her tits. He pumped harder, angrier maybe, suddenly thinking about his daddy and the iron frown he wore every damn day of his life. Did the man ever smile? Not once had Minister seen it. And why should he have? Every great, life-defining moment Eugene ever lived, he never experienced a second for himself.

He was a tool—a cheap suit.

And he got what he deserved.

Didn't they all?

What would the Miraculous Prophet, Eugene Northamm, say if he knew what his Little Snake was using his blessed boon for these days? Scamming drinks, playing dangerous politics with Injuns, and picking up roadkill to feed a city of dead fucking kids?

What good had Minister done for his god lately?

You're just a small thing. A small thing that thinks small. Guess what? Thinking small will keep you that way.

One of the few Pig lessons Minister would never forget. Eugene was a true believer too. Never did a small thing his whole life. Even when he wore his pigskin mask and hung coyote girls from the Dead Tree, mouths gagged with gasoline-soaked rags, Eugene Northamm slid his pretty knife across their throats with the flair of a desert magician.

Throat after throat after throat. Crimson dripped from crooked toes over a sea of hungry pigs waiting to fuck and feast in the bloody mud.

Throat after throat after throat.

Minister came hard. Felt himself release into her warm pocket. *If only that feeling of coming could last forever.* The pool shark gazed into his eyes, transfixed by the halcyon depth and hues of the light within. She arched her back and stretched her neck, longing for a kiss from that sweet snakeshine that was still so deep inside of her it hurt in the best way.

The engine died.

"*Oh, no, no, NO!*" Stacy smacked the steering wheel.

Liz popped up in the backseat. The eight-year-old wiped the sleep from her brown eyes and blinked a few times. She looked out of the window at the spooky, moonlit desert. She saw shadows move, and the sandy dirt looked like silver dust. *What a strange place this is.* She hugged onto Reuben, her favorite teddy bear and *bestest* friend in the whole galaxy.

Momma stared in the rearview mirror. Eyes wide, dark-circled. Chestnut hair spilled out of a haphazard ponytail. She hadn't slept since they left Oklahoma. "I can't believe this is happening!" She punched the steering wheel a few more times and tried turning the ignition over again. The engine refused.

"What happened, Momma? We're not moving."

"Gas. Should've filled up in Tucson…" After a moment of contemplation, she pulled down her eyelids in frustration. "God, w*hy didn't I fill up in Tucson like a normal person?*"

Liz squirmed nervously in her seat. "We ran out of gas? *What! Really?*"

"Elizabeth, stop. Let me think."

"But cars need gas to move!"

"Liz—"

"We—"

"*Stop talking.*"

Liz knew *that* tone and obeyed.

"Somebody'll come along. A sheriff or somebody. We'll get more gas from them. Enough to drive to Phoenix to fill up the tank." Stacy flipped open the vanity mirror on the sun visor. She inspected the make-up fading around her freshly bruised eye.

"Momma?"

"What now?"

"Are we ever going to go back home?"

Stacy rubbed her nose. Didn't know what to say. "Not for a while, baby girl," she finally said. "You're going to spend some time with your auntie in Glendale. It'll be fun to visit your cousins for a few weeks, won't it? They've missed you."

"But…what about Daddy?"

Stacy snapped the visor closed.

"I think you should get some rest now. It's late." Momma looked like she wanted to cry, but she took a deep breath and stiffened up instead. "The morning'll come soon enough. A little bit of light always makes things better and brighter. You'll see."

A swarm of Broken Kids poured into the Chapel on the Mound like a swarm of desert roaches. Busted kneecaps. Metal pulleys. Skin stitched together with human hair. Missing pieces. Swapped parts. Screws twisted into bone. Bone pushed into skin. Teeth crushed with a hammer. Nails driven through nostrils. Lifeless, black eyes that had no bottom. They only knew how to serve the Crooked Woman who made them.

One of Delora's favorite pets, Spider Girl, lowered herself from the shadowy rafters by one of her long appendages. She had three elbows on each arm and rusty hooks for hands. She wore a flowery dress to hide the blasphemous tangle of flesh that existed below her waist—four legs, each with a knee and foot. Hammered to the ball and heel of each was a board bottomed with corroded nails and fishhooks so sharp she could damn near climb any surface. Her dark, brittle hair bounced in twin ponytails. Worst of all, Spider Girl always smiled, always flashing her splintered, screw-like teeth, because the Crooked Woman had snipped off her lips and cheeks a long time ago. The creature said nothing, slipping her corroded hooks under Esther's armpits.

"Hey! Easy!"

Spider Girl ignored her plea and lifted her into the thorny

bramble of the Dead Tree. There, other Broken Kids scurried into the branches, ready to bind the expectant mother's skinny wrists and waist to the jagged bark. They fastened her feet to a pair of tall, crudely built wooden stilts.

"It's getting worse." Esther yipped through her teeth when Spider Girl placed the razorblade crown on her head. The twisted blades slit the skin of her brow, and blood, rust, and sweat dyed her fair hair red. *"Hurts so fucking bad."*

"Breathe!" Snarl shouted from the front pew. He was the conductor of this train. The boy wrapped in barbed wire was the only ghost who spoke for Delora. He had all of the power here.

Just breathe, pigfucker.

In through your nose.

Out through your mouth.

The Broken Kids parted the stilts, and her legs spread open. She dangled from the Dead Tree, posed like a broken marionette with nothing to hide. Warm blood trickled from her forehead, down her back, chest, thighs, and shins until it dripped from her toes onto the frilly shoulders of a mildewed dress. Delora lurked beneath her, black eyes upturned and visible through her shoddy veil, while her icy fingertips crept up the soft, warm skin of the teenager's inner thigh.

"In her younger days they called her Delta Dawn," Esther sang nervously, hoping that Waylon Jennings would soothe her just like it did the day Markus was born. Minister had a soothing voice, deep and full of country. *"Prettiest woman you ever laid your eyes on..."*

Her voice wobbled.

It wasn't the same.

Or helping.

The baby twisted in her belly, tearing down her birth canal like a hungry peccary. Esther drowned in waves of spiky pain and faster contractions. When she squeezed, tiny claws scratched against the red walls of her womb with blackened nails. A fish mouth with piranha teeth puckered. Black eyes. Pig eyes. Biting. Scratching. Blood in the water. Blood in the dirt. *Dirt in the River.*

Esther dug her nails into the Dead Tree's brittle bark.

"Something's wrong! *Help me!*"

Snarl was on his feet. "*Just breathe! Don't fight it!*"

Esther spat and lifted her eyes across the candlelit sanctuary. There, in the back of the desolate nave, she saw them milky eyes watching her. The eyes that wore her husband every time it felt like having a turn with her. A Father Pig. A shadow. A snout glistening with blood and covered in mud.

"*Kill it! Kill it! Killlllll iiiiittttt!*"

"You keep breathing and pushing, Coyote! *That baby's coming, and it don't belong to you!*"

Glancing down, Esther saw blood on the Crooked Woman's claws and laughed like a lunatic. "*Oh fuck…it's eating me, isn't it?*" Her head rolled. "Just let me die."

"*Fuckin' push!*"

OK. OK. OK. Esther tightened up like a metal spring, arched her back, and squeezed everything in her body as if it were a single, throbbing muscle.

"*Gahhh!*"

More spit misted from her lips.

"Again! It's coming! Breathe!"

"*Gahhhh, fuck!*"

There wasn't enough air in the world!

"*Push, Coyote! Push!*"

"*Fuuuuckkkk!*" Esther's cheeks bulged; her teeth clamped so hard she might as well be shitting out the world. Then came the feeling of passing rivers. Emptiness spreading.

Relief.

The baby was out! The new mother lifted her head, dizzy and hot, seeing sparkling stars behind her eyelids. Blood salted her eyes and tears washed it away.

"What is it?" Esther asked weakly. "A snake?"

The Crooked Woman held the newborn by its gooey hocks. She rotated the bloody bird-thing in her bony fingers, eying it with a grimbone grin. The hairless chicken squealed, its slitty lips peeled away from red gummy jaws. Tiny eyes black as pitch swallowed the moonlight. Esther's relieved smile slipped into a blistering scream until she passed out.

"*Lookey, lookey!*" Snarl did a little prospector's dance while a chorus of Broken Kids flocked around the hem of Delora's dirty dress. They croaked and drooled, bearing witness to the new boonchild. "*It's a baby girl! A Sister of Sorrow!*"

The Crooked Woman knelt to the Mound and scooped up some wormy dirt in her claw. When the baby cried for meat, she sprinkled it into her wet, gaping mouth.

"*Prick!*" Stacy flashed her middle finger at the fat trucker with the indecent proposal. He returned the gesture and taunted her with a long toot of his horn. Eighteen wheels kicked up dust and the big rig rolled on down the lonely highway without them.

Stacy smacked her forehead. Looked up in frustration and sighed on her toes. Not a cloud in the sky today. She guessed a few ticks above 100 degrees Fahrenheit. She wandered back to their broken-down Subaru and leaned against the window.

"What's wrong, Momma?" The little girl kept herself busy in the back seat, tying a red ribbon around Reuben's neck in several variations of bows and pretty knots. "Did that man have any gas? Is he gonna go and get some help for us?"

Stacy shook her head, gazing around the vast stretch of empty desert. *Who the fuck could live in such a place? There's nothing here that doesn't have pinchers and claws.* She held her hand up to block out the blinding sunlight.

"We're not in Oklahoma anymore, are we, Toto?"

Liz laughed, sucking up the last few drops in her juice box. The blistering desert was no place for a farm girl who liked chilly night breezes and shady apple orchards in the summertime. She couldn't see a single tree out here—only prickly cactus, ugly rocks, and circling vultures in the cloudless sky.

A few more cars passed.

A station wagon filled with children.

A Cadillac with a couple of old folks.

More big rigs.

Nobody stopped. Nobody cared.

Then, a rickety tow truck appeared on the wavy horizon.

"Oh, you're going to stop for me! Yes, yes, you are!"

Stacy ran into the road, arms waving wildly.

The driver, a handsome, bearded man wearing a button-up mechanic's shirt, rolled down the window. His eyes sparkled in a way that made Liz feel like hugging him forever. Momma felt it too. She clung to the side of the truck, breathless.

"Need a tow?" the man asked, smiling like Jesus.

Ghost River

2.

Something fucked with her hair. *What the hell is that?* A gentle tugging stirred Esther from a restless sleep. When she opened her eyes, Spider Girl crouched over her dirty mattress, playing with a strand of her hair. The Broken Kid clicked and giggled, passing blonde locks back and forth between her hooks. Esther growled and yanked it back with a weary frown.

"*Get away from me! Shoo!*"

Delora's pet screeched in annoyance and scuttled up the wall, ripping off a sizable chunk of plaster on her way. It exploded into chalk dust when it hit the hay-covered floor.

The teenager sat up on her elbows. The fog of sleep fell away. Sunlight crept through the broken window in the orphans' room and felt warm on her skin. She glanced at the empty mattress next to her. Minister hadn't been home yet. Still out celebrating his birthday? More likely, he was sleeping off a bender somewhere in the desert. She tried hard not to be mad at him. She'd told him to go, hadn't she? She begged him to have a little bit of fun before the dire business of a roadkill, to pretend they weren't who they were for a while. At least one of them could feel human on a birthday. It was never going to be her, and she'd grown up knowing and accepting that fact. She rubbed the itchy Pig's mark on her wrist and wanted to cut it off.

Snarl squatted in the corner of the bedroom, scratching symbols on the wood floor with a curved nail. Scabby cuts covered his leaking face. A small glint of gold swam in his only eye, the rest black as an ocean on a starless night. That bit of sparkle, that flash of color in the inky din, was Delora watching everything and everyone in Orphan Rock. "About time, Coyote." He rose from his place on the unswept floor. "Weren't sure you would live through the night. You lost a lot of blood." He grinned.

"Sorry to disappoint you," Esther replied curtly. Lost blood was right. She wore her dingy nightgown, freshly soiled with bright crimson around the crotch. She sighed, knowing she'd have a hell of a time washing it out. "Gimme some aspirin."

"Fresh out."

"Fuck you then."

"Mother stitched you up, Coyote," the boy wrapped in barbed wire said, dropping the nail on the floor. When he dusted off his hands, rusty wires struck and threw a spark. "The bleeding's stopped for now, but we'll need to keep an eye on you. Mother's concerned your baby-making parts might be broken. The birth of a Sister is not easy on a womb."

"Broken? What do you mean, *broken*?"

Snarl shrugged. "Time will tell."

Bam! The door burst open.

Minister?

Potato Sack.

The burlap-garbed grunt carried baby Markus over his shoulder and a bucket of soapy water in his grip. He set both down by her, and Esther's nose wrinkled. Markus needed a fresh diaper and bath. She was happy to see him anyway and squeezed his chubby thigh. The toddler cooed and tumbled on the floor, covering himself in hay and dust. Her Little Snake never liked to sit still, did he? She scooped him up and tickled his tummy.

Then, the laughter of children faded, and everything turned fuzzy like the picture on their television set. She could hear the pitched squeal in the back of her mind. It grew louder like a train coming at her from a deep, dark tunnel.

Snarl smiled like a viper, waiting for her to ask.

"Where is she?"

"Put up elsewhere."

"Doesn't she need milk?"

"She doesn't drink milk from tits unless you want to lose them tits." The boy stood up from the floor, looked out of the window. "Mother will nurse her in the place where she belongs. She ain't yours to fret over anymore. Never was to begin with." He turned back to her. "Where's your husband?"

Esther held Markus tightly against her chest.

"I dunno. Doing the roadkill, I guess."

The boy wrapped in barbed wire looked unamused. "Why do I think you're hiding something from me?"

She looked away, not liking the gold ripple in his eye. "I ain't hiding anything. I don't know where Minister is. In case you fucking forgot, I've been a little busy making boonbabies."

The boy worked his jaw; corroded iron barbs scraped against rotted teeth. She could feel Delora measuring her in his gaze. She didn't like secrets or surprises. After a tense moment, Spider Girl and Potato Sack followed him to the doorway. "Clean up, Coyote," he said, closing the door. "You smell like fresh shit."

ENTERING

GHOST RIVER RESERVATION

The tow truck bounced down the dirt road, a Subaru wagon pulling on the hitch. The interstate vanished in a cloud of brown dust in the side view mirror. To Liz, it was like a science fiction movie out in the desert—a land filled with alien plants and deadly animals. Sage, yucca, spindly mesquite trees, red and silver boulders, and of course, cacti. All kinds of cacti drifted by in shades of green and brown. Being a girl from Oklahoma, Liz found the cacti most intriguing. The driver seemed to know everything about them too. He named them off proudly, pointing at each type: saguaro, barrel, prickly pear, and the fuzzy cholla.

"They look like frozen people reaching for the sun." Liz admired all the many-armed saguaros. She lifted Reuben to the window for a look-see.

"Out here everybody's reaching for something," the man with the golden eyes said, smiling. Momma sat next to him in the cab. She was quiet ever since the man told her to be. But not Liz, though. The handsome tow truck driver enjoyed her company.

"You live out here, mister?"

"Sure do. Not too far away."

"You like living in the desert?"

He lit a cigarette and rolled down his window.

"Now that's a complicated question, missy."

"No, it isn't!" Liz tossed her teddy up in the air and caught him in her arms. "It's easy! You either like something, or you don't! What's so hard about that?"

"Well, that's a choice, isn't it?"

"So what?"

"Not everybody has the privilege to make one." He brushed some of his long, unkempt hair away from his sunburnt nose. "For example, you don't get to choose where you're from. It's just where you're from is all. No choice who your parents are either. In fact, most of your day ain't decided by you at all. I've been here my whole life, and only ever made one decision for myself." The scruffy man looked tiny for a second, but then he straightened with certainty. "Truth be told, you stay in a place long enough, it tells you how to live your best life. Circumstances unfold, and you just ride it out until the next wave hits. That's what I'm doing out here. Ridin' it out."

"You lived out here your whole life?"

"Sure have. Twenty-threeish years…I think."

"You sound sad about it."

"Not sad. It's what it is. I told you I made my choice."

"Well, why don't you make another and *just leave*?" The girl's face lit up like she cracked the case. "That's what Momma and I did, you know! We took a vacation after my daddy got mad again. We're going to visit my auntie in Glendale."

The driver chuckled. "Vacation? What the *hell* is that?"

Liz sat up and pointed out of the window, eyes bright and wide. "*Holy cow!* Look at that big one right there!"

"Oh, him?" The driver squinted, pinching the filter of his cigarette between his teeth. "The tall boy with all them arms?"

"Yes! *He's huge!*"

"We call him the Hydra, like that legendary Greek dinosaur with all them heads. It takes ten years for a saguaro like him to grow an inch and a half, and thirty-five years to flower. You'll need a hundred more years for an arm to grow. That's a long time, missy." He leaned into the windshield to get a better look. "So, when you see ol' Hydra there, you see something that's been living its best life in one spot for hundreds and hundreds of years. The longer it stays put, the bigger and stronger it gets. Thick roots and rock ribs don't come from wandering about. You need to pick a place. Put your feet down for a minute. Call it home and suckle on the soil a little while. Home is what changes you the most. Good or not, it'll change you."

"You mean, grow like a tree somewhere?"

"Exactly right."

Liz pondered the notion. "Maybe I'll find my place where me and my family can be happy again. Maybe we'll find that someplace out here in the desert with you, mister…"

"I'm afraid you won't, darlin'." He tossed his cigarette butt out of the open window. Sparks popped on the dirt road.

The warm, wet sponge stripped off the toddler's dead skin.

The more Little Snake grew, the more he shed. The extra dermis bunched up from her scrubbing, stuck to her fingers, and had a gooey texture like tapioca. Esther kept washing, switching to a gentler pressure when she found freshly grown underskin.

"You're going to be so handsome," she whispered, nibbling his tiny ear. "Just like your daddy."

Markus enjoyed the warm water; it increased his blood temperature and gave him a little more pep in his step. She stroked Little Snake's cheek and then shaped his hair into a tiny mohawk gelled with bubbles. Playing with him took her mind away from her new baby, her missing Minister, and a thousand other fucking miserable things that orbited her mind at any moment in Orphan Rock. This time was hers to be happy. Not a second to waste.

"You have a sister," Esther told the boy splashing in the bucket. "I don't know what I'm going to name her yet. She's not like you and me." Esther sopped the sponge down his back, peeling off a long strip of skin like plastic wrap. "But you'll need to watch out for her when you're both older. I do know that. I may not live long enough to see you grow up, but you're the big brother already. You've got a boon, and your sister does too."

The thought of Little Snake and his sister growing up together in Ghost River, keeping each other safe, was a little comforting. Least they could play. Climb up to The Needle. Hunt lizards. Do some of the fun stuff Minister and Macho used to do as kids. Back before it all fell apart.

They parked in front of an old tin-roofed shed, way off the dirt road, deep in the basin of Ghost River Valley. No paved roads, cars, or other buildings in sight.

Stacy woke up a little. "Where are we?"

"Gas station." The driver opened the door and stepped outside to look up and down the road for trouble. When he came back, his expression had hardened. Didn't look kind anymore. "Follow me. Bring all of your things."

Concern sprouted on Liz's face when she climbed out of the cab with her teddy bear in arms.

"Momma, I don't see any gas pumps..."

"Don't be rude." Stacy pulled her along by the wrist. "This nice man is going to make *everything* OK for us. Can't you hear the way the angels sing in his eyes?"

Liz didn't like the way Momma was acting. She was way too calm right now and trusted this stranger without question. Worst of all, she didn't seem to care that there weren't any gas pumps at the so-called *gas station.* Was Momma feeling OK? Angels singing? "Maybe we should call Daddy?"

Liz squeaked when Stacy squeezed her fingers.

"Don't be a mouthy child."

The little girl gave up protesting. Momma never listened to her anyway. Neither did Daddy. They always fought with each other instead. She followed the bearded truck driver to the shed. He unlocked the door with a bent key. Then, he kicked it open with his boot. "Come on, pick up your feet."

Inside the decrepit interior, dust fairies swirled between bright fingers of sunlight crisscrossing the creaky floorboards. A folding chair sat in the corner of the room next to a couple of metal buckets—one empty, one filled with murky water.

"Gimme your purse." The driver held out a rough hand with tobacco-stained fingers. Momma surrendered her handbag. "Now go sit down on that chair over there and *be quiet.*"

Stacy sat down while the stranger ruffled around in her things. Liz couldn't believe it! Momma yelled at her for digging for gum in her purse sometimes but had zero problems with the truck driver's dirty hands all over it. This made little sense. Maybe Momma was sick. She definitely needed sleep.

"Where's the fucking money? IDs?"

"In the front pocket. There's a wallet."

He found it: cash, driver's license, and checkbook. Everything went into the back pocket of his greasy jeans.

"What else has your name on it?"

"Nothing." Momma grinned. "You have beautiful eyes."

"So they tell me." The driver walked over to her, knelt beside her chair. He took Stacy's hands in his and stared deeply into her eyes. "Do you want to please me?"

"Yes, I do."

"Good. You're going to sit here until the sun goes down. You're not going to make any noise. Should nature call, you're going to piss and shit in that empty bucket. Drink that water in the other bucket when you're thirsty. When you're not pissing or shitting or drinking water, your ass stays in this chair until you see the moon out that window." He pointed at the painted mountains in the distance. "When you see the moon float above them hills, that's when you get up, go outside, and stand in that clearing over yonder. Do you understand what I'm saying to you?"

Momma nodded.

"And you…" The driver turned to Liz and Reuben, looking even sadder than he was a moment ago. "You stay with your mother. Do as she says. Keep quiet until the stars shine. Then, you follow her outside. You understand me, missy?"

"Sure do, mister." Liz dropped to the floor, sitting cross-legged. Something foreign played around inside of her, like a magical worm squiggling around behind her eyeballs. It made his voice sound like music, and his face radiate like a sunbeam.

"All right." Across the splintery room, he bent over and yanked up a floorboard. He tossed Momma's purse onto the secret stash hidden beneath the shed. Duffel bags. Sneakers. Suitcases. Toys. He looked at Liz, then at Reuben clutched in her hand.

She wrapped her arms around her best friend, squeezed, and gave the stranger the stink eye. The man considered his next move, wisely shrugged, and then replaced the board and stomped on it to make it fit again. "Goodbye, y'all, and Godspeed—"

He winced, clutching his right hand. The veins under the skin of his palm turned black as charcoal.

Delora's leathery feet kicked bones. Her toenails clicked against the floor of her stone sanctum, a magnificent cathedral cavern in The Needle of Orphan Rock.

The Broken Kids fled to escape her, scurrying to their dark holes on splints and riggings cobbled together by rotten wood and rusted bolts and thread spun from human hair. Those that still had eyes looked down when she passed. The rest faced shadowy corners, still as statues. Smashed teeth chattered in the dark while shaking shoulders slumped over and huddled together. They held hands trying to remember the dark song they were born to sing.

All that we do, we do for Delora.

She was a builder, a shaper of worlds. *A lover of children.* The spider queen of her kingdom of lost babies. She passed her knotty workbench. On it, an assortment of decaying tools and jars of bolts, screws, hinges, and nails. Dried blood stained the wood so dark it was nearly black. Leftover pieces of ant-infested flesh stretched on a nearby tanning rack.

In the bone pile beneath her nest, where she tossed all of the leftover pieces from her workbench, Mordecai, the Ghosteater, raised his shovel-shaped head. The mighty albino diamondback coiled up and shook his skeletal rattles. His blood-red eyes smoldered, his forked tongue buzzed the air.

The Crooked Woman snatched a ghostling who could barely stand on the crutches hammered through her hands. She whimpered, unable to speak through the stitches that sealed her blue lips. Without any kindness, Delora threw her into the bone pile. ***Thwack!*** The Ghosteater buried his curved fangs into the undead child's soft belly. Venom pumped into the dead girl like warm, acidic honey. Mordecai wrapped his tubular body around his kill, squeezing the ghostly breath from her spider-filled lungs until dirt burst from her lips. While it fed, Delora stroked her claw over its white scales. Mordecai was an old thing. Like she was.

Wah! Wah!

The cry of a newborn echoed through the chamber.

The Crooked Woman gazed toward the hungry mewling coming from the nest up in the high rocks, near the crack in the ceiling where the sunshine poured in. Porcelain bone *popped* through her hunched shoulder muscles, unfolding from the open back of her stained dress. Leathery skin with black, wormy veins linked the gaps between her spreading batwing fingers until speckled feathers punched through her pores like swords dropped into fluffy sand.

Whoosh!

She left behind a cloud of bone dust. The harpy ascended, passing by newborn Broken Kids. They dangled upside down from the bottom of her nest by loops of barbed wire wrapped around their bluish ankles. They would sleep until she called for them. Not a moment sooner. Until then, they would float in the shadows, while the dirt stained their empty bellies.

The Crooked Woman landed in her nest, a bowl tucked in the high rocks, weaved together by bone, branch, and wire. She folded her wings against her back, approaching a ray of sunshine that warmed the newborn that laid in the wicker-spun cradle.

When Delora picked her up, the Crooked Woman studied the cherubic creature with those dead space eyes she kept hidden behind her filthy wedding shroud. Tiny claws. Downy skin. A flat, lipless mouth filled with darkness. The chick cried for food.

The Crooked Woman pulled back her bramble and bur-tangled veil. Below scarred cheeks, her long mouth rolled open. Rigid teeth, triangular and sharp as dagger points, dripped with dirt and spit to make mud. She placed her slitty maw over the child's lips. Then, she retched until the meat, wormy soil, and rodent bones spilled from her throat into the itty-bitty mouth.

The baby bird swallowed it all.

The Ghost River Council had a quaint town hall, a brick building in the heart of their burgeoning community founded on the other side of Orphan Rock. They even had a statue of one of their famous chiefs, Leonard Larucha, with a bronze placard at its base. Minister had never been inside that lovely place. He wasn't welcome there. No Northamm was.

Instead, he drove to the old meeting spot on the cliff that overlooked Ghost River Valley. There, high above the painted landscape and wind-whipped valleys, the real business occurred—the kind neither party wanted anybody else to know about.

Macho greeted him at the truck. "You haven't slept."

"No, I haven't. Guess I'll do that when I'm dead."

"Doubtful." Macho noted his blackening hand. "Looks like you're running out of time."

Minister shot him an embarrassed look. "I'll be fine." He slipped his burning fingers into his pocket to hide the blisters. The whiskey helped numb the pain a little, but the Grim Seed would only add more gasoline to the fire in his veins if he didn't hurry up and get back home where he belonged.

"Ready then?"

"As I'll ever be."

Up the rocky steps, two older Ghost River men and a woman sat around a cold fire pit with stern, suspicious gazes. They refused to look Minister in the eye. They'd had a long history dealing with snakes from Orphan Rock and were no fools to their tricks. The middle-aged woman with graying hair spoke first. "Wallace informed you of what needs doing, Mr. Northamm?"

"Yes'm. Hear no evil; see no evil."

One of the older men spat on the ground. "*You* are *evil, you scumbag.*"

Minister raised his healthy hand in a gesture of truce. "I come in peace, friends. I'm just a concerned resident of Ghost River doing my civic duty for the community I love."

"Don't mock us," the same man said.

"More foolish than his pig of a father if he does," the other old man added, pretending Minister wasn't there. "*May Eugene Northamm rot in Hell for what he brought here.*"

"Look, fellas and ma'am, no need for hostility. I'll make sure the federal agent you're worried about goes back to his cubicle in DC satisfied that the Ghost River Tribe ain't looking to wage war on a weary nation. He'll be assured y'all keep Ghost River squeaky clean. You can count on me."

"Yes," the woman chimed in. "We'd also like the commissioner to approve our budget request for a funding increase for our educational programs."

Minister offered a thumbs-up. "Rubber stamps all around. Anything else?"

"There is." The woman looked at her companions and waited for them to nod in agreement. They did, and she continued, "In the coming days, we'll be moving some specialty resources to a location near Orphan Rock. There's a cave there, near the edge of The Pig's land. We need assurances our people can travel back and forth without concern for their safety. It will be a monitored location, but we will respect our land treaties and your privacy."

"How close are we talking about?"

"Solemn Cave."

Minister considered it. "She don't like trespassers much, but I think I can smooth the way for your people *if* they stay on the right side of the river. Can you guarantee me that?"

The woman saw no protest from her peers. "We can do that."

One of the angry men laughed darkly. "We should salt her

out like the slug she is and burn that chapel to the damn ground. It'd be a mercy to the world."

"I'd be careful making threats, friend." Minister tapped his cigarette in the wind. Ashes drifted over the cliffside. "She hears everything in Ghost River. *She is everywhere*."

"*Fuck you.* I know what she is!" The councilman rose to his feet, fists clenched. "She took my little sister. Snatched her from the front yard like she was a mouse."

"That don't have shit all to do with me, sir."

The riverfolk man's sandy eyes boiled with rage. "One day, it'll all come crashing down around you. Around her. When that day comes, I will spit on your grave."

The woman raised her hand, silencing her companion. "Enough. What is in the past, including your sister, is dead. What is in the future, unclear. What is right now is our business. Do we have a deal, Minister Northamm? Can we call it a day?"

"Almost."

She arched a brow in curiosity. "What's the problem?"

"My wallet." He shrugged. "Last I checked, it's empty."

A faded sign welcomed him home:

GHOST RIVER REVIVAL
Where Miracles Happen Every Day.

The Dodge Retriever pulled up to an iron gate with a cattle guard. Beyond it, a chunk of pristine desertscape bordered by posts of sun-rotted wood and barbed wire fences. Orphan Rock, a monolith mountain, was the epicenter of the Ghost River Valley. Visible layers of siltstone, mudstone, and shale painted the ancient landmark in red and silver shades. At the summit, The Needle, a chimney rock touched the sky

Minister pulled up the gravel drive and parked in the shrubs near their home, a stone-stacked, mortar and clay structure with all the modern fixings of a water tank, a power line, and a fancy TV antenna on the flat, adobe-style roof. Further down the road was the scrapyard and Minister's workshop, where he stripped down vehicles and sold parts for a few bucks. The other direction, down the river rock path toward the base of the mountain, was Orphan Rock proper – the old ghost town, where the bones and remnants of the Days of the Pig rotted in the sun. The old church with the crooked steeple stuck out against the orange sky like a tombstone.

The Chapel on the Mound.

Minister pulled the keys from the Retriever and watched the blisters on his wrist heal. The black veins in his arm faded with the searing pain. As always, the dirt curse disappeared once he returned to the Land Where Pigs Squeal.

He took a deep breath—what a day.

Nice to be home.

He never really knew what time of day it was in Orphan Rock. Didn't even have a clock or a watch. Couldn't read them anyway. Out in the desert, that shit didn't matter. The sunrise and sunset mattered. The moonlight mattered. Whiskey mattered. A pocketful of cash mattered. A little food, playtime with Markus, and holding Esther all mattered more to Minister than time. He strolled up the dirt path, passing by the wooden picnic table.

M+E = ME

He smiled proudly at the initials he carved in the splintery tabletop years ago. He never learned how to write but practiced M and his E's until he got them right. Pain in the ass trying to learn anything out in Ghost River, though. The little he could scribble was all thanks to Macho lending him comic books as a boy. And he didn't like to read the wordy ones ever.

"'Bout time you came home. We were worried."

The boy wrapped in barbed wire stood behind him.

Minister sighed. "Jesus Christ."

"Where you been?"

"I don't answer to you."

"You have a happy birthday party, Minister?"

"Tell her I did my fucking job. Roadkill's out by the river."

Esther sat on the old striped couch in the living room, watching television with a sullen expression. *The Matching Game.* Blood vessels burst in her cheeks, and dark ruts circled her eyes.

"I had another baby. A fucking boonbaby."

"Sorry I missed it."

"Was a girl."

Minister scooped Markus up from the floor and hugged his boy tightly. "It alive?"

"Think so. She took her away from me. Snarl won't say to where."

"Don't matter to where." Minister plopped down next to her on the couch. Little Snake bounced on his knee and hooted. "You did good, baby. If Delora's happy, it'll matter. Maybe she won't want another one again so soon. She has two snakes, and now a—"

"Snarl says my baby parts might be tore up for good. Lost too much blood, you see." Esther turned pale at the thought. "Goddamn baby girl nearly cracked me like a wishbone."

"Esther, it'll be fine—"

"Did you have a happy birthday?"

"I told you I didn't want to go. You made me."

"Well? Answer the question. Did you?"

"It was fine. Nice to slip away for a minute or two between kidnapping children and running arms for Injuns. You know what it's like to be me. I appreciated the respite."

"Did you fuck somebody else?"

"Esther, you don't want to know—"

"But I do." Her eyes glittered with gathering tears. "Tell me something good happened to you."

"All right. Something good happened."

Esther sniffled and tucked her upper lip.

"Happy fuckin' birthday, then."

"Yeah. I suppose so."

His wife nuzzled his shoulder. She didn't mind the smell of cigarettes and whiskey. "I don't even want to know what happens to me if I can't make more babies." Her voice dropped with fear. "Purpose *is* my only value to her. She'll mark another."

Minister didn't want to think about it. "Delora don't owe nothing more to The Pig. We've kept our end of it."

"What if she don't see it that way?" Esther reached over and stroked Markus' soft skull. "Delora ain't ever happy with enough. She'll want another pig baby sooner or later. You know it too. Whatever gets that Grim Seed watered is all she's on about."

"It's all we should care about too." Minister wrapped his fingers around her wrist and smiled gently. "We have to finish what we started, Esther. We ain't got no choice."

Elizabeth chased the luminous, blue-winged butterfly that fluttered through the broken window of the old shed. Poor Reuben swung in circles, while she reached and hopped, trying to snatch a little bit of flappy magic that soared just out of reach.

Momma was already standing at the window, watching the full moon rise above the desert mountains, a little bit of drool pooling at the corner of her mouth. "We have to go now," she said, pointing to the door. Liz agreed. The bearded driver gave them specific instructions to follow, and it would be rude to disobey them. He was so lovely that Jesus Man.

Outside of the run-down shed, they followed the glowing butterfly to an open clearing. Nearby, the rumble of a flowing river. "You wanna go for a swim?" Liz asked Reuben.

The teddy bear's button eyes had no answer.

She giggled. *Tough guy.*

More of those cosmic butterflies circled above the desert scrubland, providing candlewicks of faint blue light against a starry sky. Liz finally cornered one on a bush, but her fingers passed right through it. The creature dissolved in a poof of shimmering blue glitter. The little girl watched its glowing particles float away on the warm night breeze until it was all gone.

"*Whoa...*"

"*You need to hide,*" came an urgent whisper.

Liz turned in the direction of the childish voice. The sagebrush was thick, and the shadows of the desert, thicker. She held Reuben up to help her look.

"Hello?"

Maybe it was nothing.

"Why are we here?" Stacy rotated in slow circles in the clearing. Confusion spread on her face like a fresh oil spill. "Maybe this isn't right? Maybe we should leave?"

"Awww! No fun!" Liz was too enthralled by ghostly butterflies to consider it.

"*You need to hide,*" the whisper again.

Liz turned on her heel. "*Who's there?*"

In the spindly bushes, a set of radiant wings flapped on a pale, scarred arm. Shadows concealed the young boy's gaunt face. A dirty rag covered his eyes in a ratty blindfold. Liz's courage vanished, too afraid to scream. Her jaw fell open, but no words came out when a cold hand reached out and tugged on her fingers. The boy's face looked grim.

"*You need to hide, or she'll get you—*"

"I don't have my keys!" Momma threw her hands up frustratedly. "What on Earth are we doing out here? Did I fall asleep?" Stacy looked up. "*What the fuck is—*"

Wham! A shadow swooped from the sky. Stacy fell backward into the shrub, buried in a vicious storm of feather and claw. Liz tried to shout, tried to yell for help, but the boy placed his cold hand over her mouth.

"Don't say anything! She'll hear you!"

The sky monster pinned Momma to the ground. Dark wings flapped, kicking up dust and ruffling bushes. Black talons polished as knife blades, shredded Stacy's clothes apart with ferocious speed. She screamed for help, kicked her legs into the river rocks, struggled to hold up her hands to stop the violent slashing, but the bird-woman sliced through her wrist muscles until her fingers fell dead on her useless hands. Blood gushed from her nose and mouth, and Stacy gazed into the dark desert, thinking only of Liz. Little lost Elizabeth from Oklahoma.

The beast screeched loud enough to shake the hills when she pulled the beating heart from Momma's chest. Its long, toothy mouth unzipped, and she swallowed it whole. A visible lump traveled down her buzzard's throat. Liz took a steadying step backward, trying not to faint or pee her pants. Her white Keds stumbled over river rock, and it ***thumped!*** against another. The sky monster's head snapped in her direction.

"*Go! Go now!*" The boy pushed Liz away from the clearing. "*Run!*"

She couldn't feel her legs but ran anyway—no direction in particular, not even sure if the boy were nearby or not. The desert was only empty space at night—darkness in every direction. No light. No beacon. *So just run.* Her tiny legs pumped, and Reuben bounced along in her fist. All sorts of scary sounds resonated behind her, but Liz refused to look back.

No time for this. No time to stop.

Run! Liz! Run!

Whomp! Whomp! She heard the beat of dark wings. Obsidian talons pierced her shoulder blades, slicing through her purple Care Bears t-shirt like tissue paper. Liz was too frightened to feel the pain. She watched the ground fade away when the monster stole her into the night sky.

1986

3.

Ding! Ding! Ding!

The Dodge Retriever rambled down the bumpy drive toward the property line. Minister didn't recognize the yellow Buick sedan idling by the gate. They didn't get many visitors out in Orphan Rock, thanks to the riverfolk keeping a lid on the roads. They set up a checkpoint too, but it was usually unmanned. Minister could come and go as he pleased, but that was about it. The Ghost River Nation did everything they could do to keep Orphan Rock hidden from the world. This morning somebody slipped through, somebody ringing the Northamm's dinner bell. "You've got to be fuckin' kidding me," Minister cursed.

An emaciated man in the most audacious black cowboy hat money could buy held up a liver-spotted hand. Silver-toed, snakeskin boots glinted in the sunshine.

"*Wrangler Vandersloan,*" Minister announced from the other side of the iron gate, head shaking in utter disbelief. "The hell you doing here clangin' our bell?"

"Minister Northamm," the old mongrel replied, smiling. His teeth were crooked and capped in gold. "It's a fucking sight to see you again. You look like Eugene, but not them eyes. Those pretty things belonged to Clara, didn't they? Yessir, I can see her cunning in you from miles away."

Minister spat. "Don't you say her name."

The Cowboy Lizard kept his grin, pulled his aviator sunglasses down for a better look around the land he remembered. "The old country never changes, does she?"

"Oh, she's been changing plenty." Minister stepped over the squirmy bloodroot cracking through the arid soil looking for a morsel. They sprouted up all over the desert these days, part of the Grim Seed's changes. "You didn't answer my question, old-timer. *Why the fuck* are you *here?*"

Wrangler smiled like an innocent angel. "Same reason I always come back to Ghost River. *Special delivery.*"

Minister didn't hesitate to strike. Nobody rubbed him more wrongly than Wrangler Vandersloan did. He grabbed the old kidnapper's meatless shoulders through the metal bars of the gate and yanked him close enough to see the pocks on his bird-beak nose. He felt the snakeshine warm up his eyes. Breaking into Wrangler's rat skull would be a goddamn pleasure.

"How the fuck are you not dead? You ate the dirt like the rest of us. You should be ash in the wind by now."

Wrangler laughed, ***click!,*** and Minister felt a hot prick. The Cowboy Lizard held a switchblade against his belly.

Minister let him go.

"That's better," the old man said, folding up his blade. The Cowboy Lizard ducked under some nearby fencing and took a bold step over the property line. "We both know if the dirt wanted me dead, I'd be dead already." He sneered like a wild jackal, still a Pig Man after all these years. "But here I am. Still standing. Trespassing like a sonofabitch."

Minister sighed. "Why'd you come back?"

"Old contracts. One left to find."

"What the fuck you talking about?"

On cue, the passenger door of the Buick sedan opened. A young woman stepped out. Attractive. Cutoff jeans, freckled nose, red hair, and eyes greener than an Aloe Vera leaf. She floated through the tangles of barbed wire and hooked her thin arm around Wrangler's elbow. In her vibrant eyes, Minister saw a familiar shadow swimming in the deepest green seas.

Something old. Something with teeth.

She placed a hand on his chest.

Then, she was inside of him.

Crash!

The glass shattered on the kitchen floor.

Esther looked at her trembling fingers in disbelief.

Breathless.

In that dog's cage.

The other girls throwing rocks at her head.

Blood in her eyes. Stinging her eyeballs.

You fuck like an angel.

You're fit for a king.

The iron brand pressed into her wrist.

A scream she'd never duplicate.

Burnt flesh smelled like browning beef.

Markus, now ten, appeared in the doorway. "Momma?"

"*Stay out!* I just broke a glass."

"Who's that man in the cowboy hat?"

Esther sighed, sucking on a small cut.

"An ancient fucking relic long thought dead and gone."

The boy's weary mother washed her bleeding finger in the sink. She gazed out of the dingy window, haunted by days long gone. The man who brought Esther to Ghost River when she was nine years old was out there smoking around the fire ring like it was 1973 all over again. The monster who built the cages and carved the boxes and fed the girls to the Pig Men had returned.

Markus pointed outside. "Can I go run?"

"Will you be careful?"

He nodded eagerly, his sandy hair a little crooked after his last bowl cut. "Yes'm, I will."

"If Delora comes around, what do you do?"

"Run home."

"Fine. Be back in an hour."

Markus clapped. "*Yes!*"

Esther exhaled through her nose, scowling at a floor filled with lots of broken glass left to pick up. "All right then, run along and have some fun. I have a *big* mess to clean up, otherwise known as *the fucking usual for me*."

Markus zipped out of the kitchen. Esther leaned into the sink, watching Wrangler congregate with a strange woman. She was pretty. Had nice hair. Enchanting eyes. From the looks of it, Wrangler had aged fifty years in the last twelve.

But fuck, hadn't they all?

"The man who finds the lost girls is here."

Esther's fingers curled around the sink basin.

In the window's reflection, she could see the Crooked Woman standing in the doorway. Her spine stooped like a collapsed fence; her obscured face hidden behind soiled tulle. Delora's long claw clutched Snarl's wire-wrapped hand. Behind them, a cloud of horseflies poured from a fresh rip in The Dark. Suddenly, the air smelled like wet dirt.

"Why is *he* here?"

"Not your concern, Coyote."

"I thought he'd be dead." Esther put a cigarette in her mouth with shaky fingers, but it fell from her lips. "I was only able to sleep some nights because I believed him dead."

"Don't be a child!" the boy snapped with a sour tone. "Useful things shall ever find providence here."

Esther shivered and looked at the broken glass on the floor. Thought about her insides and how they were just as broken. She wasn't especially useful these days, was she?

"Did The Pig visit you last night?"

"Yes." Esther hated to think about it. "Late."

The shadow crept through their broken window like a daddy longlegs. Minister hardly made a peep when it entered his skin and turned his eyes white like milk. She laid there, too scared to breathe, as her possessed husband rose to his feet from their mattress. His expression twisted like a greedy pig. His dick hard and his smoky snout moist and sniffing the air for treats.

"Ready for me, Sweet Pea?"

Esther could only nod and then fuck him.

"And he spilled his seed in you?" Snarl asked flatly.

"Of course, he fucking did."

"Turn around."

She obeyed, careful not to step on any broken glass. The Pig's mark on her wrist itched, but she dare not scratch it. Snarl's dead eye sparkled with fascination.

"Mother says suffering quickens the seed."

"Please...*don't hurt me.* I've been good."

"Walk to her, Coyote. *Keep the faith. Show your love.*"

Esther took a careful step forward, turning white with apprehension.

"No. Not like that. Mother wants you to bleed."

"Please, I—"

"*Walk.*"

A metal hook caught Esther's braid. Minced cheeks leaked spit and dirt from a wicked grin above. Spider Girl shrieked and scuttled across the ceiling at full speed, dragging Esther along for the ride. She cried and tripped over glass shards that pierced the rough meat at the bottom of her feet. An extremely sharp fragment sliced a deep nerve, and Esther crashed into the wall, slid down, and lay there like a broken doll. The spider kept running down the hallway, a chunk of her blonde hair rippling on the hook. Esther looked around, too afraid to cry.

The Crooked Woman was gone, but not the flies.

Wrangler Vandersloan whistled.

"Wowee." He investigated his former coyote pen—the pasture where he kept the lost girls in cages. Flash floods had toppled over his stacks of old crates and chain-link fences over the years, and weeds invaded the open spaces underneath an old black cargo van wherein Wrangler once slept. The old mongrel picked up a sun-bleached ragdoll from the dirt and eyed it with a nostalgic frown. "Place has seen better times. Why'd you let it fall apart?"

Minister shook his head. "Twelve years is a long time. The climate ain't kind to longevity out here. Besides, it costs money to run a goddamn ghost town for nobody."

"Not like it used to be, eh? Filled pews and coffers?"

"Ain't got any coffers since all the Pig Men died. Now, the only asses that fill those pews on Sunday morning belong to termites. Your god's dead here, I'm afraid."

The old mongrel tipped his hat, grinning a bit. "He's still around. Watching in the hills. He's in the dirt too. You can't have Orphan Rock without Father Pig."

"Don't be ridiculous." Minister laughed nervously, scanning the dry hills for any moving shadows that oinked. "You know what happened here. Sure as shit Eugene ain't coming back, and The Pig ain't either. What's left of him can't do much."

"He still takes you over?"

Minister nodded, eyes low. "Time to time, he does. But she don't let him run things no more. Not like he used to. He's just an echo now. Something we live with out here."

"*So long as the Grim Seed spoils the earth, you, too, shall carry its burdens.*" Wrangler watched the yellow Palo Verde blooms rustle in the afternoon breeze.

"So, what is she?" Minister asked. "The redhead. She snaked me. I felt her rummaging inside my mind."

"A Sister. Last one by my account."

"How'd you find her?"

The Cowboy Lizard leaned against the dented wall of the rusted cargo van. He put his boot on a wooden casket, still carved with pigspeak symbols. "That's a long story. That one don't like being found. I'll say that much. Unlike the others, she moseyed far from Ghost River and hadn't planned on coming back."

"So, she's not dumb."

"No. She's not."

"She put up a fight about coming back?"

"Nope. Rather pleasant. Tell you the truth, seemed eager."

"What's she got to offer Delora? Makes no sense to come back to Orphan Rock for any reason." Minister chuckled darkly. "Then again, you fucking did."

"Never had a choice. As you know, I ate the dirt too. Long as I tracked her down, did what the flies told me, I never burnt. Long as you obey, you can live a long fucking time." The old mongrel's gaze swept over to the Chapel on the Mound; his expression became one of sadness and nostalgia. "Shame to have a church without a preacher," he said. "Seems wrong."

"A tomb," Minister said distantly.

"Beg your pardon?"

"A church without a preacher is a tomb."

"Suppose it is." Wrangler took off his cowboy hat and fanned his sun-scarred face.

Below the bristly nest tucked in the jagged rocks: the striking of a ballpoint hammer, the clanking of buckles and hooks, and the sobbing of a dying child.

The smell of food.

The unwashed harpy climbed down the rickety ladder spun

from barbed wire and fence posts. She landed in the bone pile near the slumbering snake. Mordecai lifted its head, flicked its gray tongue, and smelled its better. The serpent wisely recoiled and laid still as a hubcap, watching the bird-girl climb over a hundred snapped crutches. On the hunt for her next meal, the delicious stink of death led her through the bone chamber.

Mother bent over her workbench. Her crooked spine looked like tiny, balled fists punching against a stretched canvas of leathery skin laid bare by the open back of a cricket-covered wedding dress. Her spidery hands moved with precision, stitching an arm to a torso. A partially constructed Broken Kid dangled from a hook over her table, head slumped against her shoulder blade. There was a funny little grin on her blue lips.

Mother didn't acknowledge her hungry visitor. Instead, she put down her suturing needle and picked up a crescent knife. She split the child's belly open with a clean slice. Greasy innards plopped in a bucket beneath her tiny toes. The chickling from the nest licked her lips.

When Mother kicked the cold pail of slop in her direction, she wasted no time digging her claws into the cold viscera. She bit through the chewy intestine, her baby teeth still squared and poor at incising, so it took her a while to chew the best parts.

While she slurped and burped, barely taking a breath, the Broken Kid with the barbed wire around his skull watched her with that annoying smirk of his. He leaned against the cavern wall like a spy. Arms folded. His one good eye deep as a wormhole.

"You need to practice your words, Baby Bird," he said, watching her eat like a pig. "Squawking and hissing may get you fed, but you'll never run your own ranch without talking to the cattle." The feral harpy ignored him, quite happy in her guts and gristle. He looked up to the crack in the ceiling to where the sun shined brightly. "Once the Grim Seed is watered, you'll be free to build any paradise you want. You're a blessed beast, but you're a beast nonetheless." Snarl's eye tightened on the gobbling critter.

"And a beast without reason is easily hunted and slaughtered. Tonight, you'll practice flyin' when the moon rises high. Mother will teach you how to hunt. I'll teach you *some manners*."

Markus zipped like a silver roadrunner under the hot Sonora sun. He parkoured up rocks, leaped over crevices, and skipped across loose gravel like it was hard concrete. Speed was freedom. It didn't matter he didn't have any shoes. Scales padded the bottom of his toes. Nobody could keep up with Little Snake! *Nobody!* Markus was desertfolk, born and bred. He liked to move fast and was surprisingly good at it too. He could sprint from Orphan Rock to the river and back in no time. Minister taught him how. Sometimes, they ran together, and Markus loved it.

"Your daddy can run like the devil too," he'd tell the boy. "Used to beat Officer Machado regularly. Although he'd never admit it if you asked him."

The boy wished he could spend more time with his Daddy, but Minister wasn't around very much these days. Not like he used to be. Markus missed him. He was somebody to talk to, run with, and pretend they were race cars chasing checkered flags. Seemed the world was cruel to snakes. Delora kept Minister moving these days, and Little Snake grew up alone and lonely.

When he saw her, he slowed and kept a bit of distance between them. The mysterious visitor stood in the clearing near the old shed he liked to root in to find toys under the floorboards. She folded pale arms over a flannel shirt tied over her flat belly. Her verdant gaze rested on the nearby riverbank, watching the current turn the high noon sun's reflection into infinite ripples.

"Why do you stare?" she asked, not looking up from the water.

Markus gulped. "Me? I'm not—"

"Then, what are you doing?"

"Running."

"You're here to snoop. You're a terrible liar." The woman's intense green eyes met his. Markus felt a ripple of tremendous power in her scrutiny. Something inside his snake heart warned him that she was just like the Crooked Woman, powerful and dangerous. *Maybe he should run away?* He looked on the road near the clearing and saw no cars.

"How'd you get here so fast?" he asked.

"I know all of the shortcuts in Ghost River." She gestured for him to come closer with sharp bristles for fingers. The boy felt compelled to obey. He scooted down the riverbank and joined her at the water's edge. "What's your name?"

"Markus."

"I am Desyre." She pointed at the crisp, flowing water. "Markus, did you know many babies drowned here?" The desert boy squinted one eye and scratched the back of his head. She went on, "They tossed them in the water when the current ran deep. When it was shallow, they held their little bodies under until they stopped kicking. All the babies that didn't have a boon died this way, crying for dead mothers and vile fathers who hated them. Hundreds, maybe a thousand, children died right here."

"How'd you know that?"

"I'm well-versed in Ghost River history." She knelt to the current and let the river flow between her long, sharp fingers. "Do you know the stories of this place?"

Markus blushed. "Not really. Just what I learned from the Dirt Hymns. I don't read books so well."

"I'm talking about the time *before* the Grim Seed." The woman stood from the river and flicked water from her fingers. "Do you know the *real* history here?"

He shook his head.

"Just a matter of time then. The Pig will teach you. I imagine your time is coming soon."

Markus puffed out his chest. "That's not gonna happen to me. Momma and Daddy say so. We're gonna water the Grim Seed, and then we won't have to carry those burdens no more."

"Do you really think you'll have a choice?"

He shuffled his feet in the dirt. Looked at the brushy ground, watching red ants marching on their hill. "To be honest, I don't know what I have. Some days, it feels like nothing." When he lifted his gaze, the visitor in cut-off shorts was gone.

Do you ever get mad, Markus?

Mad they're drowning you here?

The boy spun around, her voice on the wind.

Do you ever want to cry, Markus?

Cry while you grow up without a friend?

Ghost River flowed under the sunshine.

Do you ever get lonely, Markus?

I bet you do.

They both looked at the bloody footprints that smeared the kitchen linoleum in crimson. Minister opened his mouth to ask what happened, but Esther seemed in no mood to give the answer they both already knew. He wrapped his arms around her thin waist and hugged her tightly instead. His wife vibrated with tension, like a bottle-capped volcano ready to blow.

"Slow down, Esther! Things are moving fast."

She squirmed out of his grip.

"*Slow down?* Easy for you to say!"

Minister tried grabbing her by the shoulders, but she broke away. She tugged open the icebox. Pulled out a browning head of lettuce and smashed it on the countertop.

"I'm sorry you have to see him again. If I had my way, I'd cut his throat."

"It's fucking fine." Esther snatched a dull knife from the drawer. "I'm an adult. Besides, there ain't a man alive that could fuck me up any more than I'm already fucked."

"Sure, baby, but it's OK to feel angry or scared…" Minister

crossed his arms, watched his wife storm by without blinking. "That man did things to you. *Unspeakable things.*"

She spun around; the knife pointed at his chest.

"So did your daddy. *So do you.*"

"That's not me doing it. You know that."

"Funny. Sure looks like you when you're on top of me."

"*Fuck you.* That's not fair. I can't control him."

"*Fuck you too!*" Esther flipped the cutting board over on the counter. A few tears rolled down her cheeks. "I'm the one she fucking hurts while you're out running around getting drunk. You come home smelling like pussy all the time. *You don't even bother to shower anymore before you get in our bed.*"

"Esther, I ain't ever done anything without your permission—"

"Shut up, you son of a bitch. I don't like hearing your fuckin' voice right now."

"Baby, listen, you're not alone." Minister lit a cigarette, tried handing it to her, but she swatted it away. "I hurt all of the time too. We all carry our burdens here, so one day we'll be free."

"No, it's not all of the time, Minister! She only hurts you when you fuck up. Me? She hurts me because *she likes it*. She really *fucking* likes it. I know why too. *I ain't worth shit to her.* Just a maid she can cut up and kick down now…I should just kill myself and be done with it. Death is better than this bullshit."

"Esther, please, let's not talk like that, OK? She hurts me too. Every goddamn day. *How many have I taken from that road? How many babies?* I see them sometimes, walking around out there. Pieces I recognize—parts of the people I scam away from their lives to keep her fed. No matter where I look, I can't stop seeing their faces. *That's my goddamn burden.*"

"Oh, I'm sorry, Minister!" Esther rolled her eyes. "So sorry for you. *I really fucking am.* As a snake, you still have some value here. Me? I'm worthless. Food, probably."

"Don't say that. Keep the faith—"

"No. I'm twenty-something years old, and I ain't been pregnant since she took the last baby away. How many times has The Pig fucked me since then? No more babies. No more boons, snakes, or whatever the fuck the last one was. I can't give her what she wants, and Delora hates me for it. *Keep the faith?* Are you fucking shitting me? Once Markus is old enough to breed for her, she's going to kill me and mark another coyote for *him*. Hell, look at that fresh piece Wrangler dropped off today. Looks like she's got some birthing hips. Coincidence?"

"Not gonna happen." Minister's hand cut through the air in defiance. "We're in this together. You and me. Esther and Minister. The Orphans of Ghost River. Can't change what the fuck we are. Can't change the world we live in. We just have to—"

"Have to *what*?" She glared at him. "*Bleed more?*"

"Sometimes, yes." Minister lifted his hopeful brown eyes and squeezed her hands. "But we have to keep going. We can't give up. *That's the only way we live.*"

Esther cackled. "You sound like a man *used to having a choice.*"

"I perceived the corruption the moment I stepped foot in Orphan Rock." Desyre stood in the chapel doorway. Her sharp fingers scratched along the rotten tops of hand-carved pews while she traveled toward the rickety pulpit. "You can see the transformations *everywhere*. The trees bleed. Animals invaded by sinister natures. Can you imagine what it must look like below the surface of things? I dare not step foot in The Dark to see it." The woman tossed her fiery hair over her shoulder and laughed. "You've made quite a mess here, Sister Dirt. But I can tell, you have not done this all by yourself. Our Sisters have answered your call, haven't they? As have I."

The Crooked Woman watched from the shadows. She held the hand of a little boy whose one eye never blinked, and whose upper lip hung from barbed wire.

"He's nearly dead," he said. "As the Grim Seed spoils this earth, the shadow is all that remains of the Pig Father. He's nothing but a servant of our will and command. His undying instinct to breed keeps our stable filled with boonchildren. He serves the Seed too. Once we have watered it, he will be swallowed by misery, and we will be free of him."

Desyre lifted a scrupulous brow. "When I left, The Pig controlled these hills. Now, something beneath the hills controls all of you. This energy has even stolen your beautiful voice, Sister Dirt. I remember when you sang to me as a child. Your voice soothed me." She walked beneath a soft tube of light cast from the hole in the buckled roof of the sanctuary. Desyre admired the bloodroots crawling up the walls. "I have seen many boxes in my lifetime, but none so mutated as this one. Where is the source of this affliction? It must be close."

Snarl pointed at the Mound. "Buried deep in the soil with the worms."

"It shares his grave then?"

"No," Snarl replied, eye glittering. "It *defiles* it."

"I see. The poison is the master here."

"All who eat the dirt will be bound to serve the Grim Seed." Snarl recited passages from the Dirt Hymns. "So long as the Grim Seed spoils the earth, you, too, shall carry its burdens."

"Oh, no. Not I!" The visitor scoffed at the notion of her servitude. "I won't be staying in Orphan Rock for long. I'm not comfortable in this wretched desert, nor is it wise for our kind to be so close together. I've created a life for myself that I much prefer to living in this dust bowl. In the world out there, I hunt, I eat, and I collect rare treasures. I savor the sophisticated life you afforded to me." She stood before the pulpit, studying the Luminarchs roosting on the crooked branches of the Dead Tree. "I have come to repay my debt to you, and I shall do that by enriching your seed. But I will not stay here and become corrupted by this malady you serve."

Snarl beamed. "You're a grower, Sister Salamander. A curator of life. Mother seeks to forget the sounds of Sisters crying—so many Sisters in the river. The Grim Seed speaks to her of a better way ahead for us all. But we are unable to satiate its hunger. Its growth will take centuries at this pace."

"This curse may become unstable if stimulated. I cannot guarantee your preferred outcome. Sister Death is a careful weaver. I may ruin her artistry."

"Time is not on our side," Snarl said, listening to Mother's whispers. "The cities of men creep closer, and the skyreaders grow weary of our blemish on their land."

Desyre scowled. "Let me put it another way, *dead boy…* All who suffer this affliction will be at the whim of a curse with an accelerated purpose." She cast a concerned glance at the Crooked Woman. "Stability will be lost. This box will crumble."

"Mother thanks you for your concern, Sister Salamander. She requests your boon in repayment for saving your life. You'll be free to leave here afterward."

"Oh, I intend to leave. I do not believe in sitting still for a second." Desyre's long fingers danced around her ears. She tore away her comely mask from her true visage: an egg-shaped skull with gray, scaly skin, and a lipless mouth set beneath two pitch-black eyes with candlewick, caramel centers. "This will take some time. Seal this place, and do not interrupt my work."

Splat! Her mask hit the ground.

Sister Salamander climbed up to the wooden pulpit and circled the Dead Tree that grew from the Mound. The glowing Luminarchs scattered from their perches when she leaned her bloody cheek against the brittle trunk. She closed her eyes. Listened to the dirt. "I am not living, I am undeath," she said after a moment of quiet. Her voice was low and rough as gravel. "*Hunger.* Never enough to eat. *Vengeance.* Never enough to kill. *Hatred.* Never enough to suffer. *Deeper.* I dig deeper into where bones rub together to make dust in a dry, cracked belly. I seek the Heart of the Desert. The Deepest Door. I will bloom in the spaces beyond where *the worms of colossus feast on the meek.*" Then her voice turned somber, remorseful, pitiful even. Her black eyes rolled up into her skull. "Yet, I cannot take root because you are cruel and starve me. You deprive me of my right to feed. *When will I be watered with a river of pain?*"

"She can hear it!" Snarl clasped his hands in prayer, falling to his scabby knees. "*She can hear the Grim Seed, Mother!*"

Sister Salamander swayed, listening to the accursed song of the soil, her black tongue licking her mouth in ecstasy. She held her hands over the dirt, and green roots broke through her skin, like blades of grass, and burrowed deep into the Mound.

"*Oh, the despair!*" she cried out while her life essence fertilized the corrupted soil. The chapel shook, and dust fell from the rafters. "*It isn't enough suffering! The land must bleed. The beasts must break. Misery is a machine! MISERY IS A MACHINE! MISERY IS A MACH—*"

Broken Girl opened her black eyes.

Everything upside down.

The little boy with the pitchfork hands was happy to see her awake. He only had one eye and a split nose with rusty tines for fingers. They swung in the drafty cavern breeze, hanging from the bottom of a giant nest by nooses of barbed wire cinched around their ankles. Other Broken Kids dangled around them too.

"Have we sung the dirt song yet?" her closest neighbor asked, a couple of soft eagle feathers strung from his hips.

"I don't remember," Broken Girl said. "Should we sing it now?"

"Yes," the boy said eagerly. "We should sing it together." He recited words to a peculiar song that she did not know. He didn't seem to mind that she said nothing.

Fascinated by her hands, she studied them in the dim light that filtered through a massive crack in the cavern ceiling. She had eight blades for fingers and a couple of bent forks for thumbs. Screws through her bones kept everything in place. A metal plate hammered into each of her palms protected her wrists.

A knife's blade captured her reflection. Her nose was a hollow hole. A hard tortoiseshell stapled tightly to her half-skull. Railroad spikes driven through it in a straight line formed a rusty mohawk: a metal rooster crown. Hinged braces lined her thighs, capped her knees, and fastened tightly to a leather belt around her hips. On her feet, she wore Keds, stained red.

"Am I pretty?" she asked, not sure what she was.

The boy gurgled blood for words.

The Broken Girl looked at the sea of shadows around the gigantic nest—darkness on all sides. Secret doors hid there, she just knew it. Something in The Dark called to her. A soft, welcoming light she could see in the deep void.

A room with windows.

"Find me," it said.

Whoosh! A scaly, giant white tube swept across the floor beneath her. A gigantic serpent rolled up in a tornado of bones. The Ghosteater of Orphan Rock cornered another puny Broken Kid who held a bloody teddy bear by his pretty red ribbon. Broken Girl studied the familiar toy. Something remembered:

Reuben?

4.

Minister slumped on the curb in front of the Ghost River Police Station. Beard scraggly. Plastic sunglasses resting crookedly on his face. He looked like he crawled out of the same gutter he was staring into. He rocked back and forth, cradling his arm, his veins black from the tip of his fingers to his shoulder blade. Beneath the char, nerves drowned in hot lava.

When Esther pulled up, Macho yanked Minister up from the sidewalk by his good arm. He could hardly stand—let alone walk—by himself. She shook her head, thinking he might puke up worms on the way back to Orphan Rock.

'*Course he fucking would just to spite me.*

Macho opened the door and pressed Minister into the station wagon. He smelled like a carton of cigarettes and a few cases of whiskey. Sweat too. Streaks of blood stained his white t-shirt and crusted around his left nostril. He refused to look at her.

"Had quite a night," Wallace Machado said, frowning in the passenger window. "Not sure what the deputy told you, but it started at the Wagon Wheel, ended up at the VFW. One of the old-timers landed a solid punch. Nose might be broken."

Esther sighed. She reached over and squeezed the Ghost River man's strong forearm. "Thanks for letting him sleep it off. You're a good friend to him."

Macho nodded but didn't crack a smile. "He spent all night screaming about his body being on fire. Said he wanted to be ashes. He's pretty far gone, I think." The riverfolk man shook his head. "Get him home. Try to keep him there. His truck's down at the VFW. Didn't want to impound it. Too many questions. Fuck knows what the boys in forensics would find in there. I don't want him driving anywhere right now, Esther. You hear me?"

He tossed her Minister's keyring.

"Yes, sir." She tucked the keys in her pocket.

"I've warned him before, and I'll repeat it to you because he *never listens*. There's a new member of the council now, the son of one of the members who recently passed. He's been looking at Orphan Rock closely, wondering why we let the trash in. Especially if the trash can't keep the bottle from his goddamn lips in public. You need to keep him on a leash."

"I hear you. We'll talk."

"They're watching me too. I can't keep letting him abuse us. Won't be good for anybody if they replace with another."

"We have a deal, *you fucking scoundrel*," Minister said, waking up from his hungover trance. "The council knows the good that I do for them! All that *fucking blood money* and that *mountain of guns* you're hiding out there..."

Macho looked at Esther, hope fading. "See what I'm dealing with here?"

"Thanks, Macho," she said. "I'll take him home now. When he's dried up, we'll talk, and I'll get him straight. I'll help this asshole see the light. I'm good at that."

Officer Machado patted the window. "I know you will, Esther. You're the best thing this bum has. He doesn't deserve you. *Not one fucking bit.*"

Esther blushed a little.

"*Fuck you, Injun-man!*" Spit flew off Minister's lips.

The little girl spun in circles in a room full of windows. Through panes of glass: rolling hills of amber wheat. In the far distance: a grove of apple trees and a tin grain silo. Momma sat on a white wicker chair, watching her little jellybean play, twirling like a top with her red jump rope looped in hand.

"Careful," she cautioned. "You'll get dizzy that way!"

The little girl laughed and tumbled onto the floor. Her brain felt woozy like she was swimming in a fishbowl. The room kept on spinning. She laughed again, hugging herself.

Bam! A door slammed shut. Heavy footsteps. Daddy stood in the hallway, his tie loose, his briefcase in hand.

"What's going on in here?" he asked.

Momma popped up from the chair and smoothed her skirt. "Paul? What time is it? You're home early—"

"It's the same time I get home every day."

"I must've lost track of time. I was reading, and we were playing—"

"Dinner isn't ready, is it?"

"No, but I can start something. Spaghetti is quick."

Momma tried to pass him in the hallway, but Daddy snatched her elbow. He twisted it, bending her arm like a pretzel. Momma yelped. "*Stop it, Paul! That hurts!*"

"*Hurts?* What hurts is when you spend all day cold-calling hardware stores trying to land an account. *What hurt*s is when your boss says you aren't hitting your numbers, even though you show up an hour early and leave an hour late every day. *What hurts* is when you come home and expect to find the food you provided ready to goddamn eat, and it ain't because your wife is fucking worthless. That's what hurts me, Stacy. *Like a knife in my neck.*"

"*Paul, please*, not in front of her. Take me to the bedroom. Do it there, OK? Not here! Not in front of—"

Smack!

Momma landed on her cheek. She looked into her scared daughter's eyes; blood ran from her nostril to the tan carpet.

"Have we sung the dirt song yet?" she asked, her mother's form twisting to become the Broken Kid with the pitchfork arms when the dream world faded away to the bone cavern.

"I don't remember," the Broken Girl said. "Should we sing it now?"

"Yes," the boy said eagerly. "We should sing it together."

The boy sang while Broken Girl pointed a knife at The Dark. "I can see it," she said. "It's there…"

A faint flash of sunlight.

A room with windows.

A comfortable place with carpet.

She grinned to see him again. A boy with filthy cloth wrapped around his eyes. He stood at the edge of The Dark and made the shape of a heart with his fingers.

Once they felt the comfortable bounce of dirt roads, Esther Northamm rolled down the window and lit a cigarette. Anything to keep calm right now. Anything to keep her from killing the man she loves. Her husband leaned against the passenger window, teeth grinding from the curse-born pain charring his arm. He watched the desert pass by with empty, sorrowful eyes.

"Minister, you need to listen to Macho."

"Yeah? Why the fuck is that?"

"He's an ally."

"The hell I have to listen to him for? Our nations have a treaty. *A deal is a deal.*"

"A treaty? Eugene shaking hands with some dead Injun ain't a deal."

"That's your opinion. What is there to say about it?"

He tried crossing his arms, but a large boil burst on his hand. He winced and then punched the dashboard before falling back into his seat like a drunken lump of sweat.

"*Fuck!* You know what I'm trying to say here!" Esther gripped the steering wheel angrily. "I'm trying to be a good fucking wife to you! *Your head's full of ghosts right now.* Woke up to some deputy telling me that my husband's in the drunk tank. All of Orphan Rock knows."

"*So what?*"

"So what?" Esther's jaw dropped in disbelief and dire frustration. "You think Delora is fine with you waltzing off as you please? Why do you keep pushing our luck? You're the bastard that told me to buck up the other day because we ain't got no choice. Then, you go and burn it all down."

Minister laughed bitterly. "I was wrong. We do have a choice." He looked at her with desperate, bloodshot eyes. "We could just keep driving. *Burn up together?*"

"Forget the fucking curse?" Esther arched her eyebrow. "What about *Markus?* Our son? You'd leave him behind like that? In that place? *With her?*"

"*Gah! He doesn't even belong to us. We just made him is all.*"

Esther slammed the brakes. Minister hit the dashboard and flopped back into his seat. He grabbed his nose. Both nostrils bled through his fingers. "You're drunk," she said with a fat scowl. "*That's our child.* The only thing we have together."

"Do we?" Minister laughed like a broken fool. "Do we have him, Esther? All that we do, we do for Delora. *All that we have, we have for Delora.* Nothing is ours."

"I'll never leave my son," she said in a stony tone that cut sharper than a diamond. "*You can, Minister.* Leave us both if you like. Go and drink yourself to death in some Mexican cantina. Turn to ashes, baby. Take this car if you fucking want to. Just let me out. I'll walk back to fucking Orphan Rock, and then I'll tell that beautiful boy *his daddy's a cunt.*"

The sobering drunk hugged his blistering arm. "You know I can't leave you," he finally said. "I just get…*sad* sometimes. So sad, I can't think of nothing else but this hole in my heart. I don't ever want to leave you. You know I can't."

"Then shut the fuck up about leaving anybody."

Minister buried his forehead in his palm.

"*We ain't dogs, Esther.*"

"Then quit fucking acting like we are."

Markus watched the Chapel on the Mound. He lingered on the outskirts of the town square, under a dilapidated gazebo, smoking a pack of Marlboros he found in Minister's workshop. The more smoke he inhaled, the less it made him cough, and the better it tasted. The boy waited patiently for Desyre, who was inside the chapel with the Crooked Woman. Two days now, the alluring visitor spent screaming in the old wooden church. The ground in Orphan Rock rumbled and cracked open with strange ferocity. Whatever she was doing in the chapel was changing things. The air felt electric. Prickled, if you tried to feel it.

Ever since their encounter near the river, Desyre haunted the young snake's thoughts. Her stories of drowning babies. Her prophecies: even worse. *The Pig will teach you.*

Markus put his hand on his chest, trying to feel his snake heart beating beneath his ribs. His daddy always told him that all snakes are born with a hole in their heart, and that hole is a door. A door for Pigs to slip through. *Could there really be a door there?*

A desert tortoise lumbered by his feet, desperate to outrun the hungry bloodroot that slithered after it across the town square. The tortoise lost precious ground.

Do you ever get lonely, Markus?
I bet you do.

Desyre's supple voice hooked into the soft walls of his mind. Of course, he was lonely. The ten-year-old never had a friend to play with in his life. He spent his days alone. Running away fast as he could, but never getting anywhere else inside of the shoebox. Other kids his age played baseball and jumped off diving boards into swimming pools. They joined Boy Scouts and set off firecrackers. They went to the mall and played arcade games and drank giant gas station Slurpees. They sat in air-conditioned classrooms and learned all about a beautiful world they'd see one day. They attended school formals, held hands, and slow danced to some oldies.

Markus would be a teenager soon.

Who fucking cares?

There's no prom in my future.

He kicked the bloodroot closer to the tortoise.

Whatever childhood he had in Orphan Rock was devoured by circumstance. Markus was born a snake. One day he would become a holy man like his daddy.

Then what?

The Pig will teach you. He'd be just another monster snatching babies from the road and getting drunk to deal with it. He'd come home late at night looking like fresh hell, and who would be waiting for him? Broken Kids? Some coyote-girl slaves? Delora? The Pig Father?

That unlife made Markus want to die. Maybe death was better. Except death was just another outlook in Orphan Rock. *All that we do, we do for Delora.*

Some fucking life.

Markus tossed another butt on the ground.

A Broken Kid studied Little Snake from the river rock path. The dead boy limped, one pathetic crooked foot over the other. His oily eyes looked nowhere, his mouth half-stitched up. So empty were the dead. Maybe they *were* the lucky ones?

Did they get lonely too? Did they even feel pain? Little

63

Snake bent down and picked up a rock and pitched it.

"*Catch!*"

Thud! The stone hit the Broken Kid square in the back of the skull. He lifted his bent nose in the air, snarled and sniffed the atmosphere. Markus stepped out of the gazebo, a fresh cigarette dangling between his lips. "It was me," he said, grinning. *"So what're you gonna do about it?"*

The Broken Kid's offered no reaction.

Markus growled and chucked another rock. It bounced off the dead boy's chest with a hollow *thump*. Still, the Broken Kid did nothing in response. "What? I'm not good enough to eat?" Another rock soared past the Broken Kid's head.

"*You're trash just like us.*" Markus picked up a smooth river rock. Large enough he needed two hands. He lunged forward, smashing it into the ear of the undead child. The blow knocked him to the ground. He croaked, coughed up beetles, bent fingers reaching for the blue sky.

Markus stood over him, eyes wild and golden. "You're just a dumb puppet, ain't you? Like we all are. Just some puppet held up by strings you can't see. And can't never cut. You don't even know you're here, do you?" The boy raised the rock over his head. "I'll never be a *shadow*. I'll never be a fuckin' pig!"

He smashed the boy's face. What remained of his broken teeth caved into his throat. White fluid leaked from his crushed nostril. He gurgled and spat out the purple tongue he bit off. Markus laughed at the sight and bashed him again.

And again.

And again.

And—

"What's the point?" a familiar voice asked from behind him. "There isn't anything inside you're hurting. There is nothing at all that feels in that pathetic creature."

Markus dropped the bloody rock and stood apart from the twitching husk of the Broken Kid. Desyre was behind him, her eyes the exact opposite of dead.

"I…don't know…"

He folded into her and sobbed. She stroked the back of his head while he cried like a child. "Markus, this is a small box," she said gently. "You've outgrown it. With your gifts, it strangles you being in a world so insignificant and meaningless."

"I hate it here."

Desyre studied the sun-bleached wood of the empty homes in Orphan Rock. The twisted rungs of wire. Window shutters that squeaked in the dry wind. "I don't blame you."

"Everything dies in Ghost River."

"Yes, it does. Dreams go first." She pushed him back gingerly so he could look into her resplendent emerald eyes. Her face conveyed measured sympathy. "The nature of any curse is the spreading malignancy of an injustice that has no obtainable recompense. That is the definition of an affliction, Markus. It never gets any better. For anybody. Only worse, until everything is rotten and forgotten in time. It will get worse here too. I have seen the future. I have fed the outcome."

The bloodroot suckled the dying tortoise.

"I can't stay here anymore," Little Snake said, eyes red, tired, and itchy with dust. "But I can't leave either. I ate the dirt. Death is in my blood. I'll burn alive if I try."

Desyre's red lips spread from ear to ear. "I can free you of that burden, Markus. Would you like me to release you?"

"You can *cure me*? So…I can be free?"

"No." She laughed mockingly at the idea. "You'll never be free. You are a boonchild who will only know boxes until the end of your life. But you can choose to be in a better one. A box that isn't corrupt. There is an exit here for you." Desyre held out her slender fingers. "Are you ready to take it with me?"

"Who the hell is that?" Esther elbowed Minister, who slept

against the passenger window. When he snapped to, he craned his neck for a better look through the cracked windshield.

"Fuck if I know..."

A mysterious couple stood at the property line near a slate-colored Mercedes Benz. A blond man dressed in a pressed, white shirt and black tie rang the dinner bell, while a thin, dark-skinned woman with glasses and a clipboard stood nearby, taking notes.

"Want me to get rid of them?" Esther asked, but it was already too late. Minister hopped out of the wagon. He marched over hot, hungover, and pissy. He tucked his black arm behind his back. The fire had receded now that he was closer to home.

"Hello!" the man said, extending his manicured hand. "I'm Davis Connelly. This is Lauren Williams, my assistant."

"Minister Northamm." He shook with his good hand, squeezing threateningly. "Can I help you find your way? Most folks that end up out here took a wrong turn somewhere."

Davis Connelly laughed. "I'm afraid we took all of the right turns, Mr. Northamm." The blond man held up a paper map. "Orphan Rock is nearby, right? The town. Not the mountain."

"What's that got to do with you, sir? Orphan Rock is private property," Minister said flatly.

Esther crept up beside him and crossed her arms.

"Hello, ma'am! I'm Davis Connelly, and this is Lauren Williams. We're from Sandoval's Planning and Zoning Commission. We represent the city council."

She shook his hand. "Well, that sounds fancy."

"It's a charmed life if you get kicks from looking at maps of water sources and power grids all day." Davis spun on his heels, admiring the desert scenery. "You've got quite the view! How long have you two been living out here in the desert?"

"My whole life."

"Mine too," Esther added.

"So, you've seen it all then? The birth of a city like Phoenix? The land rush? Industry crashing ashore? *The ebbs and flow of progress!*"

Minister crinkled his brow. "We keep to ourselves."

"Well, the Lord teaches a quiet life is a humble one." Connelly gestured at his assistant, who pulled a piece of paper from her clipboard. She handed it to Minister. He eyed the lines, the grids, the topography. Esther peered over his shoulder, completely bewildered by what she was seeing.

"What's this?" Minister asked.

"Good news, I hope." Davis laughed a laugh that Minister didn't like. Cityfolk laughter. The sound you hear right before the fucking starts.

"Go on."

"Sandoval is expanding. The city council just approved our five-year zoning plan." Connelly's finger drew a line down the paper. "That's where the canal's going to run. The other line here, well, that's where the new freeway is going to let off. We're right here." He tapped the map. "Over there, a few miles southwest, residential developments. Schools. A hospital in ten years. Some commercial spaces. The works, Mr. Northamm!"

"I know where the fuck we are," Minister said.

Mr. Connelly's smile wilted. "Excuse me? What?"

"You told me where we are like I don't know where we are. I know where *the fuck* we are." Minister made a fist. "Don't you talk down to me, *ever*."

"No disrespect, Mr. Northamm!" Davis put his hands up in surrender. "Of course, I didn't mean anything negative by it. The map can be a little overwhelming is all. Even I get confused sometimes looking at it, and I drew the damned thing."

"That freeway exit is mighty close," Esther chimed in.

"Well, yes, it'll run along the Ghost River Reservation border."

"That's private property," Minister said flatly.

"Actually, that land is part of Maricopa County. This proposal does not infringe on any agreement negotiated in good

faith between the United States and the Sovereign Nation of Ghost River. Just so happens you live between the two. Your world's getting a tad smaller is all." Connelly gave him a wink. "All good developments for progress, modernity, and invention."

Even for a ghost town, the main street in Orphan Rock was especially quiet today. A warm canyon breeze made old cabins croak. Tumbleweeds rolled down the thoroughfare, brushing past his dirty jeans. The hairy-skinned bloodroots grew more abundant the closer to the Chapel on the Mound he traveled. Some even vined up the stone foundation. *Funny.* Minister used to walk this path every day with Eugene. Today was the first time he didn't recognize the only town he's ever known. Things changed around them quickly. Twisted variations replaced the mundane. Life ate itself. Evolving at a rapid, kiss your ass goodbye pace.

The redhead.

What the fuck did she do?

He approached the Chapel on the Mound. Needed to tell Delora about the cityfolk, about the Injuns making a play without a Northamm at the table. She was going to be pissed off as hell, he knew. Might even get a whipping as the messenger but fuck it all. He wanted to get it over with at this point. He'd had quite enough lectures for one day. Between Esther, Macho, Davis Connelly, and the tribal council, he was ready for a cocktail.

Potato Sack guarded the doorway of the chapel. His bloated, black-veined arms crossed over his burlap gown and droopy belly. Ever since the redhead showed up, Delora locked down the church and nobody's seen her or the redhead since.

"I need to talk to her. Situation's changed."

No words. Just piggy snorts and labored breathing from the cut burlap of his mask. Horseflies wandered in and out of dark eyeholes and whatever was underneath didn't seem to mind.

"Fine, I'll see myself in." Minister took another step

toward the door. Two meaty hands shoved him backward with a grunt. The hungover man lost his footing, tumbled down the steps, and landed on his ass. He scrambled up from the dirt, eyes tight as bullet holes. "*Goddammit!*"

Minister charged up the stairs, shoulder aimed at the beefy bouncer. The boy absorbed the blow—didn't stumble—and wrapped his fat arms around Minister's wily waist. He squeezed while the holy man squirmed and spit. Then, he barreled down the stairs with Minister in his arms. The bulbous boy kept running, a one-kid stampede, until he crashed into a cabin wall.

Whomp!

Air exploded out of Minister's mouth. They rolled in the dirt together. Legs flailing. Blubber shaking. Fists flying. It didn't take long for Potato Sack to pin him down. His clammy, hammy legs pressed against Minister's chest. He struggled to breathe, kept coughing, choking on his own empty breaths.

Once he was pegged down, Potato Sack raised his gown. The dirty crease beneath his bellybutton (above his deformed, buttery penis) slit open, revealing a gaping mouth filled with stained horse teeth dripping with rank spit. Arctic blood spattered on Minister's face and he spat it off his lips.

Thud! A rough tongue from the cavernous maw unrolled onto the dirt square. It quickly snaked around Minister's neck. Bug-eyed, he tugged at it to let go. *To let air in!* Despite his wily nature, Potato Sack pulled him into his gnashing grin with ease. Fat motherfucker would swallow him whole…

"*That's enough.*"

The tongue relaxed. Potato Sack rolled off his body.

"Where have you been?" Snarl asked, standing in the chapel doorway with the Crooked Woman. "Which of her many needs have you been attending to all night in prison?"

The desertbilly coughed and rolled onto all fours.

He looked up, blood on his lips.

"I…uh…been…uh—"

"Enough." The Broken Kid waved his hand. "Your disobedience has not gone unnoticed. You break more promises than you keep. You're a disgrace to our traditions."

"People from the city came by with maps and grand plans." Minister ignored Snarl's endless lecturing. He looked at Delora instead. "They're going to build a freeway exit nearby. The whole goddamn city is going to be just a few miles away! The riverfolk. They signed on to the plan too. Sold us out just like that. Do you hear me? You know what this means?"

"Yes," Snarl said. "More food than we can eat. More blood than we can drink. Paradise, you ingrate. When they come, they shall water our crops with a crimson tide." Delora pointed a crooked finger at Minister. Snarl's eye shone brightly with approval. "You're right, Mother. If we're going to build a better church, *we'll need to find us a much better preacher first.*"

Minister's mouth flopped open. "But—"

Whap! the 2x4 clubbed the back of his head.

Click! Somebody locked the front door behind her. The man who finds the lost girls, The Cowboy Lizard, offered a grimdark smile from the shadows in the corner. He wore aviator sunglasses and a fat black rustler's hat. He licked across his gecko lips until they were nice and wet. "Well, well. Little Esther all grow'd up it seems. Look atcha! A supple fucking peach."

Her legs wouldn't move. She was nine years old again, looking at a scary world through a chain-link fence in a foul pen where all the girls drank water from Wrangler Vandersloan's cattle trough. She wanted to say something.

But what could a little girl do?

"It's fine, Coyote. You don't have to say nothing to me." Wrangler smiled, leaning against the door. "I know you hate me. I don't blame you either. I've spent my entire life serving pigs. I know what it means to. I know what it takes. *And I know what I fuckin' lost along the way*." He tapped the heart space on his chest. "But I also know what I'm good at. I only ever liked snatching things from people. Then, I started liking *snatching people* even more."

"Get the fuck out of my house," Esther finally said.

Wrangler took a step closer instead. "I'm the best there is, Blondie. And part of being the best is *not* getting sentimental about outcomes. Never did let feelings dull my skills. The cost of living the heathen life I always wanted here in the desert was girls like you. Still is." She backed away when he took another step closer. He stripped the sunglasses from his nose.

Esther felt the wall behind her. "What the fuck you doing, Wrangler?"

"Carrying my burden is all, Coyote. Like we all do in Ghost River." The Cowboy Lizard peeled off his cowboy hat, revealing some kind of hood on his bald head. "I have one last contract left to close. Weren't who you think it was from either. No, I don't serve *that bitch*. Never fucking did. My king is the *king of fuck*, Esther, and he's long been ready for something new." He pulled the pigskin mask over his face, a quilt of human skin stitched together with a dried pig snout. "It's time to retire," he hissed, voice muffled. "That snatch of yours is all worn out."

Click! A silver blade glinted in his fist.

"No!"

The old mongrel struck like a cobra. His switchblade lunged at Esther's gut, but she was a fast coyote. Faster than the rest. It's why the Pig Father chose her to be his bride.

He liked the chase. The bottomless resistance.

"*Got one more run in you, huh?*" Wrangler tracked her down the hallway of the stone-stacked house. "*When I catch you, I'm going to take my turn!*" ***Boom!*** He slammed against the nursery door. "*Sweetest damn puss in all of Orphan Rock. I can smell your stink from here!*"

Boom!

Esther pressed against the door, eyes searching for a miracle. *Fuck!* The stone-stacked house was built to keep people in, not the other way 'round. Small windows. No exits except for the front door. *This weren't a goddamn house, it was a fucking mousetrap! Don't panic. You're fine now. You're an adult. Adults fix problems. This is a fucking problem!*

A sleeping bag and a few comic books lay strewn about on the floor where Markus slept, but not much else. Wrangler rattled the door handle. He let out a cowboy cry.

"There ain't no other way for you, girl!"

Boom!

Esther clutched her head. Tried to stay strong.

"You fuck like an angel! You fuck like an angel!"

No. No. No. Not him on top of her. *Not the Cowboy Lizard.* A thousand other men, maybe, but not Wrangler. Never again. That one time was enough. His dick was so crooked, it only hurt. She couldn't even pretend it felt good to make him come quicker. It was a goddamn fishhook. And he hit her and slapped her and called her a nobody. That was the worst part.

Nobody.

"You fuck like an angel!" **Boom!** *"You fuck like an angel!"* **Boom!**

Crash!

The rotted door snapped off its hinge.

Esther fell backward, scuttled against the far wall.

The Cowboy Lizard stormed into the room, blade ready for the Way of the Pig. His golden teeth shone beneath his snouty mask. *"You're done howling, bitch."*

Voom!

The air split open over Esther's head. A spreading whirlpool of shimmering black ink. Horseflies—thousands of them—poured through the rift. Even Wrangler stopped his pig play, and took a measured step away from the buzzy, leaking wound in space.

Slurp!

An ebony-eyed creature dripped out of the darkness. She rose from the floor, naked death shaped like a girl, covered in patches of soft feather and pink skin. Her skull was an oval, and her long, clowny mouth curled at the edges. Owl eyes—black with golden tacks—sat beneath a spiky, feathered plume. Its legs bent at the knee, and her chicken feet scratched the floor with steely sickle talons curved like the quarter moon. She grinned, eyeing a strange new world.

"*Who the fuck?*" Wrangler stumbled back.

The girl-thing looked at Esther. She cocked her head, fingers curling into claws, teeth pointy as dagger tips. "Do you want to see what I can do to him?" she asked.

"*Yes.*" Esther quaked against the wall. She didn't dare move in case Wrangler came back to make her cry again. "Please," she added, eyes wet, "*make it hurt like a fishhook.*"

Desyre was a crack of white lightning when she sprinted through the prickly pear patches. Curved talons bit into the fractured earth and the high afternoon sun made her pearlescent scales shine like slivers of ivory. In her Salamander form, she appeared like so many different things the desert boy recognized—woman, reptile, shark—all of them *perfect*. She was everything worth chasing after. She was *freedom itself*. A promise of living a better future than now.

Markus thought about leaving Ghost River. The notion felt so foreign and poisonous, he almost forbade himself from considering it. Even if Desyre could cure him of the dirt curse, would he have the guts to go? Leave Orphan Rock behind? Then what? What about Esther? Minister?

Mom. Dad?

You'll never be free. You are a boonchild who will only know boxes until the end of your life. But you can choose to be in a better one.

A choice?

Her words were like sugar on his tongue.

A dream come true?

Minister told him never to dream.

Dreaming is dangerous.

"Run faster, Little Snake," Desyre's sultry voice popped in his head like firecrackers. He obeyed—heel to toe, heel to toe—chasing her to the property line.

There, she stopped. Her form settled into a woman again.

Markus halted a few feet from the road. Being so close to the edge of the world tightened his gut with bitter worry. His whole life he was told never to leave here. "Wait," he said, huffing. "I...I can't cross over. The curse. My body will die if I leave the land. I'll burn to a crisp!"

Desyre extended her hand to him. She offered a look of serene confidence and encouragement. "Little Snake, do you trust me? Do you want a better life?"

The boy considered it. He did. He trusted her. More than anybody, in fact. Those narcotic eyes. *Spellbinding.* She was deep inside of him already, showing him portraits of a life he'd never dreamed of before. A place filled with children, kids just like him, who played together in a lush green forest. They stayed up real late, licked ice cream cones, and chased green butterflies in a garden near a wood and plaster cottage nestled beneath a sky with two moons. She wanted to give him a better box. Why wouldn't he trust her? Why wouldn't he succumb to the offer of his sad, little lifetime? Little Snake had literally nothing to lose.

He bit his lip, pulled away from her stare, and said yes.

"Close your eyes and walk to me."

One.

Do you ever get mad, Markus?

Mad they're drowning you here?

Two.

Do you ever want to cry, Markus?

Cry while you grow up without a friend?

Three.

Do you ever get lonely?

Open your eyes.

He stood on the dirt road with Desyre.

"I bet you do," she said, cupping her hand on his cheek.

He left the goddamn box! He left Orphan Rock!

Markus exhaled and nuzzled into her soft breast. The world seemed so much bigger than ever before! Little Snake's heart fluttered. No more Delora or Pig Fathers! No Broken Kids or Snarl! Fuck boons! Fists in the air instead. Two pumps for glory. The boy was the king of the mountain. He could do anything now! Go anywhere! Be anything, just like a regular kid!

"*Whoohoo!*" he shouted.

The sudden pain started beneath his belly button. A matchstrike tossed onto a pile of dried leaves. His look of joy melted into agony. Markus grimaced, clutching his tummy when horrible fire ignited in his gut and soon that magical green forest was awash in flame. All the children were burning. The Grim Seed carved its name into his belly when he was born. There wasn't any escape for him! He broke the rules like a naughty child, hadn't he?

Naughty children suffer first in Orphan Rock.

Death was in his blood!

Little Snake dropped to his knees. Blackened veins and popping blisters climbed his hands and forearms. The inferno of suffering lit beneath his bones and boiled his blood.

Teary-eyed, he looked at the property line he crossed.

What a stupid mistake! He was never supposed to leave.

All that he did, he did for—

Desyre cradled him. She hushed him like an infant in her arms. The torment in his body—fire ants in his veins—made him seize and shake, mouth foaming with ashen spittle. Green roots cracked through Desyre's palm. They wormed into Markus' belly and he flinched to feel her inside of him, dousing the conflagration with her cool, misty energy. The cursed fire sizzled, diminished until only cold embers remained. She'd smothered it with her *life*. He looked up to say something, but his stomach worked into a knot. She held his head while he retched, coughing, and choking until he puked up a handful of wet putrid soil.

The dirt was gone.

His blood was pure.

"You weren't lying," Markus said, grinning at his guardian angel. Desyre hushed him and stroked his hair until he was able to stand again. The boy wobbled at the property line, gazing at Orphan Rock with teary, thankful eyes. "*I'm free.*"

"No, you're not." Desyre raised her hand to block the impressive sun. A couple of specks traveled the dirt road toward them—a blue van tailed by a motorcycle. "On time," she noted. Markus stood at her side when two strangers arrived. A muscular black man in a studded leather vest mounted a sleek chopper, all chrome, with burning pipes. He wore a bandanna, offered Desyre a cool nod. Strange symbols and bite marks scarred his forearms. The second man, bald and lanky and pale as spilled flour, sat in the driver's seat of the van. Tattoos of cat eyes inked over the soft, pink flesh of his twitching eyelids that he never opened.

"My Everything," he said. "Are you ready?"

"To never come back here again? Absolutely." Desyre pulled Markus by the wrist, her gentle nature gone. The groggy boy tripped and dragged his feet around the van.

She pushed him through the cargo door.

"Where are we going?" he asked.

"To a better box, Little Snake. *Mine.*"

Minister bled on the wooden cross. They hammered railroad spikes through his palms and ankles. The Broken Kids snapped their wired jaws and praised Delora as they hoisted the holy man over the Old Sinkhole in the desert. The Crooked Woman and Snarl waited at the deep gap's edge. Delora's discolored veil rippled in the breeze.

"This is not a sad day," the boy wrapped in barbed wire told the crucified man as he bled out under the brutal sun. Above them, dark buzzards circled ready for carrion to pick. "It is *exceptional* when we first discover the illusion of free will. When we look at our shackles and give thanks to the rust that stains our skin, we acknowledge—no, *give ourselves to*—the notion that not all animals have destinies. Remarkable freedom is knowing that *you never mattered at all*."

Snarl clasped his hands in reverence while Spider Girl carried over a wreathed crown made from twisted razor wire. She clicked-clacked, her tongue lolling out of the jagged hole of her sliced-up cheek. She struggled to get it on straight when Minister shook his head. "*I'm sorry!*" he moaned, skull still ringing from the blow at the chapel. Everything happened too quickly. The fog in his mind was thick as stew. "I'll quit drinking! *I swear I will…*"

Blades cut into the soft skin of his forehead.

Minister stared into the vast desert, blood salt stinging his eyes. He wanted to put his pain into words so they could feel it too—*the burdens*—the blackest fucking burdens he carried inside of his heart. The dead baby faces. A pile of tiny shoes. Another empty car seat to burn. Crushed cars. Wedding rings.

Bloody teddy bears.

Where is God?

Where is God in any of this?

Two pinkies entwined.

I'm going to run away with you someday.

He saw Esther standing across the Old Sinkhole. Her golden hair whipped in the dry wind. She wore her only dress— the same one she married him in. That was the day they ate the dirt. Days after, he made the only decision of his miserable life.

Blood dripped from his fingertips, his sweaty hair, from

his unkempt beard. He looked at the Crooked Woman. "*I opened your cage,*" he said, eyes glittering like nuggets. "*We had a deal. I did everything you asked me to do.*"

"*Cast away the sinner with the sin!*" Snarl turned toward the Old Sinkhole with Delora and the Broken Kids carried their holy man to the edge of darkness. "*Cast away the sinner with the sin! Cast away the sinner with the sin!*"

They stabbed percussively, their curved and jagged blades burying in his flesh like steady raindrops pattering on a tarp. He could only cry out blood and watch it drop into the darkness from the tip of his tongue. Colorful sunspots burst in his dying eyes. He opened his mouth to talk about love, but the world faded away.

"*Cast away the sinner with—*

.

.

.

.

A holy man nailed to a wooden cross fell into The Dark.

Smack!

Momma landed on her cheek. She looked into her scared daughter's eyes. A trail of blood dribbled from her nostril to the tan carpet. "Dark is a prison," she said, grinning with empty, opaline eyes. The Broken Girl jolted. Awake.

"Have we sung the dirt song yet?" the boy with fork hands wondered, caught in his forever skipping-record existence. Yet again, he hummed and sputtered words to a song she did not know. They hung from the bottom of the nest, little sewed up ornaments that jingled in the cave winds.

The Broken Girl gazed into The Dark around them. She could still see that room with windows—a tiny dot of light a thousand miles away from the dreary cavern.

In the bone pile below, Mordecai slumbered, enjoying the

warm sunshine. Flickering ghosts skipped and laughed in the ribs and skulls. They held hands and sang together.

In the distance, a hammer struck metal.

The Broken Girl looked at her hands. Knives screwed into bone. Why was she not like the others? Why didn't she know the song? Why did she see the room with windows? Why did she feel the need to be there? She wasn't supposed to be anywhere anymore. She studied the noose of wire that wrapped her ankles. What might happen if she were to turn right side up again?

"Find me," came a whisper. At the edge of The Dark, a Blindfolded Boy made the shape of a heart with his fingers.

Clink! The Broken Girl crunched her stomach, reached, and slashed the wire that suspended her from the branches beneath the ratty nest. Sparks fell on the Ghosteater's shovel-shaped head. The undead rattlesnake scanned the room with hungry eyes.

She looked at the missing chunk of corroded metal that her knife-fingers scratched away. A bit of excitement rattled up her spine. She could free herself if she wanted to, but not if it meant falling headfirst onto the cave floor. That would be no good at all! Then, swaying, she looked at the boy with tine hands. He mumbled, yawning. *An idea.*

The Broken Girl swung her bruised arms, gathered momentum, and when she was close enough, she grabbed one of her neighbor's pitchfork arms. "Have we sung the dirt song yet?" he asked dreamily, while she clung to him like Tarzan on a vine. Keeping one hand on the pitchfork, knives folded tight, she used her other claw to cut through the rusty wire.

Clink! Clink! Clink!

Twang!

Her legs fell past her head while she hung from the fork.

Finally, right side up!

"Goodbye," the boy said, a blood bubble bursting on his lips when she let go. *Bam!* The Broken Girl hit the floor, and her wooden splints and metal hinges held her weight without struggle.

She landed in a pile of fractured jawbones and tiny femurs. When she steadied herself on her blood-stained Keds, Mordecai rose around her, a rumbling storm of cold scale, putrescent diamonds, and a bone rattle that shook like thunderclaps. When the Ghosteater reared, her bladed fingers spread like a razor fan.

Sssst! Thwock!

Neck tucked, the Broken Girl somersaulted in the nick of time. When his slingshot head and venomous fangs struck the ground behind her, she punched her claw through rough scales. Mordecai jolted in surprise. It had been so many years since the Ghosteater hunted prey that was not a brittle husk of a thing. This Broken Girl pushed her metal fangs deep into his scaly gut. His jaw flapped helplessly when she raked down his long, tubular belly, splitting him wide open. Blue blood and rotten guts spilled onto the cavern floor, and he rolled and writhed as all sorts of parts—gears, hinges, latches, screws, scissors, sickles—poured out of his leaking belly. Parts weren't everything, however. Half-digested Broken Kids, some still moving, trying to talk, trying to sing the dirt song, gushed out of the Ghosteater in a splurt of stinky bile. One such Broken Kid lay still in slime with her arms around a teddy bear with a pretty red ribbon.

Something remembered: *You wanna go for a swim?*
Tough guy.

The Broken Girl pulled Reuben from the girl's grasp. She fastened her *bestest* friend in the whole galaxy to her blood-stained leather belt by the ribbon. Mordecai twitched, unable to coil or slither away. From in between his ancient ribs, Broken Girl sliced out his black heart. When she pierced it, a cascade of dirt, not blood, spilled from the wound like pepper. She watched his body turn into bone and then a cloud of fine dust.

The boy with cloth wrapped around his eyes waited for her at the edge of The Dark, a blue-winged butterfly on his stitched wrist. It took flight when he made the shape of a heart with his fingers. The Broken Girl walked over and dropped the shriveled snake's heart at his feet. "The Dark is a prison," she said.

"But I know the way."

He carefully wrapped his fingers around her bent-fork thumb. They walked into The Dark together. Above, a tiny voice croaked, "Have we sung the dirt song yet?"

"I don't remember," another one replied.

"Should we sing it now?"

II

Dark is a Prison

1990

5.

The bug-splattered headlights of the tow truck cut through the desert night like whetted swords. The stranded woman on the side of the interstate waved, covering her eyes to block the bright light when the old Dodge Retriever approached her broken-down sedan. "Need a tow?" the driver asked.

"God, yes! Please!"

The trucker backed up to align the hitching plate.

Middle-aged, the stranded wore an executive gray skirt, a pristine white blouse, and kept her brown hair in a neat librarian's bun. She pointed at the steaming engine of her Audi and laughed heartily. "I think I broke it!"

The driver said nothing while hooking up the tow. All business, little charm. The traveler hovered, chatting about the regular commute from Tucson to Phoenix and how she'd never had any car problems before tonight. The heels of her pumps wobbled on the uneven road.

"My boyfriend told me to try the drive after sunset. Easier on the air conditioning, he said." She sighed. "Another great idea from a man who has so few."

Other vehicles whizzed by, mostly big rigs and RVs tugging ATVs, ambling down the long stretch of the interstate highway toward the big city lights of Phoenix. The driver studied every passerby cautiously from behind a curtain of chains and hooks. When finished with the hitch, the driver told the woman to gather her things. Purse. IDs. Wallet. Anything with her name.

She rummaged around a messy passenger seat full of documents. She tucked her wallet into her handbag, grabbed some critical files, and shushed a little whimper from the backseat. "It's OK, darling," she told the baby back there. "We'll be home in no time." The infant cooed and clapped her tiny pink hands together. "All right, that's everything," she told the driver, turning around to see her reflection in the glossy window of a welder's mask.

Crack!

The heavy wrench smashed her rouged cheek. Bone splintered beneath her skin, and she couldn't see out of her left eye anymore. She stumbled to her hands and knees. Staring at the dirt, she spat up blood and pulverized molars that felt like grains of sand in her mouth. The businesswoman tried standing up, but the heel of her left shoe snapped off. She hit the ground again.

"Helfff meeh," she mumbled, her broken jaw making the words muddy as fuck. The trucker struck her again, this time targeting the soft spot on her skull. **Crack!** The businesswoman's cheek hit the loose gravel, and her arms and legs twitched in desperation. After a few more knocks to the head, she didn't move at all. The driver waited a few seconds to make sure the roadkill wasn't going anywhere. The businesswoman bled into the dirt, crumpled and still. Her breath shallow, bloody bubbles popping on her lips. She would be dead soon. No doubt about it. No time to waste, either. The moon was almost full.

Esther lifted the bloody visor from the welder's mask.

She needed to hurry the fuck up.

Delora wouldn't wait forever.

Half-asleep, Liz stirred under her staticky Strawberry Shortcake sheets while Stacy dug out clothes from her dresser drawers and shoved some in a duffel bag without care for folding. Momma looked like she'd been crying. Grape juice stained her lips a funny purple color. When she turned to tell her daughter to get out of bed—*quickly now!*—Liz saw the bruise around her eye.

It was the same color. Eggplant.

"You can only take one stuffed animal, so pick your favorite." Momma threw open the closet. Liz wiggled up her headboard and wrapped her arms around Reuben, the best teddy in the world, an amazing keeper of secrets. When she peered out the window, it was still dark outside.

"Momma? What're you doing? Where we going?"

"On vacation. To visit Auntie June."

"In Arizona?"

"Yes!" Stacy looked around her daughter's closet in a flustered panic, unsure of what to grab next. "Get up out of bed. Help me, Elizabeth! We need to go, and I can't do all of this by myself! We're in this together now."

Her daughter stood up, bare toes curling in the carpet. She rubbed her sleepy eyes, wanted to go pee first. "Momma? What about Daddy?"

Stacy froze, hunched over the half-packed bag.

"What did you say?"

"Daddy? Is he coming too?"

"Liz, you need to grow the hell up!" Stacy spun around, her teeth brown and broken. A ratty bandage slithered over her furious eyes. The color drained from her skin until she appeared bluish white, like lake ice. Everything so dark and black here.

"You talk in your sleep," the Blindfolded Boy said gently, pulling on her bent fork thumb to lead her out of the fog of her dreams. "Something remembered, wasn't it?"

"I don't know."

"You are in pieces," the boy said with a sad grin. "He will help you remember. He is in pieces too. Sometimes when you sleep in The Dark, your pieces shine like broken glass."

"How long have I been sleeping?" The Broken Girl sat up, stretching her arms and knife fingers with a yawn. "I don't remember getting sleepy."

"There is no time here," her companion replied, helping her stand again. "This is the Space Between Spaces. Where dreams can be forever if you're not careful."

"Are we safe here?" Broken Girl looked around the silent expanse, only the pale light of the Luminarch to guide them. If it vanished, there would be no way to anything.

The boy shrugged. "This place does not belong to the Crooked Woman. It belongs to another. The one who makes the tunnels. The one who connects the boxes together."

"Who?"

"The warden."

"Who is that?"

"The steward of the prison."

"The Dark is a prison."

"Yes, it is."

The two Broken Kids followed the dancing Luminarch butterfly. The boy with the blindfold never let go of her hand. The Broken Girl was happy to be in The Dark with him.

"Why're you different?" the Broken Girl asked. "You don't sing for her."

"Neither do you."

"But the rest—"

"They're still sleeping. You woke up. So did I."

"Am I dead?"

The boy laughed. "You're not alive."

The Broken Girl hesitated. She studied her knife fingers, the metal braces on her kneecaps, the shell stapled to her skull with spikes cutting the air like a Spartan's plume.

"Am I pretty?" she asked.

"No. Nothing Delora makes is pretty. Like so many shapers here, she is cruel and full of hatred." The boy tugged her along, desperate to keep up with the Luminarch.

"Who is Delora?"

"The Crooked Woman. The shaper who made you."

Something remembered: *A little body, barely alive. She hung from a hook over an old workbench, while gnarled fingers thread a needle. So many children watched from the shadows, too afraid to be seen by the crone in the wedding veil. So many children watched from the shadows when the Crooked Woman slid her knife down her belly. So many children watched from the shadows when she filled her warm empty tummy with dirt.*

"Do you remember the night she took you?" Blindfolded Boy asked, peeling Broken Girl away from her rusty hook. "The night we met in the clearing by the river?"

"I remember the hook. The children watched from the shadows."

"Before that."

The Broken Girl shook tired to remember, but she couldn't see things clearly. "I know there is a room with windows. That's where we need to go. That's the exit. It's that way."

She pointed a blade into the darkness.

Blindfolded Boy nodded, kept his hand on her fork.

"You're special, Liz. No wonder he chose you."

"Why do you call me that?"

"Does it feel familiar? I was told it was your name."

The Broken Girl looked down at the soiled teddy bear that swung from her hip. Blood and mud crusted his fur. One of his button eyes: gone. Was he her friend? Her *favorite*?

"Something remembered. *My name was Liz.*"

"He will help you remember more."

"The warden?"

"No. The prisoner."

"Do you have a name too?" the Broken Girl asked.

"I don't remember."

"How long have you been here? In The Dark?"

"I don't remember."

The Broken Girl stared into the ensnaring shadows surrounding them.

"The Dark is a prison, isn't it?"

Snarl and Potato Sack dropped through the portal of horseflies onto the silver sand dunes. The night sky made the endless, windswept desert look forged from hammered metal. They stumbled down the hill toward pillared ruins that sat in the otherwise vacant expanse. There, a shimmering oasis bordered by pale columns was in the center of a tiled veranda. Palm trees bowed over the patio. Wizened vines with white, bell-shaped blooms climbed their ragged trunks.

The boy wrapped in barbed wire approached the girl who sat near the water's edge with a hostile stare. She wore blue jeans, red Chuck Taylor low-tops, and a solid black t-shirt. Nearby, a floating radio plugged into nothing played "Disintegration" by The Cure. "Are you enjoying your sandbox, Baby Bird?"

The girl's human mask was fully grown in. She had thick, flaxen hair like Coyote, and Minister's brunette eyes. She was an underweight little thing with a fat scowl.

"I'm hungry," the twelve-year-old griped.

"That's why we're here. You'll be flying with Mother very soon." Snarl thrummed his bloody fingers in anticipation. "She's eager to see your progress on a hunt." He admired the oasis around them. "Have you shaped any more pieces of this box?"

Baby Bird sighed heavily. "No. It's boring without doors to play with. I want to learn doors."

"What about your books? Have you read them all?"

A sinister grin flashed beneath her mask. Snarl followed her mischievous gaze to the mossy bottom of the pond where a stack of books turned to sludge in the murk.

"Nope. I *accidentally* got them wet."

"Accidently."

Baby Bird didn't blink.

"Well, you'll have many years here to catch up on your studies, won't you? With our guidance, you'll do fine." Snarl waved for Potato Sack to come closer. The gorilla in the burlap gown carried a leash and a hound's choke chain. "Now, we've come to take you to Mother. Are we going to have any problems with that? *Like last time?*"

"Nah," the girl replied, jumping up. "I'm bored anyway."

Baby Bird accompanied the envoy of Broken Kids back to Ghost River. They stepped through Delora's special door into the nursery of the stone-stacked house, then through another hidden door in the hallway near the kitchen. That one led back to The Dark, the old box of the King of Pigs. Horseflies vanished when they traversed into the shadowy spaces.

Mother waited for her in the nest. The Crooked Woman peeled away the veil from her deformed head and looked to the crack in the sky. The moon was full and bright.

"I want to go by myself this time," Baby Bird said, hands on her hips. She waited for Snarl to take Delora's hand. Mother's creepy butler was a real asshole.

"No," he finally said.

Baby Bird's claws curled.

"It's not fair! I can do it myself, but you never let me try! You never let me *do anything* fun. You promised to teach me how to open my own doors and you didn't. *You're a liar.*"

"You're impatient. Once the Grim Seed is watered—"

"Why do I have to wait for that?" Baby Bird's mounting anger turned into a knowing scowl. "Wait. I know why! If I can't open doors, I can't leave this place just *like you!* I'm just another

89

Broken Kid to hang on your hooks, aren't I? A toy?"

"Our family is meant to stay together until the end." Snarl grinned, always enjoying teasing her with his arrogant dismissals. "It ain't the end yet."

Delora raised the hem of her soiled wedding dress. Her naked, unwashed body bathed in the silver moonlight. A black centipede squiggled in the bush of coarse hair between her wrinkled thighs. A few scorpions raced between her breasts. Her gold-vein eyes watched the moon. She grinned, snot leaking from her nose holes, and stretched her arms toward the stars.

Crack! Crack!

The Crooked Woman's legs broke at the knee, becoming bird haunches attached to a woman's bare midriff. Rectrices— long feather spears—spread from her tail and burst from her wing pores. Soon, dark, and speckled wings swirled up cyclones of bone dust. Her razor nails flexed for murder. The Harpy of Orphan Rock screeched, rising like a rocket ship through the chimney of Orphan Rock until she circled high above Ghost River.

Snarl smiled at Baby Bird. "Your turn."

The tow truck turned off at the Ghost River exit on the brand-new portion of the freeway leading into Sandoval. Esther rolled down the window and lit a cigarette. Country music on the radio drowned out the crying infant in the safety seat next to her.

Children were not something she recognized anymore. All of her children were dead or monsters. None of them belonged to her. Never did. *The world was just a cruel fucking place to orphans.* Believing that put new wrinkles around her eyes but almost got her to sleep at night. *Almost.*

Minister. Markus.

One is a ghost. The other gone four years now.

She parked at the old shed near the clearing and river. The Luminarchs gathered, ready to light Delora's way. Esther was dog-tired, but there was no time to rest. She hopped out of the tow truck. The gentle rumble of Ghost River nearby made her feel a little less alone. No matter what, the river never left you.

"Well, *fuck me*." She gazed in the trunk of the Audi and shook her head. The businesswoman shifted, eyes open. Small, panicked breaths. Still alive—*goddammit*—but mostly dead. Esther rolled her out of the trunk.

Good thing she weren't so heavy. Light enough to drag into the clearing by the armpits. Esther placed her in the middle of the dancing Luminarch ring. The businesswoman mumbled, but her brain was too damaged to make any effort to escape. Esther left her there in the grass, a corporate hump reaching for the stars, stuck in a maze of shattered death dreams.

Next, she unhooked the baby seat from the cab. The infant cried, voice already hoarse, but Esther refused to look at it. She didn't try to calm or soothe it either. It was just food. Like all kids in Ghost River, it was meant to be ripped up and left to dry out in the desert. She placed the baby in the bucket seat near its mother. Something in the battered woman's eyes recognized the child, and she reached a weak hand out to squeeze its knee.

Sick of it all and then some fucking more, Esther backed away from the clearing, standing apart from the faint light of the Luminarchs. *Better to keep your distance from the mess.* She shoved a cigarette in her mouth and tapped her foot, thinking about Minister despite her best efforts not to. He tried everything in his power to protect her from seeing any of this, hadn't he? He pinkie swore that he'd always do the dirty work to keep her conscience clean and tidy—those promises broken as their marriage now.

Fuck promises.

Fuck dreaming.

Pretending it's all OK was easier on the heart.

The first scream in the sky. Esther looked up.

Two winged shadows soared among the stars: a big one and a little one with matching razor grins and beetle-black eyes.

The big one swooped down first, burying its talons into the businesswoman's soft torso. She barely gurgled when dark wings folded shadow around her. Expressionless, the elder harpy put her claws on her meal's skull and snapped its neck back. Her spine cracked, and the businesswoman's mouth flopped open.

Delora's limp prey fell to her knees, a corpse set to sing the Dirt Hymn under the round moon. ***Thwock!*** A fist of obsidian scimitars smashed through her teeth and tore down her throat. The harpy's scarred face twitched as she dug into her victim's warm ribcage looking for treasure. ***Slooosh!*** Black eyes sparkled in dim Luminarch light when a half-dead heart sat on her rough palm. When she swallowed it all, and her black tongue had licked the last bit of blood off her fingertips, Delora spread her wings again and returned to the sky. Her triumphant shrieks echoed in the night as she flew toward The Needle with a fresh meal in claws.

Whoosh!

Soon after, the smaller harpy descended to claim its dinner. It was not as regal as Delora. It flapped awkwardly just above the baby basket. The peculiar Baby Bird had a black feather plume, and her wings—not one speckle of white—were black as a crow. It watched Esther for a moment, golden pupils shimmering.

Esther waved a few fingers at her.

Caw! After a second try, Baby Bird's talons snatched the plastic handle of the infant's seat, and the wailing child lifted into the sea of stars. Esther Northamm waited long enough for the quiet to come back to the hills before she dragged her weary feet to the truck. The desert was finally at peace with itself.

And silence was a sacred fuckin' sound to hear.

The compactor plate dropped, and the windows of the Audi burst. Under the full moonlight, glass fragments sparkled like diamonds on the desert floor of the scrapyard. Tomorrow she'd drive the lift and place the businesswoman's car in one of the many stacks around Minister's salvage lot—another cairn for the dead—piled up behind her dead husband's old workshop.

With work done for the day, Esther stumbled past the fire pit and picnic table (M+E = ME) into the old stone-stacked house. She paused her weary march and peered into the dark kitchen. It fucked with her that she missed it so much. Cooking. Scrubbing pots. Chasing babies. Warming bottles. Now, the cupboards filled with black widows. She had nobody other than herself to care for, and she did not like herself very much anymore.

At least the shower was something.

An experience that was just hers.

The water barely trickled out of the old showerhead Eugene put in, but Esther didn't mind. She slid a bar of soap across her bruised skin. Sure, dirt and blood washed away, but she never really felt clean. She'd been fucked by a Pig her whole life. Hurt by a witch too. Minister used to make her feel better about herself, never let her get too empty or too far gone. He had tried to save her from that after all. He opened the cage. He did it to save her fucking life. *What a waste that was.* Esther wrapped a towel around her body and stepped into the hallway.

The TV was on in the living room.

She crept along the hall, passing all the old pictures of the long-dead Pig Men. The Mound. Eugene building the Chapel with Wrangler and the rest. No shirts. Handsome, young men with grand ideas and stone hearts who wanted to be pigs come nightfall. Sometimes she doubted her life now was any better than it was back then, and that thought—that wicked little thought—terrified Esther more than anything. She still lived in a goddamn cage, didn't she? She floated around the corner of the living room and saw Minister sitting on the striped couch. He had a can of beer in one hand and a lit cigarette in the other.

Markus tumbled around on the floor at his feet.

"Hey, baby," he said, smiling. "Long day?"

Esther wanted to buckle and sob.

After she blinked, her family was gone.

In their place, Snarl, Potato Sack, and Spider Girl squeezed together on the couch, watching static and deformed images on the television. "Baby Bird will need a bath in the morning," the boy with barbed wire told her, gaze fixed on the distorted screen. "One of us will bring you into Mother's sanctum."

"All right."

Spider Girl chittered and pointed a hook toward the black and white TV. Porky Pig was on.

"Go to bed, Coyote. Don't be a bother here."

"Good fuckin' night to you too."

Esther turned back to the hallway.

Tacked to the wall was a picture of Markus, a Polaroid she took when he learned how to walk. That Little Snake charged into cabinets, chairs, even the icebox door. Always landed on his rump. Loved to laugh. Esther took a deep breath and pushed the pain down further until it hardened into bedrock again. She built an impenetrable wall with her sorrow. Nothing got in.

"He's out there somewhere," she whispered to herself. Maybe she was wishcasting, saying the words she needed to hear to keep on breathing. But why did she want to? *Because he's out there somewhere,* she told herself again. He was a snake. That bitch who took him valued that enough to cross Delora and steal away her future. All their futures, really.

Esther drifted back into the living room with a new idea in mind. She interrupted the Broken Kids' hooting at cartoons, eating scoops of bloody meat out of a popcorn bowl.

"I want to take the truck out tomorrow," she said, trying to play it cool. "Need to scout out some other roadkill areas. I'm taking too many from the same fucking spot."

"Mother doesn't like you wandering about."

"If I get caught, Mother'll starve to fucking death. Picking up somebody near the freeway ain't easy anymore. Lots of eyes. More cops. *Trouble.* We can't afford any trouble."

"You assume Mother cares about your safety," the boy replied, picking some fatty gristle from between his rotten teeth. "You can't breed. You can't snake. You can't even dog very well. In fact, you're pretty goddamn worthless 'round here. Even with that pretty pig mark, your stock ain't worth much."

Esther rubbed her wrist.

"So…she doesn't want to eat?"

"Oh, she'll eat." Snarl slapped Potato Sack's puffy hand away from the last bit of guts. "Those cityfolk across the canal are throwing up houses faster than a roadrunner lays eggs. Pretty soon, there'll be all kinds of food wandering our way—men, women, and children. We'll water the Grim Seed again and get back on track. It'll be a river of pain, you'll see."

Esther laughed. "You'll have the army of the United States of America dropping fucking atom bombs on Orphan Rock if'n you start snatching up cityfolk like that."

Snarl's frown rubbed against the wire hooks on his face. Chunky pus dribbled from his cheeks. Fury in his one good eye—Delora—but Esther didn't look away from it. She held her ground against the rodent and his mistress. What little leverage she had left stemmed from her being the only remaining resident of Ghost River who could leave the land for a time.

After a brief pause, Snarl agreed.

"Fine. Two hours. *After* your chores."

"All right then."

Esther tried hard not to show any signs of victory. She turned back to the dark hallway, walked past all those pictures of dead, terrible pigs, ready to find her lumpy mattress and a long night's sleep. Her plan was a Hail Mary, but it was better than having no plan at all. It was fucking *something*.

The Luminarch butterfly landed on a shadow. It sat on absolutely nothing, its souldust wings slowly flapping in respite.

The Blindfolded Boy let go of her fork thumb and approached the odd space in the black expanse of The Dark it occupied. He felt the air below it, and it shimmered at his touch—a ripple in the void—another passageway in The Dark. Deeper yet to go in the Spaces Between Spaces where there was no light or sound. Only the hum of emptiness. "There is a door here."

He tugged the rip apart like a window curtain, and suddenly, there was a new tunnel ahead. Not quite as dark but dim with walls made out of slippery, wet rock.

Something other than nothing, but...

Not a room with windows.

"This is the way," he said, ushering her behind him.

Passing through the mysterious portal felt like slipping into a bath of static. Frigid mud squished beneath her stained Keds, and musty air filled her stitched-up lungs. A slimy, phosphorescent mold clung to cut rocks. Behind them, more endless tunnel.

The rip shimmered closed. The Broken Girl stood in the perfectly rounded tunnel, marveling at the smooth stone walls. What had cut this hole through the earth?

"This is her box," the Blindfolded Boy said. "We're close now."

"Close to what?"

"The warden."

The boy led her deeper into the damp earth, guided by the glowing fungus and their Luminarch chaperone. The slippery walkway expanded into a much bigger junction—a cavern with dozens of round pathways and tunnels drilled into the bedrock with circular precision.

In the middle of the chamber, the boy with the blindfold cupped his hands over his mouth and shouted. No words, just a scream. His voice bounced in the infinite. The Broken Girl was confused and waited for the echo to die. She blinked.

"Why did you shout—"

The caverns shook. Blindfolded Boy held her against him

to keep her grounded as the quake intensified, rattling water droplets from the tips of stalactites.

Bam! The Broken Kids hugged tighter when the first hook-mouthed worm chewed through the ceiling, biting into the floor, its body fat as a redwood's trunk.

Bam! Bam! Another burst through, and another, and soon they lost count of them. *Bam! Bam! Bam!* Within seconds, they stood in the center of a throbbing spaghetti ball.

The Broken Girl raised her bladed fingers, grit her chipped teeth, and readied to slice through the gargantuan beasts as she did with Mordecai the Ghosteater.

"What's happening?"

Blindfolded Boy pushed down her knives.

"We need to ask for permission first. Look!"

The mass of worms, ancient devourers of the oldest earth, formed a small crack in their wall of jellyskin. A giant, lavender-hued eyeball blinked through the keyhole.

"*Who are you?*" a mischievous voice asked with childish intonation. "You stink like spoiled dirt. Death too. You've come from old places and filthy nests. What Sister do you serve? Who gave you the freedom to wander in my box?"

"Sister Worm," the boy began, "we serve no other. We are awake. We are lost."

"*You speak.*"

"We are not empty. We remember *injustice.*"

"Injustice?" The girl hiding behind the wall of worms quieted. Then, after a breath, she asked, "Why have you come here? This place is not for you."

"We've crossed The Dark to find the prisoner you keep."

"*He's mine.* She gave him to me. I keep the *pieces.*" The worms flexed in a show of warning. In a snap, both children would be crushed. "Are you trying to steal what belongs to me? What is mine is mine forever, *deadlings*. She can't have him back."

"We don't seek to take anything from you." The boy

prodded Broken Girl to step forward. "This one needs to walk past his pieces. This one needs to find the door to the Other Side that is beyond his cell. Her home is not here. She is in the wrong box and in the wrong shape."

Broken Girl looked at him, unsure. "*Other Side?*"

The lavender eye tightened in suspicion. "You were put together by a shaper, a builder of worlds. Hard to think she'd put you in the wrong skin. Sister Dirt doesn't make mistakes."

The Blindfolded Boy shrugged. "This one remembers her name. Let her by, Sister Worm. There's power in a name, isn't there? *This place isn't for named things.*"

The worm girl blinked, considering the request. "Nobody sees the pieces. You might try and steal a bit of him away. Won't do you no good, though. He's shattered."

"No," the Blindfolded Boy said. "It would be rude to steal anything from you. We only seek to pass to the door. Let him speak with this child who remembers her name."

The worm girl squinted. "What will you give me in return?"

"We don't have anything. We're broken."

"*Bah!* You're not very fun to play with then." The worms bulged, and the hole with the eye shrunk away. "*Leave.* Don't ever come back here or I'll *smoosh* you."

"*Here, take this!*" The Broken Girl held out dirty Reuben, her frayed teddy bear. The worm girl's black pupil grew wide with interest to see such a toy and red ribbon.

"*What is that?*" she chittered.

Something remembered.

"His name is Reuben, and he is a magical friend." Broken Girl held him out for her to see better. "He'll keep you safe from monsters. All you have to do is hug him."

Another hole opened. A massive hand with dirty fingernails slipped through the tangle of worms. Her knobby knuckle stroked the side of the teddy.

"The magical friend is soft," Sister Worm purred.

"Yes. When you sleep, always keep him near your pillow. You can tell him all of your secrets that way, and he'll keep them safe for you. When scary things happen in the dark, squeeze him tight, and he'll make you feel better. Wanna hold him for a minute? I think you'll like him."

The gnarled hand snatched Reuben through the greasy hole without warning. After giggles of delight, the eye lit up with pure joy. "He's got a funny nose!"

"You can keep him if you let us pass," Broken Girl said, winking at Blindfolded Boy, who looked pleased with her cunning. "I know you'll take good care of him."

"I love your little paws! I'm going to keep you *forever*, Reuben." The colossal earth-eaters shimmied apart, revealing a passage. Darkness spilled from it like a fog creeping along the muddy floor. Broken Girl slumped. No room. No windows.

Just more of The Dark.

In the corner of the bone chamber, Baby Bird wrapped her arms around her scraped shins. Her blood-matted bangs fell in front of her downtrodden face. A pile of guts and hunks of flesh with hair on it next to a stained blouse and a battered safety seat made her cranky. They were scraps. Mother always gave her the leftovers, and it *made her so mad* sometimes. *Why couldn't she ever eat the heart?* That's what she really wanted.

The heart was the best part.

The worst part was changing back into the dirty girl again, letting the fake skin and fingernails grow over her beautiful body like a disease. Looking like a human was disgusting. Why not look like a hamburger instead? Everything was so annoying. Baby Bird just wanted to keep flying, eating, and never be in another cage again. She *hated* cages. Boxes too.

The fly rip opened, and Esther skulked into The Dark. A

Broken Kid—a girl with fishhooks pinning her cheeks into a jester's smile—escorted her below the ratty nest tucked in the boulders above. Other Broken Kids scuttled past her as if Esther didn't exist, as if she were just as dead as they were. Esther never minded them, either. *She is brave,* the dirty girl thought, having learned the word recently. Brave.

To have courage, even when you're scared.

"Look at fucking you," Esther said, sighing at the mess. She set down her bucket of soapy water, towels, and clothes fresh off the line. She noticed the empty baby seat. The dirty girl watched her quickly look away from it and say nothing.

"I was hungry," the dirty girl said.

Esther smirked. "You always are."

The girl pointed a curling, bloody finger at Esther. "You're brave, aren't you?"

"Ha! Too empty to give a fuck more like it."

Her caretaker soaped her sponge and went to work. Baby Bird didn't fight the bath anymore. Even let Esther touch her with her hands. She gently scrubbed soap in her hair, untangled the bones, and used a soft sponge to clean off her other parts. Baby Bird noted her bittersweet disposition. It confused her. Her servant should be pleased to be in the presence of her better.

"Why do you smile that way?"

Esther shrugged. "A frown is a smile turned upside down. It means the opposite of being happy. It means I'm pretty fucking sad right now. I ain't got much going these days."

"Why?"

Esther was surprised at the question. "Well, there're lots of reasons why, but let's just boil it down to 'I'm stuck like we all are in Orphan Rock.'" She stroked the dirty girl's cheek but dropped her hand when the harpy noticed. Baby Bird snatched it back and placed it against her face again.

"Don't stop. I like it."

"OK," Esther said. "Whatever makes you feel good."

She held the girl for a time. Was nice to be close to something again. Something that needed her. Something fucking alive. The harpy felt it too. Mother was cruel and never offered her kindness. Esther was the opposite of that. Not cruel at all.

"You're a good mother, aren't you?"

"*Oh, fuck that!*" Esther cackled, nearly dropping her sponge. "I haven't seen my son in four years now. He's fifteen. If he's alive, that is. I can't tell for sure. I feel like he is, though." Esther looked at the floor. "Then, there's you." She shook her head. "Well, you're not technically mine, but I love you the same. And here you are, living in a goddamn cage." Her face withered in shame. "I never even gave you a fucking name when you was born. Mother of the year here."

Baby Bird looked up. "A name?"

"Yes," Esther said, twisting her sponge in the bucket. "Something to call yourself. A name lets the world know who the fuck you are. You don't wanna be girl, or hey you, or birdy. I planned on calling you Shelby. Always liked that name."

"I like that name too. You will give it to me."

"Well," Esther said, laughing, "take it. It's yours."

"My name is Shelby?"

"Why the fuck not?"

The freshly cleaned girl beamed. She waved at the Broken Kid, who haunted the far corner of the chamber, playing with her rusty scissors and a dead lizard.

"Hey! I have a name," she told the chorus of ghosts gathering in the bone chamber. Above, Luminarchs fluttered. Then Baby Bird shouted at the top of her lungs, "*I have a name!*" She smiled, feeling a surge of power in knowing she was more than just a Baby Bird now.

Her sad-eyed caretaker handed over a set of fresh clothes. "I'm glad it makes you happy, Shelby." A tiny tear rolled down Esther's cheek. "Makes me happy too. And it really suits you. It's beautiful and fucking perfect just like you happen to be."

"I'm not crazy." Esther examined herself in the rearview mirror. Recite the words again. "I know he's out there. You can help me find him."

Just like that. Say it just like that.

She stepped out of the tow truck and walked up the cement stairs. She passed non-descript apartment doors with bronze numbering until she arrived at lucky number 21. She knocked on the door quietly. Too quiet. So, she did it again. On her third knock, it swung open. Wallace Machado stood there in a white undershirt and a pair of jean shorts. He looked confused.

"Esther?"

"In the flesh. I need to talk with you. Can I come in?"

"It's been…a while."

"I know how long it's been, Macho. You going to invite me in?" Wallace looked around. Then he looked at Esther. She saw his cop gears grinding, and he couldn't hide those suspicious eyes from her. She weren't dumb and anticipated the next question. "Yes, I'm alone. What you're afraid of can't leave that land. It's just us—you, me, and all this death in my blood."

After a sigh, Macho nodded. He closed the door and pulled on the chain lock, then opened it again to welcome her inside. Esther eyed his living room. A bachelor's pad. Take-out food boxes, warm cans of beer, and an ashtray that should've been emptied a week ago.

Macho blushed. "Sorry, it's a mess."

Esther scoffed at the notion. "Did you forget where I live? This is a goddamn luxury resort." She plopped down on his faux-leather sofa and pulled out a smoke.

Macho lit her up and sat in his recliner.

"What are you doing here, Esther?"

"I'm not crazy," she said, reciting the words she practiced the entire drive over. "I know he's out there. You can help me find him." She stared at the off-duty cop with expectant eyes, as if he should know precisely what and who she was talking about.

"Who?"

"*Jesus fucking Christ, Macho!*" Esther threw up her hands. "Markus! My son. That bitch took him four years ago. The day Minister passed. Wrangler Vandersloan waltzed that whore right into Orphan Rock, and she took my boy on her way out."

"Esther..." Macho sat back and crossed his strong arms in contemplation. "I'm going to be straight with you. It's not that simple to find somebody taken that long ago. That's a lot of time. The boy doesn't even have papers—no birth certificate. No fingerprints. He doesn't exist in the eyes of the law."

"You're a cop. Cops find people."

"No...I mean...yes...some do..."

"You're the only friend I know. Fuck, you're the only person with a pulse I know too!" Esther laughed maniacally, ashamed to be herself yet again. "But I won't force you to do anything to help me. You don't owe me shit. You know what?" She stood up, headed for the front door. "This was a mistake. I'll find him myself. Drive around and knock on every damn door in Phoenix if I fuckin' have to." Esther laughed again, her voice cracking. "What else do I have to live for anyway? My place is always at the bottom of things, and there I am again."

Wallace met her at the door and pressed it closed with his hand. Esther paced in front of him, eyes wild. She was skinnier than he remembered, tired looking, but still charming in her particular way. She always had the prettiest blue eyes.

"What can you tell me about this woman? The one who took Markus? Let's get some notes down. Maybe do a sketch. Not sure what I can do to help, but whatever I can, I'll do it." Esther flinched, and a palpable relief softened the edges of her determined face. Her defenses cracked. Her complete expectation of failure failed. What was that strange feeling?

Hope?

"You're going to help me?"

"I can try, but hell, I can't guarantee—"

Esther kissed him without thinking. Wrapped herself around his muscular body. His lips were soft as warm pillows. His chin was smooth—a funny feeling because she'd never kissed a man without scruff before. She liked it. Kissed him again.

He pulled away from her, shook his head, and looked directly into her grateful eyes. "Esther, you don't have to do this. I'll help you because we're old friends."

"Shut the hell up." She traced his lips with her pointer finger. "I've got about an hour and twenty-five minutes left before my skin burns off my bones. I suggest you fuck me quick, so I can get to telling you everything I know about fuckin' witches."

6.

Cobra grabbed the tip of his skateboard, tucked his knees, and stuck the landing with a ***bang!*** Cheers erupted from the cool kids sitting on the edge of the ramp. But he wasn't done yet. No way. There was one trick left to hit, but he needed more velocity to get there. He kicked for speed, then whizzed up the half-pipe. Rocketing upwards, he switched feet, landed, and cut across the concrete to the other pipe. Back and forth, gaining momentum.

Faster. Faster. Go!

Up the ramp. Knees to chest. Hand on the nose.

Rotate one time, two times, three—

His wheels kissed the polished wood. *Perfect 720!*

The crowd went apeshit. A dozen or so moppy-headed skater kids on their feet. Clapping. Fist pumping in tribute. The young man opened his arms, took a bow, winked at the pretty punk girl sitting at the edge of the ramp, her Converse kicking the waxed wood. Skitch gave him a high five. "Nailed it, Cobra," he said, his green mohawk looking extra spiky today.

"Fucking awesome, right?" The skater kicked up his deck, a hooded cobra painted on the belly of it. The best board money could buy. All custom. Wheels. Bearings. Paint job. "Hey." Cobra leaned close to Skitch. The gutterpunk lifted an interested brow. "Who's the new girl?"

"You mean Punky Brewster?"

"Yes, you dickhead."

Skitch pondered it, scratching his chin with scabby knuckles. Then, he shrugged. "Fuck if I know. Every day more freaks show up to play in our little wonderland."

"Helpful," the skater teased. "I'll find out all there is to find out." His eyes shimmered in his skull like hidden treasure. "After I piss, that is."

Skitch winked. "Sure you will, man."

Cobra rounded the corner for the bathrooms.

Nicholas put his gloved hand on his chest. The cat eyes inked on his pale eyelids fluttered with urgency.

"You've been requested."

"Now?"

Nicholas nodded.

"All right, I'll head up after I pee."

Cobra washed his hands and looked in the mirror of the warehouse bathroom. His long bangs covered his left eye. Stubble on his chin. Just like his daddy—

"Don't think about that," he whispered, pounding on a paper towel dispenser.

He tucked his deck under his armpit and jogged up the stairs to the offices. The first floor was the warehouse—the hangout. Skate. Play music. Drink beer. Sleep where there's room if you even want to—a paradise for gutterpunks and street kids.

On the second floor, Cobra knocked on the door. Gunner opened it a crack, saw the snake, and let him in. The black biker walked over to the table in the corner and put down his shotgun. His long beard was braided in a Viking style, and a black bandanna covered his head. "Need to see the boss. She's looking for me." Gunner gestured for him to enter—fresh scratches on his arms.

Cobra strut to the far wall where he could see the shimmer in the shadow. He pulled the portal open, and red light spilled onto his skin. Crying. Moaning. Pumping techno music. He walked past them—the lost kids chained to the walls in front of bowls of dog food. They reached out to him with dirty hands and begged and called after him to let them go home. He might even recognize a few if he stopped and looked at them long enough. But why do that? Life was too short to feel bad about the way things had to be. Food is all. Everything has a right to eat.

On the other side of the pantry, Cobra found the next hidden door. He could feel the mist on his brow when he stepped into Desyre's forest. Havenarchs, the green butterflies, danced under the lush jungle canopy like emerald fairies. He traveled the stone path, hopping from one to the next until he arrived at the quaint wooden cottage nestled in the garden.

He knocked politely on the door.

"Come in!"

The cottage was never a cottage, but a room of Desyre's choosing. Bedroom. Kitchen. Or, like now, a hall of mirrors. She stood at the counter, wrapped in a plush towel. Her fair skin was illuminated by fluorescent vanity lights. A few discarded masks lay on the counter near a bloody scalpel. Desyre's black and gold eyes stared at her reflection with indifference. Long mouth, sharky teeth. Scales. Two holes that served as a nose. Cobra looked away, and she noticed his discomfort. Her long fingers reached over and pulled the skin he preferred from the counter. As it melded onto her salamander visage, soft curls of red hair sprouted from her ancient head like grass.

She was Desyre again.

Beautiful Desyre.

"Do you like your new skateboard?" She turned back to the counter, but she continued watching him in the mirror.

"Absolutely," he said. "Totally shreds."

"I'm glad. You've earned it. My cupboard is far from bare, thanks to you. You've delivered a bountiful harvest." She winked. "How do you do it?"

Cobra blushed. She always caught him staring. "I work the bus stations mostly. Lots of people come to Reno to get lost. I find 'em there. They're always looking for a nice place to crash."

"Well, we're almost done making people lost in Reno. In a few weeks, we'll migrate north. Start again. Unlike Delora, I know when to quit before trouble starts." She made a kissy face, spreading candy apple red lipstick across her pouty lips. "Besides, I believe you are ready to work on more important things for me. You're not a Little Snake anymore."

He puffed his chest. "No, I ain't."

"I want you to acquire something special for me. Forbidden treasure."

Cobra perked up. "Treasure?"

"Yes." Desyre smirked, setting her hook. "There's a man who operates a brothel a few miles outside of Vegas. A bombastic gentleman. Bit of a local celebrity, actually. People mistake him for a buffoon, but he's cunning. He's well-guarded and keeps what I want locked-up tight."

"OK. What's his name?"

"Zippo Babcock. He—"

Cobra laughed.

Desyre frowned and continued, "He caters to all kinds of clientele, but I'm only interested in his elite patrons. You'll have to look hard to find where these visitors are served. There are secret spaces there. Doors within doors."

"Is Zippo…like you? Like Delora?"

"No. He is a con man. He keeps something that creates doors hidden from the public and controls it with a special name. I want *that* name."

"Snatching a name? That's the mission?"

"One he keeps in his mind that he'll never say out loud. With your boon, you should be able to retrieve it from the *vast empty spaces of his skull*."

Cobra though about it. "He probably has a thousand names in his head."

"Not like this one. It will be guarded, and not only by Babcock. I'm sending Nicholas with you. He'll be your chaperone and my eyes on the mission."

"I'll handle it."

"This pleases me." Desyre dropped her towel. Her beautiful body on full display. He gulped. Looked down. She cackled at his awkwardness. "Do I impress you so much?"

Cobra bristled. "Uh...I..."

Desyre strutted over and placed her hand on his chest. "Cobra, you need to experience a woman. The fear in you is a weakness. You do like women, right?"

"Of course, I do."

"If a pretty face captivates you so easily, you will find your life short and miserable."

"Every time I get close to a girl, I see...*her*. I freeze up."

Desyre's emerald eyes simmered with frustration and contempt. "She can't find you here. She is a broken, obsolete Sister lost in her impossible quest for revenge against her maker. She'll never leave that wretched land. She'll spend eternity pining for a miracle that cannot come. I felt the heartbeat of her Grim Seed, Cobra. There is not enough suffering in the world to break her shackles with it. Delora will fail, and soon the natives will starve her. She has made her choice." The snake kicked the toe of his sneaker against the mirrored floor. "Speak, Cobra."

"My family. Is there a way to help them?"

"Your family is here! Those people in the desert were hardly human at all. You must always remember you were not conceived from love but as a tribute to a *pig*. Now, all that they do, they do for Delora." The salamander used the pointed tip of her long finger to push up his gaze to meet her hypnotic eyes. "Here, you are cared for. I have given you more love than you know. One day, when you're older, you *will* recognize that I have saved you from a lifetime of swallowing servitude. You will honor me in thanks and obedience as all of my lost children *must*."

"I know." Cobra shoved his hands in his pockets. "I get lonely is all, even with all these people around. My momma was a good person. My daddy too. I miss them."

Desyre shelved her anger, then offered a tiny grin. "I understand, Cobra. Humans crave connection to other humans. Good thing you're on your way to a brothel then, isn't it? Consider it a requirement of the upcoming job."

"Consider…what?"

"Losing your virginity. Don't come back the M-word, the Little Snake from Ghost River." Desyre leaned in; her moist, black tongue flicked the soft rim of his ear. "I am quite ready to meet Cobra, the man. As a reward, I will show him true *connection*."

Nevada. Brown. Flat. Crows perched on power lines.

Nicholas drove Desyre's candied apple-red Porsche 911 with brown leather seats. The odometer clicked over one hundred miles per hour. He kept his eyes clamped shut the whole way.

"One more time. What is your name?"

"Seth Lowman."

"Where are you from?"

"Dubuque, Iowa."

"What's your driver's license number?"

"D25614328."

"Your birthday?"

"September 20, 1972."

"What astrological sign is that?"

"Um…Taurus?"

"Wrong. *Virgo*."

"Fuck! They're not going to ask me that."

"And if they do?"

"I'll snake them."

"And if they're wearing sunglasses?"

"Fuck, man. I'll figure it out."

Nicholas groaned frustratedly. "Do not be naive. These are not runaway teenagers at a bus stop. These will be armed professionals paid to be suspicious."

"Fine. My daddy was a king shit farmer, recently stroked out, and I inherited a fortune. Had my butler here, that's you, drive my ass up to Vegas to have me a weekend o' hell."

"And you want?"

"The VIP Treatment."

"The VIP Treatment. Good."

"And I'm a Virgo." Cobra bowed in his seat. "Happy?"

"Always, with Desyre." Nicholas swerved between an RV and a slowpoke pickup with a hitched trailer. The young man knew extraordinarily little about the slender man who never opened his eyes. Was he really blind? Was Desyre right about him being her eyes? Cobra flicked his cigarette out of the window. Whatever his deal was, Nicholas was about as fun as a paper cut on your dick, probably why he was the salamander's favored confidant. Boring, efficient, and predictable.

"You known Desyre long?"

"My entire life." Nicholas' fingers tightened around the steering wheel. After a second of consideration, he frowned. "Frankly, I'm surprised you would ask that silly question."

"Oh, yeah? Why?"

"Because of what you are. Where you came from."

"I know where I came from, OK?"

"Yet, the tragedy of your history eludes you. Curious."

"What're you gettin' at, Nick?"

"Did you not belong to the one called Delora from the day you were born?"

"Belonged to? I guess so." Cobra glanced out of the window. The desolate roads to Vegas reminded him of home. He never minded the drab colors of the desert. People liked to complain, but there was beauty in earth tones. Resilience and timelessness. No fluff or flair. Everything dies in the desert. That was the color Cobra missed. Seeing the earth crack open and realizing you were so young. "But I had parents too. I mean, I *have* parents. I belonged to them *more*."

"That's cute," Nicholas quipped, waving him off. "Honestly, you have no appreciation for the history of any of this. You were a sheltered child then. I suppose that is for the better."

"I remember the Dirt Hymns. That's enough."

"And what did they teach you about snakes?"

"I don't want to talk about that." Cobra crossed his arms. "Prophecies don't matter when you're making your own way through things. I never believed anybody's born a slave. I mean, I left Orphan Rock. That was never supposed to happen. What'd the Grim Seed do about it? Not a goddamn thing. Why? Because I made a choice and said fuck destiny. Fuck what you think I'm supposed to be because some old desertfolk said the world was ending. Desyre showed me I could do big things. Think outside of other people's bullshit expectations. Be my own legend."

"She is quite fond of you."

"Jealous?" Cobra smiled.

"Oh no, Little Snake. I am content with my place in her world. Every day she grows more powerful, and we all prosper." Nicholas cracked a tiny smile. "I assume it's not difficult to admit life in Desyre's box is preferable to life in Delora's desert."

"No." He looked out of the window, blank-eyed. "Not hard at all, Nick. Orphan Rock was a shitty place to be."

THE LADY SHADE
SADDLE UP, COWBOY

Nicholas wasn't joking about the level of security Zippo Babcock had in place at the Lady Shade compound. Video cameras topped flagpoles, barbed wire wrapped around a chain-link fence that encircled the perimeter, and an armed guard sat in a visitor's booth. Looked more like a prison than a whorehouse. Nicholas put on his mirrored sunglasses and drove up to the gate. The gorilla attendant set down his Hustler magazine.

"Here to party, gentlemen?" He measured the occupants in the Porsche. Cobra tried to sit up, look cool…older. *Like he was totally nineteen years old and here to party hardy, man.* The security brute frowned. "I need to see some ID. Especially his." He pointed at lad, who disappeared in the passenger seat.

"Of course," Nicholas said coolly. He handed fake IDs to the guard, who removed his sunglasses to give them a thorough vetting. "We have reservations," Nicholas added. "The young man here is looking forward to receiving the VIP Treatment."

The guard's eyes flicked up at the mention. "That so?" Then, he looked at Cobra. "When were you born, son?"

"September 20th, 1972."

"In Iowa? I have a sister in Des Moines."

The shrinking teen offered a shaky thumbs-up. "Cool, man. *Rad.* Love Des Moines."

"Oh yeah? Which part do you like best?"

"I…uh…like that one spot, the…um…"

"By the way, you're pretty tan for an Iowan." The guard winked and handed the ID cards back to Nicholas. He pressed a button in his booth. The metal gate rolled open. "Valet parking at the main building. When you go inside The Shade, you'll see the concierge. If you have reservations, she'll get you situated. May all your fantasies come true, gentlemen."

Nicholas drove up the gravel drive.

"Game face on, Cobra."

Before a parking valet drove the Porsche into an airplane hangar in the distance, Nicholas grabbed his briefcase from the trunk. He joined Cobra by the front door. He marveled at the rustic aesthetic of the state's most infamous brothel—a non-discrete, windowless bunker. Some sad Christmas lights twinkled on the roof even though it was daylight and *June*. Aluminum siding and more chain-link fences sewed together some sort of RV park centipede of a building. A palm tree rotted in a pot by the front door. *Not so sexy*, Cobra thought.

"Remember, there are doors within doors here," the blind man said, sensing Cobra's confusion. A few drunks stumbled out, high fiving, rambling on about their hot escapades. They smelled like perfume and smoke. Nicholas caught the door to the dark haven. "After you, Mr. Lowman."

The atmosphere inside of the Lady Shade was smoke-stained with red-light district accents. A weak strobe light throbbed somewhere. Blown out speakers rattled. Mismatched furniture and dusty-leaved fake plants. In the foyer, a group of prostitutes tucked away their make-up bags, snubbed their smokes, and adjusted their corsets when the doorbell tinkled.

"Welcome to the Lady Shade, cowboys," purred a wizened woman who stepped forward from behind red velvet curtains that blocked the back rooms. She stood at a small receptionist's desk. Heavy perfume invaded Cobra's nostrils. He found it almost suffocating. Her hair was tall and piled on top of her head in a puffy bun. It reminded him of the bride of Frankenstein. Her flapper dress was sequined, and a lone strap fell off a bony shoulder. When she grinned, he shivered. Something about her tobacco-stained teeth reminded him of the Crooked Woman. He wished this hostess wore a veil too. She gestured to the group of sex workers hovering nearby. "What is your pleasure, sirs?"

Nicholas stepped forward.

"Mr. Lowman, has a reservation."

Her gaunt finger slid down a ledger. "What kind of reservation?" she asked. "I don't see Mr. Lowman's name on our appointment list. Is he a regular?"

114

"He's scheduled for the VIP Treatment."

Dark eyes blotted by thick mascara inspected Cobra slowly. "I see," she finally said. "Wait here while I confirm."

The concierge dipped behind the curtains. Cobra kept busy watching the prostitutes fondle and kiss each other on a cheap leather couch. They winked at him. Blew kisses. Put on a real show. One caught his eye. She was younger than the rest. Latina, maybe. Brown hair, modest lingerie, and round hips. She had the saddest brown eyes he'd ever seen on a woman.

The concierge returned.

"Everything is in order, Mr. Lowman. We need to settle up the account. Cash only for the VIP Treatment."

Nicholas lifted the briefcase. "I'll handle that."

"Wonderful," she said. "You will come with me, sir. Meanwhile, as part of the VIP package, Mr. Lowman may have his choice of our available companions. The VIP Treatment will begin after dark, so he has an afternoon to *enjoy himself* in preparation." The concierge gestured to the gaggle of women. "Please choose, Mr. Lowman."

Cobra walked over and selected the brown-skinned girl by taking her soft hand. The rest of the prostitutes feigned disappointment and then shrugged and lit up smokes.

She led him through the winding hallways of the Lady Shade. He could feel the growing nervousness in his belly for the first time. Soft moans, headboards rapping against walls, and men and women letting out cries of pleasure composed the soundtrack of the cathouse. He looked at the doors on his left and right, searching for secret ones, anything to keep his mind off of the pretty hooker who opened the last physical doorway on the left.

"Here we are," she said, closing the door behind them.

The bedroom was simple. The bed appeared clean; the lighting kept dim. Cobra marveled at the harnesses, gadgets, and paddles hung from the wall—a plethora of sex-enhancing paraphernalia not for the meek or unimaginative. A mirror hung over the bed. His hostess gestured to a small bathroom. "Wash up if you'd like, Mr. Lowman."

"Okie-dokie." Cobra slipped into the bathroom and shut the door. After turning on the water faucet, he took a second to breathe before splashing some cool water on his face. In the mirror, he studied his brown eyes and wished he could snake himself. If he could, he'd tell himself to be brave. To stop being a scared little kid. To embrace being a man. He was a long way from Ghost River. Desyre had freed him of the dirt.

Why couldn't he feel safe?

Cobra undressed. Used a warm washcloth to soap and scrub his body. Then, he wrapped a towel around his scrawny waist and returned to the bedroom. The girl sat on the edge of the bed. He caught her in a daydream, those umber eyes of hers staring into empty space as if it were home. She snapped back and forced a smile to greet him. "You're so handsome," she said, patting the space next to her. "Come sit down."

He sat beside her on the squeaky mattress.

"What should I call you, baby?"

"Mar—" He gulped. "Seth."

Her hand slid across his thigh. Excitement grew in the pit of his stomach and spread to other regions. He stiffened under his towel. "Call me Candy," she said, running fingers up his chest. She leaned into whisper, her lips close to his, *"What do you like, Seth? What sort of fantasy can I fulfill for you?"*

"I…um…don't know…I…"

Candy pulled back a little. A switch flipped. "I think I understand," she said, scooping up his tight, nervous fist. She peeled open his fingers. "This is your first time, isn't it?"

He looked down.

"It's OK. We'll go slow. Let's start with a simple kiss."

Candy pressed her lips against his. Her lip gloss tasted like concord grapes, the sweetest damn taste his tongue ever knew. He closed his eyes and cupped her breast with his hand. Squeezed it, and she giggled. He laughed too. Only when she felt him relax a little more, she dialed it up. Pushed him on his back and climbed on top of him. Cobra looked up, dizzy from the speed of her play. She unfastened her corset, letting both her breasts fall out with a beautiful bounce. "See? Nice and easy."

Her soft hand snaked underneath his towel, creeping up his thigh. A shiver raced up and down his spine. She floated down to his mouth for another gentle kiss. He shut his eyes, hugged her, and stroked her spine—jagged, rangy vertebrae—passed under his fingertips. The warmth left her almond skin. Everything around them sucked into a black vacuum and stunk like damp animal carcasses. A bristly horsefly tickled his cheek.

When he opened his eyes, the Crooked Woman writhed on his pelvis, pinning his arms to the bed with her scaly knees. Her jaw flapped open, releasing a fly trap tongue that was wet with mud. *Swink!* Spikes burst from the tip of it.

Before he could shout for help, Delora grabbed his cheeks with her sharp claws and forced his mouth open. Her razor-blade tongue slid down his throat slowly, scraping the sides of his throat, slicing open gills on his neck from the inside.

Cobra pulled back, snakeshine bright.

"*No!*"

Candy flinched, assaulted by the magical eyes that flipped over all the rocks where she kept her secrets. Golden eels slithered into her unguarded mind, hooking into the softest parts they could snap to. He watched her tragic life like a movie, and his urgency softened. She was a foster child—unwanted, abused—and taken from her home as a little girl by state workers.

"They burned me with cigarettes," she recalled. "Now, I can't feel anything at all. I'm only nineteen and that's really sad, right?" She tried to keep in the sobs. "I'm so fucked up."

"What's it like to feel nothing?"

Candy dropped a tear. "Sometimes, it's the only way to get through your day. It's easy when you're gone."

He sat up. Kept his eels in her mind fastened tight.

"Do you ever get scared?"

She nodded. "I can't sleep without pills."

"Maybe I need some pills too." Cobra stroked her shoulder. "I'm always scared. Every time I close my eyes, I think about where I came from. About how I could still be there, living that shit life, and there wouldn't be a thing to do to stop it. About what I left behind, and what's coming for me one day."

"But what if it never comes for you?" she asked. "You'll waste your life waiting for it."

"Maybe. But I'm not sure I have a choice."

"It's OK." She smiled for the first time. "Some of us never did. Having choices is for lucky people. We weren't born lucky."

For the rest of the afternoon, they held each other. Cobra felt her heavy burden lift the more he poked and prodded in her mind. He drained her suffering like infected pus, and Candy's aura grew a little brighter. Cheery even. She laughed. Told better stories about her life, and the young man listened. No need to interrupt. She was a beautiful soul. And she was healing.

A gentle rap on the door. He yanked out of her mind and Candy sat up, gasping. She blinked a few times. Looked around. Then, she gazed at the teenager in the towel.

"Did we…?" she asked. "I can't remember."

"Yes," Cobra said. "It was perfect."

Candy smiled a little, nodded, then answered the door where the old bird in the flapper dress stood in the shadows of the hallway. "It's time, Mr. Lowman. Follow me to the VIP Lounge for the reception." Cobra rolled off the bed and tightened the towel around his hips. The concierge held open a fluffy white robe. "Candy will gather your things for you. Put this on and follow me. The rest of the patrons are in the lounge."

Cobra kissed Candy's cheek.

"Thank you for everything."

Her eyes already looked sad all-over again, sorry to see him go, and fading back to the comfortable blank spaces they called home. "Come and visit me again, will you?"

The holy man said he would, but it was a lie.

Near the front entrance, Nicholas waited. The blind man couldn't look more disinterested being in a brothel. He checked his watch, which made Cobra chuckle. How does a man who never opened his eyes see anything? Fuck it. Nick was just a freak too.

"This way, gentlemen," the old hostess said, drawing open the velvet curtains behind her podium. She led them into a small cantina, a bar with more twinkling Christmas lights. A neon Budweiser sign. A few more patrons sat on couches, sipping cocktails—men and women wrapped in the same white robes. "Please, enjoy a drink while the VIP room is prepared."

The concierge left Cobra and Nicholas at the bar. The bartender, a man wearing a leather bondage mask, asked what they'd like to have. Nicholas ordered a martini. The snake, a Coors Light to stay incognito. He never much cared for alcohol. Tasted like piss. "Did everything go as planned?" Nicholas asked. "Will Desyre be pleased with your afternoon?"

"Not exactly."

The slender man sipped his cocktail, eyes clamped shut behind his dark glasses. "Well, the night is young. You may still have a chance to honor Our Everything. I wouldn't recommend letting her down. What Desyre wants is what Desyre expects to happen." Cobra sipped his beer, missing Candy already. She had no expectations. That was a nice change.

"Come on now!" With attention-sucking swagger, a boisterous man in a cowboy hat appeared from a roped-off hallway. Gold chains hung from his flashy, unbuttoned shirt; the links tangled in thick chest hair. His skin was pocked, and purple veins spidered along the creases of his big nostrils. His teeth were the biggest, whitest dentures Cobra had ever seen.

The bartender set down a whiskey, no need to ask.

"Evenin', Mr. Babcock."

"Indeed, it fuckin' is!" the man said, shit-grinning. He took his shot, wiped his chin, and then clapped his belly. "I smell my two favorite things in the air tonight: money and pussy!" They laughed, and Zippo Babcock's gaze drifted over to the curious lad down the bar from him. "Well, well, we've got a daring young cocksman here tonight. What say you, hoss? You turn out a few? Everybody gets their happy fuckin' ending at The Lady Shade."

Cobra studied Zippo's eyes. Shit-brown and unguarded. The golden eels in his belly began to swim upstream, ready to strike. Could it be this easy? *Wait for it,* he thought, trying to keep cool. "Sure did, Mr. Babcock! Came from Iowa for the VIP Treatment. Ain't been disappointed yet! You got a real classy place here." He took a cigarette from a complimentary pack of Marlboro's on the bar top. He smiled awkwardly, realizing he left his lighter in Candy's room. Pants pocket.

"Came indeed, I hope," Zippo snickered. "Allow me, young sir." The pimp scooted down the bar and flicked his wrist. In a silver snap, a flame kissed the tip of Cobra's cigarette. Babcock tucked his legendary Zippo away with a wink. "That's better. Indulge yourself. What's your name, kid?"

"Seth Lowman."

Babcock winked again.

"You're in for quite a treat tonight, son. Businessmen. Saudi Princes. Oligarchs from faraway fuckin' kingdoms. They all come here to play. The VIP Treatment is the *most sensual* experience money can buy. Take it from little old me. I've done fucked my entire life. Had it every which way twice. Nothing, and I mean shit-fuck nothing, compares to the VIP Treatment."

"I can't wait, Mr. Babcock."

Cobra leaned in.

Now!

His golden eels torpedoed Babcock's punch-drunk stare. The snake slipped inside his eyes without hindrance but hit concrete slabs laid behind his eyelids. Cobra wobbled on the stool, shaky smile, rattled by the force of the denial. Whatever was keeping guard inside the pimp meant business!

Zippo didn't seem to notice the attack, or he didn't care if he did. The notorious pimp left their conversation with a third wink and sharked the bar. He mingled with the other VIPs in the lounge. The young snake exhaled, stuffing his wounded eels back into his belly to recover and recharge. He leaned over to Nicholas and whispered, "My snakeshine can't get inside. He's got some kind of wall or forcefield up. It's blocking me."

Nicholas bit an olive off the end of a toothpick and shrugged. "Then wait until he opens the door, Cobra."

The VIPs wore blindfolds. Led through a series of doors and hallways in the Lady Shade, real and ripped in space. Cobra could feel the passage through the secret cracks—a shimmer that tickles the skin—a subtle change in vibrations when dimensions shift from one place to the next. Desyre made similar doors. Carved them right out of reality with a flick of her claw. Delora shaped doors too, but hers were fetid by the Grim Seed's curse. They attracted flies and dead kids, and most of them, according to his Momma, were remnants from the Days of the Pig.

Zippo played the pathfinder for his motley crew of eager patrons. "Now, don't any of you fret—we'll get you home safely," the boisterous man assured them. "And with big ol' smiles on your faces. That's what I'll goddamn guarantee you." They entered a final door, and Babcock told everybody to go ahead and remove their blindfolds. "Time to party, ladies and gentlemen."

Floor to ceiling, the VIP room was white, and the bright fluorescent lights above made the pallor of it intense like a hospital corridor. A boxy chamber with no furniture or creature comforts of any kind. Not even a bed. A curious symbol marked the floor— a black circle bordering triangles floating in a labyrinth of unknown runes and lines and forbidden shapes.

"Gather 'round," Zippo told his clientele. Besides Cobra, there was a couple—a man and woman—with Eastern European accents, and a muscular black man built like a boxing champ. "That's right. Stand around the circle. Don't be shy!" Zippo strut like a rooster into the symbol, belly bouncing. Silver spurs on his alligator-skin boots jangled. "Those of you who know me, know I love selling some shit to somebody. My momma used to say I was born dirty and greedy as a pig, and she weren't wrong. I've made a fortune selling the fantasy.

"Fuck, after today, you'll think I'm a goddamn Houdini, too, but I ain't. I'm just the guy in the front seat who watched his momma turn tricks in the backseat as a child. I used to hold on to the money, counted it for her in between Johns. I learned the value of sex that way, and spent my entire life traveling the world to find the *absolute best talent*." Zippo bit the tip off a fat, unlit cigar and spit out the nub. "You sophisticates paid a lot of scratch for the best sensual experience money can buy. Well, friends, rest assured, you've come to the right fucking heathen."

The ringleader stepped away from the center of the circle, revealing a mysterious woman sitting cross-legged on the floor. Her dark hair curled, draping over her brown shoulders. The crowd ogled. The European woman clapped. The black man scratched his chin, nodding.

Candy? Cobra's heart hit the acid in his stomach, and he wanted to puke. *What the fuck is going on here?*

When she lifted those tragic eyes, Cobra felt the invasion right away. She was inside of him. And it wasn't Candy. It was something else that played the part. Something old, cold, and powerful. There was no resistance to it either. Some things knew how to open doors. Other things, like Father Pig, knew how to break them off their hinges instead.

"Come to me," it said in Candy's soft voice.

Unable to disobey, he stepped into the symbol.

And into her open arms.

Crash! The world inside of the circle shattered like a crystal egg and reformed differently. Before he could do anything, the familiar sun—his old friend—warmed his brow. They stood on a recognizable riverbank, near the water's edge of Ghost River. Orphan Rock cast a long shadow over the valley around them. The smells, the sights, the symphony of cicadas buzzing in the trees— the scene was exactly as he remembered it. Candy stood close to him, nude skin sparkling with river mist. She smelled like crushed flowers soaked in warm oil.

He leaned in to kiss her, to steal just one more taste.

But those eyes.

So shallow.

Not real sadness. An imposter.

"This isn't real."

Cobra pulled away from her arms. Candy blinked, her expression blank.

"What is the matter?" she asked, head cocked in confusion.

"You're not her."

"I am whatever you want me to be." The girl stood up; her legs stretched as her body became taller, slenderer, with heavier breasts. Red curls slithered down her back.

Desyre grinned, sea-green eyes cast over her freckled shoulder. After the picture shattered again, they stood in her garden near the cottage. Havenarchs danced in the thick canopy above. A stream babbled by his feet. He looked around the box of the salamander and realized this thing was using his own mind to create fantasy. "Does this please you more?"

"No. I'm not here for that. I'm looking for a—"

Desyre furrowed her brow. Whatever it was that changed shapes struggled to comprehend. "You want me to hurt you then?

Do you take pleasure from pain?"

"What? No!" Cobra raised his hands, urging her to slow down and hear him out. "I don't want that either. I'm not here to *be with you*. I'm looking for a name. A special name."

"A name?" The creature that wore Desyre's skin considered it while her hand slid down his chest. Her fingernails scratched like ice picks. "There is power in a name. Control in a name. I cannot tell you any names." Desyre's lips brushed his earlobe when she leaned into it. "Name your fantasy," she whispered. "Whatever it is, no matter how devious or depraved, I will do as you say. *I am bound to that name*."

Cobra hesitated. Was this illusion what Desyre had warned him about? The guardian of Babcock's dirty little secrets? Was she the concrete behind his eyes that kept his snakeshine at bay? How can you battle something you can't see? If you can't see it, how can you shackle it with a name? An idea formed. He smirked. "You're bound to fulfill my every fantasy, right?"

The mimic nodded eagerly. "Yes. I must. Tell me yours."

"OK." The young man folded his arms. "I want you to show me what you really are."

Desyre hesitated.

"Is that your...fantasy?"

"Yes. I want to see what you really look like."

The mimic stepped away obediently. The garden shattered to black for a tick, until white walls and a floor snapped together like puzzle pieces around them. Back in the center of the glowing symbol, Desyre withered into a small, bruised, asexual nymph. A cowering cricket of a creature. Its large bug eyes cried fatigue. It looked like a space alien that Cobra had seen on those trashy tabloid newspapers at the gas station. Raindrop-shaped head, pasty grey skin, small slit for a mouth. Below its humanoid waist, a maddening kraken of oily tentacles stretched across the circle, pleasuring the VIP patrons. *What a sight!*

Cobra fell back on his heels, disbelieving his own eyes.

The European couple writhed on the floor near his feet. A tentacle stuffed his mouth while another pushed deep into his moist anus. His companion laid on her back and a thick limb pounded into her pussy, while another tentacle teased her pouty lips with a peacock feather. To his right, the black man hung upside down, legs tangled in squid-snakes. A barbed tail whipped his back. He moaned as tiny droplets of blood fell from his hard dick.

"Does seeing me please you?" the creature asked.

Cobra looked past its shallow, despairing gaze.

Zippo Babcock stood at the edge of the circle. Nevada's most infamous pimp watched the fuck-squid service his patrons with complete devotion. Utterly lost in his own weird fantasy, Zippo stroked his old cock like he was starting a gas-powered lawnmower. Cobra eyed the sex monster knowingly.

"It's your name, isn't it? Zippo has it. He makes you do this, doesn't he?"

"I am bound to serve a name. This man calls my name." The creature pointed a wormy finger at the brothel owner with the fake teeth. "This man is cruel to me."

He noted the purple bruises on the fragile creature's skin. "I'm sorry to hear that." He lowered his voice. "But maybe I can help you? Maybe I can give your name to somebody who'll treat you better. Can you tell it to me?"

"No, I am forbidden to speak such a name."

The teenager grinned and swept his bangs away from his nose. He was getting better at this game of tricks. "OK, you don't have to say anything. I'm gonna steal it from him."

"Steal it?"

"Yes. Where does he keep your name?"

"A name is locked in his mind."

Cobra watched Babcock mumble while masturbating.

"From the looks of it, so are you."

"I am kept with the name, yes," the creature said sadly. "I protect it."

The young man took a confident step closer. "What if it's my fantasy to be alone in his head with you? Can you unlock the door for me so I can let myself in? Can we be in there together?"

"Is that your fantasy?"

"Yes."

"It is open."

Energy shifted and Zippo snapped out of his pleasure-trance like he just got sucker-punched in the nuts. When he steadied on his boots, the spray-tanned pimp glared at the creature in the middle of the circle. "What the fuck are you doing—"

The snakeshine surged from Cobra's eyes and stabbed into Zippo's rattled, exposed mind like stiff scorpion tails. The pimp rocked on his feet and dropped his prized silver lighter in the circle. Cobra scooped it up when he drew closer to him.

I'll take that.

Inside the damp, steamy vents of Babcock's mind, the snake chased after the lone tentacle, careful not to let it get too far ahead. It rolled up like an unused garden hose, leading him to a chamber in the back of Zippo's secret spaces. There, the fuck-squid huddled in the corner next to a wooden box. *The name!* Cobra didn't wait to snatch it. He wanted the fuck out of the pimp's perverse head. The air smelled like semen here. Before he took it, the frail demon placed a wet tendril on his palm and looked solemnly in his eyes. "Will you be cruel to me?"

"No. I'm not going to read it. Just deliver it to a better person than this."

Its tentacles loosened from the box, but it still held the prize away from Markus. Its black eyes tightened, and its tiny mouth curled into a devilish grin.

"When that name leaves this mind, I will be unbound until that name is called again."

"OK. What does that mean?"

The battered nymph giggled darkly. "Playtime."

When she let go of the box, Markus fell out of Zippo

Babcock. Out of the circle too. Suddenly, moans of pleasure devolved into squeals of suffering. Tentacles tore the European woman's legs from her pelvis like a chicken drumstick while still fucking her bloody cunt with mechanical, hammering precision. Another tentacle stiffened, then drilled through her husband's asshole until it burst out of his mouth on a wave of shitguts. The barbed tentacle that whipped the upside-down man curved into a sickle and hacked off his cock in a downpour of blood. It was a pain-bringer, a dark demon of deadly instrumentation. It turned to Zippo Babcock, who watched the horror with soft dick in hand. All of its tentacles snaked toward him, wrapped around his ankles, and slithered up his legs. The pimp disappeared in suction cups.

When Cobra passed through the door ripped in space, the creature gurgled in delicious ecstasy while Babcock's voice shattered inside a bottomless scream. The pimp was right. *Everybody gets their happy fuckin' ending at The Lady Shade.*

Cobra snapped shut his new Zippo lighter, "Z.B." in carved flourish on polished silver. He smoked on the bench in Desyre's garden near her cottage, his skateboard laid across his lap. Watching the wheels spin endlessly, he thought about Candy and wondered what she'd do next with Babcock gone. He hoped she'd find a better box too. She had a good heart, and that should matter, right? She was born in a shitty situation, played her cards, survived. She deserved happiness. Like Esther—

Desyre left his mind, taking the box with the precious name inside. Cobra gulped, feeling her awesome presence leave him. He was glad to be rid of the name.

"I'm pleased," the salamander said. "Thanks to you two, I'll never have to return to Reno again." A verdant Havenarch landed on her finger blade. "Nicholas, darling?"

"Yes, My All?"

"We'll be departing this foul city soon. Make your

preparations for travel. Kill off the urchins in the park."

"All for you." He bowed at the waist. "The slender man slid by, a thralled Nosferatu on the next blood trail. He vanished through the rip that Desyre sealed behind him.

"Now, I want to hear about your conquest." She slipped around the vine-wrapped pillar, claiming a seat beside Markus on the stone bench. His bangs hung over his glum face.

"It didn't work out."

Desyre's eyes smoldered. "Why not?"

The snake didn't know. He rubbed his hands together and stared at the dirt. "Everybody's a fucking slave, you know?" he said after a breath. "It sucks. *It's not fucking sexy at all.* Their eyes are so shallow and dead inside. Not like—"

"*Mine?*"

Cobra swam in the greenest pond.

"What are you doing?"

She kissed him. Then, she let his head drift away.

"I can taste the fear. You taste like Delora."

"I'm sorry, I don't know how to stop—"

"You stop by having no fear of that which cannot hurt you and reserve it for those things that *can*." Desyre tore the garden away. They stood in the red dungeon—strobe lights, dog food bowls, crying club kids chained to the wall.

"My pantry is full of cowards," Desyre said. "Addicts to their own weak natures and fears. *Pathetic food.* Do I treat you like food? Is that why you refuse yourself to me?"

"I don't want to be this way."

"*Then, you will need to grow up.*"

Suddenly, they were in the cottage again, away from the loud techno music and sobbing runaways. A fire crackled in a stone hearth set before an ornate, four-post bed. Desyre climbed on it, her red curls falling over her pallid shoulders like lava runs. She raised her demanding eyes. "Our future requires you shed the skin of your innocence." Sister Salamander sat up on her knees and shimmied her gown off her shoulders. Cobra approached the magnificent specimen and fell into her arms. Underneath her bed, inky tentacles slithered out from the infinite darkness.

7.

Wallace Machado rang the dinner bell.

He leaned on the hood of the police cruiser, arms folded over his uniform. The approaching Dodge Retriever was just another glint in his polished sunglasses. When it pulled up to the property line, Esther popped out of the cab and wiped her hands on her jean shorts. She climbed up on the other side of the gate to talk, dry breeze tugging her blonde ponytail.

"What can I do you for, officer?"

"The council wants to meet."

"I guess that means me?"

"'Fraid so." He opened the cruiser's door, ready to climb in and buckle up. "Now is the time, Esther, so if you need to tell the boss, *chop-chop*. I'll drive." He winked.

She gave him the middle finger and sprung off the gate. When she spun around, Spider Girl's rusty hook tapped her nose. She beamed with a wide, carved pumpkin grin.

Snarl watched Machado closely.

"You heard?" Esther asked. "The fucking council. The Injun overlords. They want—"

"We heard." Snarl licked his lips, a razor barb sliced through his tongue like corned beef. "Go. Hear them out. Accept no deals. Without a snake, we have so little leverage."

"All right. That I can do."

Esther gathered her things from the Retriever and climbed over the gate. Her old boots hit the ground. In the cruiser, she gave Macho the side-eye. "Is there really a council meeting, or is this jailbreak your new fucking scheme to get laid?"

Macho laughed and shook his head. "Sadly, there's a council meeting. But that is an excellent idea, Mrs. Northamm! The dead ones never say no to a council meeting, do they?"

"No, they don't. Delora still respects the parley. Long as she don't figure out the truth about us getting fresh on occasion, you can just about pick me up anytime."

"What would they do?"

"Come again?"

"The Crooked Woman. Her dead ones. What would happen if they found out about us getting *fresh*?"

Esther shrugged. "Kill me, probably. She would've a long time ago, if'n I weren't the only slave she has left with a heartbeat and a fake driver's license to pick up her food."

"She'd starve without you."

"Think so. None of the rest of them can leave the land like I can." Esther chewed her thumbnail nervously. "Lucky fucking me, I'm suddenly *important* 'round here."

They drove to the old meeting place on the Ghost River Valley overlook. Macho filled her in the best he could along the way. "Do yourself a favor, Esther. Don't do what Minister used to do. Act humble before the council. *Be respectful.* They know the current situation in Orphan Rock. She's weak. Losing Minister changed the landscape for everybody. Without his special nature, the council sees no benefit keeping the Crooked Woman appeased out there in Pig Country. Right now, Delora's a burden."

"We've buried a lot of bodies together, our two peoples." Esther's voice had a tinge of hope. "That counts for something meaningful, right? We have a *history* together."

"It counts for little, I'm afraid. The saddest truth about history is that it's forgotten or changed with time and power. Our tribe values and protects stories for that very reason."

"Well, *fuck*, Orphan Rock certainly has a story."

"A bad one."

"All right, Macho, I'll mind my manners." When she unfastened her seat belt, his strong hand wrapped around her knee. His square jaw tightened. Voice grave.

"The tribal council is your enemy, and while we're up on that hill, *so am I.* We have all the power now. Don't act like you have any. Be humble and pray for mercy."

Esther laughed. "Why that's my fucking specialty, *sir.*"

Shelby was lying on the travertine tile by the koi pond in her oasis—a playground for children, who weren't allowed to have any real fun. Her long finger swirled in the fresh pool of water. She watched ripples spread across the wet glass with a listless gaze. So fucking restless. She was stuck in Mother's mud all the time, wearing a mask, and playing children's games. Everything felt deathly boring in this sandbox. She gazed at the empty sky, too restless to shape anything in it. *Who cares?*

Out of the cage.

I want out of the fucking cage.

This box was not hers. Mother put her inside of it. Mother, *the shaper.* The builder of worlds. *Some joke that was!* Shelby's world was just one color—shit brown—and all sand. *"You will learn to build in here. Mother will teach you the ways of your nature,"* Snarl promised her. Sounded terrific, right? Except,

Mother refused to teach Baby Bird anything. The Crooked Woman's agenda was focused only on the Grim Seed.

That old curse again.

When she was a child, Shelby believed the boy wrapped in barbed wire when he told her she was not ready for advanced lessons, like tearing open doors and building bridges between worlds. But now, a little older, Shelby was wiser and more suspicious of Mother's intentions. Knowledge was power. The Harpy of Ghost River wanted to keep it for herself.

The teenager sighed. *What can I do about it?*

Everything that made up the desert felt like a jail cell. What good is God-given power if you can't use it for anything? Why have claws if you're not allowed to cleave any muscle?

And so, the hunger remained.

That *bottomless, hellish emptiness* persisted.

And the *boredom. GAWD. The boredom.*

It kept Shelby awake at night. How could anybody sit still in the world with an empty feeling like this in their heart? The yearning for meat only ever stopped when she fed and would immediately bubble back up soon after. Always worse than before. Moreover, there was nothing she could do about the craving. No food in this prison block unless the warden tossed her a bucket of scraps and leftover tidbits of the stringiest parts. Incarceration wasn't right. Unnatural for her kind. She was a hunter, and whatever the hell she was wasn't meant to be caged!

What's that?

A Broken Kid, a girl in a pink dress with a lolling neck that never sat right, stumbling down the dunes. "What is it now?" Shelby pulled her hand from the pool, then stood up to greet her. The Broken Kid ambled between the sand-carved pillars. When she stopped, her little jaw dangled open, a dirt-flecked string of drool sticking to her ruffled shoulder. "Well? Tell me."

Swink! Shelby's claw sparked against the marble pillar.

The dead child wobbled, lost in some dirt dream.

"*You're so boring!*" The harpy marched over to the corpseling and sniffed the crook of her floppy neck. She savored the musty scent of Ghost River that wafted from the dead toy like perfume—all of the blood, the life in the muscles, the bugs, reptiles, and beasts that crawled in the hills and cracks of Orphan Rock—clung to her dress. Shelby could almost *taste* the life.

Holy fuck, a feast of flesh and hearts—and Mother *never* let her have the hearts—waited for her on the other side of this empty desert. Her hidden mouth watered.

Hearts.

Juicy as peaches.

So soft in her mouth!

Shelby growled, kicked the tile floor with her Converse and it squeaked. The twelve-year-old wasn't allowed to eat unless Mother let her. The problem was, Mother was greedy. *She was a selfish, bad Mother.* The young harpy glanced at the ripped door on top of the tallest sand dune. A door from the Days of The Pig, and only Mother and her chosen could open it. Years ago, after she crawled out of her crib and killed a man to impress her servant, Esther, Mother locked her behind it and called this cage a *gift*. But that heart was the *real* gift. The only heart she ever tasted.

Ate the whole fucking thing *and loved it.*

"Why are you here?"

The dead girl in the pink dress dropped a roll of toilet paper on the ground.

Shelby rolled her eyes. *Supplies.*

Toilet fucking paper. How about food?

Shelby shuddered with rage, ready to tear her guest's head off to make a point. She hated Broken Kids. From the dark spaces they watched her like spies. Cockroaches never getting close enough to play with and never talking unless it was the little asshole with the barbed wire smile. Worst of all, they weren't nice to Esther. This angered Shelby the most. *Esther was hers.* The Broken Kids acted as if she belonged to *them*. Were cruel at times.

And whenever Shelby saw one of them abuse her caretaker without permission, Baby Bird made a promise to murder that Broken Kid one day. *If she ever got out of the damn cage, that is!*

Across the veranda, her undead visitor's eyes appeared like freshly dug holes. Shelby looked in them and saw no bottom. Delora's eyes. Ever watchful.

Mother never let Shelby have a second to herself.

Not one goddamn second.

"Stop spying on me."

The young harpy snatched the dead girl's cheeks in her claws and stared into those vacant eyes. She aimed her temper at Delora, who watched from inside of the reanimated corpse. Fury propelled Baby Bird like a launched spear into her rotted mind. She felt part of herself transfer from physical to spirit. A new lesson had been learned. This teacher's name was *rage*.

Inside of the child, Shelby soared above a labyrinth of metal walls covered in twisting vines and purple flowers. The Grim Seed infested this husk, its malicious roots replacing dead veins with black roots. It moved her body, but something else controlled it—something named Mother.

The harpy's disembodied energy descended into the center of the soul maze, surfing on a wave of razor-edged black feathers. Mother stood in the tall grass. Arms parted, palms down. In each claw she worked a marionette crossbar with taught wires that disappeared into the grass and soft ground of the dead girl's subconsciousness. She moved the Broken Kid like a dancing puppet, yet it wasn't exactly Mother pulling strings. Not all of her, at least. Like Shelby, Delora was a shadow. A remnant.

A parasite?

"I found you," Shelby proclaimed, surprised to hear her own voice. "I want a turn. Let me control her." The eager harpy reached for a crossbar. Mother's shadow countered her move with a vicious slap to the hand. Shelby yipped, then rolled her lips under her teeth. She could feel her true face—her perfect face—breaking through fake skin, eager to gnash and bite.

The twelve-year-old backed away from the grim puppeteer, claws hardening.

"I'm sick of you telling me no!"

Shelby flew across the ground like a fire-licked canon ball. Her obsidian talons sliced through Mother's shadow, but it was less than moist vapor. She screamed, and tears rolled down her cheeks, slashing at a phantom in a yellowed wedding dress until she was gone from the dead girl's consciousness.

On the ground, her crossbars lay in the grass, the wires useless without command. Shelby picked them up. As she did, the realm of the child's mind tremored. Her body responded to her puppeteering, and Baby Bird let out a laugh to see the world through its dead eyes. She grinned, sipping power.

"Now, you're *my* pet."

Sister Worm's muddy tunnel sloped endlessly downward, slick, and treacherous, and the Luminarch struggled to light a path forward in The Dark toward the prisoner's cell. The gloom was thicker here, coagulating the deeper they descended into the strange prison. Blindfolded Boy told her stories to pass the time. One he repeated several times was about a boy born with no eyes, who was drowned in the river by his own father. He was hated because he was born imperfect. A Forsaken Kid, they called him. A boy with no name, who was tossed away.

"He had no life. No memories. Except one." The boy made the shape of a heart with his fingers. "But he came back. His father pulled him from the river to atone for his cruelty, and the boy would serve him. The boy always chose love. He wanted love to win in the end."

"Can I ask something?" the Broken Girl said. "I think it's important."

"Yes."

"You told Sister Worm I needed help crossing over to the Other Side? What does that mean? What's the Other Side? Why do I need to go there?"

"I can't tell you why you must go, but I *can* tell you that there are many sides of places to explore. Sometimes all of those sides merge and overlap, like a river. Sometimes it's hard to tell what side you're on. Sometimes there's no sides at all and you're just in The Dark."

"I don't understand."

"Me neither. But I'll try to explain it better if I can. We're on one side of things. *This side.*" He gestured to the brown, slimy walls of Sister Worm's box. "Before you were broken, you came from another side. *Ok-la-homa?* You need to get back there."

"A room with windows."

Blindfolded Boy nodded. "Everything is connected, Liz, and all of the sides have doors, but you need a map to find the right ones or you'll get lost in the hallways."

The Broken Girl considered this. A sad look withered her stitched face. Her oily eyes slid across the damp walls. "I don't know what I'm supposed to do. I feel lost here."

"You're broken," Blindfolded Boy replied. "You won't know what to do until you've been put back together again. Your real spirit is much bigger than the body she gave you. That's why we need the prisoner to repair you. Only he can help you get to the Other Side."

They wandered further into the darkness together.

"The prisoner. Does he have a name?"

"He does, but I can't say it. There's power in a name. *Control.*"

"What does that mean?"

"I don't know."

"He sounds dangerous."

"He is, and he's powerful too."

Broken Girl scraped her knife fingers along the mossy

walls in thought. "If he's so powerful, how did they catch him? Put him in a dark place like this?"

"They betrayed him. They shattered him."

"Who did?"

The Blindfolded Boy tugged on her fork, pulling her along. "That's not my tragedy to tell."

The floppy-necked dead girl in the pink dress was a skeleton key. She saw the shapers' doors and could open them with ease. The child never resisted, even when Shelby demanded she open the Pig's door that kept her locked in her drab sandbox. Controlling the Broken Kid was easy, the part she'd planted inside of her obedient mind worked the puppeteer's crossbars to match the commands Shelby manifested in her thoughts. No wonder Delora could control so many. After her remnant took command of the corpse, it became beholden to her simple desires and wishes. As their bond grew, it anticipated her wants, and Baby Bird could see through its eyes at any time.

Shelby followed her into The Dark, creeping carefully in the malaise of nothingness. She had been in The Pig's box many times, often led on a leash by Potato Sack. But Shelby had never seen it through the eyes of a Broken Kid before. They had all of the right keys to every door. More importantly, they saw every lock—even the hidden ones.

So many cuts and tears in The Dark. Even an inexperienced shaper knew this wasn't the work of an artisan. Delora was neater than this realm demonstrated. She did not shape it—living anger did, a heart so black they could breathe it in like smoke and ashes. Was there any reason for this madness?

Wet slits. Bleeding portals. Horseflies. How many rooms and worlds attached to this corrupted place? Shelby wondered if the Grim Seed could creep into other realms from here. She imagined a spider's web of dark passageways leading to a thousand weird worlds. Maybe that was the plan?

But Mother never told her the plan.

Snarl did, of course.

"Once the Grim Seed spoils the Earth, you'll be a free bird. And you'll know your boon by then. Mother is a shaper, a builder of worlds. A lover of children. What will you become?"

Shelby didn't know the answer to that, nor did she believe Mother or Snarl would ever tell her the truth anyway. She was on her own now and would handle pressing matters like an adult, such as wondering which door led to freedom, food, and *fun*.

A spotlight of bright sunshine cut through retreating shadows. Shelby ran over and stroked Pink's broken neck in approval. Her pet held open a hidden doorway to the desert. The two fugitives from The Dark stepped toward the edge of Ghost River. Those delicious smells assaulted Shelby's nose again. *Skin.* She sucked them all in, could feel the saliva production kickstart on her tongue. *Meat.* Her gaze followed her nose beneath a blazing ball of sky fire. Across the gentle river, a pickup truck drove up a twisty mountain road toward the summit. *Life.*

"I'm hungry."

Pink reached for her hand.

"I'll bring you something back. *Promise.*"

Whoosh! Shelby burst from the bushes, tearing off her mask with an echoing cry of liberation. The creature with the glitterdeath eyes moved like a cougar. She sprinted for the river, hopped across slippery rocks, and dug her fingernails into the desert soil to gain more speed. On the other side, she felt immediately lighter as if she'd crossed over into a whole new world of opportunity. No more cages. She leaned into the freedom and darted up the mountain.

The incline didn't slow her down. The brighter her hunger burned, the faster she dashed and the higher she jumped. She fantasized about the kill, about having a whole body to eat. Maybe more than one by herself! Did Mother starve her to keep her small?

Weak? *Just enough food to be a proper, dependent, and beholden daughter?* She was Dark Bird now. Beholden to no mothers.

Shelby grit her squared teeth. They broke apart in her mouth and she spat out the pieces like chunks of crushed plaster. A row of triangular incisors sliced through her red gums. The corners of her lips ripped apart, making her mouth three times the length of her false one. As she picked up speed, sharp bristles broke through the pores of her skin, slicing through her t-shirt and jeans, and unrolled into waves of black feathers. Her toes curled into obsidian sickles, and a pair of shoes fell to pieces on the gravelly trail behind the girl who had become the roadrunner.

It's time to eat the fucking world now, isn't it?

Dark Bird chittered like static on dead air.

The older councilwoman wore the most beautiful turquoise necklace Esther had ever seen. She had a strong, unbreakable gaze. To her right sat a grumpy, old man who chewed his gums and looked at the dirt. Pain and anger roiled inside of him. He eyed the Pig's mark on Esther's wrist, and she dared not scratch it. A fresh face sat at the firepit too: A younger riverfolk male whose bourbon eyes stung with venomous contempt.

"I don't care to know your name," the councilwoman told Esther, waving off Macho's introductions. "You're the last one. Once you're gone, she will have no servants left, and The Pig will have no bride. So, I will call you Last One until *you* die." She looked at Wallace. "Officer Machado tells us you have no extra abilities? Is this correct?"

"Yes'm. I have no boon."

"*Boon*," the old man said, then spat. "*That spider's nest you call a church needs a stick of dynamite tossed in the front door...*"

"So, you're a just a...servant?" the woman asked, ignoring the old man's anger. "A pretty, white slave? Leftover from Eugene

Northamm's grand experiment, are we?"

"Yes'm. I came to Ghost River as a child."

"Well, Last One, tonight you're also going to become a courier with a critical message. Will you be able to remember it if I tell it to you? It's important she hears it."

"Yes. I'll do my best, ma'am."

"Tell Delora that new developments and the inevitable march of progress toward us all have rendered our previous agreements *null*. It's a new day in the Ghost River Nation."

Esther side-eyed Wallace.

What did she mean by that?

New day?

The woman continued, "We've come to terms with our neighbors in Sandoval and have reached an important agreement in our burgeoning relationship. We'll be opening a brand-new casino near the freeway exit. Construction starts in a few months."

Esther gasped. "How near the freeway exit?"

"Orphan Rock."

Esther scanned the tribal council. Surely, they weren't this fucking stupid! But the riverfolk grinned, seemingly content with their terrible decision. Her worry sprouted like a thorny weed.

"May I say something?"

The councilwoman nodded. "Please do."

"*You'll be fucking nuts building anything on the land near Orphan Rock!*" Esther looked ill, green around the edges. "That's her land. *You fucking know that.*"

Bam! The young councilman kicked the firepit.

"*Her land?*" he asked angrily, on his feet. "You share the same nerve as the Crooked Woman. *That land is not hers.* She haunts it, like a ghost dog. Clings to it like a dead history. If she does not accept our demands, we will tighten her leash. We'll make her remember our agency."

"Mister, I don't think making threats is a good idea—"

"Good thing you weren't asked!" the man snapped. After

a frigid pause, he settled down into his seat again. "Delora will listen and obey, or there will be *war*."

"That land is precious to her," Esther said, rubbing her temples in frustration. "You don't get it! She won't just let it go because you're asking her to. She can't!"

"We're not asking, *you fool*."

The councilwoman lifted her hand to calm tension. "We appreciate your concern, Last One, but we are not interested in negotiating land ownership with you. *We will take what we need.* Now, here is the rest of the message for your masters…"

The demands were simple: The Crooked Woman. The Broken Kids. Esther. Nobody from Orphan Rock, living or dead, past, future, or present, was allowed near the casino or its construction site. "If she disobeys, we'll shut down all of the roads leading to Orphan Rock for a hundred years. She will starve. Our grandchildren will make sure of it."

Esther couldn't believe it. Macho offered no help. He looked down at his boots.

"Think about this!" Esther pleaded. "It's a big goddamn desert you have here. Enough room for a million casinos. Build it somewhere else! You know what she is!"

The councilwoman nodded. "She's a tragedy stuck in a time that's passed her by."

"No, she's much more than that."

"Enlighten us then, Last One."

"She's a fucking *predator*. She don't think like you and I think. Not one shared thought between us. *That's where everybody fucks up with her*! They think she's some feeble old spook, hunched over and frail. You shouldn't fear little old Delora, right? *Fuck.* I've watched her hunt for years. I know exactly what she can do. If you don't reconsider this plan, she'll steal your children like the old days. You don't want that again."

"Not if they don't crossover to the haunted land. She won't steal anyone then." The young man folded his arms, pleased with these circumstances. "We'll build tall fences around it. So tall even an eagle can't fly over it. No one will have access to Orphan Rock for a century. She will starve and turn to dust in time." The young man sighed and looked at the lights of Phoenix in the far distance. "We should have never let it get this far."

Esther put her hands on her hips.

"We all carry our burdens here, don't we?"

"We have said all there is to say, Last One." The councilwoman looked at Macho, who took Esther by the elbow. "Be safe in your travels. May your spirit find peace one day."

"*You're making a big mistake!*" Esther shouted, trying to pull out of Macho's vicelike grip. "*You're gonna fucking kill a lot of people! Do you hear me? You fucking hear—*"

"I'm getting too old for this shit," the munitions inspector from the Ghost River VFW complained, stacking another ammo box on the stockpile at the back of Solemn Cave. He took a breath to wipe sweat from his brow with a red handkerchief. "Wonder if I'll get some worker's compensation for my trouble? All this heavy lifting can't be good for my back."

"You'll be lucky if they buy you a round at the Wagon Wheel, old-timer!" the younger of the two riverfolk men, a tribal police officer, yelled over the rattling generator. "Speaking of a cold one, it's about that time! Let's finish this up."

"Almost done." The older man cracked open a faded crate stamped with the date 1978. He checked the .308 rounds with a flashlight. "It's critical to inspect old cases for corrosion. Rust spreads to new and old bullets like a virus. Gotta keep them all squeaky clean." He put the ammo back and sealed the case. He looked at his escort, who shined a flashlight in the tunnel leading toward the entrance. He didn't say much but looked alert.

"Something wrong?"

"Something moved."

"Probably a coyote. They live up in these rocks."

"Maybe. Seemed bigger. You almost done?"

"One more to check."

The munitions inspector popped the clasps on a gray military surplus case. Rows of hand grenades lay in compartmentalized beds. He picked one up and flicked the silver pin with his finger. "Ever throw one of these babies?" he asked. "I never got the chance in 'Nam. It's easy, though. Pull the pin, give it a throw. Find a rock and watch the boom!"

After shaking his head no, the cop thought about it. He'd played with a lot of firearms in his day, but never a grenade. Always wanted to. "So, let's throw it." He laughed, looking around the cavern filled with munitions. "Not in here, *obviously*. But they won't miss one if we take it outside."

"You serious?"

The cop shrugged. "Why not? Sounds fun."

The inspector considered it, then tucked the grenade in his pocket. "Won't tell if you don't. Let's toss it by the river."

The men hustled, gathered their belongings, and shut off the small gas generator that hummed in the corner over the cavern. Overhead, the light bulbs went dim and then dark. They chatted about baseball and headed toward the light of the cave's entrance. A shadow zipped by, clicking.

"Who's there?" The young cop's flashlight crossed over a haunted visage—lightless eyes and a jagged grin. Then, the light hit the ground. The creature was on top of him in an instant. He held up his arms to try and stop those curved talons from shredding his chest apart.

"Help! Jesus, fuck! Help me!"

The monster scooped him off the floor and held him up by the neck. Before he could grab his gun, a razor finger sliced open the skin from his armpit to his belly button. A red line bled through his tribal police uniform, and she wrapped both arms around his body and *squeezed*. His internal organs shotgunned from his belly.

143

Guts spilled onto the cavern floor, splattering blood and shit and kidney juice all over her feathery legs. The beast screeched in liquid euphoria. The inspector ran toward the light of the exit.

To the truck. Get to the truck. He didn't hear his escort screaming anymore. That wasn't a good sign. He moved as fast as his weary legs allowed. *To the truck. Get to the truck.*

At the police pickup, he tried opening the doors.

"Goddammit!"

Locked.

The cop had the keys, of course. The munitions inspector turned back to the lightless cave, sucking in a frustrated scream. Then, the monster emerged from the darkness. A human-looking thing that was decidedly not. It was a distorted creature. The drawing of a crazed child. Part girl, part bird, part something else. Her sharp talons clicked on the rock. Her long, toothy mouth dropped open, grinning like a sand shark. Her claws dripped with his cohort's blood. "Get back!" He pulled the grenade out of his pocket. "*I'm warning you!*"

The old-timer barely had time to pull the pin before she descended on him with midnight wings spread wide. Her talons tore through his quadriceps. He buckled upon bleeding knees. Her gaping, black mouth swallowed his screaming head in wet darkness, jaws crushing the walls of his skull until he felt nothing but electric love. The man's dead fingers let go of life.

The live grenade hit the dirt.

The deeper they went into the muddy hole of Sister Worm's prison, the more abrasive The Dark became until it was thick as mud. The Luminarch struggled to fly through the din; its vibrant moonglow barely shimmering like a coin at the bottom of a murky wishing well. "We're close now," the Blindfolded Boy said. "The shadow is coming."

Broken Girl stumbled beside him, metal sprints clanking against her bony shins. She couldn't see the walls or the floor anymore. Just dense, black chowder. It was like the dark labyrinth around Delora's nest but dingier, more textural, and absolutely *choking*. "It's hard to breathe."

"You don't need to."

Their Luminarch guide wasn't so lucky. The gutsy butterfly finally succumbed to the toxins of The Dark, turned grey as ash, and fell to the floor. Dead. Lightless now.

Broken Girl was too scared to move when the darkness surrounded her. She couldn't see Blindfolded Boy anymore. Her companion disappeared into the creeping wall of shadow.

"Hello?" When she opened her mouth, she felt wintry fingers reach down her throat. She gagged on cracked fingernails while circling in a molasse of darkness

Someone whispered, *"I've been waiting for you."*

More hands grabbed at her from the shadows, and Broken Girl splayed her deadly fingers. She didn't know where to stab next, so she swung her arms wildly. The void around her filled with the overwhelming stink of sweat and dog fur. Pigs squealed. Men moaned in ecstasy. The soft screams of distant coyotes howling at the moon filled the short gaps in-between madness.

"Let me go!" Broken Girl cried out, slashing at more dark appendages. They crept closer, hulking shades of masked Pig Men, and she tried to chop free from the smoky tendrils that clung to her ankles and wrists. But they were infinite—smelled of bleached horror—and yanked her down into The Dark. She felt the descent, and the cold, rough hand stifling her scream.

"Don't fight it," came that guttural whisper again. *"You'll get hurt that way."*

Broken Girl couldn't move, see, or cry out. She sunk into the heavy black—a smothering pillow that robbed her lungs of air and eyes of sight. Something pressed against her, hard and wet— a glistening snout, full of snot and mud—rubbed against her cheek. *"You ready to see the truth of things, Little Lamb?"*

Broken Girl cried and thrashed.

Clap!

The Dark vanished.

Bright light poured into a room full of windows.

"A fucking casino! Did you know?"

Macho stared out of the windshield. Shadows slid down the face of Orphan Rock as the sun hit its apex. "Heard rumors. Tribes up in the Dakotas striking it rich, letting whitefolk play their slot machines. It's been a real game-changer for those communities too. Funded schools. Hospitals. Created jobs. Natives driving Mercedes. I know how that sounds, Esther…" Macho withered in his seat as if he'd forgotten his every right to be angry. "You have to understand our position—"

"I get it, Macho. Really, I do." Esther squeezed his thigh. "Build it anywhere else." Her blue eyes spelled danger. "Don't you dare break ground out here. *She won't allow it.*"

"What choice is there? Sandoval built their goddamn freeway exit right next door to Orphan Rock! Can't change that fact, can we? The council wants every middle-class commuter coming home from Phoenix to see the glitter of gold on their horizon. That's where it's going up. We're past debate now. Delora's going to have to understand the situation—"

Esther hissed and jumped out of the cruiser.

"Hey! *Wait a minute! Esther!*" Macho chased her to the property line. She spun around, angry as a kicked rattlesnake. "Will you slow down for a second? *Please*? Let's talk."

"*Slow down?*" She laughed hysterically and threw her hands up at the sky. "I have to go tell a very fucking cranky old bitch that her land is about to get stripped away from right under her by your people. Do you have any fucking idea what kind of hell that's going to bring on me? On you?"

Macho hesitated. Esther waved him off.

"*Wait!* Maybe I can help you—"

"*Hell no, you can't!*" Esther's spine stiffened. She marched back to her lover, broken dreams in her wet eyes. "You can't help me, *and don't you fucking tell me you can!* All my life men promised me a better future *but fuck that shit.* There ain't no fucking romantic ending in this for me. No knights in shiny armor coming to save me from the dragon. I ate the dirt, Macho. *I don't get to be a fucking princess at the end of this movie. Fuck you.*"

She raised her wrist, showing him The Pig's mark scarred on her flesh. With an angry smile, she raised a middle finger before crawling over the iron bars of the cattle gate. Macho stepped toward her but halted at the property line. He looked down at his boots, making sure no part of him crossed over into the Land Where Pigs Squeal. His face looked ripped in two, both fear and shame mixed into helplessness, and Esther thought it was the damn saddest sight she'd ever seen. "See?" she said, shaking her head. "Nobody's coming to save me, Macho. *I'm what I got, always been that way too. So, let me go fucking do what I do.*"

Esther drove the tow truck back to the stone-stacked house. She didn't look in the rearview mirror to see if Wallace was hanging around. Didn't matter anymore anyway if he was. Everything on the other side of that gate wasn't real. Fake promises. A shitty TV show. More empty pinkie swears and future corpses to come. A life she could never fit into no matter how much she wanted to. She socked the steering wheel and groaned. *Slow down? What privilege he had!* Every day Macho woke up in a world that let him decide shit from breakfast to sock color.

At the stone-stacked house, Esther hit the brakes. Soon as she slammed the door shut, the children screamed in the distance. A swarm of Broken Kids rounded the corner, tripping and clacking in terror. Sparks flew as their rusty weapons skipped over stone. Curious, Esther crept along the path toward the scrapyard. She peeked around the corner, confused by the sight of Delora dancing in a circle of fresh corpses below cairns of crushed vehicles. *What the holy fuck?*

The Crooked woman slay her own Broken Kids, dismembering them with gnarled claws in rage. Their parts twitched on the ground with undeath, still animated by the cursed dirt in their hollow bellies. Her dead eyes glittered. Her mouth curled with delight. The harpy waltzed with murder and grabbed a shocked Broken Kid by the leg—he squirmed like a captured cricket—and she raked his throat open without hesitation.

The Crooked Woman was mad.

Potato Sack stood between Delora, Spider Girl, and Snarl. Her favorite pets kept their distance; even *they* looked scared. The harpy's blackhole eyes landed on her chosen ones, and she would show her children no mercy. Her shark mouth dropped open, soil and spit clinging to her jagged teeth. Potato Sack tried to step in her way, but Delora craved absolute destruction. She snatched the boy's blubbery arm. The mouth beneath his underbelly ripped open in shock when she pulled his shoulder out of its gray, fleshy socket and beat him with it repeatedly on the head.

Spider Girl stood near the shed with Snarl. They were cornered. Finally, out of luck! The boy with barbed wire looked resigned to what was coming. He tried pleading with Mother, but his fancy words had no power to stop a tornado. Then, his eye caught Esther peeking around the corner. He pointed his finger at her. She gasped and ducked behind the workshop's wall.

Maybe he didn't see me...

Delora glided around the corner, and her ghastly fingers seized Esther's ponytail. With a monstrous pull, she dragged her along the dirt path to her circle of gore. Esther crowed and kicked along the gravel, but there was no reasoning with the Crooked Woman in her frenzied state. She dropped Esther in bloody dirt and pointed at Snarl, who ran over and took her hand. Spider Girl scrambled behind them, trying to replace Potato Sack's arm in its socket, but it only fell off again when she let go of it.

Esther gazed at the Crooked Woman's horse face. Those oily eyes. That long mouth of hers. Scars that never healed. Flies with kaleidoscope wings crawling on her leathery skin.

"*Just kill me,*" Esther whispered defiantly. "You know you want to. *I'm more broken than anybody.* You saw my cage. You heard my screams. Just let me go."

"We have an emergency," Snarl said, ignoring Esther's dare. "Mother's sacred child has escaped the sandbox. Mother says she's not on the land anymore."

"Shelby's gone?"

"Who?"

"Baby Bird."

"Yes. She's gone. *Ahhh!*" Delora twisted Snarl's hand. His finger bones snapped like dry wood. The boy winced as a prong of barbed wire popped a blister on his cheek. "*Mother wants you to go and find her! You are the only one who can leave this place. You'll go right now and find her!*" Delora kept twisting, snorting behind her veil with unrelenting urgency. "*NOW!*"

Esther howled with laughter, letting her head fall back onto the gore-soaked dust. Hatred swirled inside of her enflamed eyes. "*Fuck you, bitch.*"

BOOM!

An explosion rumbled in the distant hills.

8.

Through each pane of glass, bright sunshine poured into the room with windows and purged away the choking Dark. Outside, rolling hills of amber wheat rustled beneath a bright, cloudless sky. In the far distance, a grove of apple trees and tin grain silo with a weathervane shaped like a rooster that spun whichever way the summer breeze pointed.

"*Paul, please*, not in front of her. Take me to the bedroom. Do it there, OK? Not here! Not in front of—"

Smack!

Momma landed on her cheek. She looked into her scared daughter's eyes; blood ran from her nostril to the tan carpet.

Her lips opened to speak—

"*We're not done yet.*"

Paul peeled Momma from the floor by a fistful of hair. His necktie was crooked, loose around his throat. When his fingers rolled into a tight fist, Daddy's grin looked hungry like a crocodile. Stacy withered in his grip. He aimed for her eye and cocked his elbow.

Time stopped.

A stain of black blossomed on the far wall. A portly figure bled through the hidden door, wrapped in chains, rags, and a cloud of buzzing horseflies. It had strange hands, each with three sickle fingers, and it placed them on its goat knees when it sat in the corner of the room. The prisoner kept its milky-eyes on Liz—the rest of its queer, shifting face obscured by shadow.

"Do you remember your parents?" the stranger asked, voice raspy and blunt. "Do you remember their love?" Square teeth glinted in the smog. "Sometimes, when people aren't their very best, they need to remember who loves them the *very most*."

Liz rolled onto all fours. She had fingers in place of knives. She took a second to admire her old sundress. Her braceless knees. Bare feet. A red jump rope in her tiny fist.

"I have fingers," she said.

"*And toes*," the shadow replied.

"Are you the prisoner?"

"I ain't free, if that's what you're asking."

"We're supposed to find a prisoner. Me and this boy…"

"Look around you, Little Lamb." The shadow raised a hand, and flies circled his metal crescent fingers. "This was your home. Don't you recognize where you came from?"

She scanned the scene. Something remembered. Momma and Daddy. A Fourth of July in the cornfields. Christmas carolers in the 4H Club. Barn cats chasing mice beneath a combine. An old English Setter named Rex buried in the apple tree grove in the distance. "My home," Liz whispered. "Oklahoma."

The shadow stirred with excitement. "She made a mistake, you see. She didn't make you empty enough. Not like the rest of her roaches. She left this little seed in your broken mind. A room full of windows. Here, I found you—the *real you*—sleeping in the sunshine. Like Humpty-Dumpty, I put you back together again."

The girl looked at her frozen parents. Momma's face

sliding into a scream. Paul's unblinking, bulging eyes. "Am I…dead?" she asked, feeling goosebumps lift on her skin.

"That term means absolutely nothing to me. *We are wherever we are.* Doors. Rooms. Lifetimes. Worlds. This is just one side of infinite possibilities, and we're not leaving it until we're *goddamned finished* doing what needs doing to make things right by my account."

"What things? What're you talking about, mister?"

"Settling old scores. Remedying filthy injustice for *the both of us.*"

The prisoner's cloudy gaze made Liz feel small and scared. Although he had a folksy twang to his voice, she felt little charm in this prisoner she found. "Who are you, *really?*"

The chained shade laughed. "Didn't the boy tell you the rules? You're not supposed to ask, and I will *never* say my name. There's power in a name, Little Lamb. Call me the *King in Pieces* if you must name me something because that is what I am today."

Liz put her hands on her hips, bit her bottom lip. This strange shadow liked to talk in riddles. *She hated riddles.* She liked connecting dots much better. The surprise of seeing her old home and body as if she'd never left Oklahoma in the middle of the night faded quickly. These memories joined others. Glowing butterflies that danced in The Dark. Flying monsters that ate hearts in the desert. A workbench stained black with the blood of disassembled children.

"I was killed by a woman who could fly," Liz said, chasing after dots. "She made me into a monster and hung me from a nest. I met a boy—a blind boy—and he told me I needed to come here and find a prisoner. Said that prisoner was going to help me get to the Other Side. Are we there? Did I make it to the end of the maze? Help me understand what's happening."

"Get to the Other Side?" the shadow replied, laughing, a sinister smile stretched across a pool of tarry din. "Little Lamb, I'm gonna help you do *so much more* than that."

Clap!

Momma and Daddy melted into bubbling piles of mud and brittle sticks. Pink cactus blooms sprouted from the eye sockets of their blanched skulls. The little girl in white Keds and the purple Care Bears t-shirt spun around in a sunny clearing at the edge of a flowing river.

"*Whoa!* Where are we?" she asked.

"At a door," the prisoner, who sat in the shadow of a nearby boulder, replied.

"A door to where?"

"The Other Side, of course."

Liz watched the blue current and the foamy patches of bubbles.

"A river isn't a door."

"Little Lamb," he began, snickering, "in this ramshackle box, every crack and cranny you find is a door to somewhere else. *What parts she didn't tear open, the Grim Seed carved out of my perfect world.* The Other Side is just one of many destinations to choose from. By the time we're through, you and I, you'll have worn many shapes and crossed through many doors. You'll hardly recognize yourself, and you'll thank me for it when you have your *sweet revenge.*"

Liz knelt and felt the water. Cool on her fingers. She gazed into the murky depths. "What's on the Other Side?"

The prisoner said nothing.

"Well? What is it?"

"A fugitive," he finally answered. "Somebody who wasn't supposed to slip away but did. Somebody *wicked*, who likes to poison the well. Somebody who thinks they're more cunning than I am. Somebody who is *ungrateful* and needs to be taught *a cruel lesson in love.*"

"Who?"

"Who, indeed?"

Clap!

A holy man studied the corpses of the slain children lined up on the bank of the hallowed river. The monster had torn them apart, cracked open their ribs, and ate their insides. His rifle trembled in his hands. He kept his barrel aimed at the Harpy of Ghost River, a forsaken daughter who defiled their sacred land, stole babies from their cribs at night, and who stood in the water dissolving the last of her clay effigies in the muddy current.

"You've been *naughty*, Sister Dirt," he growled. "You keep taking what don't belong to you. That can't happen no more. We've had enough of your meddlin' in things."

The demure creature looked over—part human, part bird, part something fantastical—and river water descended the skin between her full breasts, making her slender hips glisten beneath the sun. Water dripped from the sepia tips of her thick hair and bony claws. Her wings folded against her back, and her scaly hocks hid beneath the river crest.

"You should not be here," she said, licking her blood-smeared lips. "The river is *mine*." She pointed at The Needle. "The high rocks are also *mine*."

"*Those children were ours.* You stole them."

"You are cruel to them."

"I am whatever he wants me to be."

"Another slave."

The holy man opened his mouth to curse her, but a long shadow stretched across the desert floor. It slithered up his leg like a vine tunneling inside of him and busted through the secret door in his snake heart. The rifle lowered. He sucked in a deep breath through his teeth. When the holy man opened his eyes, they clouded with a sinister white haze.

"You have my attention, child," a raspy voice said, usurping the holy man's mouth to speak on its behalf. "But you won't have it for long. What do you want?"

The River Woman scowled.

"*Give me all of your children.*"

The possessed man laughed.

Time froze.

Liz knelt next to the little bodies. They looked near her age, give or take a few years. Their throats cut. Their sternums cracked open. They looked fake. Too still to be real. Dolls. Broken dolls baking under the unforgiving sunshine.

"Why'd she kill them?"

"That's like asking why clouds make rain," the prisoner replied. "Things do what they're supposed to do. This one is a *predator*. You've seen it firsthand. Don't you recognize her?"

Liz turned back to the woman standing in the river water. She didn't look familiar at all. She appeared like an angel, in fact: downy wings, pretty hair, and smooth, beautiful skin.

"No. I don't know her."

Clap!

"*How about now?*" the prisoner asked when time-shifted, and the riverbank changed into a blood-drenched battlefield. The beautiful woman was a snarling mantis, surrounded by a pile of skin-stitched, mask-wearing corpses. Her pretty face was torn off, revealing black eyes and a lipless mouth filled with rows of sharp teeth. Her finger blades stained crimson with fresh blood. Her magnificent wings spread, blocking out the sun rays above. Horror settled in the little girl's eyes at the sight of her own murderer. She backed away from the monster that ate her Momma's heart.

"You remember," the prisoner said, grinning.

Tears dripped from Liz's chin. "She…killed my momma. Took me into the sky. Brought me to a cave…"

"That's right, Little Lamb. You're a clever girl."

"What…is she?"

"She is my greatest failure." The prisoner bowed its head in shame, and a pig snout shone in the fog of flies. "She is a murderer. A plotter. A cunning bitch who killed your momma and broke me into pieces. She fooled me once but won't again."

Liz struggled to keep up. "Your failure?"

"It's never easy for a father to call his child a menace, but that's exactly what she is."

"This...*thing*...is your daughter?"

"Yes, I'm the father of many children in these old hills. Probably fathered them hills too. I didn't drown this one like I did *most* her Sisters. Should have. Just look at the devastation she caused. The savagery. I should have spared the world of her."

"She sure didn't spare me or my momma."

"You're a smart girl, and you're right. You and yours weren't spared from a horrible fate, but that judgment wasn't by my hand. I'm a lover of children, you see." The fat shadow cloaked in flies laughed sadly. "By the time I knew what she had in store, it was too late for either of us."

Liz stepped over another corpse whose ripped throat bled into the clay riverbank. "Why didn't you drown her?" She regained some bravery and stood a few feet away from the harpy's splayed fingers. Droplets of blood floated in the warm afternoon air between them. "Why didn't you stop her from doing any of this? From killing my momma and me?"

"I wanted to, Little Lamb. Planned on it, in fact. But I never got the chance."

"What stopped you?"

"She committed a terrible murder. *Mine.*"

Clap!

The striking of a match. Dry grass crackled. Spreading fire. A cave. Murals on the stone wall, stick figures in a ring around a boar. A strange scarecrow weaved from bone and branch, hanging from a wooden cross at the back of the cavern. The harpy stood next to a symbol she had painted on the ground in blood. Face obscured by shadow, the prisoner stood next to her in a place that vibrated with dark energies and deep history.

"What happened to her?" Liz asked, scanning Sister Dirt's wrinkled visage, crooked spine, and emaciated figure. Her oval face was scarred, deformed by some wound, and her head of once beautiful hair had gone bald. Her wings appeared scraggly, mostly bone with no feather for lift. In her claw, she held a shriveled heart. A dead mountain lion lay on the floor of the cave nearby, torn open. "She's not pretty anymore. She's the Crooked Woman."

"This is what bottomless hunger looks like," the King in Pieces replied. "She's a fiend. Never enough meat to fill the belly of a shaper. No matter how much *love* you give to her, she wants more. *Ungrateful termite.* Her appearance mirrors her black heart."

Liz studied the mural on the wall. Etchings in stone shaded by charcoal. A great-winged bird grappling with another in the sky above a floating *jellyfish*? The little girl squinted her eyes, but she couldn't read the shape any other way. "Where are we?"

"One of my sanctuaries."

"Why?"

The prisoner pointed a sickle finger at a hole in the cavern ceiling. Liz followed his gaze and could only see blue sky. "Always keep your eyes up, Little Lamb. You never know what's circling above the desert, looking to pick the meat off your bones."

Clap!

Whoosh!

BAM!

The giant buzzard dropped through the crack in the cavern like a bunker-buster missile. She landed in the center of the bloody symbol, wings wrapped around the rest of her body like dark armor. Her feathers turned gray and then dandered away in the breeze like fresh ash thrown from a fire. Skeletal wings fanned out before folding tightly against her shoulder blades. Her bird legs started at the knee, attached to slender, nude hips. Sister Death wore an exotic mask, Eastern in features. The buzzard's black hair floated on the gentle cave wind.

"Sister," Death said. "You've summoned me by name. Called me to the place I swore I would never come to again. Speak of your burdens to me, so I may leave from here."

The deformed harpy stepped into the light, exposing her gnarled visage. "I seek a Grim Seed to spoil the earth. I seek retribution, Sister. I cannot shape it myself."

Sister Death took a moment to look at her kindred's poor appearance. "I see. They've wounded you. But why choose this path? You are capable of building another."

Sister Dirt hissed, "I am going to take everything from them! They are cruel to children. They are cruel to us. He is the reason why coyotes howl in the hills at night."

"You are no fool, Sister Dirt. You are the best of our sisters. A builder, a shaper of worlds. Would you see this box defiled? You would seek absolute destruction of your home?"

"That is my request. Will you honor it?"

Sister Death didn't blink, her sparkling brown eyes became eddying pools on a porcelain mask. "*A Grim Seed will cost your life,*" she whispered, leaning toward her sister.

"Be it so."

The buzzard woman looked surprised. "Is vengeance so important? This is an unthinkable sacrifice you'll have to make. Yet, you do not hesitate at all!"

Sister Dirt rested her bald head against the soft shoulder of her kindred. "I want him to suffer for all of the children, for our Sisters. Will I witness it?"

"The end of life does not always mean the end of existence," Sister Death said, stroking Sister Dirt's wrinkled head. "But know you will be in shackles until the curse blossoms."

"Sister, time is unfair to us. As we speak, they are hunting me. Will you share your boon to help me kill our father? Will you help me scrub his stain from history?"

Death smiled sadly. "I shall grant your request and share my boon, but you will carry my burden for it. You will be a ghost that serves the seed until *misery is a machine.*" Sister Death paused to look at the mural on the wall. Men throwing infants into a winding river. "But know this, sweetest Sister of all, to purge a king from his kingdom, will take more resilience than you can offer. You will need the other Sisters to share their boons too." Sister Death faced Sister Dirt. "I ask you once more, are you willing to pay the toll to spoil this land?"

Dirt looked at Death, eyes steady and sure.

"Will our father suffer?"

Sister Death grinned with black beetle carapace teeth. "Eventually, it will destroy him."

"Then, yes, I am sure."

Clap!

"She hated you."

"Yes," the King in Pieces agreed. "She was *confused*. Overtaken by emotion. A misguided child who misinterpreted my absolute love and kindness for cruelty."

Doubt spread across her face. "Mister, if you're willing to kill yourself to get revenge on somebody, *that's real hatred right there*. There's no other way to see it."

The prisoner snorted. "Are you surprised? Did she not murder you in cold blood? Did she not eat the heart right out of your sweet momma's chest? You've seen her cave full of dead children. Yes, Little Lamb, Sister Dirt is full of hatred. Chocked full. With selfishness on top of that. The Grim Seed was a desperate move by a troubled woman who couldn't help herself. She wanted more than she was entitled to have."

Liz eyed the prisoner with deepening suspicion. There were too many dots and not enough lines to draw a clear picture. "I know you're not telling me something."

A sinister expression bloomed on his shrouded face. "I'm telling you exactly what you need to hear to get to the Other Side. What other details matter to you?"

"I don't know. But I think you're lying."

The fat shadow bristled. Jagged boar tusks glinted from gummy jowls before being concealed in the thick marmalade of the rolling dark again. Liz swore she saw a smoky grin.

Clap!

The air smelled like sawdust inside of the newly constructed chapel. They prayed to the Dead Tree, the crown of the Father Pig. A teenager hung from the branches. Her blue eyes barely opened, and her forehead bleeding beneath a crude crown made from twisted razor wire. Another girl—brunette, white dress, wedding veil—put dirt on her knees before the podium. She interlocked her fingers in prayer, keeping her face downcast. In the pews, naked men in pig masks sat quietly with stiff erections. They waited for their turn. Silent. Good Pig Men.

The bearded man—the holy man from the riverbank—preached from behind the pulpit. He wore a mask too. Skin stitched together with a fat, dripping pig snout over his nose. Next to him, an iron brazier filled with smoldering coals and a molten-tipped branding iron. He walked to the battered girl hung in the Tree and placed a knife against her throat.

The door flew open, and the men in the chapel fell silent.

"*You,*" the holy man said, pig-possessed eyes alarmed to see the crooked visage of a ghost it remembered. "You're a fool to come back here. *Twice a fool* for interrupting my blessed wedding day. Won't be merciful to you this time, child. You've crossed your last river."

The Harpy of Ghost River said nothing. Bony fingers burst from her crooked shoulders, linking together with thick cartilage to provide lift. Men in pews hit the floor hollering when she swooped over them, soaring toward the rickety pulpit with fiery, black eyes.

Whomp!

She landed on the Mound before the Dead Tree.

The girl hanging in the branches—the blonde runt—watched her with hopeful eyes.

"*Get out of my house!*" The holy man yanked the branding iron from the coal-filled brazier. He raised it over his masked face, ready to smash in the harpy's deformed skull. Then, he stopped to cock his head in wonderment.

A tiny black seed sat in her dirty palm. Small tentacles reached hungrily for the soil before her fingers wrapped into a greedy fist around it. She smiled at the holy man.

Wham! The crack of split rock echoed off the desert mountains like a gunshot.

The wooden rafters in the sanctuary shed sawdust.

When the harpy pulled her fist from the collapsing hole she punched in the Mound, thousands of brown roaches and scorpions skittered out from the oldest earth. The mind-snaked bride shook waves of venomous insects from her dress, waking from her dream. Before she could scream for help, the monster's claws curled over her mouth. **Crack!** The Crooked Woman made a quick fist and crushed her cheekbones. The bride moaned and sobbed while the creature studied her squashed face. It looked *so much prettier* behind the tulle of her veil. The fascinated harpy stripped the magic shroud from the dying bride's head.

"What did you do?" The holy man watched the discoloration of the soil spread across the Mound. The desert dirt turned dim as the midnight sky. He stumbled, looked dizzy, and dropped the molten branding iron. *"What the fuck did you do?"*

No time to waste. The deformed monster cut the bride's neck open with her finger and bled her onto the Mound like she was a human watering can. Black veins spidered up the Dead Tree's roots, suckling from the fresh blood spill. This was only the beginning. It would take so many more throats to water the Grim Seed. But it would be worth it in the end.

Every drip.

Every drop.

More poison staining the Land Where Pigs Squeal.

The holy man clutched his chest in agony, and the parasite struggled for control of his host. A boy stood from his pew, walked over, and picked up his daddy's sharp knife.

He looked at the harpy. Then, at the runt in the Dead Tree.

"*Minister, what do you think you're doing?*"

The boy said nothing and slashed the holy man's throat.

"You've made quite a home for yourself here," the King of Pigs said from The Dark that surrounded the cathedral hidden inside of The Needle. Mesquite trees weaved together with cactus ribs, bones, and desert grass into a nest high up in the cavern rocks. Wicker effigies hung from the underside of the tangle from thin strings made of human hair.

Delora worked silently, ignoring the demon, sewing together a bundle of brittle sticks. She didn't look at him, nor did he expect her to. "You're still a builder, a shaper of worlds. At least, some part of you still is." Father Pig knelt, picking up a small arm that had been sewn to a rotting shoulder that lay by his hooves. "I see twisting mesquite together isn't enough for you anymore." He dropped her necromantic craftwork out of the nest. It struck a pile of bones below where a mighty white serpent coiled in the sunshine. "You and I need to have a *conversation*."

Father Pig raised his arm. His three sickle-shaped fingers, sharp and polished, sprouted from a hairy wrist and forearm that throbbed with black veins. His jowls curled in pain. "The Grim Seed is a cancer!" He stepped out of the shadows, wearing his true form. "One I cannot cure or curate for another to endure. It's mine, and it's changing me." His pig eyes watered in sadness. "The Dark is changing, child. I'm poisoned, and *you don't care*."

The harpy rummaged through a pile of junk, chittering like a greedy rat looking for a gold coin. She wore the white dress and the wedding veil she stole from The Pig's dead bride.

"*You fucked me with it, and what did you get in return?*" Father Pig's hoof kicked a clay child, and its straw body burst. "Trapped in a cage? You must be so lonely, sewing dolls together in The Dark all day. *Nobody to talk to while I die.*" He surveyed the nest with disgust. "You're an animal now, Sister Dirt. Feral as a bobcat. You've even lost the Other Side, haven't you?"

The hideous woman in the pilfered dress ignored him.

Saliva dripped from his whiskery chin. *"When I'm dead, what will you do? WHAT WILL YOU DO?* Serve the Seed? You're a fucking fool. You built a prison for yourself is all." He laughed madly. *"How does slavery taste, you bitch?"*

"Your time is over, Swine King," a childish voice said. The desert demon sneered when a ripped-face boy limped out from a hole in the cave wall. He was naked—just skin and bones. Barbed wire wrapped around his inflamed body and his wounds had stained purple with rust. His one eye was black, but there was something energetic inside of it: something potent that glowed in the darkness. Father Pig didn't blink. The desert demon recognized the boy and growled at him with disgust.

"How are you alive, piglet? I did not perform this resurrection!"

The harpy held out a hand. The boy walked over and took it. "You have no more miracles," he said. "Mother has poisoned your grave, killed your flock, and your land will become a machine to suffer the world. You look frail, Pig Father. The curse makes you weak."

"Quiet!" The cavern in The Needle shook. The nest croaked. The Dark flexed. Dust fairies whirled in a tornado of glowing speckles. A kaleidoscope of Luminarchs rustled free from their perches and flapped away. *"I am the age of filth,* and the *only* overmaster of this domain—"

Scrreeeecccchhh!

The Pig was gone in a tsunami of hooks and feathers.

His sickle fingers ripped into her empty breast while the Crooked Woman scooped him up in scaly arms and carried him through hidden doors, fly rips, and grim tears in the fabric of The Dark. Deeper. Further. More doors. Dark hallways. No light. Then there was dirt, tunnels, and glowing moss. Another box. Hidden from him. So deep, it had no name.

Wham!

They crashed into a floor of slimy bedrock.

Father Pig shattered like a precious vase. Smoky shards of stained red glass. Silver tusks without a snout. Broken hooves. A red heart so sanguine it looked like a shard of obsidian.

The Harpy of Ghost River wobbled on her chicken feet. Her talons clicked on mossy stone over to the remains of the Prophet of Filth. She picked up Father Pig's head by a floppy ear.

"That's my girl! *Feels good to be king, don't it?*"

The primordial earth trembled around them in the circular tunnel. Giant worms burst from the walls, surrounding Delora in a prison of moist tubes. "Sister Dirt," a childish voice sang. "What have you brought me to play with?"

The boy wrapped in barbed wire held the Crooked Woman's gnarled hand. He stroked her bony knuckles with adoration. Behind them, other Broken Kids clamored, walking on stilts and splints, or crawling on hands hammered through with nails. Two living souls followed the dead—the Holy Boy and the Runt of the Litter. They held hands, kept close.

Delicious companions.

Their gloom parade passed by piles of rotting corpses. Devoured parts of Pig Men and coyote girls turned yellow under the sun. The vultures circled above, waiting to snatch a strip of meat from the slaughter of every living soul in Orphan Rock.

They passed the Chapel on the Mound, and the soil beneath their bare feet groaned as the Grim Seed spoiled the earth and twisted its dark roots ever deeper. It searched the soil for suffering and discovered rich veins of blood that ran toward the Heart of the Desert.

Along the way to the sacred riverbank, Broken Kids smashed Father Pig scarecrows and dreamcatchers. They celebrated. Hoisted their crude weapons. Mumbled dead whispers, half-formed thoughts and pieces of worldly reflection poured from decayed, stitched lips.

At the river, The Crooked Woman waded into the water carrying The Pig's head.

"What comes from dirt must be cleansed," the boy wrapped in barbed wire preached loudly. The Crooked Woman dipped it in the water. Tendrils of tar ran from the Pig's neck muscles, turning the river black as runoff from a coal mine. Then with a toothy, satisfied smile, she let it go. The jabbering head bounced along the river bottom, carried by the current until it was swallowed by the hidden door. She turned back to her devoted congregation on the muddy bank of the river, her eyes hidden behind a white veil. The boy who seized her hand beamed.

"The old religion is dead," he proclaimed. The audience eyed one another in disbelief. "You are orphans, each of you made so by dirt and death. Together, we'll raise a new god, build a new church, and suffer the world for a better paradise to come!"

The crowd on the riverbank cheered.

Clap!

"She threw your head in the river?" Liz asked, holding up her hand to blot out the bright summer sunbeams. "That's why you want me to go to the Other Side, isn't it?"

The prisoner's chains rattled. He sounded close enough to kiss. "King in Pieces, that's what I am. But handsome as it is, it's not my head we're after. It's what's *inside* of it."

"Your brain?"

"No, Little Lamb. Inside my skull is what can never be spoken. Without it, I can't put myself back together again." *Pig breath.* Liz spun around, and he was not behind her, but she could feel him everywhere. He haunted every shadow in the desert.

"Your name?"

"Now we're cooking with grease."

Liz sighed. Too many broken pieces. "I still feel like you're hiding something."

"Don't matter if I am. Knowing extra details won't change what needs to happen next. You want your life back? You want revenge for your dead momma? I'm the only one who can give it to you. We need to work together, you and me. *Just do what you're told is all.*"

"Didn't she kill you already when you had your head?" Liz laughed at the notion of a talking pig head. "What's getting it back going to do for you? She'll just kill you again."

"Don't worry about me, Little Lamb. I'll take care of mine. Always have. But you? You're a prisoner too. Just like me. Except you have something I don't..."

"Yeah? What's that?"

"A choice to make. We get that head back, and we'll both be free again. Me? I'll pick up where I left off around here. You? You'll get that lovely room with windows, except it won't ever end. That'll be your home again and *forever...if you please me.*"

Liz considered his offer. She scanned the savage desert. Dust. Prickly cactus. Hawks circling overhead looking for carrion. Dry, lung-rotting wind. Every breath was heavier than the last. A riverbank full of dead children danced under the sun.

Broken.

Everything rusty and broken and reaching...

"Everybody's reaching for something out here," the driver with the golden eyes said.

"All right," Liz said, crossing her arms. "I'll try."

Sickles rested on her shoulders from behind.

"I knew you were special. First things first, you need to break your own chains. Look into your darkest secrets and find where she hid the dirt. Then you need to spit out every rotten speckle of it until you're sacred again. That's the only way out of The Dark for you. I hope you're ready, Little Lamb."

Clap!

"Paul, please, not in front of her. Take me to the bedroom. Do it there, OK? Not here! Not in front of—"

Smack!

Momma landed on her cheek. She looked into her scared daughter's eyes; blood ran from her nostril to the tan carpet.

"We can be strong," she said sniffling. "We—"

Daddy's big hand grabbed her blouse and plucked Momma off the floor. She hit her knee on the coffee table, then toppled against the wall and leaned against it.

"Stop it!" she screamed.

Fists balled, Paul stepped over Liz. The bottom of his business shoes looked so big from underneath them. Momma rolled along the wall, trying to outpace him with no luck.

"Stop it, Paul!" Stacy grabbed the bronze clock from the fireplace mantle. She missed her target. It shattered to pieces on the far wall. *"Get the fuck away from me!"*

"I don't know why you make me so goddamn angry, *but you do*." Daddy slapped her head. *"Why can't you be a good wife?* Get your shit together around here? Lord knows you spend enough money on books and make-up. Pick up a vacuum sometime and say thank you."

Momma shoved him. "I want a divorce!" Paul smiled at her weakness.

"That all you got, *sugar plum?*" he asked, lunging after her. He snatched her by the wrist. Momma let out a sharp yelp when he twisted her elbow.

"Leave me alone!"

She stumbled toward the hallway and the kitchen.

Daddy's jaw clenched and he followed, chewing in anticipation. "I'm going to hurt you, *you dumb fucking cunt!*" He rolled up his sleeves, and Liz watched his shoes pass over her a second time. She held up her hands, stretching the red jump rope into a straight line. It hooked on his shin, caught him off balance, and then both of Daddy's big business shoes floated in the air.

Crack! His skull struck the top of the coffee table. He hit the carpet, rolled on his side, and gazed at his precious daughter.

Blood gushed from his forehead like a waterfall.

Momma ambled over and took the jump rope from her hands. Liz let it leave her fingers. She watched Stacy crawl on top of him, looping the rope around his neck.

"Come here," she said, looking at Liz.

Liz said okay, trembling.

"Open your hand, baby."

Liz did as she was told and lifted her empty palm. Stacy leaned forward, parted her bloody lips, and coughed up a small pile of dirt that landed in her daughter's hand.

"Go play in your room now, Little Lamb," Momma said, wiping her muddy chin. "Go show Reuben what you found. He'll be proud of you like I am."

Liz backed away down the long hallway. With every tiny step, the room with windows shrank into darkness. She watched Momma yank on the jump rope until Daddy stopped kicking.

Clap!

The Broken Girl pulled her tongue back and looked at the stinking pile of desecrated soil on the metal plate bolted to her wrist. A fistful of dirt with smoky fingers that reached back for her mouth. She let the soil fall from her hand. When it touched The Dark, it vanished. *"You did it! You broke the curse!"* Blindfolded Boy squealed, returning to her side again.

"That was inside of me?" she asked. "Something remembered found it inside of me."

Opaline eyes and white teeth appeared over her shoulder. The King in Pieces. *"Any who eat the dirt will be bound to serve the Grim Seed until misery is a machine."*

"What does that mean—misery is a machine?"

"Let's not find out, Little Lamb. Can't be good."

The Broken Girl settled into her doll body and thought about the room with windows. It faded like a dream. She clung to the girl's hidden secret. "Liz killed her father."

"No," The Pig replied. "The awful woman did."

"The mother?"

"Yes. That selfish woman stole a hard-hustlin' daddy from a daughter. A provider from a family. A *king from his kingdom.* Sounds sort of familiar, don't it?"

Broken Girl looked at the foggy ground, trying to remember. "But that's not what happened. The man was cruel to his wife. She ran away to save her child. She loved her child. The man was heartless and deserved to die."

Blindfolded Boy interrupted, "I feel *trouble!*"

Blue light approached. Soft at first, but then brighter and brighter as it traveled down Sister Worm's tunnel, cutting through the dark milk of the prisoner's cell. The retreating darkness exposed chains attached to a glass body and jars filled with sharp crimson shards. A ruby rock shaped like a heart sparkled on the end of a hook attached to a rusty chain.

"What is that?" Broken Girl's finger-knife aimed at the growing orb of light.

"Luminarchs," Father Pig replied. "Souldust. Sister Dirt is coming and it ain't gonna be pretty when she gets here."

"What?" Broken Girl spun in circles, trying to find the King in Pieces in the din, but it was too thick to see anything. "Why is she coming here? *Is this a trap?*"

"No time for questions!" the shadow snapped. "She's realized you and I have a special bond now, and she's come to take my heart away. Can't let that happen, Little Lamb."

"*Your heart?*"

"Listen to me. If you want to fix this filthy injustice and free yourself from prison, you'll take that heart off that hook and carry it to the Other Side right now. There's not one more detail that matters until you get that far. *Go!*"

The lights drew closer.

Hundreds of glowing butterflies. The Crooked Woman moved amongst them like a vampire in fog.

"*Go!*" Father Pig barked again. "Take my fuckin; heart,

and *don't you dare break it!*"

Broken Girl looked at Blindfolded Boy, who urged her to do something—anything! Her metal braces clanked when she jumped up to pluck the heart off its hook. It was frigid and heavy, and she felt like she couldn't carry it for long. She'd freeze to death first. *I'll be you guide.* The voice came from inside of her. Filled her mind with the buzzing of flies. So cold, so numb. Ghostly fingers poking out of a pond of static.

She snapped out of her trance when Blindfolded Boy wrapped his hand around her bent fork thumb again.

"We have to run, okay?"

"Okay," Broken Girl said in a daze.

The King in Pieces parted the darkness before them. Another tunnel appeared, leading away from the sphere of light and the wicked harpy who was lurking closer to the cell. Broken Girl and Blindfolded Boy sprinted through The Dark as fast as their dead legs and splints could carry them. Behind them, Father Pig squealed and laughed and cursed Delora's name, and everything shook and started collapsing behind them.

Broken Girl looked over her shoulder and saw them on the hunt. Broken Kids. Carrying corroded tools with sewn-on faces and patchwork bodies. They howled. Sang for blood.

Blindfolded Boy tugged her along. "Faster!"

They ran uphill to a dead end. A small hidden door shimmered along a rock wall. No bigger than a coat zipper "Go," the boy said, pulling the portal open in a cloud of buzzing flies.

"You first."

"Only room for one. You have to go now!"

Broken Girl turned around. "*What?* But—"

"*GO!*"

The Broken Kids charged into the dead end. Ripped faces with screw teeth. They clawed for her. Snatched her by the wrist. Stabbed their weapons into her body. Stitches ripped. Braces bent. So many teeth biting into her skin. She floated by Blindfolded Boy in slow motion. They tore off his bandage, revealing no eyes or sockets. Just a flat brow and scarred forehead. They scratched the bluish skin from his back and bit off his ear. While they ripped him apart, he kept a kind smile, held her in his arms, ushering whatever was left of Broken Girl through the secret door—

He whispered into her ear, "When you're feeling small and ready to quit, *find me*."

—and into the light.

9.

The tinny ring in her ears faded. So did the twinkling rainbow spots behind her eyelids. Whatever exploded in front of Solemn Cave was the dead man's doing. The impressive magic power came from beneath him. *The mighty boom that shook the mountains.* He absorbed it, shielding her from *most* of the searing metal, but not all. Hot shards jutted from cuts on her scaly shins. Grimacing, she plucked out the pieces she could.

Food would make it all better.

Food was life.

The Dark Bird crawled over to the magician's corpse. She turned him over with a grunt. All his clothes melted around the singed skin that engulfed the detonation. She slipped her claws into the wound and pulled out some of his sloppy insides. Even though his guts tasted like pure bliss, she had to spit him out. Pieces of shrapnel cut the insides of her cheeks.

"*Blah!*"

Ruined! She dropped the dead boomwizard, and then took

a second to pout in the afternoon sunshine. She stroked her black plume in frustration. She finally breaks free from Mother's cage, hunts worthy prey, and her prize is ruined by spells. *What if her boon was fucking everything up?* Mother never warned her about magic. Neither did that little shitheel Snarl, who she imagined laughing at her, that dead eye of his sparkling with a bloody tear. She could hear his voice saying, *"Told you, you weren't ready. You're just a dumb Baby Bird."*

Shelby's claws hardened into blades, not ready to give up. Returning memories and the smell of additional blood pushed aside disappointment. There was another meal close by, wasn't there? Maybe the younger man didn't cast magic on his meat before he died. Shelby frowned and pulled the largest metal chunk from her thigh and tossed it aside.

In the cave, Dark Bird collapsed by her first victim. She used her sharp fingers to crack apart his ribcage, admiring the buffet of fresh organs set on the table of his spine. *The heart.* She smiled when she pulled it out, snipping off the major arteries with scissor fingers—blood spurt in the air like squeezed ketchup. Finally, after all of these years, she could eat *the best* part again.

Shelby stuffed it into her froggy mouth. When she chewed, blood spurt over her guppy lips. She giggled from embarrassment and wiped her egg-shaped chin. The heart tasted like...*power*...like drinking gasoline! That was the best way she could describe it. The rest of the meat tasted like energy, but the heart? It was the core of things. Power. Life. Healing. She could feel it hit her stomach, the empty place, and for but a moment or two, it felt warm and full. Dark Bird fell onto her rump, drunk on flesh and blood. She didn't want it to *ever* end.

But it did. *More. Shelby wanted more.* If she could eat enough hearts, she would never be cold again! She could shape galaxies! That was a goal! *More. Shelby wanted more.*

Dark Bird stood up. Felt strength course through her body again. Regenerating scales pushed any remaining shards of metal from her hocks. Wounds zipped up with fresh skin. Bristles retracted. Her talons flattened into toes. Her regal plume fell limp, becoming sandy hair again that laid upon the bare shoulders that swallowed her folded wings link by link.

A nude girl covered in blood walked out from the dark of Solemn Cave. Her brown eyes shone with fierce vitality. She climbed a nearby rock to survey the sunlit valley below. For the first time in her life, she saw what was on the other side of Orphan Rock. There was a modest town just a few miles away. When she inhaled, she could smell the musk of humans on the wind. Her mouth salivated. She would go to that village of men and she would eat all of the hearts she wanted there. As many as it took to make the fire in her belly last forever.

That is what Shelby wanted.

More. Shelby wanted more.

Esther howled with laughter, letting her head fall back onto the gore-soaked dust. Hatred swirled inside of her enflamed eyes. *"Fuck you, bitch."*

BOOM!

An explosion rumbled in the distant hills.

The Crooked Woman wrapped her bloody fingers around her throat and lifted Esther from the ground. The coyote didn't fight, only smiled at the dead eyes behind Delora's filthy veil. Her feet dangled off the ground, airway collapsing when the harpy squeezed her icy grip.

"Do it, you fucking bitch. I want to die."

Delora's maw curled into a devious smirk. Her grip tightened, and Esther closed her eyes to welcome the end of her shitty life. Yellow sparkles pulsated in the blackness. Her head felt empty, dizzy, full of nothing but fading whispers of life. Finally, time to let it all go. Time to lay her burdens down and disappear.

Then, falling! ***Thud!*** Hard ground.

Esther wailed, pounding her fists in the gravel. "*Goddammit!* Just fucking let me die! I never believed your promises anyway. You fooled Minister, but *not me*."

Delora extended her hand. Snarl seized it.

The boy wrapped in barbed wire listened to Mother. He nodded, quite obedient after watching his brethren butchered in a fit of rage. His one good eye tacked onto Esther.

"The boonchild," he began, "doesn't only belong to Mother. She came from your womb. Would you lose another child just to prove your disobedience?"

"The fuck you say?" Her eyes pinched into venomous slits. Torrid embers of hatred ignited in her gut. "*You told me never to think of her like that.* You said she was *never* mine."

"Mother wants you to know what's at stake here. Your *daughter* is in danger if you do nothing. Time is running out to find her. The dirt curse will kill her if the humans don't."

"*My daughter?*" Esther stood up, wobbling and dizzy. Her sweaty, blonde bangs fell over a maniacal smile. "*My fucking daughter? Fuck you. Fuck all of you!*" She reached for Delora and placed her hand on her gelid breast. The Crooked Woman was emotionless. "I have given you *everything*. My husband. My son. My childhood. Every time I think I'm ready to be free from this fuckin' jail cell, you tell me another lie. Something you pretend is mine, so I do what you want. But nothing is *really* mine, is it?" She leaned into the harpy's bloody veil. "*IS IT?*"

Delora waited for Esther to stop. When the angry coyote did, she pulled her trembling hand away from the harpy's bosom. All of Orphan Rock watched patiently as she smoked and paced and cursed under her breath. Then, she let go. A long exhale. Time felt heavy. Her head too full of garbage to sort. Doing nothing was easier. Obedience was even easier than nothing.

Esther growled and stomped away.

Snarl called after her, "Coyote, where are you going?"

"I'm going to find my *fucking* daughter!"

The brittle scarecrow, a life-sized puppet shaped from mud, sticks, and human bones, broke off of the ancient cross in the cavern with the petroglyphs. The ramshackle doll's knees clacked together but remained standing. It looked around the familiar cave with two holes in a clay face for eyes. Although Delora's bloody symbol was long faded, the girl inside the golem recognized this was the very same chamber where Sister Dirt called Sister Death and traded her life for a Grim Seed.

So weird...

Liz felt a new body, but it was stiff and awkward like stale licorice. Cumbersome like a suit of armor. Even the Broken Girl felt less fragile...and she was sewn from rotting pieces.

Careful...nice and slow.

She practiced using her new legs. They swung like tree trunks, and she stumbled when she walked. Her arms stiff too. Baked clay anchored with ancient bone and mixed with brittle desert grass. When any part of her rubbed against the rocky outcroppings, fissures formed, and parts crumbled off.

At the mouth of the cave, she pushed through sage bushes toward the daylight. Thorns ripped cloth and grass from the scarecrow's appendages. It seemed everything in the desert was hellbent on breaking her down. This vessel was falling apart fast.

Doesn't hurt, though...there's no pain in here.

She gazed down into the Ghost River Valley. A dizzyingly steep flight of natural steps descended the cliff face. Ghost River sparkled in the distance—the door to the Other Side—wherein the King in Pieces' head journeyed to a place unknown.

"That's far away," Liz said grimly. Her voice sounded like a muffled whisper spoken in a closet. She could pull back from the golem's eyes as if they were part of a telescope on a scenic overlook. When she did, she felt her own body again. Heard her own voice. Curled in her ghostly fingers: A Pig's heart, little more than a shriveled piece of reddish-black stone now.

You keep that close, Little Lamb, a chorus of flies sung in her mind. She tucked it into her pocket.

When Liz peered through the golem's eyes again, she filled the awkward vessel like putting on her father's oversized raincoat. Its stiff neck creaked, surveying the darkening sky. Thick clouds gathered over the distant mountains. She could feel a hard wind push against her new body. A storm was coming.

"*Scrrawwwwk!*"

Broken Kids.

They shrieked from the cavern behind her.

There must be another door, a portal to The Dark there!

"*Whoa!*" Liz stumbled down the first rocky step. She misjudged the distance and fell to her knees. Her left hand, no more than bundled sticks, snapped off. She landed on her hip. Mud broke, twine frayed. An arm fell dead.

"*Scrreeeckkkk! Ro! Ho!*"

The yipping of a pack of dead children drew closer. Liz tried to stand up, but her leg barely moved. Her broken arm flopped without control. Oh, she was not good at driving this stupid scarecrow at all! Liz wanted to cry.

Couldn't she just disappear?

Something remembered.

"*We can be strong,*" her mother had told her in a room with windows, nose bleeding, a mad man towering over her.

The Broken Kids climbed down the red rocks. Cracked feet skipped over stone. One of them walked on rickety wooden stilts, surveying the overgrown mountain trail below through thick lenses bolted to his eye sockets like swimming goggles.

She squeezed under a rock shelf, watching them pass by. A fat Gila monster—a black and orange-spotted lizard—shared the tight crevice and licked its rough jaw. She watched the Broken Kids stab bushes with pitchforks and search behind boulders along their way toward the river. When she couldn't hear them anymore,

Liz rolled out from her hiding spot.

There'll be more, she thought, looking over the scarecrow's clay shoulder to the King in Pieces' hidden cave. *I gotta move faster.* She lumbered down a few more steps to a fallen saguaro cactus. Sturdy ribs jutted from rotting skin with barbed needles. Liz thrust one of the ribs through her damaged wrist until it felt secure enough to snap off. She pointed her newly extended arm at the ground and put all of her weight on it.

Luckily, it held.

Using her new crutch, the girl in the golem carefully moved down the mountainside—step by careful step.

The desert swarmed with danger.

The darkening skies did too.

The Dodge Retriever sped down the backroads toward the bridge over Ghost River. Esther's scabbed elbow hung out of the open window. Sparks flew from her fingertips—a cigarette ripped apart by the wind. The marmalade sunset over the Ghost River Valley smeared her sunglasses in orange light. Minister's old shotgun sat in the passenger's seat. Loaded.

What did she feel?

What was this exhilaration in her stomach?

The bravery of the damned?

Flickering fool burning out?

"*Fucking daughter,*" she said, wincing at each syllable.

Minister grinned in the rearview mirror. That Burt Reynold's smile. "*Golly, she plays you like a fiddle.*" She ignored him. His golden eyes sparkled, and he continued, "That child has little to do with us. I ain't the daddy, and you ain't the mommy. *We just made her is all.* Why can't you just accept the truth for once? Why can't you learn you're meant to be alone?"

"Fucking truth? *Truth is you broke your promise.*"

"So, that means you get a free pass to fuck my best friend?"

"You left me behind. Said you wouldn't ever do that."

"She killed me, Esther! What choice did I have?"

"But you did have a choice, you fucker!" his wife hissed, flicking her spent butt out of the Retriever's window. "You *chose* to open her cage. You *chose* to serve the Grim Seed. You *chose* to bring me along. You *chose* the bottle over keeping your family safe and look what happened to Little Snake."

"Bring you along?" Minister shook his head, long hair hanging in front of his dead man's eyes. He laughed in disbelief. "This was *all* for you! Everything I ever done, I done for you!"

Esther lit a new cigarette. Her hand trembled.

"Yeah, well, maybe you should've just let me die in that Tree." She blew smoke out of the window. "Your plan didn't work out too fucking well for us, did it?"

"Well, I disagree. *You're still alive, ain't ya?*"

Minister's handsome image faded from the backseat. Esther punched the rearview mirror and groaned with exhaustion. The desert road ahead was empty.

No more thinking about the painful shit.

The blast. The crack of dynamite.

Focus on that to find Shelby!

Only one place she knew in all of Ghost River had that kind of firepower. Solemn fuckin' Cave.

The girl inside of the twisted scarecrow watched another patrol of feral Broken Kids descend the rocky steps and switchbacks on Orphan Rock. She used her cactus rib hand to push down the branches of the sage bush, spying on her hunters.

The first group, led by the lanky boy with the stilts, made it to the bottom and turned around. Now they merged with the second group of deadheads that spilled out from the King in Pieces' cave. A freakishly large Broken Kid led the second search party. He wore a burlap gown and a sack over his head with two dark eyeholes. He was missing an arm. His shoulder socket leaked white liquid around a bed of gray and decaying cartilage.

They assembled on the cliffside, completely unaware that Liz had smashed herself into a tight little ball between two rocks a few dozen feet away. A fat sage bush provided some camouflage from which she could watch her enemies in secret. One of the Broken Kids, a girl with a railroad spike driven into the side of her neck like the bolt of Frankenstein's monster, poked the bush with her pitchfork when they passed. *Thunk!* Liz felt the impact of the prongs punching into her golem's side. Stabbed hay didn't hurt at all, so she kept still and silent. The dead girl didn't stop to investigate any further. Now, she stood with the rest on the rock, eyes scanning the rocky staircase for their little runaway.

Liz's time in The Dark already felt like a dream. The patchwork body she wore…the Broken Girl…it all seemed like an old t-shirt she grew out of years ago.

She had been one of them, hadn't she?

A mindless husk. A worker bee. A slave.

She thought about the room with windows. The little bit of herself that the King in Pieces found and rebuilt in secret. Another life. Two lost parents, now phantoms.

Did these kids have another life too?

Where did she snatch them from? What happy day? What desperate situation? Did people cry for them somewhere? Or were they just forgotten orphans tossed in a river?

Ghosts.

For the first time, Liz felt the grim weight of being an orphan too. Her parents died. Her body died. Her spirit was a tiny and flickering thing, with only a few filaments of memory left. Even if she could escape the vast desert, there was nowhere to go. No dress to wear to homecoming. No future wedding day.

So, she would go to the Other Side instead.

She would do what she was told.

What else is there to do?

I'm just like them, she thought bitterly. But she served another interest now. Liz had seen what life was like for a Broken Kid in Ghost River under Sister Dirt. Never again would she serve that vicious crone. She would take her chances with the Other Side and the King in Pieces instead. No. She didn't trust him at all, but there were no other voices to guide her.

What did she have to lose?

Nothing. Like she was. *Nothing.*

After some time, the Broken Kids disbanded to resume their hunt. The big boy in the burlap gown led a few dead runts down the mountain. Pitchfork Girl followed others back up the steps to the cave. The Boy on Stilts posted on the rock, searching the Ghost River Valley with those thick magnifying lenses screwed to his skull.

When the wind whistled, Liz rolled out of her hiding place and crept toward him. The Boy on Stilts turned around just in time to catch her jab her cactus rib hand into his flayed chest. His stitched arms struggled for balance, flapping like a chick trying to learn how to fly. Instead of up, he fell off the overlook.

His body hit the rocks far below.

Liz looked further down into the valley. She could see the burlap-gowned goon waddling toward the base of the mountain. She was about halfway to the river from the looks of it.

She needed to keep going and move faster.

The gathering storm clouds overhead told her so.

Esther peered through a tall chain-link fence. A fresh corpse bled out onto the ground near a police truck parked inside the gate at Solemn Cave. She cupped her hands around her mouth and called out, "Anybody there?" No response. "Hello!" she yelled louder. "*Shelby? You in there?*" Nothing but singing cicadas replied from nearby Palo Verde trees.

The fence around the Solemn Cave complex was about ten

feet tall, wreathed in barbed wire at the top. Climbing over seemed a painful proposition. "Well, fuck it all then. I'm going through."

Esther climbed back into the tow truck, spun the steering wheel, and backed it up to the gate. She hopped out and hooked the tow chains to the chain-link and gave it a tug. Secure.

"Here goes nothing." She pinched her cigarette in between her lips and shifted the transmission to drive. She stomped on the gas pedal, let it all go. Tires spewed gravel.

Crash! The fence buckled.

She hopped out of the cab to admire her devastation. The weather was changing for the worse, getting darker outside as blood orange clouds threatened a monsoon near dusk. She'd been a desertfolk her whole life and knew that the pretty clouds above were harbingers of bad fucking situations. *Gotta hurry.* Esther grabbed a heavy flashlight and Minister's shotgun. She climbed over the collapsed fence, carefully avoiding the razor wire.

The first corpse, an older riverfolk man dressed in civilian clothes, lay face up in the dirt. A swarm of ants blanketed his eyes. Something didn't sit right about the scene, however. All of the juicy parts Shelby would have devoured were left behind.

"Why didn't you eat, Baby Bird?" Her flashlight circled a mysterious crater, a ring bordered by burnt dirt.

While moving toward the mouth of the cave, Esther passed an empty guardhouse. She shined her light in the dingy window. Hadn't been used in a while from the looks of it. Further into Solemn Cave, she found the second corpse. This one made sense to her. Pieces of a young Ghost River man. All of his insides scooped out of his chest like soup from a bread bowl. She recognized the uniform he wore. Tribal cop. Not good news.

"*Shelby!*"

She wandered deeper into the cavern and searched behind every ammo crate and peeked under every tarp. The missing girl wasn't there. Shelby had already gone.

When she emerged from the complex in the cave, Esther

met a more threatening sky. The wind had already picked up—the corpse by the police truck now coated in dust.

"Fucking monsoons," she said, shaking her head at the overlook. The town of Ghost River appeared haunted when the salmon and gray thunderheads rolled over the valley.

The dark thought stabbed her. Shelby would be there. The allure of people to eat would be irresistible to a harpy. All the riverfolk. Meat. The old folks. Meat. The children. Meat.

She'll hurt somebody—all the somebodies, in fact!

Esther shivered remembering half-dead, starving eyes under a sinister quilt watching her across Wrangler Vandersloan's coyote pen as a child. *Meat is life. Creation eats life.* She clamped her eyes shut, trying to forget the pathetic creature in the cage.

No, she thought. *This isn't your fucking problem. Besides, Wallace and those assholes never did shit to help you. They let Eugene Northamm keep you prisoner for The Pig. They knew what he was doing out there, didn't care, cut wise deals with him, and now it's time to pay the price for their sins...*

"Do you want to see what I can do to him?"

Baby Bird grinned.

Esther looked away from the Ghost River village. She took a deep breath, then rubbed her temples. *Yes, I wanted to see it.* She couldn't shake the image of her little Baby Bird eviscerating Wrangler Vandersloan in that dark hallway of the stone-stacked house years ago. The way her bladed fingers sliced through his belly made Esther smile. The way she forced him down on his knees while she pulled out his heart made her tingle. He couldn't do shit to stop it, could he? She cried against the wall of the nursery. It was *beautiful* to watch, another lost girl breaking the man who found so many. Then, Wrangler became Macho, limp in Shelby's bloody arms, and Esther ran toward her truck. Not Macho. She could eat everybody else but him.

"Who's that, Mommy?"

Alyssa tugged on Misty's t-shirt. The Ghost River woman followed her daughter's finger to the bloodied and dusty naked girl walking toward them from the desert.

"*Chris!*" Misty yelled through the screen door of their trailer. "I need you!"

A muffled voice: "What?"

"Come out here! *Right now!*"

The stranger stood across the front yard. Smiling.

"You need help?" Misty asked. "Are you hurt?"

"I'm hungry," the girl replied.

The screen door opened. A bull-chested man in a Metallica t-shirt stepped outside. "What the hell?"

"I'm hungry," the girl repeated.

Misty followed Chris across the yard. Her husband was brave and always ready to help. "She just showed up. Walked out of the desert looking like *that*."

The gore-drenched visitor didn't move. Chris opened his hands, held them up in peace when he approached. "You hurt?" he asked, stepping closer. "Do you need a doctor?"

The desert wanderer grinned, watching Alyssa hug Misty's thigh. Her daughter, who was only four, said the girl looked funny. Her eyes seemed weird, sort of sparkly.

"Where'd you come from?" Misty asked.

She pointed at Solemn Cave.

Misty shook her head. "That's near Orphan Rock. Nobody lives out there, darling. Where do you really live?"

"Maybe she wandered over from Sandoval?" Chris addressed the bloody girl, asking, "Is that where you're from? Sandoval? Was there an accident near the canal?"

"I'm hungry," she said a third time. "I ate something earlier, but now I feel cold and empty again." She raised her hand, and although her incredibly long fingers looked like claws, the charred skin and the bubbling blisters on her palm stole the show.

Misty took a step back. "I'm sick. I need to eat more to get better." She studied Chris. "You're a big one, aren't you? Beefy."

"I'm going to call the police." Misty turned back to the trailer. "Keep her out here, okay?" She pulled curious Alyssa by her skinny wrist for safekeeping. The little girl groaned but followed. Misty had always feared that the closer Sandoval crept to their lands, the white kids would sneak out into the desert to party along the river. Do drugs. Light fires. Park and fuck.

"*Nuggghhh.*"

A juicy, guttural gasp.

Misty froze, turned slowly back around. Alyssa screamed when her father's skull disappeared inside of the naked girl's gaping mouth. The way her lips stretched and snapped over his neck reminded Misty of a snake devouring prey twice its size. Blood squirted from his broken skin while her serrated teeth sawed through his spine. Hanging from her mouth, Chris's body flopped and kicked, and then jerked awkwardly one last time.

Crunch!

He fell to the dirt. Headless.

"*Jesus!*" Misty panicked and yanked Alyssa inside the trailer. Her daughter was screaming and crying and trying to unlock the door to go back for her stepfather.

"Don't you open that door!" Misty screeched, the telephone sitting in the crook of her neck. She dialed 9-1-1. Could barely hear the operator. Alyssa wouldn't stop shouting.

Outside, savage claws cleaved skin while rising winds whipped at nutmeg hair.

Wallace sighed and let Esther inside of his apartment. She sank onto the couch, unable to find the right words to say. Macho kept his distance and folded his arms impatiently.

"You only come by when there's a problem."

Esther looked at the floor. "Well, guess what? There's a

fucking problem."

His gaze bored into the ceiling; his head shook slowly. "You know, I've been thinking a lot since the last council meeting. About the way things are between us. I'm done. We're…*done*."

"All right then."

Macho deflated. "See? That right there! You're never connected to an outcome. Good? Bad? You just float through it all, don't you? Nothing ever gets close to you!"

"I don't know what you want me to say."

"That you give a shit?" Wallace made fists, shook them in anger. "Fuck! Why are you the way you are?"

Esther laughed, tossed her hands up in contempt for the stupid question. "Why is anybody the way they fucking are? *Shit* happens, you turn out. Christ, what is the matter with you?"

"Are you really that dumb?"

Her jaw clenched. "The fuck you say to me?"

"*You don't realize I love you?*" Esther flinched to hear Macho say it. Those words shredded her open like bullets, made her bleed. "I think about you all day long, worrying about you living in a goddamn nightmare! My whole life I've heard the stories of Orphan Rock. *Nothing but sorrow comes from the Land Where Pigs Squeal.* Now? I can't sleep unless I know you're safe. You're a goddamn ghost, Esther Northamm, and you're haunting my head." He rubbed his bloodshot eyes, and his voice dissolved into a whisper, "Why can't this be any different?"

"Macho…"

Esther's words trailed off with the crackle of static.

"*…Officer Machado…do you copy…*"

He turned his exhausted gaze to the bedroom and sighed. His police radio sat on the dresser next to his display case of medals from Vietnam. He stepped in the room, closing the door to answer dispatch in private. Esther buried her head in her hands. She feared Macho might break one day. That he'd come to realize he slept with a phantom. A thing without history. Without creed.

A desertfolk girl. The kind that'll break your heart because they must. A coyote marked to howl in the hills until the day she dies. *Love? Her?* She was a ghoul like the rest of the pathetic creatures in Orphan Rock. No better, no worse.

When Macho's bedroom door finally opened, he stepped into the living room, buttoning up the shirt of his uniform.

"I have to go. Assault in progress."

Esther jumped up. "By Orphan Rock?"

"Yep." Macho slung his holster over his shoulder.

"I'm going with you."

"No, you're not. You're going home."

"Macho, please." Esther pulled on his arm. "Listen to me. Something escaped from Orphan Rock this morning. We have to go and get her back before she hurts a lot of people."

Macho tugged his hand away, looking annoyed. "What are you talking about now, Esther? Nothing leaves Orphan Rock, except for you. Now get back there before you burn up."

"This thing can."

"What thing? You're not making sense."

"It's like Delora, except she isn't bound to the land. Like me, she can go where she likes...for a time. She'll kill a lot of people too. She don't know no better. She's just a kid."

"Esther, it can't be like Delora."

"I'm positive she is. I've cared for her a little while now. I wanted to tell you this, but..." Esther choked up. She hated keeping secrets, hated coming clean even more. "When Minister told you I lost my child it was a lie. When she was born, Delora took her from me. Kept her locked up in a special cage, raised her to be just like her. She's my *daughter,* I suppose. I spray her with a hose sometimes and comb her pretty hair." Esther rubbed her belly. "I made her in my tummy. Right here."

"You what?"

"Macho, I—"

"Why wouldn't you tell me this?" Hurt made his jaw

tremble. "What about the danger to my people?" Macho paced, shaking his head. "I'm next in line to be chief of police, Esther! If it's what you say it is, a Sister of Sorrow like Delora, then that thing is a goddamn menace and needs to fucking die tonight."

"Macho, please, she's my child."

"I'm done." Macho opened the door. "*Go home.*"

"No. I'm going with you."

"The hell you are."

"Try and stop me! Arrest me, you big fucker!" She stomped over to him, held out her wrists, showing him her scratchy pig mark. "Well? Go on. Cuff me, *tough guy.*"

"Jesus Christ, why are you like this?" Macho asked again, half-laughing in resignation. "*Fine.* You tail behind me in your truck. You don't get out unless I say so. We clear?"

Esther kissed his cheek. "Love you too."

III
Monsoon

10.

The wall of ruddy dust loomed like a billowing titan: a towering, slow stalker that swallowed the desert expanse of Ghost River Valley in a rusty-brown haze. Sand in your eyes. Sand on your tongue. Dry lightning surging in the clouds.

Visibility worsened fast. First, she couldn't see the river or the valley from her perch on the mountain's high steps. Then, she couldn't see the base of Orphan Rock. Lastly, she lost sight of everything more than ten feet in front of her. Sand cloaked the mountain in gritty fog. The wind blasts tore through crevasse and branches. Deafening. Liz spun in place. Which way to go?

Down. To the river.

With her cactus crutch and stiff legs, she tried to pick up the pace. The howling wind was a brutal enemy and resilient in its quest to shove her over the cliffside. She imagined her body bursting like a ceramic pot on boulders below. In Oklahoma, Momma used to keep flowers in ceramic pots on the front porch filled with...

filled with…

Liz tried to remember the flowers. She could see Stacy in her gardening gloves, scooping soil with her spade, but the flowers had no blooms. Only stems.

Crack! Whoosh!

Above the girl trapped in the scarecrow, a mature mesquite tree toppled and rode an avalanche of loose gravel down the mountainside. Boulders gathered more boulders along the way.

Soon, half the mountain raced in her direction.

Everything quaked and tumbled, and dirt poured over the cliff's edge like floodwater. Liz clung to the nearby wall, pressing the scarecrow's fragile body against the rock. When she felt her shape crumble under the duress of crushing debris, she yanked her eyes from the golem and cried out in frustration.

The little ghost curled up in the dark corner of her shell. She didn't want to look. Didn't want to see what just happened. Didn't want to gaze in those dim eyeholes and see only the darkness of dirt forever. *Am I buried? Crushed?* She'd haunt the earth beneath the ground for more than a thousand years if that were the case. The King in Pieces never told her how to escape this vessel. Maybe there wasn't an exit. Maybe getting to the Other Side was the only way to something else.

"Why can't it ever be easy?"

Liz wanted to cry, but her tears were smoke.

Macho's cruiser sped through the streetlights in Ghost River proper, siren squealing in the dusk. Esther stuck on his tail the best she could despite the wind pushing the Retriever all over the road. Luckily, the coming storm kept most other drivers inside tonight. The smart ones, anyway.

The trailer was a few miles outside of town, right at the edge of the desert. Esther parked behind Wallace. Hard to tell what was happening with the sandstorm tearing the world apart. Macho stepped out of his cruiser, wind whipping through his black hair. He pulled out his handgun and looked at Esther. She couldn't hear his words, but she read his lips.

Wait in the truck.

She reached for the door handle. Then hesitated.

Wait in the truck.

Of course, Wallace would say that. He's protective, means well, and a complete fucking fool to think she would listen to him. Seemed optimistic that she could sit still and wait for shit to happen to her like Minister did. Always doubted her ability to handle the worst of things by herself. *Guess I have a type after all. Assholes and underestimaters.*

Macho approached something or somebody on the ground. It was getting harder to see him. Soon he would be lost to the wind, and everything would be left to…fate? Esther never liked fate. Fate had this funny way of fucking her over every time. She felt that door handle again.

Wait in the truck.

What if Shelby attacked Macho?

Wait in the truck.

She didn't really know Wallace at all—she'd just kill him!

Wait in the truck.

What if Wallace shot Shelby because she scared him?

Wait—

No, she thought. *This ain't gonna work his way.*

Esther picked up the shotgun and pumped it. "Fuck it."

She pulled the handle and hopped out of the truck.

"I told you to stay inside!" Macho shouted at her above the storm's howl. More purple lightning flashed, still no thunder.

"I can talk to her! She trusts me."

"Jesus Christ!" Macho knelt next to the husk of a riverfolk man that was lying in the front yard. Ribs hollowed out. Head missing. No way to tell who it was.

"It's her," Esther said, looking around in a circle. Dust cut into her eyes like microscopic knives. They crept toward the trailer; guns pointed at the front door struggling on its hinges in the wind. Macho tried to take the lead, but Esther slipped ahead. "Please, let me go in first. She knows me. She won't attack me. I can talk her out of there without any more bloodshed."

The riverfolk man could only agree to her terms. Protocols meant little in Ghost River these days, if ever, and even less to a Northamm. "I'll be right behind you. She makes any sudden moves, I'll shoot her in the head. I fucking promise you, Esther."

"All right then. We move slow. No surprises."

While screams and broken glass filled the ghostly hallways of her home, Liz laid in her bed with Reuben and told him all of her secrets. The trick was to keep talking, singing, laughing through the fear so no pain could bleed through. Reuben built a wall and tried to guard her childhood behind it – a fading thing, a dimming flame, and a broken butterfly.

The girl in the scarecrow hated feeling small—feeling afraid—feeling unable to stop her parents from hurting each other or making her cry. She hugged her skinny knees and felt only scabs where her teddy used to be. Reuben made it better for her. She should have never given him away. That stupid Broken Girl had no idea how important he was in making her feel brave.

Something remembered:

"*We can be strong*," her mother said, blood on the carpet.

A surge of confidence and anger lifted the broken butterfly to her feet. Small things could be strong too. In the hollow prison, she approached the golem's eyeholes, terrified she would confirm the avalanche had buried her far beneath the earth.

Darkness, but not the crushing black she expected to find, greeted her. Some light ahead. Branches moving in the wind. The mesquite tree had fallen top of her! Its trunk pinned her cactus rib crutch to the ground but did not crush her body.

Liz yanked until she felt the pole snap into a wooden shiv. She used it to part the web of gnarled branches surrounding her. Strange to celebrate crawling, but she had learned that life and death were only a series of strange feelings anyway.

When the battered golem stood from the uprooted tree, the rain fell in fat, juicy droplets—a few at first—and then, the downpour. Rainwater made rocks slippery, and Liz struggled to guide her clunky legs down the steps without falling and washing away. Oddly, the scarecrow's appendages seemed to loosen up in the rain—squishier and more natural to bend. The water was a lubricant! This information brought some relief to the passenger until Liz felt her broken arm fall off her shoulder. The ghost in the golem picked it up to see why. The clay glue that kept it all together dissolved and ran down her body like candle wax. There was no shelter. No place to hide.

She peered into the Ghost River Valley. In the basin, she could sort of see the river again now that the rain washed the dust from the sky. It would be dark soon, though, and that would make the trek even more precarious.

Lightning flashed, followed quickly by the first clap of thunder. There was no time to stand around pondering moves. If she didn't make it to the river swiftly, she'd fall apart.

Broken dishes on the floor.

A kitchen table knocked over.

Blood smeared across the linoleum.

Splatter on the walls.

A television set played local news.

Toys on the floor. Barbie dolls. Scattered crayons.

Glass crunched under her boots. Esther felt the pit of her stomach turn into an acid factory. The wrecked home was too quiet for comfort. She might already be gone.

"Shelby?" she called. "You in here, baby?"

Thunder rumbled. Heavy rain drummed on the aluminum roof. Wallace followed her into the living room while Esther turned the corner into the nook of the kitchen. The discovery was grim. The body of a riverfolk woman was on the floor. Her sable eyes stared at the popcorn ceiling. Her hollowed torso was split apart from sternum to pelvis. The corded telephone dangled from the cradle on the wall. *Irk - irk - irk.* Busy signal. A large knife lay just out of reach of her outstretched fingers in a coagulating pool of blood. Macho fell in behind. *"Goddammit."*

"She didn't feed," Esther said, pointing at the glistening red coil of the riverfolk woman's intestines. "Something spooked her. Maybe distracted her. She might still be here—"

Crash!

Macho pointed his gun down the hallway.

Esther walked ahead of him, raising her shotgun.

"Shelby? *That you?*"

Water raced underneath her twine-wrapped feet, each rocky step a flowing waterfall. All the hard clay dissolved from her form. Only bones, twine, and bundles of sticks kept her rickety scarecrow standing. Every step was a small miracle, and if Liz didn't fall, a blessing to boot. She slid in the mud, collided into jagged rocks, and wriggled on her belly, step to step, if needed be. Stopping, even for a second, was a death sentence. Even stumbling was progress toward the bottom. She gritted her teeth and howled in fury. She hated her crumbling body. The cruel weather. Her jackal-eyed father. Not caring anymore about her vessel made it easier to move with abandoned caution. The golem of the King of Pieces wasn't going to make it to the Ghost River any other way. She might as well tear it all apart if there wasn't any hope left.

She had to keep going.

To keep that hope alive just a little bit longer.

To be strong too.

She stooped over a large step. Rainwater channeled around it and poured over the edge of the lip like a burst pipe. The trail had blown out in the storm, and the ground below would be a devastating force if she dared jump to it. Alas, there was no other way. Liz dropped the scarecrow to its knees. She kept her muddy elbows on the rock and dangled her threadbare legs over the edge. She wiggled a little lower, trying to shorten the gap between her and the crags below. The slick mud on her elbows created momentum. The little ghost in her brittle ceramic pot braced for impact. This might be the end of her brave adventure, after all.

"Please don't let me fall apart now," she whispered in the dark closet of her vessel. After a deep breath, she let go.

Esther crept down the narrow hallway of the trailer, listening to raindrops pattering on the aluminum roof. Family pictures hung on both walls, lining the humble home with recollections of rich history and love. A comely riverfolk family. A man, a woman, and a child. The little girl had a toothy grin— Mickey Mouse ears on her raven hair. Esther tried not to think about the little one. Mom and dad died already. Maybe the child hid. Maybe she ran away. Maybe...

Wouldn't that be a sight?

The Northamms in Disneyland.

They passed an empty bathroom with vanity lights blazing over a mirror. Hairspray on the counter. Brushes. Toys in the tub. Then a bedroom. Esther nosed the door open with the barrel of her shotgun. An unkempt bed. Blurs of rainwater reflected across white sheets from the soaked windowpane. Macho hovered behind her, nodding her on. Nobody in the room.

The last door in the hall was partially closed. A piece of paper pinned to it with clear tape. It was a drawing of a stick-figure princess wearing a golden crown and carrying a magic wand with a shining star on the tip that radiated with rainbows.

NO BOYS ALLOWED.

"...hungry...burning me...play with me...".

Esther halted, hearing the fractured voice on the other side of the doorway. Macho heard it too. At her side, he flipped the safety off of his handgun. He gestured ahead, wanting to take the lead. She mouthed no. Instead, Esther inhaled and pushed the door open slowly, so as not to spook what was on the other side. Light from the hallway bled into the darkness of the child's bedroom.

The blow was not what she expected, but it was fierce. A robust and clammy boa constrictor caught the scarecrow's waist mid-air and hurled her against the cliffside with a heavy grunt.

Bam! Her golem shattered against wet stone. Bones broken. Twine snapped. Clay in glops.

The mammoth boy with the potato sack mask looked down at her—head cocked, water running off frayed, filthy burlap. His one arm rubbed his hungry belly as lightning crackled in the dusking sky behind him. Liz struggled to control what was left of her battered form, but what could she do? The Broken Kid was a bull, and she could no longer feel her golem's legs.

A hungry mouth split open along the greasy crease of Potato Sack's distended tummy, revealing a grin packed with rows of yellowed, square teeth. His tongue unfurled from his lips like a fire hose and wrapped around her ankle. Liz turned upside down when her fragile body was plucked from the ground until ***snap!*** the scarecrow's leg popped off.

She slammed into the flagstone and nearly lost her connection to the rest of the golem's form. She felt nauseous in the spinning dark as the wrecking boy grabbed at her floppy arm. Liz poked at him with her wooden shiv, trying to fend him off. She had little strength and never broke his rubbery skin. Her feeble attempts prompted the snorting monster to catch her pole arm and break it in half with one fist. Liz bellowed in the forlorn darkness.

There was nothing left!

Both of her arms missing.

Her only good leg too.

The sticky tongue wrapped around her shin, and again she felt the ground disappear from underneath her. Liz, trapped in a crumbling torso, stared at the tunnel of teeth and the black hole her ship headed towards. There was no way to reverse course. Would the dark inside his belly be any better of a place to spend eternity than buried under a mountain?

She didn't want to find out!

Thunder echoed above.

A growing crescendo of a wayward river drew closer.

Potato Sack howled in triumph when Liz's golem slipped between his oily lips. His pig teeth bit into her vessel and chewed through branch and clay with pleasurable grunts. Liz made fists and screamed for justice, but who would hear her in the belly of a beast like this? Outside of her golem, a low rumble turned into a deafening howl until she felt the god punch of a tempest.

Suddenly, everything vanished in a roaring wave of water! The ghost clung to the golem's eyes, dizzy as it made her watching everything swirl in the ruddy murk.

Rocks, trees, even the porky Broken Kid, all swept away in the flash flood's tidal wave that started from the top of Orphan Rock and spilled down the mountainside into the valley.

When things leveled out, the current slowed and shallowed. The torso of her soggy golem hung from the thorny branches of a dead tree over the river. She dangled only a few feet from her watery destination. There wasn't any time to regroup, however. Broken Kids stormed from horsefly rips and sprinted at her from the desert scrub. They shrieked, waved weapons, and dreamed of murder. *Don't panic. We can be strong.*

Liz summoned all the agency she had left in her battered body. She stretched her golem's neck for the water.

Sluuurp! The puppet's shattered spine withdrew from its

muddy torso like a sword. Gravity did the rest of the work.

Bloop! A clay head hiding the little ghost dropped into the Ghost River slipstream and dissolved into a brown cloud.

A mad-eyed harpy drenched in viscera perched on a child's twin bed. Her scaly arms blistered with burning veins that crept up her neckline. Her sharky mouth chomped and licked, gnawing the tendons off of the little girl's arm bone. The rest of the stolen child was cradled in her feathery arms, just a floppy doll for Shelby to love and play with in the dark.

"*Drop her!*" Macho pointed his handgun at the creature. "Right now!"

"She's *mine!*" the harpy hissed, gathering the little girl's body against her blackening, curse-burnt chest. The tiny victim groaned and spat up more blood.

"It's me, Shelby." Esther stepped in front of Macho's unbreakable stare. He did not lower his weapon. "You're hurting, baby girl. I see it. I know how it feels too. Bad. Like you're on fire. Let's go home. You'll feel better there. I promise."

"*But…*" The dark monster with the crow's eyes wavered, considering the strange feelings that fueled her instinct to listen to the human. "*Being hungry feels so much worse…*"

Shelby bit into the little girl's shoulder, pulling fresh muscle from bone. The child screamed, her little voice already broken. Behind Esther, Macho boiled.

"*Drop the girl, or I'll shoot! Last warning!*"

The harpy frowned as lightning made her bloody lips glisten in the din. "I don't like you at all," she told Wallace scornfully. "You wanna see what I can do?"

Smiling like a devilish clown, Shelby slipped the trembling child's head into her wet maw like a lollipop. The little girl's soft moan muted when the harpy's lips closed around her thin neck. When Shelby bit down—***crack!*** —the girl's tiny body twitched, then went limp in her feathery arms.

Macho howled in horror.

He squeezed the trigger.

Boom! Gunfire and nearby thunder rattled the trailer.

Officer Machado dropped his weapon and stumbled into the bedroom. He crashed into the Barbie Dreamhouse and then crumpled to the floor. The back of his skull bled out.

Esther stood in the hallway, blinking, holding the butt of her shotgun like a cudgel. Dark Bird simpered to see her loyal servant and chewed happily despite the fire in her veins. A bullet hole smoked in the wall just a few inches from her head.

The Dodge Retriever bounced down the washed-out roads leading back to Orphan Rock. Everything muddy, lots of downed branches. Some stars pierced the dim clouds overhead, breaking through the storm front. Esther smoked while watching the road. She liked the way the air smelled after rain.

Shelby sat charring next to her, a beach towel wrapped around her nude body, the dirt curse blisters on her skin struggling to heal. She reached over and took a cigarette out of Esther's soft pack and lit up. Esther didn't like seeing her little girl smoke but didn't say a word about it. The twelve-year-old brooded with a familiar mix of frustration and apathy. She was a prisoner too. Like the rest of them. On top of having a cage, she had a little body that struggled to contain the tornado within it.

"You can't do that again. Run away like that."

Baby Bird rolled her eyes. "Don't tell me what to do."

"I'm not bossing you around. I'm trying to help you."

"Help me what? Starve? Maybe die from boredom?"

"Deal with it. Your life. It ain't pretty, but it's yours."

"Stop talking."

"No." Esther swallowed hard. "You need to listen. The more you fight against what you are—just another fucking slave—

the harder your life is going to be. Trust me, Shelby, there are some pretty things in the world. Not many from where we sit, but *some*. The only way she'll let you see them is if you do what you're told. You need to follow the rules. Play along."

"You don't own me," Shelby said. "Neither does she."

"*Fuck it all!* Do you know the trouble you've caused?"

"I don't care."

"You killed five people! A child! A cop! There are consequences for that shit."

"Like what?" Shelby folded smoldering arms after flicking her half-smoked cigarette out of the window with disgust. "I have a right to eat. You're just like Mother. Always saying no."

"You're feeding frenzy cost me the only friend I got left."

"The skyreader? *Oh, fuck him.* I'll eat him next."

Smack! Esther's palm met Shelby's cheek. The girl flinched, brought her fingers to her mask, and the corners of her lips tore apart in anger.

"Go ahead, Baby Bird! *Fucking kill me.* Rip out my heart and stuff it in your fuckin' mouth. *Christ knows,* can't get nobody else around here to do it. Might as well be you."

Shelby's claws hardened, but then she deflated in her seat. A tear ran down her cheek as the curse singed her neckline. When Esther tried to wipe it away, Shelby let her.

"Is she going to punish me for leaving?" The harpy asked after a moment of quiet, her skin streaked with rainwater and blood. "I won't let her put me in a cage again."

Esther sighed, then shrugged. "I don't know. Don't think Delora will be too keen on you roaming free. Especially after what happened. You broke the rules. She don't like that."

Like a scientist, Shelby studied her blackened arm and the ochre veins that ran along it. "It's not as bad as I thought. The burning. The empty is worse. The boredom is worse."

"Well, the dirt curse don't feel good, and it never stops." Esther looked at her own hand, the tips of her fingers felt warmer.

"You want out? Join the club, baby girl. Nobody gets out of Orphan Rock until Delora gets her way with things. So, play it smart and help her water that fucking Grim Seed, will you? In the meantime, it's better to obey the rules. Hurts less that way." Esther paused, and looked at the wet road ahead. "Truth be told, I was thinking about just letting you fucking go today, seeing if you could survive. I dunno, maybe with your boon you could heal yourself enough to be free. But you're not ready."

"Not ready for what?"

"*He could have shot you.*"

"That man didn't scare me."

"All you cared about was eating that little girl. You acted like there was nothing else happening around you. *That's scary shit.* You couldn't control yourself."

The girl waved her off. "I could've stopped anytime."

"I hope so." Esther tossed her cigarette from the window. "Otherwise, you're no different than Delora. I want you to be with all my heart. *Make better choices.*"

Shelby looked out of the window. She was done listening to servants.

Back home, Esther parked on the drive to the stone-stacked house. The Crooked Woman stood at the fire ring. Flames cast dancing shadows on her discolored veil.

"Better let me go first," Shelby said. "She's going to be in a bad fucking mood."

Baby Bird reached for the handle when Esther's arms draped around her. She cried a little. Nuzzled into her towel. "I love you, Shelby. Probably don't mean much to a thing like you, but I do. Don't let them fucking take anything from you, because they'll *take it all* if you let them."

Shelby wasn't sure what to say. Humans were batshit odd. She reached over and patted Esther's cheek with an awkward grin. Then, she slipped out of the car and let her towel drop. Baby Bird marched to Delora with more poise and confidence at twelve years old than Esther ever had in her thirty years of life.

At least she's got that.

Several rogue embers burst from the firepit when Delora grabbed her by the wrist. Baby Bird tried to run, tried to change shape, tried to call for help, but it was too late. *So quiet in Orphan Rock now,* Esther thought, after watching Delora and her gang of Broken Kids leash Shelby and lead her into a large horsefly portal to The Dark. *So fucking quiet to be away from it all. If you stop listening, you can't even hear the coyotes howl.*

Esther slipped the shotgun barrels into her mouth.

So quiet to be leaving so soon.

She closed her eyes.

Just a little quieter.

I want my last thought to be as empty as me.

The passenger door opened.

Somebody pulled the shotgun from her lips.

Esther looked over slowly, tears running down her cheeks.

Shelby?

His eyes darker than she remembered. Deader now.

"Even though I walk through the valley of the shadow of death, I will fear no evil, for you are with me." Minister took her hand, wearing that Burt Reynolds smile she loved.

A horsefly flew out of his nostril.

Esther screamed.

IV
Minister

11.

They stabbed him with shears. They bit him with cracked teeth. They drove railroad spikes through the bones of his wrists and ankles. They drank his blood and chewed his gristle. They called him a sinner. They cast him out from the only home he'd ever known. Now he was falling. Dying. Going deeper into The Dark alone. Every holy man needs to die to be reborn.

Wallace once told him that the Old Sinkhole was bottomless. Decades ago, his people would punish the worst criminals in their tribe by throwing them in. "Some spirits are so foul, it's better to let them fall forever than risk returning them to the world of the living," he explained. "That hole runs deeper than Hell, and it's got just as many demons living in it."

The holy man absorbed those words, folded them, and tucked them into his heart. His spirit was foul, wasn't it? Many times a murderer. Adulterer. Drunkard. Shitty father.

All that we do, we do for Delora.

He screamed.

Not in pain, but in torment. A primal hatred of self. Delora was the symptom, not the cause, of his spiritual necrosis. Eugene taught him well, hadn't he? Taught him how to be an empty man, how to disappear, how to run away when the screaming starts.

Scoot along now, boy.

Don't tell nobody what you saw here.

The entrance to the sinkhole above was a vanishing pinprick on a mile-long sheet of darkness. There was nothing else for his weary eyes to see. Minister Northamm made fists and tried to squeeze the blood out of his ruptured wrists.

The sooner he died, the sooner he could be forgotten.

1968

Crash!

What was that sound?

Minister sat up and rubbed his sleepy eyes.

The boy wiped the hay off his only shirt and stumbled into the hallway of the stone-stacked house.

Crash!

The shattering noise came from his father's room.

Minister placed his ear against the wooden door. The biting tone in Eugene's voice, the furious ranting, and hollow thuds against the wall warned of an angry Pig.

Crash!

More broken glass.

"Dad?" Minister put his hand on the door. "You OK?"

Eugene's angry voice went silent.

The boy tried the handle. Unlocked.

His father stood naked at the window—three of its four panes broken—still wearing his pigskin mask. Blood covered the rest of his gaunt body, even his penis, which was hidden in a bush of wiry pubic hair. His knuckles bled, shredded by the glass the Pig punched. He stood in a sea of dangerous shards that sparkled like gemstones in the morning sun.

Then, the eleven-year-old saw the body on the floor.

Naked. Cut up. Bound with wire. Teeth marks on her thighs. Whole chunks of muscle missing from her body, including her left breast. The knife Eugene had used on her the night before lay on the floor in a puddle of purpling blood. That grim rock of nervousness tumbled in Minister's gut again.

Another dead coyote.

"She wasn't the one," Eugene said, staring out the window.

Minister exhaled raggedly. "So, Momma doesn't have to pass the mark yet?"

The holy man shook his head. "Not today."

His father looked away from the shattered panes. He removed the pigskin mask, a patchwork hood made from human dermis, stitched together with thread spun from long strands of hair. Eugene's weary expression told the tale of last night's Coyote Run. His stern face flushed from exhaustion, his salt and pepper beard soaked with sweat and blood.

He dropped the mask on the floor.

"The day is coming when you'll be standing right here," his father began, bare feet crunching on broken glass. "Ain't easy carrying a pig's burden, you know? You're a snake. *Pigs swallow snakes when they want to.* You won't ever be able to say no."

The boy shivered. "I know, Dad."

Eugene laughed, taking a cigarette from a pack on the rickety dresser pushed against the wall. "He's *your* daddy more than me." The holy man lit up. "I just made you is all."

Wrangler Vandersloan stood in the living room. The Cowboy Lizard wore a black rustler's hat and a gold belt buckle the size of a dinner plate. Aviator sunglasses hid his mousey eyes, and a dirty muscle shirt did little to conceal the prison tattoos on his lanky arms. He smiled to see the Northamm boys up and at 'em that morning.

"Well?" The man who finds the lost girls clapped. "We celebrating or cleaning?"

"Cleaning," Eugene said glumly.

"*Damn!* She was the last one!"

"Guess you need to go and find some more."

Wrangler sighed through his birdbeak nose. "He ever tell you why?"

"Why what?"

"Why he doesn't like 'em?"

"No, he don't. He just don't like 'em enough."

Wrangler scratched his chin. "Feed, fuck, fury. Way of the pig."

Eugene massaged his temples. "That's how it goes."

Wrangler hovered for a minute, looked antsy.

"What is it?" Eugene asked.

"Might as well hear it from me."

"What the fuck is it, Wrangler?"

The Cowboy Lizard licked his sun-scabby lips. "Problem down at the river. She snatched another one."

"Goddammit!" Eugene punched the wall. "Another one of ours?"

"Took him last night. Left pieces of him on the beach."

"Fucking perfect." The holy man paced in the living room. "When Father Pig finds out, there's gonna be trouble. She ain't following the rules. Feeding off our flock wasn't the deal. She gets the ones we give her. She don't get to choose like that."

Wrangler smiled behind his sunglasses. "How you wanna

play it then?"

Eugene collapsed onto the couch and stared at the cracked ceiling. "Fuck if I know," he finally said. "Don't let nobody near that river. Curfew at sunset. 'Specially for the runts."

"You got it, boss." Wrangler clicked his boot heels. He tipped his black hat at Minister and Eugene and left through the front door.

"You going to see her today?" Eugene asked the boy sitting at the kitchen table.

"Probably. You want to come with? She asks about you! We can go together."

"Not today. We're digging trenches around the Mound. Wrangler knows a fella that'll get us enough timber for the chapel project. Them Pig Men are ready to hustle to get scaffolding up."

"All right," Minister replied, slumping a little in his seat. "Anything you want me to tell her?"

His father worked his jaw for a moment. "Tell her...I love her and that, one day, we'll run away together."

"You want me to lie?"

"With all your heart, Little Snake."

The boy traveled the river rock path to the clearing near the base of Orphan Rock. Pig Men shouted as pickaxes and shovels clanked against the rock. They struggled to penetrate the ancient desert crust around the Mound. The moon wasn't out, so they weren't wearing their masks or chasing coyotes. No, they pretended to be *civilized men* for the moment. They chattered about the river—another stolen baby taken from The Pig's litter.

Minister said nothing and strolled by. The Pig Men watched the holy man's soft boy wander away from another hard day's work with clear disdain on their scruffy faces.

"Hey, Minister!" one of the Pig Men hollered. "You're looking scrawny, boy! Pick up a shovel and start digging. Let's put some meat on those bones, eh?"

The men howled with laughter.

Minister kept walking, hands in his pockets.

The boy liked to be alone or with Clara. He didn't care for Eugene's Pig Men or Wrangler Vandersloan. Arrogance and cruelty were traits the King of Pigs sought in his devotees. This camp was chockful of men with shitty tempers and loud, terrible opinions on everything. Minister had seen them kill their kind out of pettiness before; he even watched a man bury a hatchet into the neck of another man around the campfire while drunk on whiskey.

These men were dregs, called from all over the country and desert to serve Father Pig. Over the years, their clan of criminals grew, and then Eugene started preaching. A traveling preacher who could raise the dead! A *real* miracle worker in a world full of charlatans. Of course, Eugene wasn't responsible for any real miracles. The King of Pigs handled those. Eugene was his skin to wear. Just like he would wear Minister someday. *All snakes are born with a hole in their heart. That hole is a door.* A door for the King of Pigs to enter so he may breed boonchildren, preach, and serve cruel Pig justice. One day, Minister would be his holy man.

Wrangler kept the coyotes and some livestock in a pasture next to his black van. A moldy trough for table scraps. Another filthy basin nearby for water. The girls and the old goats ate from the same feeders. They shit on the same desert grass. The chain-link coyote pen was empty now. The pigs chased them last night, and nobody came back to talk about it.

"Morning, Minister," a sweet voice said.

In a separate pen under a blue tarp for shade, his momma sat on a folding chair. Compared to regular coyotes, she lived like a queen. She had separate food and water, a couple of blankets, and shade with books to read. Being the chosen bride of the Pig Father had some perks. Clara welcomed her boy over, and she hugged him through the cage. "Eugene sends his love, Momma. He can't wait to run away with you soon…er…*someday.*"

"Oh? That's nice to hear, isn't it?" Clara smiled, her brown eyes looking tired and a bit droopy. "So, I'm guessin' the last coyote wasn't the one he was after…"

"No. She's dead."

Clara sucked in a breath through her teeth. She scratched the itchy Pig's mark on her wrist. "Well, I suppose that means we'll have more time together. That'll be nice, won't it?"

"You don't sound so sure."

His mother laughed, tossing her greasy auburn hair in the air. "Oh, I'm sure. I'm always happy with you around. You're my baby boy, Minister." He looked at his beautiful momma and wanted to keep her in that cage forever. She was safe behind that chain-link fence. At least she'd be somewhere he could always find her. She wouldn't be dead on Eugene's floor.

"It's OK, Little Snake. I'm not scared to die." She looked around nervously. "Can you keep a secret?"

Minister watched her slip her hand through the links of the cage. Her fingers folded into a fist, except for her pinkie. Minister looked at it, confused. Clara wiggled it.

"Go on," she said. "Wrap your pinkie around mine."

Minister sniffed. "Why?"

"You're going to promise me something, that's why. A pinkie swear is a sacred promise, you know. You can't break it. If you do, you'll have a hundred years of bad luck."

His pinkie coiled around hers. "OK, now what?"

"Promise me that you'll keep my secret safe."

"I promise."

Clara leaned in, barely able to contain her excited smile. "I'm not scared to die, because I'm *moving on.*"

"You mean, to Heaven?"

"No!" Clara shushed him. Her dirty knees bopped up and down on her folding chair. "I'm going to a different place entirely. A *different world*, he said."

Minister blinked. "Who said? What world?"

Clara peeked over her shoulder to make sure Wrangler wasn't snooping. "There's a boy who comes around sometimes. One of the pig runts, I think. Don't know much about him. He told me that there's a woman who lives in the river. *A lover of children.* She helps people in cages escape. Said she'll help me too."

"Help you escape to where?"

"Don't matter. It won't be here, right?" She smiled. "That's enough for me." His momma placed her other hand on his. "You want to come with us, Minister?"

"But…where are we going?"

"*To the Other Side.* To a land where the pigs don't squeal."

The boy's name was Gilbert. He was an odd duck. Book smart and liked to prove it with fancy words and annoying speeches and arrogant looks. Minister stayed away from most of the piglets just as much as he did their fathers. Most of them didn't grow up anyway. Soon as they got too needy, they disappeared. The truth was the men would always have a Feast of Pigs soon after one went missing. Plenty of fresh meat to stew up. Origin? Nobody cared.

But Gilbert stuck around. Played his cards right enough to still be amongst the living. Maybe it was because, like Minister, he was a loner and minded his own. Never made a fuss or took more than he was allowed to have. He gamed it smart, accepted his future. No complaints. Big smiles for the Pig Men.

When Momma told Minister that a kid came to her with that crazy offer to leave Orphan Rock for another world, he thought of Gilbert right away. That weirdo always looked over his shoulder. Plus, rumor had it he wasn't all correct in his mind. Had a reputation for talking to himself, spooking people.

That morning, Gilbert gunned through the blossoming town square of Orphan Rock, a small western hovel in the middle of God's great desert. The rest of the men hadn't stirred from their bedrolls yet, so he moved with purpose. Every now and again, he looked over his shoulder, and Minister kept a careful distance to not be seen. Gilbert traveled on the path toward the river. The misfit boy carried a potato sack for a satchel.

Minister tailed him to the old shed near the clearing by the Ghost River. He hid in a grove of bushes several yards away. Gilbert slid his schemey-gaze around the area to make sure nobody was looking. Once he was confident nobody was watching, he knocked on the door. Minister squinted, surprised to see it open. Nobody lived in the old shed—it was too close to the river. Father Pig never liked any of his men or children near it. People went missing when they did.

A naked boy, bulbous and pasty, opened the door and waddled out of the abandoned prospecting lodge. Minister cocked his head. Something didn't look right about the big oaf. Before he could get a better look, Gilbert pulled a trinket out of his sack and handed the burlap over. The goliath grunted and shimmied the bag over his...*head*? Not long after, a freakish girl with four legs crept out, her knees and feet rising and falling in a delicate dance. She wore a filthy, tailored dress, and her hair was in tight pigtails. Her arms absurdly long that bent as if she had three elbows on each.

Minister quivered, remembering the Dirt Hymns.

Pig Boy and Spider Girl were famous Forsaken Kids amongst the Pig Men of Orphan Rock. Just a couple of the many disfigured children tossed in the Old Sinkhole after they were born to appease Father Pig's obsession with vanity. One was so big it killed its momma coming out, and the other had four legs, crooked like a grasshopper's hind. A girl. Who else could they be?

The misfit crew moved with purpose, and Minister followed as they hiked down to the river's edge. He couldn't get close enough to hear anything useful, but he watched anyway.

They stood on the clay bank of the Ghost River, holding hands when a resplendent woman with slender fingers and long, brown curls ascended from the current. The River Woman.

Minister got nervous even seeing her. Ain't nobody supposed to see her and live to tell the tale about it.

Gilbert handed her something. A small toy? A doll? She grinned, patted his head, looked happy. Then, the oddball children clapped their hands and sang for her pleasure.

"When she comes, we must obey.
Sister Dirt, we come to play.
When she finds us, sing and sway.
In the stream, we'll wash away.
Don't be cruel, and don't you cry,
We'll see our friends on the Other Side."

Pleased by her adorers, the woman said farewell and wandered back into the river. She carried the clay doll with her. Gilbert and the Forsaken Kids turned around and walked back to the shed. Minister didn't wait to see what happened next. Whatever they were up, Father Pig wouldn't like it.

He sprinted back to Orphan Rock, planning to say nothing about what he saw. No good would come of it if he did. Forsaken Kids? They'd hang him for heresy. Wouldn't be the first time occupied nooses adorned the mesquite trees of Orphan Rock.

In town, Eugene snatched him up by the shirt as he tried running by. Minister panted, hoping his Daddy wouldn't make him explain himself. Lying to the holy man was a crime in Orphan Rock. Didn't matter if you were kin. But he pinkie swore to Clara and he wouldn't break his promise to her for anything.

"The hell you doing, boy?"

"Running."

"*Running?*" one of the Pig Men, dragging some lumber, scoffed. "That tenderfoot?"

Eugene smirked and puffed up his chest. "*Watch yourself, Frankie.* Northamms are the fastest breed of desertfolk there is." He clapped Minister's bony shoulder in support. "My boy will be a King Pig one day, chasing down coyotes in the blink of an eye. You mark my words. He'll kick up dust."

"Yeah?" the heckler went on. "I'll believe it when I see it, Preacher Man. Never seen this snake lift a finger." The Pig Man scowled at the boy. "Looks pretty soft to me."

Eugene frowned. "Twenty dollars."

"What?" Frankie asked.

"I'll bet you twenty dollars my boy catches a coyote on the next run. He's old enough to try." Eugene patted the boy's back. "Ain't that right, Little Snake?"

Minister felt his stomach hit the ground.

Coyote run? Me?

The man dragging the wood beam dropped it on the dirt and walked over to Eugene. He spat in his hand and offered it with an arrogant smirk. The holy man grinned and shook it.

"Say he catches one," Frankie said. "Is this lightweight boy of yours brave enough to go through with it?"

"Yes. It's time he followed the Way of the Pig."

The Pig Man clapped with glee.

"*And its time I make an easy twenty dollars.*"

Minister stood alone while Eugene and the Pig Men returned to their trenching project under the blistering sun. He always knew his daddy would make him chase coyotes sooner or later. He just didn't want the day to ever fucking come.

The holy man threaded the eye of the needle. His boy was all thumbs when it came to sewing.

"*Oww!*"

Eugene shook his head while Minister sucked the blood off the tip of his finger. "Slow down and make the stitches tighter. Skin don't tear easily, so don't be a soft hand with it. Go ahead and pull with some muscle. Tight."

Minister admired his pile of dried flesh on the kitchen

table. Hand-picked off the tanning racks where Wrangler skinned the prettiest coyotes. It was supple and treated. Some hair on the pieces. Different colors too. Even red. Freckles and moles, and some skin so pristine it looked like plastic. He cut them and laid them out in the shape of a face with holes for his eyes, nose, ears, and mouth. But he struggled with the stitching—all thumbs.

"What's it like when he takes you over?"

Eugene lit a cigarette and leaned back in the wobbly wooden chair. "You mean, when I become The Pig?"

"Yeah."

"Well, you'll find out for yourself one day, that's for sure. But it's like going to sleep. You just sort of die. Lights out, until its lights on again." Eugene blew smoke. "Sometimes, he shows you things he's proud of. Things he's done. That's about the worst of it. Seeing the mess." Eugene scratched the back of his head. His father's eyes: vacant. "That's a lie. The worst part is you don't even get the satisfaction of it. He keeps that *all* for himself."

"Satisfaction?"

Eugene leaned forward. "Coming, boy." He laughed. "You never get the blood rush in your nuts that you want. You fuck so many yet feel no pleasure. After a while, you sort of just don't care. Me? I'm celibate in Orphan Rock. Ain't never felt your mother. I'm a holy man, I guess." Eugene lifted his can of beer to his lips and took a swig. He offered it to Minister, who took a tiny sip. "That's another lie. I have friends in town that know how to show me a good fucking time when I come 'round. Sometimes it costs money. Ain't no shame in paying for a little tenderness."

"*You...pay for sex?*"

"How old are you now?" Eugene slurred a little. His father liked to drink a lot at night.

"I don't know for sure, but Momma said I was born over ten years ago."

"Jesus Christ, feels like yesterday."

"I guess so."

"I was thirteen when I did my first Coyote Run. 'Round your age. Was scared to death too. My knees locked up, and I got all dizzy and sweaty. Never caught one. Not even close. I wish I had, though. After that run, The Pig had his turn with me, and he ain't ever stopped since. We all carry our burdens here."

Minister made some progress on his needlework. A couple of pieces of skin finally stitched together nicely. His father admired his handiwork, even smiled a little bit.

"What are these marks?" The boy pointed at the strange carvings on the skin. "Some kind of language?"

"Pigspeak," the holy man replied. "They help quiet your mind so you can focus on important things. During our rituals, we are always empty-headed."

"Important things like what?"

Eugene snubbed his smoke. Before he replied, a car horn honked from the front yard. The Northamm boys popped up and peeped through the kitchen window. Wrangler Vandersloan. The Cowboy Lizard leaned against his midnight van. Eugene walked out to greet him, always eager to see the fresh crop of lost girls. Minister followed behind him.

"How'd it go?" the holy man asked.

"Grabbed what I could. See for yourself." Wrangler motioned for them to follow. They walked to the back of the van, and the kidnapper popped open the cargo door. Minister counted five girls gagged and bound on the floor. Other Pig Men gathered around to see the fresh meat. Eugene whistled and ordered them to get busy rounding them up for caging in the coyote pen.

Minister stepped back. He'd seen hundreds of coyotes come through Orphan Rock his whole life, but none he was going to chase in a run. The new batch of lost girls coming out to appease the Pig Father were in their teens. Some younger.

"*Let me go!*" a blonde girl screamed and slipped out of her blindfold. Minister watched her closely. She was real scrappy, with skinned knees and ice-blue eyes.

One by one, eager Pig Men carried the girls to the pens. Minister walked next to Eugene. The holy man always liked to oversee the caging. If he weren't around, the men might decide to take a turn on the girls, and that was against the rules.

While the girls stripped down and waited for the hose, Minister wandered over to Clara, who watched from her pen across the yard. She watched the caging with indifference. Minister never understood how his momma never cared that any of these women might replace her, and that would be her end.

"When is the run?" Clara asked the boy.

"Tomorrow night, I guess."

"You're not excited?"

"No," Minister replied quickly. "I mean, I know we have a tradition here, but it doesn't sit right with me. Daddy doesn't *ever* seem happy with any of it. He's in a trance or in the whiskey all day." Fear flashed on the boy's face. "I think that's my future too. I dream about it sometimes. The things I see in The Dark. It hurts my heart to dream."

Clara squeezed his hand. "I'm sorry, but it won't ever get any better for you. That's why you should come with us to the Other Side. You can lay down your burdens at the water's edge and forget your pigboon there. We can be a real family."

A tear dropped from Minister's eye. He shook his head defiantly. "I'm a snake, Momma. How else am I supposed to be?"

"*Kind.*" Clara pulled him toward her cage, and she hugged him tightly. The boy felt better in her arms. "I know you are. Eugene was too. He was the *sweetest damn man* I ever knew. Then he became the King of Pigs, and the man I loved was gone. The Pig will never give him back. He won't give you back to nobody either, Minister. *Come with us to the Other Side.*"

"All right, Momma. I'll think about it." Minister held his mother for a few ticks more. A tiny lizard scuttled over his shoe. Little critter had someplace else to be and fast. He let go of Clara and pushed the bangs out of his teary eyes. "It sounds too good to be true, don't it? The Other Side?"

"Maybe it is," Clara said in a hushed tone, "but it's the *not knowing* that gives me hope. I know what's here. So do you. Even Hell is better than Orphan Rock."

The King of Pigs smashed his smoky fist into the makeshift pulpit to calm the crowd in the town square. Any light inside of his mask was gone, and so was Eugene. Only milky eyes, veiled by shadows and flies, watched the Pig Men gather around the Mound. Fire pits burned in the Valley, lighting the hills as sunset radiated blood orange waves across the sky.

The Pig Men wore their masks too. They carried spears, scythes, rope, sickles, shovels, and pitchforks. The butts of their weapons thudded against the ground in unison. They snorted like boars and cheered for the Father Pig, who savored their devotion like honey. Five young girls knelt before the Dead Tree, all snaked by Eugene, wearing coyote pelts.

"What will we do tonight?" the King of Pigs asked, voice booming in the dark.

"*Feast!*" ***thud*** the crowd chanted, banging their weapons against the stone under the town square. Minister stood in the front row, the second smallest Pig Man near the Mound. Another tiny piglet was standing near the back. Like Minister, he wasn't moving a muscle to frenzy.

"And what else?"

"*Fuck!*" ***thud***

"And we do it all with?"

"*Fury!*" ***thud***

The King of Pigs opened his arms.

"Yes, swine. *Feed, fuck, and fury!* The Way of the Pig!"

thud**thud**thud

The Pig Father grinned, and a phantasmal snout and tusks greeted his congregation before returning to the din of flies. He

219

raised his hand. Three smoky sickles scissored the air.

"I'm the King of Pigs," he began, walking amongst his devoted who parted for him to pass. "I am the Prophet of Filth. And you are all my brood. You have appetites that cannot be sustained in a world that denies you the divine ritual of *domination*. Since the dawn of time, men and gods have sought to control that which we desire to command. To bend. *To break.*"

The King of Pigs squatted beside the tiniest coyote in the pack. That little blonde critter Minister saw at the van. She wouldn't look at him, just kept praying like a good girl while he stroked her cheek with a dirty, cracked fingernail.

"Those politicians and preachers and churches all tell you to cage your primal nature. The hunger you were born with. *They call it a sin. A sin! They call it barbarous!* They ask you to *defy what you are!* Hunters. Men who work hard for an honest cause and just can't ever catch a fucking break in their miserable lives." His hand shot into the air. Sickles swished. "But not you! Oh, no. *You're not like those soft men.* You're wiser than they are. You remember the value of being strong. The afterglow of a feast. The way a woman feels beneath you and under your fist. *That is true power and my boon to you if you will serve my appetites.*" *thud**thud**thud* "That is what tonight is about, Swine Children. Reclaiming your roots as *men who do not fear* their given instincts to take, have, and destroy. Put your faith in me and I will share my feast with you."

"*Feast!*" *thud*

"Give me your backs in daily service, and I shall let you fuck a worthy companion."

"*Fuck!*" *thud*

"And do not question my appetites or wants, and I shall share my greatest boon with you. *Fury.* With it, you will be capable of *absolute destruction.*"

"*Fury!*" *thud*

"Now, as the moon rises over this sacred Mound, you will

impress me with your thorough domination of any coyote that I do not choose for myself." The Pig Father stood at the podium again. "That leaves four to claim. Touch my choice and you will suffer the consequences. After all, *I only take one.* You get four, *you greedy little pigs.*" The desert demon cackled.

"*Feed, fuck, and fury!*" the crowd chanted. "*Feed, fuck, and fury!*"

The holy man hidden behind the horseflies glanced at Minister. The boy saw the wink. It chilled him to hear a whisper beneath his pig mask: *Peek-a-boo, I see you,* it said like a teasing child. *Soon, I'll take my turn with you too.*

Howling for help, the coyotes scrambled up the base of Orphan Rock. Thorny branches scratched the skin off their arms, and sharp, loose rock cut the bottoms of their soft bare feet. But they had to keep running. They had to hide. Fresh on the hunt, the Pig Men came for blood and flesh, their snorts and catcalls louder than their footfalls beneath the dark desert sky.

Minister ran with them, inspired by the dark passenger in his mind. The voice—raspy and deep—that begged his feet to move. It spoke to him of smells.

Can you smell their fear? Each one has a different scent. That stink should offend you. Does it?

"Yes," Minister whispered, inhaling through his mask.

Then run faster and catch one. Make it yours. Command it to smell better before you fuck it. That sound. *That voice.* Minister knew that it wasn't his own. These dark thoughts hid underneath a pig's mask and stirred his heart with every beat.

One day, all of this will be yours.

At first, Minister tried to reject the voice of The Pig, but the more it kept on talking, the more he kept on listening until he was not sure what thoughts belonged to him. He was forbidden to take off the mask during a Coyote Run, a grave offense, and the boy was not eager to face Eugene's wrath for trying.

When he was deeper in the brush, the howl of the first captured coyote rung out in the hills. The King of Pigs had made his choice. The Pig Men snorted and hooted in a gesture of respect and excitement. Now the hunt for the rest began.

Minister didn't know what to do or where to go next. For the first time in his life, he didn't dare run anywhere. If he did, he might find a lost girl and that—

The smells.

He inhaled them. His mouth watered.

Four coyotes left to find.

Pick one. Don't think. Smell and devour.

The Way of the Pig.

Minister caught the scent of one—it smelled like old urine kept in a jar in the sun—and his legs moved toward it. He held on to her offensive fragrance in a world full of sights and stinks that came alive under his magic mask. Everything smelled so foul. But nothing more so than a filthy coyote. Their fragrance worse than a dead skunk. His eyes watered with desperation to destroy it.

Run, boy. Run!

A second coyote yowled in despair, and the Pig Men serenaded the moon. Minister's heart raced. The closer he got to the source of that sweet stink, the more the voice taunted him. Called him names. Told him lies. Tried to make him mad.

I don't think you're weak, Minister. I just can't believe you have what it takes to be a king. I mean, look at where you came from! Your momma is a hound in a cage. Your daddy is a piss-leg drunk. You? You're just a small thing. A small thing that thinks small. Guess what? Thinking small will keep you that way.

"Shut up."

Why? I'm trying to help you see a better future for yourself. The Way of the Pig. Feed, fuck, fury. But I'm sorry, little child. I don't think you're man enough for me.

"I'm a man, *all right?*"

Are you? Will you be brave enough to take what you want from a coyote? Will you be man enough to destroy her afterward? I guess we'll find out, won't we? Right. Now.

Minister burst from the bushes and locked eyes with a trembling girl hiding behind a red and silver-veined boulder beneath a stringy Joshua tree. The brunette wrapped in pelts had dirt on her cheeks and shook her head when she saw the boy in the pig mask step into the silver moonlight.

"*Please!*" she squeaked. "Don't hurt me."

Well, Mr. Man?

Minister picked up a large rock.

"*I want to go home. Please!*"

The boy took a step toward her.

"*Why are you people doing this to us?*"

Kiss her with that rock, then kiss her with your lips.

He raised the stone over his head, ready to crack her dirty coyote skull. All he could smell was her stink. It made him so angry, he could hardly see straight.

"*Finders keepers!*" a shrill voice stole the moment, and a hefty shadow barreled by Minister. The other Pig Man drooled under his mask, lording over the cowering girl. He cocked his head, watching her sob. His erect dick swung side to side and thumped on his thigh. Before she made a run for it, he snatched a chunk of her hair and pulled the quivering mess to her feet. She cried as he pushed her against the rock. Every time she tried to squirm away, he hit her with his fist and laughed.

Are you just going to let him take your prize?

Minister lingered behind them.

The Pig Man snorted and fumbled, trying to get her still enough to fuck.

"No! Stop!"

"*Shut up!*" the Pig Man barked, pulling her grimacing face away from the boulder before smashing it back into it. She coughed, choking on broken teeth and salty blood.

"*Losers weepers,*" Minister whispered, smashing the rock in his hands down on the Pig Man's skull.

Thud! He popped off the girl and stumbled awkwardly, legs kicking out like a rooster on fire. The Pig Man gurgled, pissed himself, and then he collapsed. Minister dropped the heavy rock and his hungry gaze drifted back to the boulder—to *his* prize—but the coyote had already escaped into the dark desert.

Go get her! Get her! Get her!

Minister stalked his prey while she limped toward the river. She staggered along the washes. His snakeheart raced. His lungs burned air like gasoline. Her potent stench called to him as no other thing had. He needed to *destroy* it. He watched her stumble up ahead, looking so beautiful bleeding. Pictures of what he wanted to do to her flicked by in his thoughts. Surely, they weren't his, as he had never imagined such horrors before.

Whomp!

Minister buckled in the dirt. Somebody ran over him like he was a downed tree trunk. A couple more naked shadows overtook the wounded coyote in the wash, snouts dripping.

What happened next, he did not see. The concussive ripples behind his eyelids turned into dancing black spots that filled his mind like an uprooted anthill until everything was covered in darkness. Then, he couldn't smell anything anymore.

Still dark, but much later:

Minister groaned and licked his dry lips. Hot as hell in the desert, even at night. The boy sat up. He let his vertigo settle, forgetting where he was for the moment.

The pig mask still chattered, called him ugly names, and shouted cuss words. He peeled it from his sweaty head. The symbols that marked the skin on the inside of it glowed faintly.

Better to keep it off.

Then slowly, and in glitchy pieces, memories reformed.

The hunt. A coyote. Somebody smashed the back of his noggin. He looked ahead where the girl had disappeared under shadows, and there was somebody else there. Somebody who didn't seem to notice Minister knocked out just across the wash. He crept over, keeping his head down. *A Pig Man, but smaller than most. What was he doing to the body? To the dead girl?*

Snap!

The broken branch gave up the game.

The figure crouching near the defiled coyote spun around, holding a small knife.

"Who's there?" he asked, voice familiar.

Jesus Christ. Minister stepped out of the bushes.

"It's me. I'm done running tonight."

The little Pig Man hesitated.

Held in his other hand: a crude golem made of clay and wicker. He sheathed the knife. Then, Gilbert pulled off his mask. The boy looked scared to see him like he just got caught rummaging through the cookie jar. His hood wasn't like Minister's either. No pigspeak symbols on the inside.

Counterfeit.

"What are you doing to her? What's that doll for?"

Gilbert tucked the effigy behind his back.

"Nothing. To both questions."

"I saw you at the river. I know you speak to the Woman. I also saw them Forsaken Kids with you. I don't know how, but I know that's who they was." Minister walked over and grabbed Gilbert's wrist. The boy yipped when he yanked it over and looked at the clay golem, its cloth wrappings stained in wet blood. Then he looked at the dead coyote girl, bleeding out in the sand.

"What're you doing for the Woman?" Minister let his wrist go. "And why does my momma think you're going to take her away from Orphan Rock? You hypnotizin' her?"

"No." Gilbert cracked a devilish smile. "We're taking her because she deserves to be free. *Now leave me alone.*"

Before Gilbert turned away, Minister's eyes glimmered like sun drops. The piglet flinched but couldn't escape when the snakeshine burrowed into his twisty mind.

"Start talking."

Gilbert nodded and dropped the bloody doll, eager to please the halcyon eels hooked into his thoughts. "We serve Sister Dirt. She is a shaper, a builder of worlds. *A lover of children.*"

"What are you doing for her?"

"We collect the dead ones." Gilbert knelt to pick up the small effigy. "We put them inside the vessel. I try and gather all the coyotes if I can find what's left of them. I'll collect Clara, too, when it's time. She's going to die soon, you know."

Minister's fist tightened when the odd duck mentioned her name. "What does the Woman do with them in the river?"

"Sends them to a better place than here."

"The Other Side?"

Gilbert rubbed his hands. Beamed.

"That's right. *Paradise awaits the worthy.*"

Minister kept him snaked and talking until dawn. He listened to all the strange stories Gilbert had to tell about Sister Dirt and the ghosts inside of the enchanted dolls they ferried away to The Other Side. The Forsaken Kids who found the Deepest Door, who Sister Dirt brought home to help her. About desert demons and unruly Sisters and forbidden revolutions brewing beneath the hot desert sands. When he'd heard enough gibberish, he pulled his shine out of the smug boy. When Gilbert snapped out of it, he was alone in the gulch, talking to the chirping wrens.

Minister sulked back to Orphan Rock. He was dog-tired and listening to Gilbert's tall tales made him queasy in the belly and sick in the head. The hot mid-morning sun was already climbing in the sky. He opened the front door of the stone-stacked house, tossed his mask onto the ratty couch, and hung a right turn down the hallway toward the nursery and his pile of hay.

"Minister."

Eugene stood in the doorway of his bedroom.

The boy shuddered to see the tall shadow of a man, remembering the morning after a Coyote Run always resulted in the immediate removal of a corpse from Father Pig's room.

"Come here, boy." His father held open his bedroom door. Minister took a deep breath. *Just get through this and he'll let you sleep for a spell.* Rest and a new life are all he wanted.

The boy rounded the corner of his Daddy's room and looked at the pigspeak symbol on the floor. There, on the bloodstain of a hundred destroyed futures, sat the little blonde critter. Although he'd never seen it, he imagined the seas to be as blue as her eyes. She was not beaten, nor cut into pieces.

"She's chosen," Eugene said, putting his heavy hand on the boy's shoulder from behind. "She's too young still, even for The Pig. We'll keep her on until she's older."

"No." Minister backed away, wanting to puke.

"Man up." The holy man put his pig mask on the dresser, and he stared out of the broken window. "It was never going to be any other way for her, *or you, or me.* The sooner you let go of your broken heart, the better off you'll be 'round here. Father Pig will keep you numb. He's a *benevolent* god that way."

"Why won't you talk to me?"

The rude desertbilly boy looked up from the rock then spat. He went back to whittling a cactus rib spear without so much as a word. The little critter folded her scratched arms. She gripped the chain-link, her sandy hair blowing in the dry wind.

"You keep watching me. It's really fucking weird if you don't talk to me. Nobody here fucking talks to me!" The coyote sat on Clara's old chair next to a pile of Clara's old books. She spat just like Minister, but it landed on her foot. "*Shit!*"

He laughed. Minister caught himself feeling good again for a second and then shut down faster than an engine without fuel. The scrappy girl walked to the edge of her cage.

Minister tried to ignore her, but she lingered.

"What's the point?" he finally asked.

"Point in what? Talking?"

"I can't save you, so just shut up."

"Thing is, I don't want to talk about shitty stuff. I'm sick of crying about shitty stuff." The girl rubbed her wrist where the fresh pig mark festered. "Let's talk about normal people stuff."

"*Normal people stuff?*" Minister scoffed at the notion of *normal* found in any scenario in Ghost River. "That's my momma's cage you're sitting in. She's dead. I spent the last ten years of my life coming here. I...I'm used to feeling good here, so I come back and hang around until I feel better. It's getting less, though. How's that for normal people stuff?"

"What's your name?"

"Why?"

"Can't you answer a goddamn question?"

"Minister."

"Well, that's an oddball name, *Minister.*"

The boy shrugged. "Most kids here don't even have one."

"You a kid priest?"

"No! It's just a name. Not everything means something, you know. Sometimes things just mean nothing and that's all there is to it." Minister leaned back and opened a pack of Marlboros. Eugene cut another deal with the riverfolk and cigarettes flowed through Orphan Rock like dollar bills. It was currency. Holy Man's son got his cut. He lit one and tried to puff like a man, but he coughed and clutched at his chest like a child.

"You're a fucking pansy."

Minister gasped, still red from choking. "*Pansy?*"

"Purple flower where I'm from. *Delicate.*"

"I ain't no flower. *I'm a snake.*"

"That so?" The girl stuck out her hand. "Give me one. I'll show you how it's done."

The boy popped a fresh smoke in his mouth, lit it, and handed it over to the coyote. Up close, what he thought was dirt on her face was a scab. She eyed him suspiciously, smoked without coughing, and then said, "Well? Ask if you want to. You look like a moron just standing there."

"What happened to your head?"

"Last round of bitches threw rocks at me. But they ain't returned."

"They won't. They're dead."

Esther let that sink in. "Well, finally some *good fucking news*."

They laughed, and he warmed up to her. The boy sat down where he used to, close to Clara's folding chair. The girl relaxed a little too. Probably just wanted a friend. Guess they both did.

That morning, they smoked four and a half cigarettes together, unearthing the only treasure worth finding in all of Ghost River. From a distance, Gilbert watched them with a tiny smile.

1990

The crucified holy man in the razor wire crown spun like a top into the Old Sinkhole. Along the way to death, he fell through the Deepest Door into a massive cistern far into the belly of the oldest Earth. Static tickled his skin until the shift in dimensions stung. He clung to fleeting life, too afraid to let go just yet, too amazed by the oldest piece of Ghost River history there was to find. The Heart of the Desert. An empty, black lung so loud in silence it hurt his ears with nothing. This was the stain in the dirt from where the Age of Filth and its first prophet were born. The dark realm whispered of in the Dirt Hymns.

Whoomph.

The hilt of his wooden crucifix sheathed into the silty bottom of the Heart of the Desert like a dropped blade into a sand garden. Minister jerked. Iron spikes pulled through his hands, ripping holes wider, but they kept him tacked to the wood. His bones snapped—arms, legs, back. He didn't feel the pain, though. He was beyond suffering now—a genuine holy man.

The Dark around him shifted. His eyes did not deceive him! Pale indigo light, a halo of blue angels, guided her toward him—a boy wrapped in barbed wire by her side.

"Gilbert," Minister said, spitting blood. "*You asshole.*"

"Welcome to where it all began," Snarl said, grinning. "Fitting we're here together, isn't it? Our beginning is also where it's *all going to end.*" His one eye slid across the gloomy expanse. "The Deepest Door. Where Gods gather in their conquests." He grinned. "Mother has a question for you."

"*Shoot.*"

"What's a chapel without a preacher?"

"A *tomb*," Minister replied, blood dripping from his nose.

"Yes. That's what we have here. A tomb. And we need a chapel."

"What—"

"And every chapel I've seen…has a fucking holy man *worth a shit.*"

Delora shook off her confidant and placed a bony finger to Minister's mouth as if to shush him. He couldn't protest when she parted his salty lips. He couldn't even gather enough life to cry out when her finger blade sliced through his bottom lip and chin.

"*Nughhh.*"

"You said *anything*, Minister," Snarl said. "Mother

remembers your promise. Time to deliver our Rapture."

The harpy raked down his throat, chest, and belly in a straight, slow line. His intestines unfurled down his legs. It didn't feel real—his own parts gushing from his belly—and luckily, Minister didn't live long enough to feel Delora reach between his wet ribcage to cut out his scaly snakeheart.

The snakeshine died in his eyes.

Two broken lightbulbs extinguished.

The Luminarchs gathered around the Vile Hibiscus—the single lavender bloom of the Grim Seed, hidden deep in a tangle of thorny bloodroot that weaved a gnarled sanctuary in the putrid Dark. The eldritch bloom grew from the petrified body of a silver-tusked carcass that rotted on the Heart of the Desert's floor, some ancient devil that fell into this world from the Spaces Between Things. When the Crooked Woman approached it, the Vile Hibiscus' silky petals unfolded, revealing dozens of ghostly hands reaching out for the heart of a snake.

The Harpy of Ghost River placed the holy man's warm organ in the flower's gentle grasp. It closed in delight, and the Luminarchs thrummed in the air with buggy glee. The tremor of change came hard and quickly. Metal clanked, rocks loosened, and giant, moist shadows shifted and burrowed into the vacuous black of the earth lung. The transformation of things accelerated, and new shapes began to mold from the shadow.

When the Vile Hibiscus unwrapped, the twinkling Luminarchs vibrated with joy to see a Vile Heart sitting on a velvety petal. The Minister's heart, enhanced. A special heart indeed. Black, with white worms that crawled through the rotting tissue. Delora took her latest boon from the Grim Seed, and it pumped in her leathery hand. It, too, served the dirt now.

Time to build a worthy preacher from the broken.

Time to sing the Dirt Hymns to all who would offer their pain to be saved in the name of her vengeance.

V
Revival

1993

12.

GHOST RIVER REVIVAL
Where Miracles Happen Every Day.

Minister wiped the paint off his brush with a rag. The old sign looked reborn, vibrant, and welcoming after being battered by twenty years of harsh desert weather.

"Not too fucking bad," Esther said from the dirt road, holding her hand up to block the sunshine. "Almost looks new…two decades later. *Fuck.* Brings back memories, don't it?"

Minister looked down at the property line, unable to cross it to join her. He licked his dry lips, looking fevered by the heat. A few horseflies buzzed around his sweaty head.

"New religion ain't the same as the old one," he finally said, twitchy fingers buttoning up his flannel shirt, hiding the terrible scar that ran down his neck and torso.

"You think it'll work? Building a better mousetrap?"

The holy man didn't look so sure. "Ain't going to be easy bringing the flock back to Ghost River. We're competing with the golden calves now." He pointed at the casino sign shining near the interstate. "Guess we need us some mice to find out."

Her husband tried to light a cigarette, but his hands shook too much to use a lighter. Esther walked over to help him, but he was a proud man and waved her off.

"Minister, it's all right. Settle down and let me help!" He relented and let light his cigarette.

As the days passed, the man she married withered in undeath. Sometimes he couldn't remember anything that mattered. Whatever Delora did to him years back scrambled his wires, and Esther struggled to keep him together. Gaunter than he used to be. His beard scragglier now and brittle as tumbleweed. He wore sunglasses, and Esther was grateful. The worst part of him now: his eyes. She didn't like looking at them. When she caught a glimpse, all she saw was bottomless hunger.

"We've got company." Esther held her hand up to block the sun that glinted off a windshield up ahead. "Behave."

The beige sedan pulled up next to the Ghost River Revival sign. The window rolled down. An older man in a Hawaiian shirt and thick glasses said hello. His wife slept next to him, a larger woman, drooling against the passenger window. The man looked confused by just about everything.

Esther glowed like a friendly sunbeam. "Howdy, folks."

"Excuse me, but we're lost. Where's the casino?"

"You just passed it." She pointed back the way they came. "It's the gigantic circus tent with the big, flashy sign. Hard to miss, honestly, but seems that's what you did."

The man looked unsure of what to do next. His magnified eyes locked on Minister who said nothing, smoked and shivered while flies laid eggs in his greasy hair.

"Is…he feeling all right?"

"He's just fine," Esther replied, patting Minister's trembling shoulder. "Too much sun is all."

The driver craned his neck to read the freshly painted sign. "Ghost River Revival? What's that mean?"

"It's a…*church*."

The visitor's confusion deepened. "Church of what? Latter Day Somethings? Baptist? You one of them hippie New Agers from San Francisco?"

"No, sir. We're *non-denominational*."

"So, a bullshit church?"

"Pretty much," Esther said, lighting up a cigarette for herself. "You folks religious?"

"Little bit. Catholic on Easter and Christmas."

"Well, you might like seeing our little Chapel on the Mound. It's a bit of a historical site for the faithful." Esther watched her husband salivate with hunger—black spittle pooled at the corner of his lips. "I know! Why don't you two stop by and grab a map of Orphan Rock while you're here? Might help you find your way around. Y'all look thirsty, too, and we've got the best lemonade in all of Phoenix waiting for you." She gestured to the open cattle gate. "Turn left and park at the visitor center. That's the stone building just down the drive. If you find yourself in the scrapyard, you went too far." Esther winked. "Go on now. The kids will take care of you when you get there. No doubt about it."

"Well, we *could* use a map. Came all the way from Apache Junction to play slot machines. My wife has a lucky touch." He patted her knee. She snored and shuffled in her seat.

"I don't doubt it, mister." Esther looped her arm around Minister, who drooled on the soil and grinned like a vampire. "You two found us after all, so it must be your lucky day."

The visitor rolled up his window and took Esther's advice. His sedan cruised over the property line toward the stone-stacked house at the end of the drive. Minister twitched with urgency like a dog pulling on his tether to get at a steak.

"Well, goddamn," she said, impressed. "Caught ourselves some mice already."

But Minister didn't say anything. He darted across the desert toward the stone-stacked house. His undying hunger fueled him to run fast, arms pumping. The man always needed to eat. Esther sighed and put the lid over the can of paint. She cleaned up after him. After all of them. *Nothing ever changed.* Snarl leaned against the painted post, smearing it a little.

He grinned. "Flies to the ointment."

"But they're always old," Esther noted. "That casino sure reels them gray hairs in."

"The elderly folk have their purpose too. We have mouths to feed. More importantly, a Grim Seed to water." Snarl looked impatient. "Mother wants you to chaperone Baby Bird to the meeting today. The tribal council owes us some *restitution.*"

Esther moaned. "*Fuck.* All right then."

She turned to follow Minister home. A family of quails ran beside her. The mother had two heads, and she wasn't surprised to see it. The Grim Seed changed things. Made everything a little weirder the more it rooted beneath Orphan Rock.

"Coyote!"

She turned back to Snarl.

"So you know, they're not going to be happy with what we want next. Make sure Baby Bird minds her temper. We need the skyreaders to keep playing nice."

"Yes, sir," Esther said, saluting. She trekked toward the stone-stacked house in the distance, watching Broken Kids strip the old folks out of their sedan through broken windows.

The sun was a wavy silver smear in the infinite black of the river. She kicked and swam for the light in a body she remembered. *Her body.* Not some scarecrow, or some sewn dead girl with a tortoiseshell helmet. No. She felt Liz's legs. Liz's arms. Her everything…working and under her command. When she broke through the surface of the Other Side, she gasped for air and felt her lungs fill up with some sort of life again.

The celebratory experience was short-lived, however. The current swept her downriver, and she swallowed gulps of cool water, trying to keep her head afloat. She flailed, but the current was strong and pulled her under like the flash flood did at Orphan Rock. An uprooted tree in the water gave her something to hold on to. She fought against the flow, inching along the trunk until she was able to collapse on the muddy bank.

Liz looked at her old blue jeans, white Keds, and her purple Care Bears t-shirt. All soaked but remembered.

When she looked up, a white sun shined above her head. The sky was like an image on black and white television. Not blue, but grayscale. Colorless. Bleak. Dismal. There was no variance in hues here as if somebody had forgotten to paint the world after it was created by a crooked old monster on a riverbank. *The Other Side.* She raised her hands. Her fingers waved like smoky tendrils, then sharpened like knives, and then they settled into soft childish fingers again. Shifting forms. *What was she now?*

Something remembered.

The Pig's heart! Not in her pocket. Liz's stomach roiled. She must have dropped it when she went through the door. It could be anywhere. Maybe back in Ghost River on the Other Side of this Other Side. God, it was all so confusing to keep track of!

I'm in your breast, Little Lamb. Yoo-hoo!

The voice again. She felt the beat of her heart. Bitter. Foreign. *Spiky.*

"You tricked me," she said.

Trickery is what pigs do. Confluence is what rivers do. We all played our part. What matters is you're here, and you've got a lot of work to do. So, let's go get my head.

"*Yurphh…wahh…*"

A tiny creature—a fetus-looking thing covered in a beetle's shell with squiggling, black roots for fingers and hollowed eyes—crawled out of the river toward her. The deformed crawbaby reached for Liz, pulling itself along the clay. Its little fish mouth opened blindly for food.

"*Weeelllgggghh.*"

Whack!

A hunting knife pinned the baby to the ground like a butterfly on a bug board. It cried out, puked up white bile, and died face down in the mud. The blade withdrew from the corpse and hovered near Liz's face. A drop of white blood landed on the tip of her nose. She blinked as a shadow fell over her.

"What fucking world you from, *demon?*" a twangy voice asked. The scruffy man held the knife close to her throat. He wore overalls and a straw hat. He stared at her with chalky blue eyes. The color reminded her of a Luminarch wing.

Careful, Little Lamb. These folks are dangerous.

"Don't hurt me!" she said, raising her hands.

"*Have mercy!* It talks! Been a while since a talker crossed over. You got any last words, *Ms. Mouth?*"

"Please!" the little traveler cried. "I just came down to play by the river is all. I think I got lost and fell in."

Don't lie. He knows what you are.

"You're a bad fucking liar, *Ms. Mouth.*" His blade scraped along her cheek. The desertbilly squinted for a closer look at her. "I seen you come out of the river with my own two peepers. Yes, I did. Came right through the door, didn't ya? You're from the Other Side, and you can't convince me otherwise."

"*The Other Side?*"

"And youse a dumb fish too." The desertbilly laughed, pressing the blade down against the skin of her throat a little deeper. "Shame I have to bleed you out."

"*What have you caught there, Norman?*"

The man recoiled at the stern voice and pulled the knife

away from Liz's neck. An older woman stood on the hill leading down to the riverbank. Arms crossed over her rubber waders, and she scowled like she meant business.

"Just another fresh fish is all, Maggie! I was just about to clean her and add her to the pile!"

Liz gazed at the woman. "Help! I'm just a kid!"

Maggie hooked her thumbs around her suspenders. She let out an audible sigh. "Norman, she talks?"

Norman looked at the ground. "Yes'm."

"You know the rules, *you goatfucker*."

Norman's jaw clenched. "Yes'm." The wily man sheathed his blade and pulled the visitor off the ground. He grabbed her by the neck, and his fingers felt like ice. He pushed and scooted her up the riverbank. The woman's face was weathered and colorless. The same strange blue settled in her hard eyes.

"Tell me the truth." Maggie squeezed Liz's cheeks hard. "If you lie to me, Norman will slice you up like the Unclean thing you are, and I'll let him do it without a second thought. We don't like your kind 'round here. You understand?"

Liz nodded.

My kind?

"Where you from?"

"I'm...from Oklahoma."

Norman rubbed the back of his head. "*The fuck is that?*"

The woman shushed him. "Did you come out of the river?"

"Yes."

"From the Other Side?"

"*This* is the Other Side, isn't it?"

The woman cackled. "There's only one Other Side, and it ain't this one." She waved her hand. "Come on. Put her in the truck. Let Pilgrim make the call." Her ghostly eyes turned to granite. "You behave now. We don't suffer fools here."

The Broken Kid, Pink, helped Esther through the portal over the sand dune. Her head rolled in every direction except straight up, and her dry, shriveled tongue lolled at the side of her mouth. Esther swatted Pink's hand away as the child tried to lead her to Dark Bird over the sandy dunes of her mystical box.

"I know the fucking way," she growled.

Hard rock music blasted from the oasis. That new CD player again. It seemed like the only thing those tiny, silver records were good for was being loud. Shelby splayed out on her waterbed beneath a blacklight poster of the Cheshire Cat. Palm trees bowed around her veranda. Vines wrapped white columns. She wore sunglasses and stared into the cloudless sky above.

When Esther approached, Shelby craned her neck. Black lipstick. Powdered face. Two masks on.

"WHAT?" Dark Bird shouted.

"I need to take you to see the Injuns!"

The fifteen-year-old shook her head. "WHAT?"

"I NEED TO TAKE YOU TO THE INJUNS!" Esther made a tomahawk gesture with her arm. Shelby threw up her hands, rolled off the bed, and turned down the music.

Esther sighed, relieved by the quiet. "Jesus fucking Christ! What band is that? It's all noise and screaming."

Shelby lit a cigarette. "*Nine Inch Nails*, and its fucking genius."

Esther didn't know that band. It wasn't no Waylon Jennings or Merle Haggard, so she eyed Shelby's cigarette stash instead. A stack of cartons piled in the corner of the veranda along with all the junk food, CDs, and computer games money could buy. Shelby noticed her nicotine-starved look.

"Take what you like. The riverfolk keep it coming."

Grateful, Esther scooped up a carton of Marlboros. *Make that two.* "I'm supposed to take you to see the council soon."

"I know. Mother's creepy butler told me."

Shelby climbed off the jiggly mattress and puckered her

lips in front of an ornate vanity mirror, framed in gold and silver. She ran slender fingers through freshly chopped, black-and-blue dyed hair. Esther reached out and stroked it.

Shelby tensed but allowed her touch.

"I still can't get used to it. Was so long and pretty…"

"I like this better. The color rocks."

"All right then. Long as you like it, fuck it."

While Shelby primped, Esther stared at a color television that floated over the pond. MTV was on. *Headbanger's Ball?* Whatever the hell that was! More edgy-looking men with guitars and angry snarls. She side-eyed her daughter. Shelby was becoming a young woman, wasn't she? She'd always been mature, but now her body matched the attitude. And the attitude had style. She was more confident. Not a little meat fiend anymore. She was collected, poised, and cunning as a cat.

She was a predator.

With power. Real power.

In Orphan Rock!

"Ready, Betty?" Shelby asked, dressed in a plaid mini-skirt and a ripped t-shirt. Then, she slipped into a black hoodie that spelled MISFITS on the back with a giant, white skull.

Blood on their faces.

Pink sinew in their teeth.

The Broken Kids frenzied, devouring the sleepy, plump woman first—carving and ripping out chunks of thigh and butt meat, while she laid in the dirt, lost in the bliss of being saved from her sorrow. Minister drank the man now, his gray hand resting on his forehead. A crooked grin stretched across the holy man's cheeks while squiggling worms burst from his palm and burrowed into his victim's skull. Minister sipped his pain. Saved the old man's soul too. And from the look of the mesmerized, widening grin on his wrinkled face, the old codger loved it.

Esther patted her husband on the back when they passed. "Enjoy your meal, baby."

Dark Minister only smiled; wolf eyes hidden behind cheap plastic sunglasses glittered in the sunshine.

"Can I drive?" Shelby asked.

Esther looked around the empty desert and tossed her the keys to the brand-new Chevy Blazer that sparkled on the drive. Why not? The council gave it to Baby Bird for Christmas. They flattered and spoiled her to keep her happy.

"Easy on the brakes," Esther said, admiring the teen's progress on the road. She picked up everything fast, didn't she? "Don't give people whiplash by tapping on them pedals."

Shelby chuckled and turned up the radio. "Esther, I eat people." She winked. "Who gives a fuck?"

"Can't argue there."

They cruised by Orphan Rock Casino, a big top circus tent of loud noises and activity. Cityfolk in RVs, liner buses, and cars poured off the Ghost River freeway exit to try their luck. They turned into the parking lot underneath the glittering sign, all looking to strike it rich in the hot Arizona badlands.

Baby Bird watched them with a curious stare. "Why do people gamble? You always lose, right?"

"You're asking the wrong fucking person. I've never had a dollar to gamble with my whole life and still lost anyway." Esther laughed. "But if you held a gun to my head and forced me to guess, I'd say it's because people like to suffer, so why not do it under some glitter and glitz? All them flashing lights and whistles take the sting out of gettin' robbed, I suppose."

"Huh." Shelby shrugged. "Fuckin' people."

"Fuckin' people," Esther agreed.

They took the side roads to the sacred meeting spot on the overlook. Shelby parked a safe distance from the police SUV. The newly minted Chief of Tribal Police, Wallace Machado, waited by the ride. Esther shivered every time she saw his loveless eyes. The disdain still hurt both, even after three years. That monsoon was an ice block that dropped between their lives. Except it never melted, no matter the heat involved.

"Chief Machado," Shelby said, curtsying in mock respect.

Wallace returned the gesture with an unflinching glare. Esther saw the hatred burning in his heart for her. It was all over his tired, aging face. He'd kill her right now if he could.

Can you blame him?

She murdered five of his people.

Some scars were timeless.

"Come with me," is all he said.

Wallace pointed up the trail to the overlook.

Liz couldn't believe her eyes. They looked like jellyfish in the colorless sky. Translucent tendrils—fatter than gasoline tankers—vacuumed up flora and fauna into their toothy mouths. Inside their hollow saucer heads, blue sparks flickered like lightning in a bottle. Hundreds of stories tall. Just like the picture she saw in the mural in the King in Pieces' cave.

Something remembered.

"We're not in Oklahoma anymore, are we, Toto?"

No, I'm not, Liz thought. *The Other Side.*

The Pig's heart fluttered in her tight chest.

Sister Dirt created everything here. This is her box to pay in. When she started it, it was nothing but sand and dunes. I only ever let her shape here, so she would not wander far. It's important to keep dangerous animals caged. Let them think it's not a leash around their neck and they won't bite.

What about that shrimp freak on the beach?

The river is a door. Sometimes trash slips through.

Trash? From where?

I've got a lot of tunnels connected to strange places. Few of them are still open. Even Delora can't find them all.

It's all gray here. There's no color.

She never finished. Killing me was more important.

Norman sat in the back of the flatbed. He kept his knife out and never took his eyes off the little girl who had crawled out of the sacred water. The woman in the waders—he called her Maggie—drove the gray pickup truck.

Next to Liz, a half dozen dead things—*the trash?* —bled out like the crawbaby that died on the riverbank. These creatures were not quite human, but not so distant from them that Liz didn't feel the horror of murder when looking at the corpses.

From the overlook, Esther saw the Orphan Rock Casino—a mirage of pizzazz and good times—luring folks into dangerous nights with tricks and treasure. Since Shelby engaged with the riverfolk on behalf of the Crooked Woman now, Esther wasn't recognized around the firepit anymore. She was vapor to them now. Even Macho didn't see her. Fine by her anyway.

All eyes tracked to the teenager dressed in dark clothes and haunting make-up. They knew exactly how dangerous she was. Even the arrogant young man on the council minded his manners and held an uneasy smile to see her. Esther scoped out security. More than Macho lately. A few other armed riverfolk men lingered in the background. They feared Dark Bird.

As they fuckin' should.

The councilwoman greeted Shelby with a practiced grin. Her hair was grayer these days, yet her eyes still sharp as broken crystal. "I trust the latest round of supplies we've delivered are sufficient and please you?" she asked, beginning the parley. "Why are we congregating here today?"

Shelby lit a cigarette. "I want to discuss the roads."

All three of the council members shuffled nervously around the pit.

"What about the roads?" the woman asked, failing to

conceal her dismay. "We've taken down the checkpoint. As discussed, traffic is free to come and go to Orphan Rock."

"That's the problem. There isn't *enough* traffic."

"You want more people?"

Shelby grinned. "I do indeed."

"But there are larger issues at play to consider." The councilwoman folded her arms. "We've renewed our agreement with you. We will not intrude upon Orphan Rock, and we pay you for your cooperation in protecting our interests in exchange for no disruptions. If wayward souls seek comfort and spirituality on your land, that is their business and right to do so. The way of nature. But large groups of missing people will not be sustainable for either of our two communities."

"We're going to expand one way or the other," Shelby said. "And yes, you will continue to pay us in cash and supplies. We'll be investing in outreach to grow our community. You will do nothing when people come to visit us. Further, we'll be requiring a fifteen percent cut of all revenues from the casino going forward. Consider it an investment in restoring historical sites and treaties for future generations to enjoy."

"*Worse than the mob,*" the oldest riverfolk man growled, his brunette eyes rested on the ashes in the pit.

Shelby smiled. "Could make it twenty."

The councilwoman raised her hand, trying to slow the negotiations. She exhaled through her nose. "We'll consider your proposal, darkling." She turned to her companions. "But as a partner, and *friend*, I must offer you some unsolicited guidance. Our people, our tribe, and our politics are congenial compared to our neighbors in Sandoval. They watch our people with a telescope. The Mormons already detest our casino, and they grow in power in the state legislature. If by chance, something unsavory happens, and we lose our treaty with them, none of us will eat this winter." The woman looked at the Ghost River Valley over the cliff. "We're not the enemy. We share the mutual goals of self-sufficiency and dignity for our ways and traditions."

"Those sure are lovely words," Shelby said, clapping slowly and mockingly. She glanced at Esther across the fire. "But I've heard the stories of the past. When we had little, you threatened to starve us out. Let's not pretend we are partners or friends. *I am the deathbringer here.* I will eat all the hearts of your beautiful children. And you can't stop me from doing it. I'm not Delora. I'm not bound to serve any land. I'm a shaper, a builder of worlds, and your fucking worst nightmare."

The men standing in the shadows butted their rifles against their shoulders. Esther looked at Macho. She caught him staring back. Instead of recognizing her, he pointed his gun at Shelby.

"We have much to discuss," the councilwoman said, eager to end their meeting without bloodshed. "While we work out details, we'll continue to honor your requests."

"Glad we could come together and see things *my way*," Dark Bird replied, the honed hedgehog quills that broke through her skin softened and quickly retracted.

Maggie's pickup truck approached the cattle gate at the base of a blanched mountain that looked like Orphan Rock, except it wasn't. This Other Side was a mirror image of what Sister Dirt knew in life, down to The Needle. A couple of blue-eyed broadnecks carrying rifles stood behind a small barricade erected from wood posts and strung together with barbed wire curls.

"How'd the fishing go?" one of them asked.

Maggie picked her teeth with her finger. "Caught a few. Tossed a few. Brought back a keeper."

One of the men peered into the bed of the truck and shot Liz a look of contempt that made her feel small and worthless like the strange dead things next to her.

"Unclean, eh?"

"Most definitely," Maggie said, throwing her thumb over

her shoulder. "Popped out of the river. This one talks if you can believe it. Don't know how she came to be here."

"That's above our pay, Maggie. Take it to the holy man."

"Mine too. Thank shit for that."

They laughed, and the guards waved her through.

After a short drive down a gravel road, they parked at a stone-stacked house. Further out, several cabins abutted the base of the piped mountain. Down in a dry riverbed, a city square and a chapel sat in the middle of it all, looking like a black and white postcard from the Goldrush era. Beyond that, Liz could only see the monstrous jellyfish creatures scouring the whitewashed valley for the ancient bones buried in the sand.

Is this a copy of Earth?

This is whatever she wants it to be.

"Pilgrim's at the picnic table," Maggie said, crawling onto the bed with a large sack in her hand. "Why don't you go introduce them while I bag the rest of the scum?"

Norman sniffed. Rubbed his knuckles on his nose.

"All right then. Let's go, Ms. Mouth."

A few more men sat near a fire pit, playing cards at a rickety picnic table. They laid down their hands to see them coming. Wary blue eyes watched Norman prodding a stranger along the walkway with a knife. Liz could feel their hatred for her, just like the guards at the gate. But why? What did she do?

One of the men, a tall vulture with a thick beard, stood up. "What's this now?"

Norman pushed her ahead. "Came out of the river, Pilgrim. Unclean."

"Clearly." He scratched his beard. "Why'd you bring her here? Put her with the rest in the cages."

"Because she—"

"I came from the Other Side," Liz interrupted, prompting a gasp from the other men.

"*She talks,*" one of them whispered.

"*Is this some kind of a joke?*" another wondered aloud.

Pilgrim, their leader, said nothing.

He circled Liz, eying her head to toe. "Your eyes give you away, you know," he finally said, putting a silver flask to his lips, then holding it up so Liz could view her own reflection. She leaned in to look. Her eyes were deep red, almost black. The same hue of the King of Pieces' jagged heart in her chest. "Only question is, do we kill you like the unwanted stray you seem to be, or do we let you plead your case before our perfect god?" He cocked his head, turned to his men. "All of the misbegotten orphans shall come through the water with liberated voices," he began preaching. "If they can sing, make a place around your fire for them." He turned to Liz. "Have you sung the song yet?"

Something remembered.

"I don't remember," Liz said. "Should we sing it now?"

Those azure eyes didn't blink.

"*Do it.*"

Liz cleared her throat, desperate to remember the words to that strange song the dead children sang in the Crooked Woman's den of sorrow. Somehow, words spit out from her lips:

"When she comes, we run away.
Hide and seek, we always play.
When she finds us, look away.
In her nest, she'll make us stay.
Don't be scared, and don't you cry,
when Delora comes, the babies die."

The men at the table said nothing. Liz could only hear the wind howl across the barren, colorless valley. Behind her, white tumbleweeds rolled down a path of gray river rocks.

"Heresy," Pilgrim whispered, leaning in closer to her. A devious smile curled at the edges of his mustache. "You did come from the Creator's world, didn't you?" He turned to Norman. "Put her in the Quiet Box while I speak to the Lumenchild."

And with that, the bearded man strolled away.

Lumenchild?

Not now. Watch out!

Crack!

A boot to the back of her knee.

Strong men pinned her down and tied her ankles and wrists together with rope. She screamed when Norman slipped the broomstick under her hogtie. Then, they carried her away from the stone house like a dead pig ready for a fiery spit.

Minister floated along the river rock path, a lurking phantom of bottomless need wrapped in a halo of horseflies. The holy man's toes barely scraped the ground while he levitated over dry earth. He savored the fresh suffering that pumped through his Vile Heart, and his head rolled on its neck, aimless in elation.

He swallowed it all, didn't he?

Two lifetimes worth of misery.

Divorce. Death. Delicious infidelities.

Not a drop of suffering wasted.

Look at the beautiful people.

The Dark Minister waved to the cheering crowd standing on their clean porches in Orphan Rock proper. So happy to be here in Eugene's paradise, weren't they? They wore their pig masks and snorted with pride to see another holy man come to town.

But Minister was not like Eugene anymore.

No. He weren't some simple snake, some bootlicker, who raised stillborn babies from the dead for a few bucks and bones on the carnival circuit. No errand boy for the Injuns, either. He was an important man in Orphan Rock now. He was *the preacher*. He could lay his hands on anybody and make them come. He could drink out their pain like water. Make them empty. Turn them into blessed, beautiful husks without shame or guilt—a real healer!

Dark Minister was a Jesus Man.

The shade wrapped in a cloak of buzzing horseflies ascended the church stairs. The doors parted for him, and he drifted through the simple nave of the Chapel on the Mound.

The Crooked Woman prayed over dirt as she was prone to do, chewing soil and scratching symbols into the earth. Two fresh husks hung from the Dead Tree by their ankles. Blood poured from precision cuts along their necks, soaking the soil, watering the seed. Above, a giant spider that looked like a girl skittered back into the shadows of the rafters to watch him approach the pulpit.

Delora stood, spine cracking, to face her orphan grim-faced orphan. Her dead eyes and long mouth grinned behind her veil. Dirt and worm juice dribbled from her chin.

She offered a bony claw.

Something remembered.

Every drip.

Every drop.

More poison staining the Land Where Pigs Squeal.

The holy man clutched his chest in agony, and the parasite struggled for control of his host. A boy stood from his pew, walked over, and picked up his daddy's sharp knife.

He looked at the harpy. Then, at the runt in the Dead Tree.

"Minister, what do you think you're doing?"

The boy said nothing and slashed the holy man's throat.

Eugene's body tumbled over the Mound. Blood lapped from his neck like milk from a tipped carton. The soil turned darker, and whatever the Crooked Woman had planted in the Mound hurt The Pig badly. His shadow squealed and fled from the holy man, and now Eugene was dead in the dirt. She kept her promise, didn't she? The Pig Father was not invincible after all! Sure, the boy knew with Eugene dead, he would be the door, and The Pig's shadow would, one day, come for his turn. But that would be his burden for later. He looked at the meager girl in the tree, bleeding with that horrible crown on her blonde head. For now, The Pig would not have his way with her.

They fucking won.

The Forsaken Kids walked up the aisle in the sanctuary. Pig Boy, Spider Girl, and of course, their leader: odd duck Gilbert. Minister hadn't seen Gilbert for years. The boy went missing not long after his first Coyote Run. From the look of it, he hadn't aged a day. Minister shivered to see the curls of barbed wire that wrapped his fingers and arms now.

"Our new day dawns as The Pig's long dusk ends," Gilbert said, walking over to the Harpy of Ghost River. They held hands over the bloody corpse of a bride. "We must bless this fertile land in a crimson tidal wave of devotion until we are all clean again. Mother will show us the way."

Spider Girl ambled up the Dead Tree to undo Esther's bindings. The scrappy blonde moaned, fell from the thorny branches, and landed on the Mound with a soft thud. Didn't take long for her to scramble up to her feet. Minister knew she was strong, and even with the bruises on her knees, the most beautiful flower to ever bloom in the arid gulches of Ghost River.

At the Mound, the children knelt and held hands.

"What comes from dirt,
must be cleansed.
Give my life to make amends.
Bleed this heart,
Escape damnation.
On my knees,
Suffering is salvation."

After the Dirt Prayer, the children opened their mouths to receive a special blessing. Delora ladled cursed dirt over their lips with her cupped hands. Gilbert and the rest of the Forsaken Kids ate the poison without question. But Esther hesitated and caught Delora's ire. The Crooked Woman looked at the Holy Boy as if to test his conviction to their new purpose. Her claws curled, ready to end the runt who was afraid to believe in promises.

"Esther?" Young Minister held out his hand to her. A small pile of dirt in his palm. "You need to eat it like me. Watch me do it. Then you do it. Together or not at all."

The coyote shivered but said OK.

Together they ate the dirt, a poison surged in their guts, and the runts and freaks cried as a lover of children watched the tiny veins on their hands and wrists turn black as tar.

But now, in the same chapel decades from that day, Minister took hold of Delora's hand once again. She led him to the Mound. He placed his free hand on top of the soil. The holy man felt the heartbeat of the Grim Seed beneath his palm. Stronger, but ever hungry, was this new god beneath their feet. He reached deeper into the dirt, letting the tips of his fingers crack open. Black, whipping roots slithered into the dark loam.

The Dead Tree creaked, and the cursed Grim Seed spoiling the earth moaned in gluttonous delight. The Seed suckled the sorrow Dark Minister collected in his Vile Heart.

"Of course, they'll pay!" Shelby said, recklessly parking the Blazer after doing a few donuts in the dirt. Dark Bird always bathed in the afterglow of a tribal council meeting. Didn't matter who feared her, so long as somebody did. She loved the power, the dynamics of total submission by the weaker players on the stage. "They don't have a choice. They know the only thing keeping me from turning that casino into a bloodbath is a fistful of cash and a carton of smokes." Shelby flipped her new hairdo and tossed Esther the keys. "Besides, the young one likes me. His attraction smells like old sweat. I caught him looking at my ass, you know. Maybe I'll fuck him before I eat him?"

"Don't you dare." Esther, still flush from Dark Bird's joyride, closed the Chevy's door and checked to make sure she could walk straight. "That's *all* we need."

Shelby grinned like the Devil, her powdered face glowing under the silver moonlight. "I'm so kidding, Esther. *As if.* I'm not a heathen. It's totally gross to kiss your food."

Delora and Minister stood at the fire pit. Snarl held her gnarled hand, his one good eye flickering in the flame. Minister wore sunglasses, and a thick cloud of flies buzzed around him. Fat ones squeezed from his nostrils and skittered over his lips.

"What? We having a family meeting tonight?" Shelby smacked a fat wad of bubblegum between her black lips.

"Mother wants to know if the skyreaders accepted her terms?" The boy wrapped in barbed wire looked at the electrified casino in the distance. "Will they send more meat?"

Shelby blew a big, pink bubble that burst on her chin. "Not looking promising," she said, twirling the rest on her finger. Delora wheezed frustratedly, her veil rippling. Shelby continued, "The council said if things get out of hand out here like they did in 1973, and too many go missing, the US government will drop a bomb, shut down the slots, and freeze tribal aid forever. That's pretty much what they said. Can I, like, go now?"

"They have no faith," Minister grumbled. His mouth flapped like a ventriloquist's puppet. "There can't be no revival without blood to soak the Grim Seed that—"

"Spoils the earth," Shelby cut him off. "Christ. He's a broken record, isn't he?"

Esther couldn't argue. "He fucking is."

Snarl cut in after Delora squeezed his hand, "Mother's not pleased with this development. If we can't attract people, we'll have to take them from the casino or go back to roadkilling. The Grim Seed must be watered. That's all that matters now." The boy kicked a bloodroot that recoiled at the touch of his barbed flesh. "The dirt beneath us begs for liberation."

Shelby rolled her eyes. "*Gawd.* Even a few more geriatric strays won't be enough, will it? Look around you, man!" A couple of Broken Kids fought over an old pelvic bone. They gnashed teeth. Pulled it from each other like dogs fighting over the last bone on Earth. Shelby tossed her hands up, laughed bitterly. "You people act like you've built Noah's Ark out here, and you're ready for the animals to line up two by two. People aren't going to come to a shitty ghost town just because it's here. Not enough, anyway. What you expect to happen is a delusion. Years of failure and you want to keep doing the same old shit."

"Watch your tone, Baby Bird!" Snarl hissed.

"Dark Bird." Shelby stepped toward him with a commanding stare. "And I'm not listening to Mother anymore. You're relics from a time past you by." She looked at Minister too. "*Both of you* are stuck in a world that's never going to slow down enough for you to catch it again."

Minister scoffed as three horseflies took flight from the tip of his nose. "If you have a problem, take it up with Eugene's pig council. They make the rules 'round here."

Shelby frowned. "Wrong time zone, buddy."

"Quiet." Delora's gaze rested on Shelby. The Crooked Woman's dirt-stained tongue slid across her stretched mouth. "Mother would like to hear your plan. She senses invention in you. You didn't come home empty-handed, did you?"

The teenage harpy tossed her gum in the fire, lit a cigarette, and took a deep pull. "Nope. The riverfolk aren't going to give us more land, traffic, or bodies. That's a fact. They much as said the flow we get is all they can give. But…" Shelby raised her pointer finger, "they are flush in a resource we can use to our advantage *right now* to fix our predicaments. *Cash.*"

"Mother has no interest in money."

Shelby laughed. "And that's *exactly* why you all have been sitting in this goddamn desert your whole lives! Money can be used in a lot of different ways to improve our position here. And they're going to start giving us more of it than we'll ever need."

"Need for what?" Snarl looked at the shiny new Blazer

parked in the gravel drive. "More fancy cars?"

"No, that's not what we're going to do with it." Dark Bird crossed her arms over her hoodie and stared into the dying fire. "I have a plan. And you're going to listen to me and do exactly what I say. We're going to get back to our fucking roots, water that goddamn seed, and get on with our miserable lives far away from this dusty shithole in the middle of this Fuckedtopia."

Esther cocked her head. "What're you driving at?"

The shadow-eyed girl turned to the glowing aura of Sandoval's night lights that hovered over the desert like a half-halo on the horizon. "Let's bring a little faith back to the lost. Light a beacon they can't ignore. Let's welcome the flock back to our little church in the hills. But let's be *smart* for once, OK? We need a miracle to get their attention. A big fucking one."

The ghost-eyed men loaded Liz into the wooden casket. Hard as a rock. No padding or a blanket. Strange markings carved into the poorly sanded redwood. She laid on her back with her hands and ankles bound in constrictor knots.

"Nighty night," Norman said, looking down on her from outside of the Quiet Box. "Gonna keep you here until Pilgrim and the Lumenchild decide what's best for you."

"I didn't do anything! *Please!* I'll be good—"

"Sweet dreams, *Princess Fishcake.*"

Boom! The lid dropped.

Darkness spread like ink in water

"*Wait! No!*"

Dead space. Silent as air. She couldn't hear anything at all. No locks, no voices. Just nothing. The strange symbols glowed a little every time she made a noise as if they absorbed it. Elizabeth kicked the lid. She pressed her bound hands against it. Screamed as loud as she could, but biting silence pushed back hard.

Even her Pig heart made no murmur. No peep at all.

I am floating.

I am nowhere.

I am no one.

Those thoughts did not belong to her. She searched an expanding black universe. When she lifted her hands, she felt no rough wooden walls to the Quiet Box anymore.

Just a sea of silent, black emptiness.

I am floating.

I am nowhere.

I am no one.

Soon, she couldn't tell if her eyelids had opened or closed or if she even had eyes at all. Her hands disappeared too. No fingers or knives to push, and no legs or toes to wiggle.

Everything sleeping. Gone.

I am floating.

I am nowhere.

I am no one.

Liz was alone in the dark again.

Why do you cling to yourself?

And once more, the dark was a prison.

13.

Burt fed his last twenty bucks into the Lucky Lucy slot machine with what little hope he had left. He pressed MAX BET over and over and over until it was *indeed* all over, and he was fucking broke. The middle-aged, pot-bellied divorcee stared at the three reels with betrayal stinging his wiry eyes.

The whole goddamn thing is rigged.

"Are you done with this machine, sir?" the older woman behind him asked. She wore a pink baseball cap. The plastic bucket in her hands overflowed with jingling coins.

"Just a minute." Burt sucked down the last of his complimentary rum and coke. It was all watered down here. Worse than Laughlin. "I've got one more buck somewhere." He fumbled in his pockets, looking for an elusive bill.

The old woman persisted. "Excuse me. There aren't

enough machines. If you're not playing, I'd like a turn."

Burt cast her a sour side-eye and thought about smacking those thick glasses of hers right off her nose. Why did everybody think they could push him around? Did he look like a sucker?

"It's unlucky anyway," he said, stumbling off the stool. When he stood, the room spun. The cocktails, weak as they were, made his head soft and his bladder heavy. While the pushy old bird shuffled around him, taking a seat on his warm stool, Burt twirled in place. So many lights and noises. The clanking of big winners and super jackpots. It seemed like everybody carried around a plastic tub of Indian treasure.

Everybody was a winner.

Everybody except for Burt.

He ran his hands through his balding mullet and looked past all the laughing faces, gawking at him, pointing, thinking that him spending the last twenty dollars to his name was just desserts for a loser like Burt. That's what losers do, after all.

They lose.

The old woman in the pink hat reached up and gave the slot machine's handle a strong pull. 7 7 7. The sirens went off, and the red light on top of the Lucky Lucy pulsed in the smoky tent. Burt nearly cried watching coins spill out of the bottom of the machine in an endless stream of golden future.

Jackpot, baby!

Techs ran over. A crowd gathered instantly. Eyes watched, green with envy. "Oh my god!" the woman said, turning around and smiling at everybody. Even Burt. "I won!"

"That's my money," Burt said, opening his palm, revealing the crumpled one-dollar bill that should've bought the winning pull. "Hey!" Burt grabbed the nearest Native-American cashier who was wearing a magnificent bolo tie and rolling over a cashier's cart. The man spun around, looked at Burt's hand.

"Excuse me, sir. *No touching.*"

"But that's my money…that jackpot's *mine*." Burt lifted

the crinkled dollar bill. "She stole my turn!"

"Sir, the video footage confirmed who played the win." The cashier pointed at a black dome surveillance camera hanging from the frame of the gigantic tent. "Now, go find something else to play. Keno is running all night long. Drinks are free."

There was that look. The pity. Burt felt it burrow into the pit of his chest where it detonated. His fingers squeezed the cashier's arm. "Didn't you hear me, c*hief? That money's mine.*"

"Security!" The cashier motioned for a couple of Ghost River men in black suits and earpieces to intervene. They grabbed Burt by the arms and pulled him toward the exit—his boots slid across the floor like a cartoon character being tossed from a saloon. Everybody stared at Burt, the Loser.

"You redskin bastards!" he shouted. "Does taking our money make you feel strong? Well, you ain't strong!" Burt spat on the carpet. "We took your land, didn't we? Killed your people? *That's right, we fucking did! AMERICA!*" He whooped and patted his fingers against his lips to make a mock battle cry.

He hit the curb outside.

Flashbulb. Polaroid camera.

"You're done here. Don't come back."

Burt laughed. "*Did you just steal my soul, Tonto?*"

"Go home, asshole."

The guards turned back to the casino and left Burt in the parking lot. Even outside, he could hear jackpots and the joyous cries of winners. The casino was a blurry hotbed of activity tonight. Cars. RVs. Tour buses. Motorcycles. Burt felt like he couldn't focus. Didn't even remember where he parked. *First things first,* he thought. *I need to take a good long piss.*

He glanced around for a good spot, pushing the thought of peeing on the casino out of his foggy brain. Spending the weekend in a tribal jail didn't sound very glamorous. So, Burt stumbled around the fence toward the dark desert. When he got far enough into the bushes, away from the lights, he dropped his pants. Let it all go. Felt the sweet, warm relief of urination.

"*Goddamn heathens*. Rigging all the games—"

Icy-cold fingers slipped into the meat of his shoulder. Burt let his dick go. Pee dribbled down his leg. He heard the flies:

> if they make you mad
> it is because they hate
> you more than you
> hate yourself they take
> everything from your
> kind now because they
> think you're to blame
> for their suffering but
> you know better,
> because you are a
> smart man who suffers
> all of the time and you
> could teach them a
> lesson or two in
> suffering couldn't you

Burt took a deep breath. *The flies.* They were right.

He looked over his shoulder. Black desert under a full moon. A childish giggle and a rustle in the bushes. A couple of rocks landed at his feet. Burt blinked, looked past his pissed-soaked jeans to the grenades that lay in the dirt by his toes.

At first, he flinched to see them but quickly calmed to see they weren't live. He took one in each hand. The flies told him to hold still while tiny shadows zipped out from the brush. Giggling as they ran by, little fingers pulled the pins. Burt squeezed the igniter switches and stood in the desert near the casino.

Even from way out here, he listened to the celebration of winners. Winners who needed to lose it all to know *exactly* what Burt felt like every damn day of his miserable life.

The faint rumbling grew louder. At first, Liz couldn't place it in the thick fog of darkness in the Quiet Box. The symbols began to glow around her—a constellation of presence. Walls. Ceiling. She stretched her bound arms. Her fingers felt prickly again.

A rush of fresh air. A crack of sunshine.

Liz gasped.

Pilgrim's bearded face peered into the box.

"How long until she snaps out of it?"

"Few minutes is all," she heard Norman reply. "She ain't been floating long. She'll be dizzy until she ain't."

"Get her out and moving around." Pilgrim's suspicious gaze measured little Liz. "You gonna make trouble if we let you walk on your own? You gonna try to run or fight?"

Play nice.

She shook her head, somewhat grateful to hear the King in Pieces in her thoughts again. Hearing anything—even flies—was better than the nothing in the Quiet Box.

Sweaty Norman and a couple of Other Ghost River roughnecks lifted her out of the magic coffin. Her body quivered like Jell-O. How long had she been sleeping? Years? Days?

Lifetimes?

She wobbled in place while Norman sawed through the ropes around her ankles. Liz's legs were stiff and felt too numb to stand on for long. When she tested them out, she stumbled and tumbled around the gray-toned clearing. Some of the ghost-eyed men even chuckled when she fell over and skinned her knee. When she steadied, Pilgrim led her toward town.

"So, where we going?"

"To see the Lumenchild," the holy man replied. "He wants to meet you." His tone almost seemed friendly, but Liz shivered to sense a coldness in the man just beneath his grin. "Most of the Unclean are tossed in the sinkhole. *Those we don't eat, anyway.* I'd say you're quite *lucky* for a trespasser."

"Unclean?" Liz sniffed her armpit. "Do I stink?"

Pilgrim laughed. "It means you came out of the river, but you weren't chosen to be here. You're an interloper, a wayward soul in a land that wasn't built for you. If you were chosen by the gods we serve, you'd have eyes like we do. You'd know the words to the song of The Creator." His expression darkened. "We know you're from the Age of Filth. From the Land Where Pigs Squeal. This world ain't for you. The Lumenchild will decide your fate."

"What's a Lumenchild? Some kind of preacher?"

"No, child. I'm the preacher. The Lumenchild is God."

Liz followed Pilgrim along the river rock path toward the town square. They passed a side-yard in which Maggie flayed catches from the river. Sad, black-eyed creatures moaned in cages and pens. They weren't human, but they cried for help like they were. No two the same. Worms for fingers. Tentacle tongues. Alabaster skin with beetle shell wings. Tails and fins. Maggie gutted one with a skinner's blade, a dead merwoman hanging from a wooden cross spiked in the field. Her wet innards splattered on the dirt while Maggie whistled and hollowed her out.

"You're not very welcoming to strangers."

"We don't need to be," Pilgrim said sharply. "If you ain't with us, you're food. That's how we keep the filth out."

Residents stood on the porches of their gray cottages. Men held their grayscale wives. Wives held their grayscale children. Liz saw disgust in their phantasmal eyes when they watched her pass. *They're like Broken Kids*, she thought, only they looked prettier. Instead of a Crooked Woman, they obeyed hatred here and followed a holy man that craved supremacy.

Ahead, a little chapel with a steeple surrounded by a well-manicured desertscape. A hitching post. The front doors open to the elements. People drifted along, eyes glowing for God.

Pilgrim gestured for her to climb the stairs first. "Welcome to The Chapel on the Hill. This is a sacred house of worship. You're lucky to be let in, Ash Eyes. Behave yourself."

It's an abomination.

Jealous?

Every day, Little Lamb. Every fucking day.

Gray sunlight filtered through the recently washed windows. The swept wooden floor had a waxy sheen. The pulpit polished with shiny oil. Other Siders sat in pews, heads down in reverence to the Silver Tree on the Hill. Soft pale grass and colorless wildflowers grew around the roots of the white, argent-leafed tree. Sparkling butterflies with white wings circled the boughs. The air smelled fresh and full of sweet pollen.

"Sit down and listen to the prayers," Pilgrim said, ushering her to an empty pew. "Close your eyes and hear the orphans sing. He will come when he's ready to meet you."

The holy man hovered until the little ghostling obeyed. She didn't want to end up in Norman and Maggie's fish yard, so she closed her eyes and listened to the congregation chant.

"What comes from dirt,
 must be cleansed,
 give my life to make amends—"

"Unclean One." A charming voice. Impish.

Liz opened her eyes to see God.

The woman in the pink hat who stole Burt's jackpot boarded the coach headed to Sun City West. She and a couple of other seniors hobbled up the special needs ramp—all smiles and war stories from their evening with the slots. Everybody was a winner in Orphan Rock tonight. Everybody but—

Burt slipped in just as the door closed. The bus driver sized up the haggard stranger. He smelled like urine sprinkled with shit flakes. She didn't like his crooked smirk.

"Wrong bus, buddy?" she asked.

"I think this is the winners' bus, actually."

He grinned wider, held out his hands.

A live grenade in each.

"OK! Easy, man." The driver put her hands up in surrender. "We have a lot of good people here—lots of loved ones. Don't do anything crazy. Just tell me what you need, OK?"

"Close the door and drive right the fuck now." Burt stepped up the stairwell. The flies in his mind swarmed, whispering instructions. "Head out of the parking lot. Hang a left. Keep driving." He eyed the dashboard radio. "Call for help, and I'll shove one of these boom-bombs up your asshole."

The bus driver nodded, closed the door, and pulled away from the curb of the Ghost River Casino.

In the cabin, a crowd of older folks chattered like children. Burt pointed at the woman who pilfered his jackpot, sitting near the back. "There she is! *Tonight's big winner! Judy Jackpot!*"

Her smile faded. "Oh! Hello again. Did you forget something…?"

"Matter of fact, I did." The loser bowed with a jester's grin. "I forgot to *congratulate* you, darling." The bus turned left from the parking lot, headed toward the desert. "How'd we all do tonight? Everybody win, I hope?" The drunkard strut down the aisle toward that stupid pink hat of hers. He dragged a grenade along the tops of their seats so they could all see it.

"What's that in his hand?"

"Oh, my goodness. Is that a toy?"

"…got a goddamn grenade! Two!"

"Where're we going? The freeway is that way—"

"Shut up! Let's not get ahead of ourselves!"

The panicked whispers quieted. The madman looked over his shoulder through the darkened windshield of the bus. The flies in his mind agreed with his assessment.

"That's far enough," he told the driver. "Park it and take out the keys. Don't you dawdle now."

The coach rolled to a stop in the middle of nowhere—pure

desert, dark as midnight. Burt pointed at the jackpot winner. He smiled. "Come with me, my dear. The night is young."

At first, she didn't budge, but then the rest of her peers turned on her.

"*Don't upset him!*" somebody hissed.

"*Do what he says, Eileen.*"

The big winner slipped her frail arm around the bend of his elbow. Burt helped her up, still grinning. "Let's step outside and get some fresh air. It's a lovely night to celebrate."

The big winner didn't know what to say. Her friends prodded her along, offering nods of confidence. The bus driver opened the door to the shadowy landscape.

"Careful now! Watch your step, Judy Jackpot." Burt politely helped her down the stairs. He looked at the driver. "Toss the keys out of the window. *Right now.*"

The keyring hit the street.

Before disembarking, Burt smiled at the crowd. "Now I'd like you all to kindly watch tonight's next big winner. *Me.*"

A gaunt child squatted on the Hill, pale as the clouds outside the ornate rose window above his silver-crowned head. Large butterfly wings opened and closed on his bare back. Both his lustrous eyes and wings glowed Luminarch blue. Skinny arms dangled between his spread knees and long claws, black at the ends, twisted into the soil. A triangle-tipped tail thumped on the wispy grass behind him. The handsome beast grinned, pristine teeth pointed and sharp. Around its pallid neck, it wore a talisman: a shriveled pig head weaved with feather and bead.

Liz's dark heart pounded to see it.

Is that it?

Sure enough. Handsome, ain't I?

Twin guardians flanked the boy god on either side of the Silver Tree. Tall and slender, they wore shimmering cowls and tunics spun from mercurial chain. Sharp sickles rested against their breasts. But the weapons weren't the reason Liz's knees knocked in fear. Not even close. Instead of mouths, the guards had clacking, wet mandibles, and the insectoid faces of grasshoppers.

"Well?" the boy god spoke, his voice echoing in the chapel. "Are you going to say something?"

She gulped. "Are you the Lumenchild?"

"So, it is true. You speak." The boyish thing on the Hill sat on the trimmed grass beneath a halo of white butterflies. His skin was smooth, without blemish, and fragile as frosted glass. The grinning child wore no garments but had no parts to be ashamed of that Liz could see. Like a Ken doll. "That is one of my names, yes. What is *yours*? Do you even remember if you have one?"

Tread carefully, Little Lamb. He ain't like the rest.

"I'm Liz."

"Liz."

"From Oklahoma."

"I am not aware of that world. It must not be significant." A white butterfly landed on the tip of his claw. He eyed it with bored fascination until it crumbled to silver dust.

"Why're you keeping me prisoner?" The little spirit took a step toward him. The other phantoms in the church vanished, their strange incantations less than a whisper in a half memory. "I proved I came from the Other Side. I sang the song."

The Lumenchild templed his sharp fingers. His childish features turned smug. "You came from the river. That is true. But you are unwelcomed here by your own confession. The song you sang to us is *blasphemy*. You sang from the Dirt Hymns. You were not sent here by loving hands. No, *demon...*" The boy leaned forward, his azure eyes sparkling threateningly. "You are not an ally. You are a harbinger of the Age of Filth. There is rot in your eyes. You come from the oldest crack, and in your shadow hides a menace. I did not believe my holy man's stories, but he did not deceive me about you. Admit what you are, and I will show you a merciful end. Resist, and you will know pain."

He can't see me. Don't you dare confess.

"*You're right*," Liz agreed, taking another step closer to the Hill. "I *did* come from the river. Momma and me were kidnapped by an evil man. He brought us into the desert. I don't remember much, but I think he killed us."

The Lumenchild didn't blink. His devilish tail beat the ground. He cradled the side of his cheek in palm, looking half-amused by her act. "I see the burden of a murderer in you."

"Me?" Liz feigned laughter. "*I'm just a kid!*"

The Lumenchild pointed at Liz's breast, to the spot in which the Pig's heart thumped. "I see the burden of a liar in you."

"So, what if I am? Everybody lies. *Even you, I bet.*"

What are you doing, Little Lamb?

The grasshopper guardians turned from their posts at the insult. Their cricket jaws clicked and rubbed together.

"I make the truth here." The Lumenchild rose to his feet. "Just as I weave every miracle in this world, I am also the answer to *every question*. I have bestowed paradise to the faithful to dominate in my image." The godling's eyes scanned the horizon. A tempest roared across his darkening eyes. "*I create all things.*"

"*Another lie!* You're so bad at this game!" Liz cackled at his arrogance. "You didn't build this world. *Be honest!* The Crooked Woman did. She's the real creator here. Your flock murders innocent things that come from different places so you can play pretend king and rule by fear. But you're just another toy, aren't you?" Liz put her tiny hands on her waist and kicked out her hips. "You may be prettier than the rest of them, but you're still just a Broken Kid who belongs to a nasty old witch."

Little Lamb, what the fuck are you doing?

Judy Jackpot was frail, not hard to push into the road. Beneath the starry sky, Burt kicked her calf gently. She buckled to her knees on the dusty dirt road. The man filled with flies slapped the pink cap from her head and pressed a grenade against her brow. She whimpered and trembled on her knees.

"Please." She held up shaking hands. "Just tell me what you want from me. Do you want the money?"

"I want you to admit what you did."

"What I did? Son, I—"

"That was my jackpot. I had *one more dollar*."

The woman shook her head, unsure of what to say.

"You don't care, do you? Nobody ever cares." Loser Burt looked at Orphan Rock Casino and saw a glittering Gomorrah in the dust basin of Ghost River. *"Everybody's a winner."* He lifted his dark eyes to the bus. "You all watching?" he called out. The seniors peeped through the windows on the left side of the liner. "Don't blink – *you'll miss the boom!*" Burt gazed down at Judy Jackpot. "I'm sorry," he said. "This is how the world ends."

His grip loosened on the grenade trigger.

"What the hell is that?" somebody screamed.

Faint blue light spilled out from the bushes and bathed the dirt road in a mystical aura. Burt blinked, half entranced by the flies in his mind, and kept the grenade pressed to her brow until he, too, saw the light appear above the shrubs. When he witnessed the gaunt holy man tacked to a wooden cross, arms outstretched, floating above the cactus in a fog of pale luminous light, Burt's arms dropped with his jaw. Off-white blood mixed with brown rust rivered down the floating miracle's body and dripped from his crossed ankles. His bearded head hung low in serenity. Souldust butterflies formed a living halo over his razor-wire crown.

"It's you!" Burt dropped to his knees.

The Jesus Man floated above the road, letting his calm radiance soak over the shadows of the dark moment. Then, just like *that*, he faded back into the penumbra of the desert.

"Follow me," a voice cut through fly wings.

Loser Burt scrambled to his feet, forgot about Judy

Jackpot, and dashed into the scrub. He called for The Jesus Man to come back! Ran as fast as he could, trailing the specter into the shadowy barrens. He cried in exuberance and didn't care that thorns ripped his new pants open. *It was a miracle!*

Judy Jackpot watched her terrorist disappear into the cactus patches, hollering until he was gone. She quickly rose to her feet and staggered toward the bus fast as her new hips would allow. The driver urgently pointed at the keys on the road. She scooped them up. When she boarded the bus, her friends swarmed around her, so *overly concerned* about her safety now. ***BOOM! BOOM!*** When the grenades exploded outside, she was the only one on the liner who didn't scream in horror.

You get that head! Get that fucking head!
I have a plan.
It's not working, Little Lamb!

The Lumenchild's guardians moved around the Hill, sickles ready to cleave flesh from bone. The butterfly boy with the devilish tail laughed. "Clearly, you are not impressed. My power here is absolute, yet you challenge my divinity with lies. You are Unclean. It was a mistake to allow your filth in my house."

Liz laughed. "If you had any *real* power, you wouldn't need that magic necklace." She pointed at the King in Pieces' head. "I think you'd be just another silly bug without it."

He'll kill you, you fool! Just like those meat piles you passed by outside. Do it now. Snatch the head while you can! You don't have any time left for games—

A sharp claw cut into the air. The Lumenchild's guardians halted, heeding his command to stop. They stood perfectly still, watching Liz with mirrored eyes. The godling lifted The Pig's shriveled head from around his neck. "You think this silly trinket is my power? *Do you really think that?*"

Liz shrugged. "Dunno. *Probably is*."

The Lumenchild bellowed with laughter at the offensive notion. Playfully amused, he tossed his talisman on the Hill. He brought his knuckle to his chin and paced on the grass in thought. "Now, what kind of miracle should I perform for you? What would impress you? A magic trick?"

The ghostling said nothing. She shuffled a little closer to the necklace instead.

Take it...

"Ah, I know!" The Lumenchild clapped. "We'll have a good old-fashioned *resurrection*. The dead shall walk again at my command. Would that impress you?"

Another step closer to the prize.

"Maybe," she said indifferently.

TAKE IT!

"Or I could cause an earthquake. A tremor so powerful it could topple a mountain into pebbles and dust! That would impress you very much, I think. It's quite impressive, yes."

"It *might*." While the boy mused, her little fingers tiptoed through the blades of grass on the Hill until she felt the bristly skin of The Pig's head brush along the side of her index finger.

TAKE IT! TAKE IT!

She reached for the thread...

Whomp!

Suddenly, the Lumenchild landed inches from her nose. Bony fingers curled around her wrist. He frowned with ire and disappointment. "I suppose we'll have to settle for a *simple* magic spell today. *Conjuring a filthy pig thief.*" He tapped his claw on her heart, eyes brightening. "*Tah-dah!* Caught one."

Liz tumbled into his expanding blue gaze.

Something else was in her mind.

Something uninvited.

No! NO! NOOOOO!

A furious force pushed back against the invader's assault, but the Lumenchild entered her mindspace with ease.

"What do we have here?" the godling hissed. The Lumenchild pinched Liz's cheeks even harder, forcing her gaze to meet his. Inside of her splintered thoughts, a boy with butterfly wings searched the deepest shadows for parasites. He was determined to find all the secrets hidden inside her. The growing pressure in her lungs made it hard to breathe.

"*Come out, come out, wherever you are,*" he said, wandering deeper into Liz's sacred spaces. "I have your name, and now I'm going to take your heart." The Lumenchild studied the dark expanse around him. "You can't hide, Piggy. She made me just like you. She is wise and knew you would come one day. I am the Answer to your deception. Show yourself and hear it."

The boy with butterfly wings turned to see the flicker of creamy eyes in the din. "Ah! There you are! Should I say your name? Should I dominate you?" Hooves scraped against darkness, and steam billowed from a slimy snout. The Lumenchild wasn't alarmed. "You're cornered. Don't be shy, Pig Father."

The Pig vanished again, and the boy appeared amused by the game of hide and seek.

"You can't run away from your name!" he howled with laughter. "I call upon you, the King of Pigs. Obey my command! I shall make you obedient by shackling you to your rotten history." The boy's lips parted, revealing two rows of jagged piranha teeth. "Hear your name, Por—"

Splat!

The Pig's fist filled the Lumenchild's mouth. Liz's back arched when it tore from her chest, punched through her bones, and pinned the boy's tongue down. The bristly arm stretched longer, pushing deeper into the boy's gagging, wet throat. The boy god retched, trying to pull the hairy, shit-covered arm out of his mouth with feeble claws. But The Pig was hellbent in his cause and desperate. Liz could do nothing except look at the hole in her chest near her foreign heart that widened as the bristly back of a Pig Man burst free from her body. While the waifish godling shuddered helplessly, it spilled into him. Liz closed her eyes.

Much better to be in The Dark right now.

"Yes, ma'am. That's what I saw. Jesus. The Lord. He flew right over those bushes and called that lost man home. Saved Eileen's life, he did. We all saw it. Every single one of us. It was a miracle. *Praise, Jesus. The Lord hath returned.*"

"And you say he flew?" the officer asked, eyebrow arched, scribbling notes on her clipboard. The elder pointed at the freshly painted Ghost River Revival sign.

"Yes, ma'am. Right over there. By the bushes."

Wallace walked the road. His deputies interviewed everybody on the bus. Same story down the line. The Jesus Man wearing a barbed-wire crown led a lunatic with grenades into the desert where he blew himself up. Grenades. Just like at Solemn Cave. What were these Northamms up to? What game was this? Clearly, pissing off the council was the prize. Ever since that young reaper got her wings, Wallace couldn't put his finger on their end game. They had money. They had privacy. They had food. What more could a bunch of ghouls want from the world?

At least, as children, he and Minister could enjoy life under the sunshine for a damn minute. Play early in the morning and stay out way past bedtime. They shared laughs, even a couple of warm Coca-Colas. Wallace thought about Minister a lot.

Even missed him. Esther's situation aside, Minister had been his best friend. A shitheel, but a good-hearted man. They came from different worlds, circling close to one another, but met to play in the middle underneath the same blue desert sky. As grown men, they kept the peace, messy as it was. Now, with the Dark Bird haunting the lands, Esther hating his guts, and Minister dead as a doormat, Wallace felt shut out. That was never a good sign. No news from Orphan Rock was the worst kind of news. Meant scheming. Now suddenly, all this talk of a Jesus Man.

Macho had a bad feeling. The cop feeling.

Something was bubbling under the brittle crust of things. Then, the dinner bell rang.

"*Holy shit!*" Officer Machado held his firearm in place and jogged over to the Channel 10 Action News wagon. A pretty reporter with auburn hair twisted into a bun clanged the bell while her crew pulled strips of masking tape and prepped boom mics.

"This is private property, ma'am."

The woman adjusted her tight top and gave Wallace the side-eye. "You're the chief of tribal police?"

"I...yes..."

A handheld recorder danced under his nose. "Will you go on record, Chief...?"

"Machado," he said, watching the Chevy pull out from the stone-stacked house, heading his way down the gravel drive. The Northamms approached. More bad omens. "I'll be happy to give you a statement, but let's do it away from private property."

He ushered the reporter a few feet away, but it was too late. They had spotted the Chevy also. It crept up to the gate, and the Dark Bird and Esther stepped out.

"Can we help you?" the Dark Bird asked. She was dressed conservatively for once. Her black-and-blue hair in a neat ponytail. A skirt and plain white blouse. Macho had never seen her wear white before. She was carrying a thick book.

The Bible? Now he'd seen it all.

"I'm Courtney Philbin, Action 10 CBS News." The reporter slid a business card in between the bars of the cattle gate. The Dark Bird eyed it, then Macho. Wallace shivered when he felt her eyes cut across his throat. She wasn't happy to see him. "We're covering the incident that occurred last night at the casino. Have you ladies heard of what happened there?"

"Heard?" Esther laughed. "Shook the fucking mountains last night. From here to Gila Bend."

Courtney smiled sweetly. "Can you tell me more? Maybe

we can do an interview on camera?"

Dark Bird stepped in front of the recorder. "Normally, we would refuse, Ms. Philbin. We're a private, religious community here. Keep to ourselves mostly." The Dark Bird paused to consider her next words. "But with all these *miracles* happening around here lately, it's getting pretty tough to fly under the radar. Might be time to go public with our best-kept secrets."

Courtney Philbin swooned. "Miracles?"

"Oops." Dark Bird looked at Esther, who shook her head. "I probably said too much. Forget about it." They turned back to their Blazer in unison. "Have a wonderful day, Ms. Philbin."

"Wait!" Courtney reached through the bars of the cattle gate; her red nails outstretched like cat claws trying to snatch a canary. "Let's do one interview! How about that? See how it goes? If you're comfortable with it, might get you on TV..."

The Dark Bird chewed on it for a moment. "All right, Ms. Philbin, but let's do it up at the house." Her lips bent into a spidery smile. "Quieter. Less eyes. We're a shy group here." Dark Bird winked at Macho and turned away. "Esther will get the gate."

The reporter clapped, spinning around quickly. "Let's move, people! Roundup! We got news to make."

Wallace said nothing as the CBS crew loaded into their van and drove toward the stone-stacked house. Esther stayed back to lock the gate after looping the chain twice.

She didn't look at Macho once.

He wasn't surprised by her avoidance, either. Not really. They split hard after the Dark Bird killed that family. He watched that little girl's head get swallowed, and then he saw the same thing happen to Esther. There was no need to even talk about it. Sometimes when things are over, you just feel it. No going back to whatever was. She chose the Dark Bird anyway.

He took a deep breath. Couldn't spend another minute thinking about Esther Northamm, or her family of murderers.

Time to get back to the *other* crime scene.

But his heels wouldn't move.

What are you up to?" he asked, breaking the tradition of silence between them. Her steely blue eyes met his. Didn't blink when she dug in her pocket and retrieved a cigarette. Didn't blink when she lit it. Nor did she blink when she exhaled in his direction. Esther looked at him like he was just another ghost she once knew. Then she turned around and walked away.

The room with windows spiraled.

So did the face of her father, Paul, who looked down on her with an amused smile. She loved getting so dizzy, his little Elizabeth. She never seemed to settle in one place for long.

"Careful, you'll get sick." He scooped her up from the ground, hugging her tightly. Liz whooped when he tossed her up and down, catching her in his strong arms.

"Honey, don't make her puke." Momma laughed from her wicker chair. She set the novel down on her lap and folded her hands on her knees. "You're home early today."

"Well, it's such a fine afternoon! Why not sneak out and spend it with my two favorite ladies?" He carried Liz over to deliver a sweet kiss to Stacy's forehead. *Mwuah!*

And his pig snout dripped.

Shifting. Out of focus. Liz blinked, traveled through the static of competing realities, still dizzy from spinning in that silly old room with windows she knew so well. When her vision settled again, she was in the sanctuary of a pretty little church in a world that had no color at all. Black blood pooled on the polished wood floor around her. She lifted her head to see the yawning injury on her chest. She gasped for air, hyperventilating, seeing what was left of herself. Just pieces. Meat. Tatters. Her torso cleft in two from her shoulder to her belly button.

Her guts looked like gray, slimy hotdogs.

Terrified, she scanned the Chapel on the Hill for answers.

Other Siders lay butchered in the pews. The Lumenchild's guardians hung upside down from the Tree on the Hill. Their mandibles barely twitched as their cut throats bled out onto the colorless grass. Then, there he was. The Lumenchild himself, standing between them, but he was not the same creature she remembered. A black mass wrapped his torso in obsidian. Ashen veins coursed through his blue wings, and his eye sockets were pits of tar with tiny dots of milky pus floating in space.

"*I did it, Little Lamb!*" The Lumenswine raised smoky sickles in victory. "I am no longer *separated*. Whole again! Heart and mind in a brand-new body of my own!"

The little ghost looked at her broken vessel. "I did what you asked," she said, coughing up salty blood. "I want…the room. You promised me the room! Let me go back to my life. Please, mister. I'm tired of seeing all this…death…"

The Lumenswine hopped off the Hill and fluttered over to the bleeding ghostling on the floor. He brushed a gore-soaked sickle over her petrified cheek. "You're a daddy's girl at heart, ain't ya?" His pig breath stunk like rotten eggs left in the sun. "You did real fine by me, Little Lamb. *Real fine.*"

"I…want the room," she said again, voice weaker.

"So, go," the Pig's putrid eyes glimmered. "Enjoy your room with windows. You've earned it."

Clap!

"*Paul, stop!*" Stacy rolled down the dark hallway outside of Liz's bedroom. Daddy lumbered after her with balled fists and whiskey swishing in a half-drunk bottle. He stopped in his little baby girl's doorway, a towering villain in a cheap necktie. When their eyes met, his stare looked like spoiled cream.

"Go to bed," he growled, wavering on his feet. "You want to be disobedient too?" His free hand tugged his leather belt from his waist. It flopped on the floor.

"No, Daddy. I'll be good."

Paul shook his sweaty head. "I don't know why your

mother likes to make me feel so bad about things, Elizabeth. I really don't. It's in her nature, I think. Don't you grow up to be like her, you understand me? Don't you grow up and think you're a bigger person than you really are."

"OK, Daddy. I won't." Liz pulled the comforter up to her nose when he marched down the hallway, belt in hand. *Slam!* The master bedroom door shut and locked.

In the darkness under her Strawberry Shortcake sheets, the little girl listened to everything breaking again. Muffled shouts. Nasty words. Screams of agony after the crack of leather against vulnerable skin. She held Reuben to her cheek, crying into his tawny fur. *Make it stop. Make it stop.*

This is not what she wanted.

Make it stop.

This is not the memory she wanted for her forever.

Make it stop.

Liz put her pillow over her face and screamed.

Crash!

Shards of gray stained glass rained on top of her. White sunshine poured into the sanctuary from the shattered rose window above. Dying on the floor in between two worlds she never wanted to be a part of, Liz watched the Lumenswine escape through the hole. The possessed boy with butterfly wings soared over the Other Ghost River Valley like a crow. He hovered for a moment, extended a sickle finger, and ripped open a black portal in the sky. When the flies absorbed him, he was gone.

That sneaky pig thief! What had she done?

"You promised me a room with windows! *You promised me!*" Liz laughed at the futility of her pleas.

Bang! Bang! Boom!

The chapel doors broke open, and the bearded holy man stormed the nave along with Norman and a few Other Siders with sticks and rifles. Pilgrim sprinted to the pulpit. Despair filled his face watching the Silver Tree wither and brown. He spun around, eyes ablaze with hatred. "Toss the murderer in the sinkhole," he said. "Cast the sinner away with the sin."

Courtney stepped out of the satellite relay truck. The Action 10 News reporter looked like she'd just hit the lottery. She greeted Shelby and Esther with a wide grin. "Ladies, I just spoke with my producers. *Amazing news.* They want you on the six o'clock news. Primetime interview with Durbin and Grace. The whole hour is dedicated to the Ghost River Incident."

"Well, isn't that generous of them?" Dark Bird hugged the Good Book to her breast. She smiled at Esther playfully. "Sounds like we're going to be famous, doesn't it?"

Courtney splayed her fingers in excitement. "Ok, there's a lot to do to get ready. So, don't mind us. With your permission, we're going to get everything set up." Courtney snatched the elbow of a lanky boy, early twenties, who was wearing a Jane's Addiction t-shirt and carried a bin of wire. "It'll be like we're not even here. Where can Jake set up the cameras for the interview?"

Esther hovered close to Shelby, her arms folded. "*This is a bad fucking idea. Don't let them wander alone.*"

Dark Bird waved her whispers off. Her mind played elsewhere. She liked Jake's face. He had rock star hair. Spiky, with a lot of gel, and no direction in mind. Plus, he had some tats. Shelby liked that too. "Sounds perfect," she said. "Go ahead and have *Jake* here carry the gear toward town. Just down that path a ways. Look for the church. Stay on the road now." Shelby smiled. "Don't want to lose Jake quite yet. *Dangerous creatures live in the desert.* Rattlesnakes and...*such.*"

Dark Bird and Jake exchanged flirtatious glances, and Esther wanted to puke right there on her boots. After Courtney and the help left, Esther turned to Dark Bird. "You're moving too fast. You really want the world to see what's happening here? Don't you think the Injuns are going to revolt?"

Shelby sighed. "*Coyote*, you can't stop a river rock from rolling downstream. That's how they get round. Besides, the sooner we get that Grim Seed watered, the sooner we'll get rid of Mother and this goddamn armpit we call home. To do that, we need more people. To get more people, we need more buzz. We're in show business now." She watched a Broken Kid peep around the corner, scabby snout in the air. "Fuck, those little shits are going to get us pinched. I told her to back off for now."

"Delora? Never."

Shelby extended her hand, waiting for Esther to put a cigarette in it. While she did, Dark Bird pondered the consequences. "Well, if she wants to jump the gun, this won't work." She rubbed her brow and sighed. "Goddamn old people are in such a fucking hurry. Still, I guess you're right. Mother's cockroaches might blow it. C'mon, let's make sure our guests aren't fucking snatched up by the world's dumbest repo men."

Shelby and Esther followed Courtney and Jake along the river rock path toward the center of Orphan Rock. They stood in the town square together. Courtney turned in circles, taking it all in. "Well, this looks like a movie scene. A spaghetti western like my dad used to watch. This is totally amazing, ladies."

"Have your pleasant-looking servant put the camera by the chapel," Shelby said, pointing at the wobbly old church. Jake listened, smirked a little. Didn't ask questions. Shelby *really* liked that. He dropped off the bin and whistled back down the path to get another load as a good pet should.

"It's a...*rustic* chapel," Courtney replied.

"Number one destination in all of Orphan Rock. It's the oldest building here." Shelby looked at Esther, and they nodded together. "And it's where most of the miracles happen, Ms. Philbin. It's where people see...*him*."

"Him?" Courtney asked.

"The Desert Christ," Esther said, eyes-rolling. "The fucking Jesus Man. What the fuck you're here for!"

"Ah, the specter the people saw on the bus…"

Shelby nodded. "That's right, ma'am. What people saw people saw correctly."

"So…he isn't a ghost? The Ghost of Jesus?"

"Can't say what he is for sure." Dark Bird dropped her voice. Courtney leaned in. "Sure seems like he's supernatural. He has some special gifts normal folk don't have. But he's also a man too. You'll have to ask the old spook. He comes out after dark. The Jesus Man is unlike anything the world's seen."

"But how is this place so empty…?" Courtney brought her knuckles to her chin in consideration. "I've covered everything from UFOs to the pope's face manifesting on a burnt piece of toast. People flock to this sort of thing." She surveyed the empty ghost town. "I'll have to get you in touch with my financial planner. At least get yourself a cart to sell some t-shirts."

Shelby chuckled. "Oh my, Courtney, our family has kept this land private for a long time. We never looked at it any other way than keeping some things sacred in a profane world."

"Well, ladies, after tonight, you better buy some t-shirts." Courtney pointed at the Chapel on the Mound. "We're going to make this little church famous. Probably both of you too. Say, how about we go inside and take a peek? Maybe shoot some b-roll? Introduce me to the Man…if he's amenable."

"Not much point yet," Shelby replied. "The good stuff always happens after dark. Here's a thought, though. Maybe we go inside *together* while we're on television later…"

Courtney's expression ignited like a newborn star. All her buttons pressed at once. "You mean, we'll *crack it open*, just like Geraldo did with Al Capone's vault?"

Esther's face scrunched up in confusion.

"Who the fuck is Geraldo?"

"I don't know much about show business, Ms. Philbin," Dark Bird rested her long fingers on the reporter's shoulder pad. "But I think going into that chapel tonight, live on TV, would certainly give your audience something to stay tuned for. It's all they'll talk about. Ratings gold? Is that what they say?"

"*I love it!*" Courtney clapped. "Who can I talk with so I can get all of the history here? I need everything about this chapel, other Jesus Man sightings, the town, the myths, the lore…"

Other Siders spit on her body, called her Unclean, and wished her dead. Even the ghost-eyed children threw stones. Norman carried what was left of her through the town square of the Other Orphan Rock, and the town gathered to pay their respects to the Girl in Pieces with hatred and anger.

"*Murderer!*" they cried. "*Cast away the sinner with the sin! Cast away the sinner with the sin!*"

She was too tired and broken and small and betrayed to fight back anymore. Liz had seen the room with windows the King in Pieces vowed to give her, and it was always terrible in the end. He promised her lies—an eternity of joy—like a carrot on a string, but her joyless memories were full of fear and violence. She was better off imagining her own happy days in The Dark where her daddy was a kind man, a loving husband, and a good father. Not a tyrant. Not a pig. Not the kind of man who only made things a little better just to make them worse than it was before.

Momma poked her head in the doorway.

Paul and Liz hid underneath their pillow fort.

"What should we have for dinner, you two?"

Daddy tickled Liz's tummy. "Oh, I think we should have guts and eyeballs! What do you think, Eli?"

She laughed. Hugged him around his belly.

"*Ewww!* How about spaghetti instead?"

Momma thought about it. Nodded with a Betty Crocker smile. "Whatever makes you happy, darling."

Paul yawned, stretching his long arms. "How about I get changed, and we'll go throw the Frisbee outside before dinner?

Would you like that, Little Lamb?"

"Yes, Daddy," the little ghost whispered while the Other Siders raised her body over the Old Sinkhole. Then she became the Frisbee, tossed away into the echoes of The Dark.

And tonight, we'd like to end our broadcast with something special. A bit of local flavor, if you will, from Orphan Rock in Ghost River, Arizona. Action 10 Reporter, Courtney Philbin, spent the afternoon with residents who claim the mythical 'Jesus Man' is just part of the family.

[studio laughter]

Courtney, can you hear us?

Courtney pressed her earpiece in.

"Sure can, Durbin. Thanks, Grace. We're in Orphan Rock, an old ghost town nobody would ever know existed unless you accidentally stumbled upon it by luck or chance. It's here, just up the road, where members of the Sun City West Group Retirement Home witnessed a miracle. Per eyewitness accounts, a man who looked like Jesus Christ was seen floating in the sky.

"It was this man that led their dangerous assailant into the desert where he later perished by a self-inflicted and fatal wound. We'd never heard of the Jesus Man before. Turns out, he's a bit of a local legend. Well, local, if you happen to live in Orphan Rock like Shelby and Esther Northamm do. These ladies grew up surrounded by miracles and blessings every day. Take a look."

The pre-recorded package played on the monitor.

Courtney turned to her guests.

"You two ready for primetime?"

Esther sure as shit didn't like the bright lights and hated the woman padding her down with powder even more. Shelby was in her element, looking particularly smug and punky. She had her eyebrow piercing in. Esther couldn't believe Dark Bird did it herself with a safety pin. She got Minister's senses, it seemed.

Some days she couldn't see herself in her at all—especially days like today when she was full of confidence and power.

Shelby gave a thumbs-up. "We'll do our best."

"It'll be great. We'll chat for a few minutes, and then we'll take a walk into the chapel. Simple. No sweat." Courtney held her finger up to her earpiece again, nodded. "One minute until we go live," she said loudly. The grips and make-up girl finished up and scampered off like Broken Kids in the sunlight.

"Thanks, Grace. I agree! Getting to know the history of this area made for an educational afternoon." Courtney gestured to her interviewees. "Shelby, Esther, thank you so much for opening your home to us. Such an amazing piece of history."

"It really is," Shelby agreed. "Orphan Rock means a lot to us. We've spent our lives out here preserving tradition while bridging cultures with our Ghost River neighbors on the other side of the Rock. We may be divided by a mountain, but not in spirit…"

Watching Shelby hypnotized Esther. So poised and eloquent. She'd come so far from that mewling, dirty bird, and it was intimidating to think about. At fifteen, she spoke like a fancy diplomat, captivating her audience with charisma and confidence. Whatever she was, if it was indeed an old thing like Delora, she was wise already. But Esther shivered. There was more to it than wisdom. Something dangerous that Esther feared. Maybe it wasn't confidence at all. No. The look was of a lion. Dominance.

"Esther?"

Courtney.

"What?"

"When was the first time you saw the Jesus Man? Childhood? Is that right?"

Minister dropped the knife. Eugene fell face-first into the Mound. The boy spun around, and the Crooked Woman stood there with her hand out to him.

Esther blinked, trembling a little. "Yes, I first saw the Jesus Man when I was a little girl. Saw him in the chapel behind us. He saved me. Always looked after me since then."

"Sounds like he had quite an influence on you."

"Well..." Esther looked at the camera. "Wouldn't be here without him. I can say that much for damn sure."

The interview wrapped up. During a commercial break, Jake and the field crew positioned around Courtney and Shelby in front of the Chapel on the Mound. "Shelby tells me there isn't much room in there, so the crew should hang back except for Mike on camera and Jake on boom. That about right, Shelby?"

"Yes. Esther will hang back too," Dark Bird added. "Just the four of us will take the tour. More intimate that way."

Esther lit up a smoke. Fine by fucking her. She weren't no TV star. She wandered over to the make-up tent and watched the monitor with some of the other television people.

After commercials, Durbin and Grace bantered in the studio. Esther couldn't really hear what anybody was saying. Volume was too low, and her anxiety screamed.

The camera switched to Courtney and Shelby in front of the chapel. They walked up the porch stairs. Courtney kept turning over her shoulder to talk to the camera. Esther didn't know much about her, but this woman could run her mouth without breathing. Shelby was talking, too, while unlocking the door. They kept a light on her. She asked Courtney if she was ready to go in. Esther read that one on her lips. Courtney said yes, and Shelby slowly opened the door to the drab nave.

The cameraman turned on night-vision mode. Everything looked green and fuzzy. Glowing, white crickets hopped across the wooden planks of the dusty floor. Esther noticed Courtney's eyes radiated like truck lights. Shelby's were black and bottomless as if the camera had pierced her mask.

Something happened. Nobody moved. Tighter as the tension built, the crowd around Esther gathered around the monitor. On-screen, Courtney craned her neck. *What did she see?* Then, she urgently waved her cameraman to get a shot.

Get a shot!

The frame wobbled and zoomed in to the back of the chapel. There, hovering in the branches of the Dead Tree, was the Desert Christ. He bled rust over the Mound, his eyes mirroring Shelby's—black holes—in the gaze of the emerald lens.

The crowd chattered around the monitor. Rumors started. Conspiracies. Wild gossip by nobodies without a clue.

"I don't know what the hell that is!" one of the gaffers replied, leaning closer to the screen. "Do you see wire? Come on! Are you guys fucking seeing this bullshit? Gotta be fake."

Esther folded her arms. *Geniuses.*

Of course, Courtney wanted to get a better look at the floating holy man. She put the *action* in Action 10. The lanky figure welcomed her by opening his arms and floating down to the pulpit. The Jesus Man never raised his head from his chest. Courtney crept forward, continually reassuring the audience she was okay while she swatted pesky flies away from her face.

At the pulpit, his bony hand touched her head.

In a flash, Courtney seized, shaking like she was being fried on a buttered skillet. The camera panned upward, revealing a radiant holy face that loved people so much he would heal all their wounds and invite them into his Vile Heart. Fingers clasped, Courtney dropped to her knees. The camera hit the ground when the Jesus Man's palm cracked open, black worms reaching...

"Esther?" Young Minister held out his hand to her. A small pile of dirt in his palm. "You need to eat it like me. Watch me do it. Then you do it. Together or not at all."

The live feed went dead.

"Shit!" TV technicians scrambled to re-establish the connection with the camera feed. The make-up girl ran toward the chapel, shouting for help. Durbin and Grace look confused.

Esther didn't budge. She smoked.

No need to fret now. It was all out in the open, wasn't it? Not some. *All of it.*

Just like that…they were fucking famous.

14.

High atop the Aegis Tower, with its needle touching the ever-gray clouds above Kilgore City, sat a penthouse suite with a hidden door that led to a secret garden where emerald butterflies twinkled in twisty boughs of ancient trees. Beneath the canopy was a simple wood and plaster cottage with an old chimney that spewed ash and ember near a babbling stream and garden. Behind the cottage door was whatever she desired, the one who it belonged to—the one who took the children from the streets.

Today it was a cosmopolitan apartment with gold-trimmed furniture. A young man named Cobra sat at the edge of a hand-carved bed. A white sheet covered his bare midriff. Puffy scars and bite marks muraled his skin, a story of years of vicious pain and sadistic pleasure. On his muscular back, a fresh tattoo of a hooded viper. When he behaved, he could do as he wished. Tonight, he watched the news on television.

Miracles. Jesus Man. His mother on TV!

Who was that other girl with her?

What the hell was happening in Ghost River?

Cobra ran scarred hands through his dangling brown

bangs. He tried to remember his real name—almost forgotten now and always forbidden to say aloud. *"You have a sister,"* Esther *told the boy splashing in the bucket. "I don't know what I'm going to name her yet. She's not like you and me."*

The seventeen-year-old squinted his chestnut eyes, and he could see it. His Everything could not cut away all the memory in his mind. Some top-secret things he kept hidden from her in a special place she never roamed. Dangerous, yes, but he couldn't let them go. The faces of his family. The memories of his youth.

The unfamiliar girl on the screen was edgy, pierced, and exuded a dark allure. But underneath the make-up and hair dye, he recognized his mother. She had the soft, yet strong features of Esther Northamm, except for her caramel eyes.

They were snake eyes.

"What an absolute mockery," Desyre said in a dull tone. She sipped a chalice of blood and leaned against the pillowed headboard. "Seems like my Sister is getting horrible advice these days. Predictably, exposure will guarantee unfavorable outcomes for all of them. Once the world sees you, it'll never look away." Desyre's exhaustion with Ghost River was palpable. She sighed. "Although crude and filthy, Delora had a perfectly sustainable box. Now? She has too many eyes on her. Disaster is coming."

The salamander wore her pretty mask, but Cobra could see beneath it now. The illusion of beauty was just another tactic, a sword in a sheath, easily employed to seduce and subordinate. The more he pleasured her, explored her horrific dark fantasies wrapped in black tentacles, the more he saw through her disguise. Beneath her porcelain skin and verdant eyes, a lizard waited. An unkind creature who suckled obedience more than tenderness. He'd watched her grow even crueler over the years too. Gone were the others, his gutterpunk friends and skater kids. She devoured them all and only seemed hungrier for it. Now, only Nicholas and Cobra tended to her. With each day, she grew madder.

Desyre set down her glass and crossed her pallid arms.

"When your time is up, turn off that trash and come back to bed, Cobra. I've not yet satisfied my appetite."

He looked at the teenager on the screen, a few years younger than himself. *"Are you my sister?"* he whispered, but Desyre heard it—she heard everything in this cottage.

She cackled. "Oh, *Cobra!* That girl is more sister to me than she'll ever be to you! Poor chickling, she only has Delora to learn our ways from. *She's fucking doomed.*" The young man said nothing. Ash from his cigarette landed on the floor. "They did an exceptional job, by the way." The salamander studied the fresh cobra tattoo that stretched from shoulder to shoulder on his back. "Did it sting?" She perked up. "Tell me about the pain."

"No. Not really. I felt *nothing.*"

Desyre frowned with disappointment. Cobra was in one of his moods again. She was weary of his negativity. The sheet fell away from her pale body. Curls of crimson hair dangling over her shoulders, she crawled to him like a tigress. He felt her long, sharp fingers wrap around his scarred shoulders from behind.

"Why do you let them haunt you?" she asked, kissing his neck. "I have given you the best box, haven't I? Your only task here is submission to me. Why do you cling to the desert?"

"It's not that," he replied. "I'm fine."

She bit his earlobe, drawing blood. "You're lying to me."

Cobra stood up. He wiped the crimson drip from his collarbone. "It's not like that," he said glumly.

Desyre rolled onto her back. Rivulets of red hair fell off the bed in waves. Her mesmeric eyes stared at the ceiling with boredom. "Then answer this: why should we spend one second of our eternity thinking about a world we're not part of anymore? I am just as much a Ghost River Orphan as you are, but I do not keep any memories from there. I said my goodbyes, repaid my debts. Memories are anchors. They will always pull you to the bottom of the sea. Let them go, cut yourself free, and embrace your service. You will find peace wearing my leash."

Cobra tried to suppress his trembling and shook his head. "Something is happening in Orphan Rock. I can feel it prickling underneath my skin. Something bad."

The salamander scowled with condescension. "Yes, you foolish child! *Death throes* are happening at Orphan Rock! What you're seeing isn't the start of something. It's the end of everything there. *Little Snake,* we're getting as far away from Ghost River as we can. You'll have to let it go."

The young man raked his fingers down his cheeks in frustration. "Don't call me that."

Desyre's cruel eyes flickered with disapproval. "Then don't act like one." She flicked her wrist. The television screen cracked, and the picture died with a fizzle. "Now, undress."

When she had her fill of his flesh and tentacle, she told him to leave the cottage, so she could feed. Cobra said nothing, blotted the blood from his skin and gathered his clothes. Outside in the garden, Havenarchs glided on a cool breeze. Red flowers bloomed among fat leaves. He hopped on rocks to cross the stream and dipped his hand in the running water. Fresh cuts bled through the skin on his back and soaked his t-shirt. He washed more of his own blood from his hands. Couldn't feel a thing, could he?

Dead as fuck here. God, he missed the desert. Running through the empty heat to nowhere. *That was life.*

He slipped into the red dungeon where dirty food bowls scattered across the floor. An Asian girl, some raver kid with hot pink hair, was little more than a sunken-eyed skeleton chained to the wall. She was the last of their reserves. Desyre would want to leave soon. He'd served her long enough to know when she craved a new destination. Eating all the food was a sign.

Through another tear in folding realities, the young snake steeped back into the penthouse suite on the top floor of the Aegis Tower. More gold trim here. Tassels. Gleaming green marble and gaudy brass fixtures. Nicholas sat at the polished oak table by the window, drinking in the moonlight. He faced the neon Kilgore

City skyline, his eyes twitching in captivity.

"Cobra, join me for a nightcap? Bourbon." Nicholas pushed the bottle toward him. The young man plopped into a leather chair and took a swig. He barely felt the fire in his belly. *Numb. All numb.* "And how is Our Everything this evening?"

He wiped his scruffy chin. "Fed and fucked."

"Very good."

Nicholas scooted the ashtray in Cobra's direction. They drank. Cobra smoked. Storm clouds slid across the moonscape. The skyscrapers looked like tombstones in a foggy graveyard.

"Can I ask you a question?" Cobra snubbed his cigarette with a pensive, empty stare. "It's kind of weird."

"Fine. Be weird if you must."

"Have you and Desyre ever…you know…?"

Nicholas snorted. "Oh, Cobra, I would never. I am not worthy of that. She chooses her partners. I was never chosen."

The young man remembered the biker before him, Gunner, a strong and formidable man. After the heist at The Lady Shade, when Desyre took Cobra's innocence, Gunner disappeared. Although he'd never ask, he knew what happened. The salamander had little connection to her old toys.

"Probably a good thing." Cobra pressed his leg against the glass window. "Do you ever get tired of living to please her? I mean, do you ever want something for yourself?"

The cat eyes on his lids twitched wildly at the thought. "No. To both questions. The greatest gift given to me by Desyre is I no longer have to care about anyone but her." He smiled. It looked genuine. Creepy, but honest. "My life became simpler when she found me. *Less pain.* I've learned devotion is an exquisite form of meditation. Give yourself away to her."

Cobra glanced at the city lights.

"Did you see the news today?"

"No." Nicholas watched the first raindrops fall on the window. "I have no interest in current events unless Our All commands it. When you don't pay attention, it isn't there."

Cobra laughed. Nicholas was hardly a person. In the years they'd worked together, he never ceased to surprise the young man with his ability to ignore life. "Do you even dream, man? I mean, what the fuck do you do for fun?"

"Dreaming is dangerous," Nicholas said. "Dreaming is a cruel exercise one in our situation must avoid. We cannot allow any temptation to pull us away from our grander purpose."

"That's exactly what my daddy used to say." The snake leaned back in the chair, remembering Minister. "Dreaming is dangerous. Said it hurt his heart to dream."

"Your daddy was a wise man." Nicholas put the cap back on the bottle. He looked ready to retire for the evening but did not stand up. Something weighed on his mind. "Cobra," he began, his expression grim and severe. "Sometimes, I fear you think this is going to be better for you one day. If you keep expecting things to change for yourself, you're going to suffer needlessly. That one day is only today and then tomorrow and the day after that. All for her. Nothing else was ever real for you."

"Nah," Cobra said, playing with the silver lighter he stole from a whorehouse baron years ago. In the flame, he saw a scrappy little boy running across the sun-drenched barrens with his daddy. Sprinting, he laughed, knobby-kneed. "Don't worry about me, Nick. I know what's real. I just can't ever have it again."

Dark Minister woke up in the blackout tangle beneath the Dead Tree. Entwined people sprawled across the chapel floor. A heap of thighs and skinned elbows jutted out of an unholy rubber band ball made of strangers and body parts. Some alive. Some maybe alive. Some definitely fuckin' dead. All empty. The holy man so full of suffering he could barely stand.

He swallowed them all. Not a drop wasted. And in return, he held their pig faces into the dirt—blood and semen and dead crickets—and fucked them hard until he was empty too. The black roots that cracked through his strong calves milked despair into the soil. The news reporter squatted in the corner. He'd fucked her too. Stuck his dick right in her ass, and she buckled in delight. It was a gesture of healing and renewal for both parties.

"I'm so hungry," she called out from the shadows, lips covered in dirt. Her head twitched; her lipstick smeared across her cheek. "I could eat a baby. *Does anybody have a fucking baby?*"

Urine waterfalled between her toned thighs.

Minister squirmed out of the fleshy nest and leaned against the pulpit. He felt sick and dizzy, his greasy hair sticking to his forehead. He looked around the Chapel on the Mound, admiring the fine crowd this morning. Folks from far and wide packed the sanctuary. Men dressed in their Sunday best sat upright in clean pews wearing their lovely pigskin masks.

"What are you waiting for, son?" Eugene asked, standing behind him. Black ants spilled from the old wound across his throat. "These people came for a sermon! They didn't come here to die. They came here to feel better about themselves *first*. All the good ministers make you happy before they bleed you out." Eugene leaned in. "*Now, squeal like a pig for your daddy.*"

Minister cleared his throat.

"My momma died in this very chapel," he began, voice escalating. "She was strung up in this Dead Tree behind me. I watched her die and then I fucked her body like a Pig. I didn't want to, believe you me, but they made me do it. Forced me to. Beat me when I said no. Told me that my god demanded all his devotees taste his abandoned bride before she was burned up. A reward, they said. A blessing for the faithful." Dark Minister's eyes watered. "That's how I lost my innocence, you see. That's how I learned that the old god was a cruel one and needed to die.

"*Suffering is salvation.* My sweet momma told me them words all the time. I never knew what it meant until I died and weren't free. My service to the Grim Seed had just begun. I had to bleed more to find my freedom. Had to swallow y'all first."

The pigs in the audience didn't stir.

"Dig deeper, son," Eugene whispered in his ear. "Feel your words. Talk about love. Everybody wants a happy ending."

"Love?" Minister's eyes hardened as he surveyed the packed house. "In Ghost River, all the love that we share is pain. We carve it up into bloody little pieces, and gulp by gulp, we swallow it all. We're used to being fat, happy piggies, eating the disgustin' slime that people feed us and call love. But what is love really? What else is it 'sides the poison stinging our fuckin' tongues!" Minister tore at his own throat in agony. "*Love is poison, and we give it to our babies unconditionally the very second after they're born.* I'm sorry, friends, but we're villains. There are no more babies left to love here! Good riddance too. Why invite children into a future that smells like gasoline?

"Cities. Progress. Men and machines. *I can smell ALL that shit from here!*" Minister kicked the pulpit and paused until the echo died. "Is our way truly lost? Will the creeping death of modernity kill the last real magic on Earth? We sit in this desert, where the Age of Filth began, but not because we want to. We come here for different reasons, and those are not important to anybody. They never fuckin' were to begin with. WE ARE HERE TO SERVE AND SUFFER!" Minister pounded his fist. Then, he bowed his head in prayer. "In your name, Pain, I am an executioner of doubt. Those who seek to know you will find a barren valley in me, and I welcome their seeds of sorrow for I shall grow a better garden for all to harvest in your name. Amen."

When he looked up, the pews were empty.

Courtney Philbin clapped from her dark corner. "You're a peach, Minister! Such pretty words this morning!"

He glowed beneath the rose window, brow sweaty. "I made you empty, didn't I? Does this bring you joy?"

The Action 10 News Reporter giggled like a mad scientist. "No! *Everything is getting so much worse.*" She rubbed her bloody hands together and screamed until her voice shattered.

The circus came to Ghost River, and nobody had a plan to deal with the invasion.

Miracle seekers arrived from across the country. One by one, they turned off the Ghost River exit, passed the casino, and flooded the dirt roads leading to the shitspit town called Orphan Rock. When traffic slowed to a halt, they set up folding chairs and tents, tailgating in the brush, waiting for their turn to visit the Chapel of the Desert Christ. Opportunists walked down the line of parked cars, hawking Jesus Man buttons, water bottles, and t-shirts. The local police tried to keep the roads around the casino open, but the traffic was impossible to regulate.

Shelby held court at the picnic table near the stone-stacked house. She anticipated some buzz after the news broke on CBS, but she did not expect the national media brushfire. The line of cars was so long it disappeared beyond the hazy horizon.

"Well, we can't stare at them all fucking day, can we?" Esther paced around the fire pit. "Can't let them in neither. Where're we going to put them all up, Shelby?"

Dark Bird hid behind expensive sunglasses and smoked, letting the fumes drift away from her lips like a movie star. She sprawled on top of the picnic table, soaking in some rays. When bloodroot vined up the wood tried to bite her ankle, she kicked it away without any bother. "What's your point?" she asked.

Esther continued, lips tight and worried, "Way back when, years before you, the Pig Men built houses. Worked together to make shelter. If there ain't order in camp, or a goddamn mission statement, this revival is going to fall apart. Especially when the bleeding fuckin' starts." Esther paused to think about it. "Eugene Northamm was a lot of things, and a shithead legend among them, but he was also a firm hand. The Pig Men listened to him. Minister ain't that guy. He's a haunt now anyway."

Shelby snubbed her smoke, sat up, and pulled down her sunglasses. "You should manage it."

Esther blinked. "Manage fucking what?"

"All of it. Orphan Rock. You're in charge." Shelby waved down the college boy on the camera crew. Jake bopped over, carrying a bin of television equipment from the Action 10 satellite news van. He looked confused when Shelby reached in and tossed Esther a walkie-talkie. She took another one and clipped it to her leather belt. "Do you have more of these magic radios, Jake?" she asked, batting her eyes. The intern nodded. "Then get them."

"What the fuck can I do by myself?" Esther scanned the land, studying the mass of people waiting to pour into the front gate. "Running a camp ain't easy. Takes a workforce. Security. Capable hands. Organization. A goddamn schedule and three lucky miracles tied to a hopeless prayer."

Shelby sighed. "Yeah, sure. I'll talk to Mother. Her minions can work behind the scenes at your direction. Just keep them out of sight, OK? Those dead fucks will spook all the meat away. Meanwhile, I need that television crew in the chapel to—"

"They're husks," Esther interjected. "He sucked the smarts right out of them. They're gonna tear each other apart, Shelby. Best to clean them out for the pantry. Once Minister empties them of all their sad stories, what's left don't function so well."

"We're not looking for a debate, correct?"

"Suppose not." Esther bit on her knuckle then shook her head. "But it won't work. Can't reason with a husk, so I doubt you can control one for shit. Besides, they'll endanger the plan. They're too fucking wild. And I'll need muscle that'll take orders. When Eugene used to recruit Pig Men, he'd go to the train yards and fight clubs. He'd find men good with their hands. Some vets too. Quite a few lads preferred kicking up dust out here. Fucking us coyotes sure beat shitting in the jungles of 'Nam."

Jake returned with an armful of radios. Instead of leaving, the boy lingered nearby. He'd become a bit of an infatuation for

Shelby after she saved him from the chapel. Pulled him out before Minister could stick his dead dick in him. Looks like he wanted to continue their strange dance, too, but Esther was in the way. She liked to hover, worse than Mother's creepy butler sometimes.

"Esther," Shelby began, pointing at the road, "there's a sea of able bodies out there. Go pick a few big boys from the crowd and have Minister help them see things our way."

"All right then," Esther agreed, padded her walkie-talkie. She headed out to recruit. Meanwhile, Shelby turned to the intern who stood nearby, pretending not to look her way.

She could smell desire on him. It stunk, like cat piss.

"You're not leaving, Jake, so why pack up?" Shelby put her combat boot up on the picnic table. "You looking to run away from us already? *We're just getting started here.*"

Jake blushed a little, looking down at his dusty shoes. "I don't know what I'm supposed to be doing! Guess that's my specialty, though. Nobody ever tells me what's supposed to happen next." He chuckled. "Sucks being the free intern. Pay is even worse. I'm pretty expendable, actually."

Shelby was intrigued. "So, you're a servant?"

"Fucking-A," he said, sitting down on the picnic table next to her. Brazen move. She offered him a cigarette. "I mean, aren't we all slaves to something? The Man? Big Brother? Fuck, I don't know. All I want to do is make music videos for MTV. This is what they say you have to do first. You get some shitty gig in a cross-section of the industry you want to work in." He sighed, lighting his cigarette. "Got any better ideas for me?"

"I just might," Dark Bird said with a wink.

Wind chimes. Crystal tones.

Liz sat up, rubbing her eyes. Her legs dangled off a meticulously cleaned workbench, topped with glass jars, polished nails, golden hinges, and gears. The painted cave vibrated with an energy she could feel rattling her bones. A fresh breeze rattled metal effigies—ornately crafted and jeweled figurines—hung from braided chains on the underside of the tidy nest above.

Something remembered:

"Have we sung the dirt song yet?"

"I don't remember. Should we sing it now?"

The bone chamber! Liz shuddered. This was *the same* cavern on the Other Side where the Crooked Woman kept her demented vulture's nest! There in The Dark, she broke and remade children and fed the weak ones to undead rattlesnakes. But it wasn't the same. A less corrupted replica, maybe?

Terror struck hard when memories pinched her brain. Liz grabbed a nearby hammer from the bench. She felt braver with it in her hand. Wherever this was, whatever place or time, she wasn't going to wander around empty-handed. She'd learned that monsters are very real on Every Side of Things.

Monsters.

Something remembered:

A pig crawling out of her throat.

Betrayed, lying on the floor of a church—a little girl torn to pieces and left to die again.

Thrown into The Other Dark like trash. And now?

And now?

Thinking about all the twists made her head ache.

Liz rolled up her Care Bear t-shirt to reveal her tummy, whole and healthy again. But that made no sense. The Pig ripped her to shreds! Burst through her body like it was an overstuffed piñata. Where were the scars? The stitches? Her fingers danced on her pristine skin – it shimmered like a pool of water.

Why do you cling to yourself?

"Yikes!" She hopped off the table, stifling a scream. Liz recognized the voice. In The Quiet Box, right before she went to sleep. *Why do you cling to yourself?* it had asked then too.

Nothing is real. Get out of my head. Nothing is real. Tears came. *Not now. Not now, Elizabeth. We can be strong. Please be strong.* The Dark reached for her, flexing fingers from every ancient crack in the cathedral cave. She turned in circles as the shadows drew closer. Soon, The Dark flooded from all directions, lapping along the clean stone floor until there was only an exceedingly small spot left to stand in an infinite ocean of onyx oblivion. Liz chewed on her thumbnail. She didn't want to go into The Dark again! The Dark is a prison! The Blindfolded Boy led her through it before. She couldn't remember the way. Could she ever hope to find an exit on her own? Or would she only descend deeper into nothingness or find some worse Side than this one?

"What am I supposed to do?" Liz shouted.

Her voice carried, echoing in the expanding void.

Then, the little girl's eyes grew tight and curious to see a small glimmer of light approach. It was insignificant as a flickering candle. A little white butterfly. A tiny speck in a universe of nothing. It soared and swooped and loopty-looped as it navigated the sea of shadows toward her. When it landed near the edge of The Dark, wings slowly lifting and dropping in repose, Liz crawled over to it on hands and knees. With her nose near the angelic creature, she reached for it with shaky fingers. "Are you going to help me, Little Friend?" the ghostling asked softly. "I'm lost. I don't know where to go." Her fingertips brushed the icy sheen of The Dark, hard, and impenetrable. Black glass.

Why do you cling to yourself?

"*Raarrggh!*" **Boom!**

The beast charged over the butterfly and smashed against the barrier protecting Liz from the corrupted nothingness of The Dark. The ghostling yipped in fear. *What the heck was that?* She only saw it for a split second before it barreled back into the dim spaces. A hairy beast, snouted and snorting with tusks and spit-covered jowls, stomped in the din. Flickering white eyes made her think of the King in Pieces. Her little heart nearly popped.

Crick! Crick!

She pulled her hand back when the glass cracked.

Crick! Crick! Crick!

The fissures on the forcefield grew. Liz wanted to run far away from the breaking window holding back the infinite gloom. But there was nowhere to go! Dark is a prison. She felt incredibly sad to see what was left of the butterfly on the other side of the window. The pig thing had trampled it to dust. "You're too small," she whispered. "There was nothing you could do."

Crick! Crick! Crick! Cri-cri-crick!

The monster stalked her from a distance, waiting for the glass to weaken enough to break through. Liz could only sit back and wait for it to happen. Inevitable, right? No more doors to throw open. No rips to find. It was time to let the ghouls have her. Eat her. Kill her once and for all. What could she do to stop it? She was just a little dead orphan now.

She folded her hands and placed them on her lap. There, she felt the wooden handle of the hammer, and she stroked it in thought. *You're a murderer, Liz. First, you killed your Daddy. Then, Momma had to run away to protect you and she died too. You let Blindfolded Boy die in the prison, and then you smuggled a Pig into a world that didn't belong to him. You helped him butcher all those people in the chapel. When you're around, everybody always dies.* Liz turned the hammer in her hand. *Maybe it's time to do* something *to help* you *die instead.*

The filthy pig-man fanned his sickle fingers and aimed the thick dome of its skull at Liz. Its bony hoof scratched against shadow. It charged. Liz howled and swung her hammer at the window, ready to help the devil make his way through. She couldn't stop the stampeding tragedy. But she could help it happen. She was going to break it all down.

Let The Dark come in.

Crash! As the hammer and the demon collided against the black glass—**time froze**—shards tinkled, suspended in the air. Liz's face mirrored the hellion—wild, hungry, and desperate. She couldn't even move her eyes or soften her snarl. She stood face to face with the grub-covered pig. She looked just like it, didn't she? In the milky pools of its eyes, she saw her own face.

Why do you cling to yourself?

A shimmering laceration opened along the wall of black glass. Slender fingers snatched her by the scruff of her neck, and Liz felt the tickle of static as they pulled her through another doorway. Bright light. A hard stone floor. She yelped, rolling into a velvet armoire, near a crackling hearth in a comfortable and colorful abode. She scurried to her feet, hammer ready.

"Don't hurt me!" she pleaded with the tall figure looming before the open portal. When the elegant woman turned around, her cognac eyes sparkled with venerable power.

Thud! Liz's hammer hit the floor.

Sister Dirt.

The Harpy of Ghost River smiled to see her.

Minister Northamm puked into the toilet, retching up piles of slithering worms that spilled over his cracked lips like rotten spaghetti and meatballs. The jet-black eels with fish heads and barracuda teeth circled in the rust-ringed bowl, snapping at air, trying to climb over the lip to freedom. When he flushed, they screamed in despair and disappeared into the septic tank.

In the cracked mirror over the sink, he opened his mouth to see the horror show. His loose teeth wiggled, and his graying gums bled. Strands of his brittle hair fell into the sink basin.

"You've never looked better, son," Eugene said behind him wearing a pig mask, his dirty fingernails resting on Minister's shoulder. Horseflies rattled against the mirror. "You've got real conviction now. You have the look of a genuine holy man."

Minister drooled and then wiped the black slime from his chin. "It hurts, Daddy, when I eat their pain. Even though it tastes like nails, I always drink it all like a good boy. Not a drop wasted, even though it's killing my fuckin' snakeshine."

"Then it's working," Eugene said proudly. "You're more than just a boonchild now. You're a conduit to greatness—a prophet of loss. Your heart is better than mine ever was. There ain't no doors or exits to it. It belongs only to you now. You can save them all, you know. You can heal the sickness that plagues a world filled with false idols and the heresy of invention. Outside of this desert, the world cries for salvation. You feel it too. I know you do. You taste the despair. You know a *rapture* is best."

A gentle knock on the bathroom door pried his mind away from the rhapsody of madness ringing in his ears. Eugene was gone. The flies in his head too. The faucet left running.

"*Minister?*"

Esther.

He washed the blood and black vomit from his chin and beard. "Hold on now. I'm almost finished."

"Will you let me in? I need a favor."

"No! I'm indecent."

She laughed. "I've seen worse."

The door handle rattled.

"OK! OK! *Hold your horses.*" Minister dried his gloomy face on his sweaty undershirt and took one last look in the mirror. His eyes soured into a brownish-gold, and when he cried, he cried tears of blood. As pretty as he was ever going to be.

When he unlocked the door, Esther barged into the bathroom. She found him hunched over the sink. He didn't want to face her, but she could see his reflection in the mirror.

"Won't lie. You look bad."

"I know it." His fingers curled over the counter so hard, one of his rotting nails snapped off. "The more sorrow I eat, the worse I get. I'm too full, baby. The suffering…*it fills you up.* Sometimes, I get lost. I don't remember where or who or what I am. It's worse than being drunk."

Minister buried his head in his black-veined hands.

"I know it's hard. Wish I could help you. *I really do.* Wish I could take your place." Esther touched his frigid cheek and turned her husband to face her. She mustered a smile despite the sick look in his eyes that broke her heart to see. "I guessed a long time ago that when she brought you back again, it was only to make me lose you fucking twice. She's a bitch like that."

"She really is," Minister said, returning the playful smile. But it was short-lived, and the gloom parade marched across his pallid face again after a tick between them. "I don't know how long I can keep on. Carrying all this burden is making me fall to pieces. That Grim Seed is a greedy son of a bitch. The more I feed it, the more it wants. What if there ain't enough?"

Esther shrugged. "Then, there ain't enough."

"And all of this is for nothing?" Minister snorted at that depressing thought. "Fuck it, I guess." He laughed.

"Fuck it is about right," Esther replied, putting her hand on his elbow. "You're a good man. Mean well. No matter what, don't you let go of that. Stay kind if you can." Esther held out her pinkie. Her husband wrapped his around it.

"What's this for?" he asked, squeezing.

Esther placed her other hand over their sacred wrap. "Long ago, you made a promise to me, and here you are still keeping it. So, I guess I'll make you a promise too. If it hurts more than you can handle, you tell me." The dire thought cracked her voice a little. "Just give me a look if you can't talk. I'll see it in your eyes. *I promise* I'll make sure it's painless in the end."

Her husband rubbed the bloody tears from his eyes. She kissed his cheek, tasted the bitterness of death, and she gave him a confident look anyway. "I told you we're gonna run away someday. Find us a better life than this."

Esther put her head against his chest. "Guess what? I finally decided where we should go."

Minister pulled back from her arms, surprised.

"Yeah? Where?"

"Egypt."

"Egypt?" He hollered with laughter. "*What the hell?*"

"Fucking Egypt, OK?" Esther replied defensively. "I want to see that Sphinx, all right? It's like a fucking cat *and* a person all smashed together. Don't you mock me."

Minster winked. "You've been spending too much time in the sandbox with Dark Bird."

"Maybe, but she keeps me entertained. Knows all kinds of things about faraway places I want to see one day."

Minister took her hand, remembering she came for a reason. "What did you need? *A favor?* I know you didn't just show up to make me smile the way you always do. Better tell me now, before I slip away again, and you can't find me."

"Recruits," she said. "Found some muscle to help out around here while we open up for business. I need to snake them. They're a little wily. Can you make them take orders from me?" She patted her walkie-talkie proudly. "I'm the boss around here now, you know. Shelby put me in charge of the camp."

"Well, look at you!" He beamed, proud of her. "Sure, I can do that. Should be a little more magic left in these ol' eyes."

"But can you control yourself? I need them snaked, not swallowed."

"Yes'm," Minister replied. "*Boss lady.*"

Esther punched his shoulder. "Shut up, you."

Together, the Orphans of Ghost River walked down the hallway of the stone-stacked house. Esther wasn't used to how clean it looked inside the old place. Shelby spent some money fixing it up. Gutted the living room, added comfy chairs and a table with touristy pamphlets. A water cooler. A small counter for concessions connected to the kitchen. Fresh carpet and wild wallpaper patterned with tiny black skulls (Shelby's pick, of course) made the interior feel presentable.

"Hardly recognize the old place," Minister said.

"Maybe that's a good thing," Esther replied.

Outside, a gang of bikers stood around the firepit: strong men with bandannas, tattoos, earrings, and beards. They wore leather cuts. On the back of their vests was a profile of Jesus Christ with a thorny crown and halo. Along the top, the words *Sturgis Fall Saints* was stitched into the hide. They folded their muscular arms as they watched the Jesus Man approach.

"Afternoon, fellas!" Minister said, putting a cigarette in his mouth. "I hear you're interested in miracles. If so, you've found the right place and the right guy."

"The blonde hottie offered us a private tour of the chapel," one of the burly bikers said, unamused. "Are you the man they call Desert Christ? The one from TV?"

"Well," Minister began, "first things first, you can call me Minister. Secondly, park your bikes over there. I'll take you into the chapel on foot. I can guarantee you fellas this much: once you see our little slice of paradise, you'll never want to leave."

Liz backed against the wall.

Sister Dirt, who had donned her prettiest mask, stood across the cozy living quarters with her honeyed hair tied up in neat buns. She wore a clean frontier dress, beaded, and feathered. Her amber eyes glimmered with power and peace. "My child," she said, "you've come a long way to find me."

"*You're dead!*" Liz shouted in disbelief. "You killed yourself to make a Grim Seed! *I saw it!* You killed yourself, and then you killed *everybody else!*"

The woman made a temple with her bony fingers. She drifted toward her hearth, picking up a poker to stir it. "That's not *entirely* accurate. Do you often trust Kings of Pigs?"

"I've never met one before! Just like I never met whatever you are *either!*" Liz readied her hammer, waving it awkwardly in front of her face. "You killed my mother. You killed me. *You turned me into* a *freak!*"

Sister Dirt showed no emotion. "You were simply food, I'm afraid. As were many before and after you."

"I'm not food! I'm a little kid, *you asshole!*"

Liz blushed and covered her mouth. The River Woman pinched her lips and continued poking her smoldering logs. The flames of the fire did not reflect in her false eyes. "Nothing can change the past. I am a shaper, a builder of worlds—a lover of children. But creation is messy and comes with a cost. Your life fed a part of me, yes. I will not deny the cruelty of nature. But the creature that haunts the Other Side is not what you think it is. She is a ghost too, and she haunts the rusty corridors of my revenge."

"You mean, *kill the King in Pieces.*"

Sister Dirt bristled. "*Of Pigs.* Yes. And he was dead, until you—"

"He was *separated.*"

"Very well. He was *docile* until he talked a crumb of a ghost into smuggling a bomb into my box. Now he's stolen two of his three components back and taken the Lumenchild with him. The orphans here will blame you for that. Do not expect any kindness from them. I do not blame you, however. You were too naive to know any better. Exploiting a child is easy."

"You cut my fingers off. He freed me from The Dark, helped me get here, and I've got my body back now." Liz crossed her arms. "I don't care what problem you two have with each other. I want to go somewhere happy now. I'm done."

"He betrayed you, didn't he?"

Liz scuffed the floor with her shoe.

"What did he promise you?"

"He—"

"*Paul, please*, not in front of her. Take me to the bedroom. Do it there, OK? Not here! Not in front of—"

"…I don't know. My old life back, I guess."

"So, he seduced you with false promises and fantasy.

Child, that life is gone. The Pig enjoys bewitching the meek with the illusions of miracles. But he has long been unable to shape anything more than poisonous words." Sister Dirt turned from her warm fire. "He is a menace. An oppressor."

"*So are you.*"

"No, child. You're mistaken." Sister Dirt's eyes darkened. "I am a wounded Sister. One of many who suffered under his laws and punishments. I watched him drown hundreds of children. Saw my own Sisters murdered and burned just for being born. I spent my life in that river helping souls flee his cage."

"Lady, I've died a half dozen times in your boxes and tunnels and Other Sides." Liz's hammer trembled. "I don't know whether or not I'm human, a ghost, a monster, or some scarecrow made from grass. Don't tell me what *you* are. I know what you are. You're an awful meat grinder. That's what you are."

Sister Dirt chuckled, returning the poker to its ornate metal stand. She faced Liz, unflinching. "Do you think you're any of those things now? Do you even know what you are?"

"I'm Liz. Short for Elizabeth. From Oklahoma. I helped Momma kill my daddy, and we ran away to Arizona. Then, we got taken by a man. That man fed us to *you*."

"What did you do for your birthday last year, Liz from Oklahoma? Do you remember your presents?"

"What?" Liz bit her lip.

"How about your favorite childhood game?"

The ghostling searched her mind. Deep as she could go. Only gray fog answered her questions. Her brow creased when she glared at the River Woman, fear blooming in her eyes.

"What are you doing to me? I can't remember."

"Because those memories are gone now. They don't belong to you anymore." Sister Dirt's dress brushed the floor when she knelt to the quivering girl in the corner. Her claw gently stroked Liz's cheek. The little girl's hammer shook, but she did not pull away from her. Somehow, she sensed kindness in the monstrous woman—the love of a mother. "Child, we are not what we're named, where we're born, or what roads we've walked in our lives. That's the decor. Layers of false identity that we shed like lizard skin as we pass from one life to another.

"The King of Pigs exploited a fraction of life that was left behind and made you believe it could be yours again. But...you are not Liz. Liz is dead. Her story is over. Neither are you any other thing you've pretended to be on your journey thus far. *You are everything and nothing at once.* A spirit is a potent material. Focused energy. In one form, it runs in one direction for so long until it burns out like a comet. But that *energy*, that precious will, can be reborn and rekindled and reshaped like clay."

Liz shook her head and pushed the harpy's hand away. "No, you're a liar! I have to be *something.* You keep putting me back together again. You wouldn't do that for *nothing.*"

Sister Dirt offered a knowing smile, stood, and walked over to a tall cheval mirror with gold hinges. She flipped it toward the little girl in the corner, so she could see her true reflection. Liz's knees buckled upon seeing her visage in the pane of polished glass. She screamed so loudly, her ears popped

"Yes. You are indeed *something* again." The corners of Sister Dirt's lips unzipped link by link to reveal a ferocious smile. "You are my finest creation. And I *have* given you a name. There is great power in a name. You are now called *Vengeant.*"

In the far distance, jagged mountains topped with crystalline castles with tall turrets and tie-dye banners that stretched a mile long rippled across a cloudless sky with three blazing suns. Pink, the dead girl in the dirtiest of dresses, waddled up the white sand dune to the horsefly door.

The intern circled in the travertine oasis.

"Dude! How is this *even* possible? Three fucking suns? Sand dunes? Are we in Tatooine? Holy shit, look at that fucking thing!" Shelby watched him with mild amusement. Humans were so easily entertained by the fantastic, even if the fantastic was the leash around their throats. "Is this some kind of extra-dimensional portal? Holy shit, this is a fucking holodeck, isn't it? Man!"

"This is whatever I want it to be." Dark Bird walked over intricately carved tile to put her foot upon the waterbed. A red lava lamp blurped on the headboard behind her. "Well, are you going to unlace me, or do I need to command you?"

"Oh, yeah, sure!" Jake bounded over and untied the laces of her Doc Martens. He looked at the TV floating over the pond. MTV. The power cord dangled in the water.

"This is so fucked up! Mind blown, Shelby."

Everything in her sandbox was exactly the way the harpy wanted it to be. Soft pillows on the floor. Lit candles on top of gigantic speakers with a CD-player. An electric guitar and amp sat near a bongo drum. Hundreds of cigarette cartons—the Northamm treasure trove—piled on the sand underneath ancient palm trees that swayed in the cool desert breeze.

Shelby grew impatient with his gawking.

"It's a work in progress," she said flippantly. "I'll totally find a new place once I move out. There isn't enough space here for what I really have in mind."

Jake rubbed the back of his head. "Space?"

"Yes. Between things. You'd better pay attention, Jake. If you're going to be my servant, you'll need to learn that I don't like to repeat myself." She rolled her eyes and huffed impatiently. "You're not very good at unlacing boots, either."

"Sorry, ma'am." He winked and pulled one oxblood boot from her dainty foot fast as he could, and Shelby raised the other. "Why the hell would you ever want to leave? Can you make your own food? Just disappear here…you know…forever?"

"Jake, this is a cage. I don't like cages." Dark Bird giggled when Jake tickled her foot unexpectedly. "Far as food goes, no. For that, I have to order a little *take-out.*"

The intern finally tugged off the other boot. Shelby told him to put the pair *neatly* on the small ivory pedestal she shaped in the center of the atrium. On his way back, he knelt next to the pond that gently bubbled. Water flowed through his fingers.

"Wet," he said.

"You were expecting dry?" Shelby lit a cigarette and patted the empty spot next to her on the waterbed. "Come, tell me about the bands you like. Impress me."

"Oh, is this a test?" With a sly smirk, Jake dropped down next to her. He scooted close enough, their thighs touched. Shelby watched the distance between them disappear. "If I fail, I don't get to be your servant forever? Or what?"

"Currently what we're determining, yes. Now, tell me about the bands you admire. Careful, Jake, disappoint me, and I'm going to fucking eat the heart right out of you."

The intern laughed. Shelby did not.

"Hardcore! Love it!"

Jake pulled out his soapbox, happy to pontificate about the groups that mattered in life, and the music videos in his head that the world needed to see. He spun wild stories about getting tossed out of a few night clubs that Puff Daddy owned. He went on about this one girl he knew that gave head to Marilyn Manson at a Pantera concert. Endless mosh pit escapades. Backstage romps. The intern had a story for everything and everyone, including his own nasty cocaine addiction that he'd survived after OD'ing twice in high school. It was strange she would enjoy his company, but Jake was part of the gritty rocker world she dreamed of.

"…and Billy Corgan came right through the Taco Bell drive-thru in a Porsche. Motherfucker ordered a bean burrito. Just one. My friend was in total fucking shock and forgot to charge him. And, yeah, he fucking drove away. *Burrito bandito!*"

Shelby's heart fluttered.

Jake was perfect.

He noticed her itty-bitty grin.

She noticed he wore a bit of mascara around his hazel eyes.

"Why're you looking at me like that?"

"Like what, Jake?"

"Like you want to eat me?"

His hand slid on top of hers.

Jake had rock star eyes, didn't he?

Rock star eyes, rock star hair.

He was the one.

"No." Shelby bounced up. "I've decided *not* to eat you."

The intern looked befuddled.

"Um, do you want to make-out or something? I mean, I thought—"

"Thought what?"

"That's what you meant by me becoming your servant. Like, it's a sex thing, you know?" Jake looked around nervously. "Dominatrix-like shit. I'll do anything for you."

Jake bit his bottom lip. Tried to hypnotize her with his supermodel pout. Shelby clutched her knees, bowling over with laughter. His smile faded into a confused half-frown.

"*Oh, Jake!* When I say servant, I mean you're going to *serve* me like an *ant*." Her true eyes flickered behind her mask. Jake stood up from the bed, suddenly nervous.

"Hey, it's cool! I should head back to the bus anyway." Jake looked around the Dark Bird's sandbox, not sure where to go next. "The crew's probably looking for me…"

"The crew isn't looking for you. The crew is dead. I decided to save you from that fate because I…want somebody to talk to. Somebody who likes what I like. *Sit down.*"

"Shelby, this is getting fucking weird."

"You're not leaving. *Sit down.*"

"Fuck you, bitch." The young man pushed past her, tracking the footprints of the girl in the pink dress to the magic puddle of horseflies they pooped through.

Shelby came up behind him, the corners of her lips ripping

apart. Her claws stiffened. Jake spun around and spied needles bursting through her skin. He dropped to his knees in horror.

"*I'm sorry! So sorry!*" He lifted his hands in a truce, whimpering. "I'll be your servant. *Whatever. Just stop that shit!*" He pointed at the mask falling off her ghoulish grin.

Shelby flexed her claws and raked a nearby column. **Swick!** Chunks of rock from deep, hot scratches landed in the koi pond with a fizzle. When Dark Bird settled, her lips knitted together with scaly sinew. The bristles that broke through her pores retreated, leaving behind thousands of tiny red droplets on her skin. Her plume became raven hair again. And the girl in the denim miniskirt and the tattered tank top still held fury in her eyes. "Look what you made me do," she growled. "I'm all a *mess.*"

Jake followed her gaze to a nearby towel draped over a bongo drum. "I know! I'll clean you! *Don't worry.*"

"Thank you, Jake." Shelby looked indifferent as he gently dabbed her bloody body with fresh spring water. It felt nice to have Jake around. Shelby might keep him forever.

Or not.

The road to Orphan Rock had clogged up with traffic, but with Coyote's newly found leadership, the cars started moving again. A couple of Sturgis Fall Saints stood at the property entrance checking in visitors. Another roughneck Saint helped park their cars in the fields, guiding the curious into tight rows like an air traffic controller. While guests unpacked their suitcases and backpacks, he pointed all new visitors to the freshly spruced-up visitor's center—free lemonade AND fresh baked cookies.

Shelby and Jake passed out maps, urging folks to walk into Orphan Rock to visit the Chapel on the Mound as soon as they settled in. People traveled from across the nation to receive a special blessing from the Jesus Man himself, and the line of miracle seekers stretched down the river rock path.

"There's plenty of space available," Shelby said. "Take a map. Bunk up. First come, first serve for the cabins. Newly renovated. Welcome, seekers. Plenty of room for camping."

She watched Jake hand out fliers too.

The young man was teachable and obeyed.

Power was fucking easy, wasn't it?

And humans so meek.

Just tell them what to do, and they do it.

Esther worked the line at the Chapel on the Mound. She kept the beefiest Sturgis Saint at the doors. The walkie-talkie on her hip crackled with problems she always had a solution for. Felt good to be needed. Turns out, she was pretty damn good at making decisions and bossing people around. It was *almost* like she didn't grow up in a cage. Almost.

"Only one at a time to see the goddamn Minister," she told the pressing crowd. "No cutting in line. Heaven's not going anywhere. Neither is he."

Face by face, people filed in.

More kept coming.

Always more.

It seemed like everybody on God's Green Earth wanted inside the dirtiest old church in America. Nobody cared that nobody who walked in ever walked out again.

Minister thundered and flopped at the podium, a wily prop wearing a holy man's razor wire crown. He fucked and preached and fucked some more while preaching. He bled rust on the thirsty. He sprayed cum on the hungry. His left arm hung limply at his side, black roots bursting from his fingertips, searching for the soft, hungry soil of the Mound to fertilize with faith.

He just needed more.

And he took them—more—sucked them—more—ate them—more—let himself slip into their minds and bodies— more—and he carved out all of the juiciest sufferings he could find for himself. Then, when they were free from sin, guilt, and pain, he scooped dirt into their mouths. The Grim Seed changed them quickly, its dark spores paralyzing free will and spreading thoughtless euphoria throughout their bodies. His flock of husks moaned and screamed in tongues, releasing themselves from a lifetime of burdens and suffering in a ravenous orgy of joy.

Some rolled in the mud like catfish. Others stood still and rubbed their dicks with dead eyes. When they were empty and saved and ready to be delivered, Snarl and his henchmen led them into The Dark so Delora could treat them properly.

More.

More.

More.

"*Whiskey!*" Minister bellowed.

The Spider Girl lowered a bottle of rye whiskey from the webspun rafters. He took a long swig, hissed, and shouted **hallelujah!** Whiskey splashed all over his bloody face, and he felt clean again. He had no pupils anymore—just pools of rotten, reddish muck that looked like wet paint, and the maggots that fell from his nose landed on the backs of the broken he saved.

Another day of rain.

Desyre planned on leaving Kilgore City now that the pantry was bare. She uttered details that Nicholas scribbled on a notepad like a trained seal. Cobra was bored to death and ignored them. He watched the rainwater trail down the penthouse window instead. He admired how the droplets zig-zagged, merged, and channeled along the glass. Little rivers cutting their own paths.

He looked at his reflection. His silhouette was blurry. He

could see Desyre and Nicholas standing behind him more clearly than he could see himself. After a moment, it was only the slender frame of the blind man looming behind him.

Cobra turned around.

"Something up?"

"I regret to inform you that Our Everything no longer enjoys your company. You lack the gratitude she requires to move forward. Your service to her is no longer required."

"You mean…I'm free?"

"No, I'm sorry. That was never on the table."

Before Cobra could stand, the rip opened beneath him. Fierce salamander claws pulled him into a hole of static.

The Crooked Woman watched rows of Broken Kids march the empty husks through The Dark. They followed obediently, dirt on their tongues, minds enthralled by the Grim Seed. Vile Minister gathered all the water from the harvest, and she sowed the seeds in the eldritch crater of the Heart of the Desert.

The Age of Filth had begun, and Dark Bird's plan: a smashing success. The harpy's black tongue scraped along her dead lips like pulled Velcro. It was nearly time.

Snarl looked up from her hand. His scabby face twisted by concern. "Mother? *Are you sure about this plan? There are risks to defying Baby Bird. She will not be pleased…"*

Thwack! Snarl dropped to his knee, white pus and purple blood gushed through his wire-wrapped fingers. Delora flicked his skin from her fingertips and said no more to him.

Macho drove down the opposite side of the road, passing by hundreds of faces in cars—white, brown, and black. Old people. Couples. College kids. Children.

The fucking children haunted him most.

He saw her in the backseat of every car that passed. The little girl in the mouth of the monster. The horrifying way her eyes quivered when she realized she was being eaten alive. The soft **snap** of her neckbone. He punched the steering wheel.

This was going to end badly.

There was no doubt in his mind now.

So many happy faces drove toward certain oblivion— white, brown, and black. Not red, though. For that small blessing, Wallace Machado could breathe a little.

Chad Ryan

15.

Vengeant stood in Sister Dirt's tall mirror. Liz from Oklahoma was no more than a stranger to her now. A small piece in the larger puzzle. Whispers of Liz stitched into her ghostly flesh from silky despair. Broken Girl, too, woven from bones made of splintered cactus ribs with fingers like scimitars. Her body was bulky like a golem, broad of shoulder and back. The metal braces on her legs were shaped from gold. Eyes, the color of dying fire, sat beneath the porcelain skull of a broken-horned bull. Vengeant flickered before her maker, all shapes combined—girl, broken, and a scarecrow—into a new and ferocious beast. *Vengeant.*

Sister Dirt stroked the bull's horn.

"You are pieces of all things remembered. An amalgamation of the shapes written on your spirit." The harpy admired her phantasmal kachina doll. "You are nearly ready to face the Pig Father. He is more powerful now, but so are you."

"The Pig is in The Dark," Vengeant said, its voice fuzzy like static on the radio. "It tried to break through The Dark to steal away the littlest spirit. Glass protected her."

"I protected her," Sister Dirt replied sharply. "And that was not The Pig in The Dark. It was a lesser Swine. The Age of Filth has begun, and they crossover from their prison. They've long wanted another box to befoul. Pity they've come to mine."

"The Dark is a prison."

"For pigs and their ilk, yes." Sister Dirt placed her chin on her knuckle. She sighed in contemplation. "It is unfortunate things have been accelerated so quickly. This box was not supposed to be found. There are no exits here. I fear the Pig Father has compromised our location. Once The Dark spoils a box, it cannot be cleansed. The pigs will poison this garden too."

"How did he take the Lumenchild?" Vengeant wondered, watching its maker pace. "It was a god, wasn't it?"

"It hardly matters now, but the Lumenchild was to be my antidote for the Pig Father. A kinder creation for these wayward spirits to worship here. I am not interested in the devotion of children. But the children are quite insistent they needed something to worship. So, I shaped the Lumenchild to be a living deity, just as the King of Pigs was once. They are of the same design." A look of regret passed over Sister Dirt. "It was a mistake to replicate the heart of a god. There is always a hole there. A door where cunning parasites slither through."

"The Lumenchild demanded death and sacrifice, Mother Dirt. Its flock hunted and murdered wayward souls who came to this colorless world. It was not innocent."

"Alas, even in my perfect box, devotion beyond compassion ruled the day. Humans, even the spirits of humans, cannot resist their temptation to dominate in the name of a myth. It doesn't matter. They are lost already. The pigs will shackle them. Our focus must be on destroying the Lumenswine now."

"How do we defeat him?"

"I am not sure there is a way."

Vengeant's scimitar fingers flexed. "We can be strong."

"I made you brave for a reason, Child." The River Woman patted Vengeant's feathered shoulder with a flash of pride in her brunette eyes. "Gather that courage for what is to come."

"You shattered him. He can be hurt."

"The Grim Seed weakened The Pig enough to draw him out of The Dark. Once he showed his true form, he was dismembered to keep all his parts separated. Name. Heart. Shadow. A Pig is always a king weaker in pieces, you see, but clearly, it was not enough to scour him from history. He resonates with the Age of Filth, and you can't stop what is to come from that." Sister Dirt turned away from her pet and folded her arms in disappointment. "Until the little ghost found her way to him, he was nothing but a mindless shadow used to breed boonchildren for the Grim Seed. A slave whipped to build his own coffin. Through trickery and youthful naivete, his pieces found their way home. Now, he will reclaim his shadow. When that happens, he will be strong enough to perform his greatest resurrection. One he has spent centuries crawling from The Dark for."

"He has escaped, Mother Dirt. There is a door written in the sky. The littlest ghost saw it above the chapel."

"Yes, I should have known." Sister Dirt walked the ornate woven carpet before her fireplace. "As I said, I shaped the door in the river to be a one-way journey—a tunnel for the damned to escape the cruel. There was to be no exit for anyone here, including myself. This, too, was to be my final paradise." The elder harpy's expression showed more hope than was expected. "But he has revealed to us the way out! The Pig predictably allows arrogance to reveal his secrets. What was hidden is now found. His door! So, we will work together to follow him through it. You will hunt the Lumenswine while I prepare for the events to come." Vengeant stood perfectly still while the tip of the harpy's sharp finger carved a sacred symbol into the dome of her bull's skull. "Know that I have paid dearly to see him suffer. And I will not stop until misery is a machine, Vengeant. Do you understand me? Suffering is our salvation too. We must fight for justice."

"Yes, Mother Dirt. I will hunt him. I will kill him."

The harpy grinned, the corners of her painted lips ripped a little, struggling to keep her widening smile hidden. She dabbed the blood from her mouth. "Go then. Play with your form. Feed on those who brought malice into my box with their zealous intolerance. Practice on their corrupt shapes. If they ask you why you are killing them, tell them you are an angel, and the Creator has deemed them unworthy of living in this unlife. Then, go to the Chapel on the Hill. Your final boon is there."

Passengers in idling cars gave the chief of tribal police the stink eye when Wallace Machado cut the line at the cattle gate leading to the Ghost River Revival. Esther stood on the other side of the Blazer, arms crossed over her tank top, scowl planted firmly on her face. A couple of leather-vested goons hovered behind her, keeping suspicious and steady eyes on Johnny Law. Judging by their various tattoos, Macho could tell they were hardened men, perhaps even gang members. Clearly racists. But that was the least shocking and dangerous thing about them.

"Spit it out, man." Esther put her hands on her hips. "As you can plainly fuckin' see, we're busy today."

Chief Machado handed her an official notice.

"We're shutting it down. All of it."

Esther briefly studied the paper. Made absolutely no sense to her. "Too many words. What's it say?"

"Notice of eviction. Court-ordered. You've got twenty-four hours to remove all non-residents from Orphan Rock. Which, by the way, is everybody squatting on that property that's human and alive, excluding you. This circus is over." He took a step closer to his ex-lover and lowered his voice, "Listen to me. The council seeks a peaceful resolution to this. That Dark Bird is putting us all in danger with this shitshow. Our neighbors in Sandoval are getting rightly uneasy about folks coming out here to do God knows what. Shut it down before things escalate."

"People have the right to practice religion. Don't you skyreaders know that?"

"Esther, whatever it is you're up to needs to stop."

"Up to?" Esther put an unlit cigarette between her lips. "If you and the council are so fucking concerned about what we're up to, why don't you come on in and see for yourself? We've got nothing to hide here, Chief. You've seen all our cards."

Macho shivered uneasily. "That won't happen."

"Oh, that's right. You're scared." She cupped her hand and lit her smoke. She exhaled into the wind.

"This isn't a game. I know you don't know much about the world outside of this barbed wire fence, but I'll tell you how it works. You have *exactly one* opportunity—this opportunity—to undo this mess. Send these folks home. Keep the TV cameras away. Then, live the rest of your life with the cadavers you choose to, in quiet. That Dark Bird gets paid, the Crooked Woman gets fed, and you can play the fool all you want out here in No Man's Land until the day you die. It's time to put your thinking cap on, Esther. Don't care how powerful you think that Sister of Sorrow is, but she won't last long with the National Guard breaking down your brittle little doors. Clear them all out. Twenty-four hours. I'll be by tomorrow, and I expect to see these roads clear."

"Oh yeah? We're exercising our right to peacefully ensemble, *you prick!*"

"*Assemble,* and you have a lovely day, Mrs. Northamm." Officer Machado politely tipped his hat and walked back to his SUV without looking back to see Esther fuming.

Techno music wobbled the rivets in Desyre's pantry. Strobes flashed. A disco ball rotated above, casting white twinkles on a shit-stained floor. The salamander liked her food strung out and sleepless. She'd say that tortured meat was more tender. He'd walked through the kennels hundreds of times on his way to her secret garden. After a while, Cobra got used to the moaning, the sickness, and the horrid smell. Now, he was the one in the cage.

He wondered what offense finally drove Our Everything to this conclusion. Maybe it was always going to be this way with a dominant like her. She was ambitious, liked to keep the world on its toes. But he had only ever served her since she stole him from Ghost River. He followed the rules, kept her foodbank filled, and pleasured her with his company. He bled for her, had scars from her, and never asked too many questions. So why kill him off now? Had Gunner asked the same question years ago?

Maybe there weren't no good answers, he thought. Creatures like Desyre and Delora played by their own set of rules. Managed powers and concepts larger than he could catch in his mind for more than a second. They valued service and obedience. Cobra gave them *and* his childhood to Desyre. He did the worst things for her, only to be betrayed. Maybe he was the dumb one. He'd seen her operations shrinking over the years. She used to surround herself with devotees, but they all slowly vanished from the inner circle, until it was only him and Nicholas left.

Soon, it would be only Nicholas.

On cue, the blind man stepped through the portal. They'd been partners for three years. Cobra had even considered them to be friends. The thin man in the suit said nothing and walked over to the hose, unraveled some, and handed the spout to his prisoner.

"Drink, if you care to."

The boy in the kennel leaned in and lapped from the cool stream. When he finished, the man with the cat-eye tattoos on his eyelids looped the hose back on the hook.

"How long do I have?" Cobra asked.

"My Everything ate a few nights ago. It won't be long until she hungers again."

The captive snake poked his fingers through a hole in the kennel. "Does she always do this?"

"Do what, Cobra?"

"Kill off the talent? First Gunner. Now me."

"I do not question Our Everything. She always makes the

right choice. She is wiser than I will ever be."

Cobra laughed bitterly. "Well, who's going to fill the kennel when I'm gone? Don't seem wise to kill off your only snake. I'm the pied fucking piper, man, and you know it."

"My All will provide the perfect strategy." Nicholas paused to explore a strange thought. "You know what, Cobra? I think your troubled family inspires her in some peculiar way. They've proved there are new ways to hunt without stealing. People will give themselves freely if you build a better box to entice them." Nicholas sighed. "I will admit, I've traveled with Our Everything for many years, and this box will be hard to leave. I've grown fond of the cosmopolitan lifestyle."

"Oh, yeah? *Fuck the city.*"

"Well, you won't have to endure it much longer, I suppose." Nicholas pulled open the doorway to Desyre's secret garden, and Cobra could see the Havenarchs flapping amongst the fireflies in the trees. The bald skeleton grinned eerily. "I can only offer you this advice. Close your eyes. Fill your mind with images of the blessed salamander. She will bring you comfort during your final hours. Anticipate her hunger. *Her saliva wetting you.*"

"Let me talk to her, Nick. At least give me the chance!"

The slender man stepped through the door without saying another word. ***Bam!*** Cobra kicked the wall of the kennel.

Esther looked mighty peeved this morning. Shelby groaned and pulled a pillow over her head to see her caretaker coming down the dunes, grumbling about something. Always too early when the shit tide rolled in from Orphan Rock. She held a piece of paper and stomped past Jake, who was chained to a nearby column in the veranda. He curled up on an ornate rug like a Persian cat. When he lifted his teary eyes to say meow, Esther shook her head and marched over to Dark Bird's waterbed.

"We need to talk."

"Jesus. Can it wait?" Her daughter sat up, raven-blue hair staticky from the pillow. She was wearing both an oversized black Stone Temple Pilots t-shirt and a frown this morning.

"No, it fucking can't wait." Esther handed her the notice. "The Injuns are making a move against us. Macho says we got twenty-four hours to vacate Orphan Rock."

Shelby yawned. "Or what?"

Esther considered it, frowning. "Can't tell you for certain, that son of a bitch Machado said that Sandoval wants to bring in the goddamn marines. Says they'll force us out."

Shelby rolled over. "Ignore it."

"Really?"

"What can they do to us? What would be worth the price of crossing me? The council wouldn't dare."

"The casino, maybe?"

Dark Bird chirped with laughter. "As if! They operate at my pleasure. Destroying that flappy tent would be too easy. The skyreaders knows what I'm capable of. They fear it."

"So, we're ignoring the notice then? Can we do that?" Esther paced, torn in two. A bad feeling she couldn't shake lingered in the pit of her gut. "I know Macho won't send any of his people on the property. They're scared of us. But, what about the National Guard? Can we just…ignore them too?"

"Totally. We can do that. They're bluffing anyway. Seeing if we are weak enough to jump at every shadow that says *boo*." Shelby reached for the electric guitar she kept next to her bed. She crossed her legs and plucked out the first few chords of "Today" by The Smashing Pumpkins. She glanced at Jake, pride in her masked eyes. "See, Jake? I'm a quick learner."

"You sure are, My Excellence."

"*Eminence.*"

"Right. My Eminence." Jake bowed and wiped the sweat from his brow. "Sorry." The chain around his throat rattled.

Shelby blew a kiss in his direction. "So sweet."

Esther kept milling around. A storm gathered in her head. Shelby noticed and didn't like it.

"What else, Coyote? Cat got your tongue?" She smiled at her new pet again. "Speaking of, Jake, should I pierce my tongue? I think it might look cool…"

"So cool," Jake said, his voice cracking a little. "Can I have water now? Maybe some food? I'm so hungry."

"I don't know, Shelby." Esther exhaled, trying to find the words to match her anxiety. "This feels like the start of something bad. I have this instinct. Call it maternal or fucking genetic or whatever, but I have it. I know when stuff ain't sitting right. I got that feeling now. It's because I'm a mother, maybe."

"*Gawd.* What is your point?"

"My point is that you put me in charge of the compound for a reason. Made me a leader just like Eugene used to be for the fuckin' asshole Pig Men. Thing is, Eugene used to get bad feelings, too, and they were usually right. Sometimes, he wanted to talk them out with people he trusted. He did that before bad feelings for him became big fucking problems for everybody else in Orphan Rock. He used to have meetings called war rooms to work out plans. Maybe we should do something like that?"

"War room?" Shelby put down the Stratocaster and beamed. "That sounds *fucking metal*, Esther! Yeah. Let's have a *war room*. But let's make it for after eleven, OK?"

Vengeant's claws sparked on the rocks. On all fours, she ran like a mountain lion, tearing through the hueless barrens at blazing speed. She weaved through the electric tendrils of the floating jellyfish creatures that moaned above. The golden braces on her legs pumped like pistons, and she felt like a launched rocket with limitless fuel. Whatever Mother Dirt carved into the bone of her skull granted her the power to change forms. Now, she felt more like a proud lioness than a child. And whatever she felt, her form became. Her boon was shapeshifting.

Vengeant was a vigorous, amorphous creation. She felt connected to the application of her body. The tools to inflict carnage all made sense, but she did not feel a connection to what she was, or who. That information was pure static. With nothingness came little burden to care.

Or question. She had her commands.

Find The Pig.

The Other Siders saw the phantasmal feline gunning for them—a missile of claws and fangs—and she aimed for their makeshift barricade at the cattle gate.

"Shoot it!" one of the desertbillies shouted, pointing at the ghostly streak of light blazing toward them.

His partner snapped up his rifle just in time for four knives to swipe across his torso. The gun hit the ground, and so did his twitching arm. Before he could scream for help, Vengeant punched a hole through his face. Blue and gray brain matter shot across the gravel drive leading up to the stone-stacked house. Chunks of smoky goo landed with fat *splats.*

"Get away, *filthy abomination!*" His partner sprinted toward town for help, waving his straw hat wildly in the air. Before he got too far ahead, Vengeant pounced. His head hit a rock, and she pressed him so deep into the dirt his neck snapped.

Crack!

Crack! Crack!

A bullet struck her in the leg, tearing through her shifting form, passing through a thigh stuffed with nothing but smoky scarecrow hay. She roared and bared her teeth at the dim sky, howling not from displeasure or pain. Her cry came from a different place. The place where you can't feel any pain at all. The *real* Other Side of things where you go to disappear.

Vengeant lowered her bull horns and buried her razor toes in the dirt. She aimed herself at a group of Other Siders, including Norman and Pilgrim, who ran toward town with their rifles blasting against their shoulders. She charged after them, slicing through the dry air, dodging bullets, and closing the gap. The men shrieked as she tore them down. One by one, they fell in tatters.

Practice with your new form.

The last defenders gathered in front of the Chapel on the Hill. Pilgrim and a group of brutes had set up another shitty barricade in front of the porch. They stood behind plywood wrapped in barbed wire, rifles at the ready. Her fire-kissed eyes didn't blink when she approached them.

"*What are you?*" Pilgrim glared at the shifting beast. "What do you want?"

"*Unworthy one,*" she replied, knife fingers scratching along the ground. "I'm here to save you from yourself."

Pilgrim laughed bitterly. "Save us? You've laid to rest some of my best men. Now you're standing in front of our sacred church. Blood drips from your fangs like a vampire."

"The Creator is not pleased with you. You've betrayed her vision with your intolerance and cruelty."

"Vision? What vision is that?" Pilgrim glanced around the pleasant town square. "We've kept order for her, built a nice life for ourselves here, and served our godchild well. The Creator may have opened the door for us, but we, the Chosen, have made supple the land. Kept our paradise pure from maledictions." He turned to his men, who steadied their weapons. "Let us have our church in peace. All our people are inside. Women. Children. *Orphans.* Would you suffer the meek and innocent?"

Vengeant stepped toward the holy man.

Norman pulled the bolt on his rifle.

"Your paradise is lost," Vengeant declared. "The Dark is here. The Pigs stir below the crust of the soil. Your deaths are mercy that you do not deserve, yet I will deliver you."

Her knife fingers glistened in the gray sun.

"Shoot!" Pilgrim yelled.

Crack! Crack! Crack! Crack!

When the smoke from their muzzles faded, Vengeant stood before them unscathed. She faced Pilgrim, the holy man who led a regime of cruelness and intolerance in the name of some false purity they invented to create power. If you did not look like them, you were food. These ghosts forgot where they came from, didn't they? Rescued as children from a life of slavery and oppression only to bring it here to fester was malpractice. Mother Dirt was right. These were the sorts of dangerous thinkers that did not deserve an eternity of existence on any Side.

Bam!

Her sweeping kick landed like a thunderclap, and the crude blockade collapsed on top of the foolish men who built it. They cried for mercy, buried beneath a woodpile and tangles of razor wire. The more they struggled, the more their skin sliced open. Fish caught in a nasty net, already cleaned by unforgiving blades. Luminous blood spilled on the grey, cracked mud.

Pilgrim gasped like a crawbaby, his eyes losing their ethereal glow. "Why…did you do this to us?"

"All that I do, I do for Mother Dirt."

At high noon, the Ghost River Revival war room convened in the Chapel on the Mound.

"Nobody gets in here until we're finished," Esther instructed her biker muscle at the door. She scanned the long line of desperate people, ready to lay their sins down at Minister's dirty feet. "Not one fucking person who wants to live bothers us." She flicked her cigarette butt. "This is a sacred thing we're up to in here, and I don't want any fucking about. You hear me?"

The Sturgis Fall Saint nodded and folded his arms.

"Good," she said, shutting the door and twisting the deadbolt.

Inside the sanctuary, Broken Kids scuttled around like busy ants, dragging the rest of the dead and the mostly dead husks into The Dark. Minister was lying on top of the Mound, beneath the Dead Tree. Tiny black filaments wriggled from his cheek, needling into the acrid dirt like wily whiskers. He wore cheap, crooked sunglasses while pumping misery into the soil in waves.

He smiled to see her take the podium.

Delora and Snarl haunted the shadows. The Crooked Woman held his puffy hand while the boy wrapped in barbed wire watched Esther with some amusement. Esther knew he expected her to trip on her own dick, and she wouldn't give him the pleasure of that happening. Not today.

Shelby lounged in the middle of the chapel, already bored, smoking with her oxblood boots propped up on the pew in front of her. She stared up at the ceiling, watching Spider Girl play with a dead toddler for a doll. Jake tended to her like a good servant, waited on the blood-soaked ground at her feet, rolling the head of one of his supervisors with shaky fingers.

Somewhere in the nave Courtney Philbin, Action 10 News Reporter, scrounged through heaps of defiled bodies, collecting pretty bones to put in her mouth.

This was a fine council, Esther thought. *Good as any Eugene ever gathered. Better, probably.*

"Listen up! I call this war room to order!" Coyote smacked her palm on the pulpit. Once the crowd settled in, watched her with curious eyes, she began, "First things first, I want to congratulate myself for not killing nobody the last few days. It weren't easy getting everybody into all them cottages and tents, all right? So, thank me very fucking much." Esther paused, waited for nobody to clap. "Second, the riverfolk gave us twenty-four hours to vacate the land. *Our land.* They're trying to shut us down."

Delora wheezed.

"Mother wants to know if they still live. If so, why is that?"

"They live because I say so," Dark Bird replied, casting a nasty look at Snarl. "I told Coyote to ignore the order. We've got the power here. What can they do to us?"

"Close the roads," Minister said quietly from the Mound. He stretched his arms outward. "That's how they used to choke Eugene out. They'll close the goddamn roads, and then they'll send the campers home. If there's resistance, they'll tap the feds to help them clean up. That means bullets and bombs."

"*The feds?*" Shelby snorted, rolling her eyes at the idea. "The riverfolk don't have the balls."

"That's where you're wrong, Dark Bird," Minister continued. "They won't have a choice when it comes down to it. They need Sandoval more than they need us. The riverfolk ain't dumb. They understand where their future is. Hard pill for them, but they swallowed it. No choice, really. Hard to say no with a gun to your head and your children lined up next."

"Bullshit. *They do what I say.*"

"Not now." Minister peeled himself from the dirt. The black roots wriggling through his cheek slithered back into their pores. A cloud of horseflies descended upon him. The holy man limped next to Esther. He gestured to the pulpit, a request for permission from the Boss Lady of Orphan Rock. She nodded and made room for him to lean against the dais. "Listen now, because I don't know how much longer I'll be able to tell you what I know about life in words that make any sense, but I'll try. I've dealt with the tribe a long time. They don't want us endangered.

"Believe it or not, they used to protect us. Helped us put a lid on 1973 when Eugene died, and Delora ordered the slaughter of the pigs. For those of you too young to remember," Minister looked at Shelby, "there was a shit ton of corpses we had to make go away. I had to become their man after that. I was glad to, really. They're good people, and we're their scar too."

"They treat us like garbage," Shelby said, rolling her eyes again. "You're just a sentimental corpse."

"Sometimes, they do. But what relationship is always roses and bouquets? Them riverfolk have always known the trouble with this land. They don't like it, but its their trouble too.

And they don't like showing it off, neither. That's where we're fucking with them, see? We're forcing them to flip over the rock beneath which we all fucking live. Where the biggest worms are kept. Them suburban folk in Sandoval don't much like looking at our scrapyard from their pretty balconies, do they? Cause trouble, and we might as well light ourselves on fire because scrutiny is the fuckin' calamity that we can't survive." Minister eyed his wife, put his dead hand on top of hers. "You remember that city councilman years back? The one with his maps and future plans?" Esther nodded. Mr. Davis. Seemed like yesterday. "Well, it's the fuckin' future now, and it was never gonna be for us."

Dark Bird slapped the pew in frustration. "Jesus, this is fucking tedious." She glared at Delora. "How long until this goddamn Grim Seed is watered? That's all we need to worry about, right? All this history and bullshit is for the birds. I mean, figuratively speaking. I really don't give a fuck."

"Hard to judge," Snarl said. "Three or four days at the pace we're going, but things are happening now. The earth is spoiling at an accelerated pace. Transformation is nigh."

Shelby smirked at Delora. "You're fucking welcome, *Mother*."

"Don't get cocky, Dark Bird," Snarl warned. "We're not ready for war yet."

"So what? War doesn't happen fast. There's a lot of bullshit before the bombs drop." She paused to let Jake light her cigarette. "The way I see things, we have to hold them off for a few more days. At the rate we're saving souls, we'll have it wrapped up by the weekend." Shelby turned back to the pulpit. "I think we can manage that. Right, Coyote?"

"Maybe. But we need to move faster," Esther replied, taking back the pulpit. "Macho made it clear. We don't have three or four days before the Injuns pull the plug. Twenty-four hours is what we got. We need to let as many people as possible in before they shut down the roads. Otherwise, we may not gather enough to water the Seed. We won't get a second chance."

Shelby cast a bitter look at Minister.

"In other words, less fucking and more sucking." She settled on Esther again. "You think the human carrot can handle it? Doesn't look like he's holding up very well."

Minister wobbled next to her. Blood, dead crickets, and crusty cum caked his beard. "I'll be *just fine*, don't you worry about me," he said. "I was *built* for this moment."

Esther squeezed his hand. "Next, I think we need to take our message straight to the people. Freedom of religion is a hot fucking ticket. Where's that newswoman?"

"In The Dark, pigs bite you before they suck on your tits," a demented voice squeaked from the shadows. Courtney Philbin peeked over a splintery pew. She pinched a fat scorpion by its barbed tail and let it scramble on her tongue. When she let it go, it skittered down the dark hole of her throat.

"What do you think, News Lady?" Esther called out to the husk in the back. "Your bosses at the network willing to air some of the good work we do here?"

"Sure thing, chicken wing! It's all spectacle and bullshit anyways!" Courtney opened her arms in bliss before disappearing behind the pew again to eat more bugs.

"All right then," Esther replied, feeling more confident than before. "We're going to pick up the pace before they close off the roads. Save as many lost souls as we can, fast as we can. We'll use the power of television to slow things down, gum up the cogs, and try to buy us some time with the Injuns."

"That's the spirit!" Shelby clapped her knees and plopped her boots down on the bloody floor. "So, are we good here? Do we have a plan? All of this strategy is making me hungry."

"Almost," Esther replied. "One more issue we need to address before it's too late. We're dealing with Injun cops at best, federal agents at the shit end of things. We're talking SWAT teams, helicopters, armored men with lots of—"

"Guns," Minister answered.

"Right." Esther gave the holy man a wink. "*Guns.*"

Grim but resolute, the slender man in the pinstripe suit appeared in the red dungeon. He flipped the switch on the wall, and the brain-punching techno beats and eye-melting lights ceased in the pantry. "My All has decided to dine on snake this evening," he told the prisoner. "Are you ready to nourish her?"

Cobra lifted his head from his knees, and his bangs fell over his cobalt eyes. "So, she isn't willing to talk, huh?" He looked at the ceiling. "Guess I'm fucked."

"It is not for us to question how nature chooses to sustain itself." Nicholas walked over to the wall and grabbed a metal collar and chain leash. "You will die so that she will live. This is as it was always meant to be. A perfect circle."

The electric prod crackled a warning in his hand. A spark that could drop a wild horse flickered in a flash of blue.

Nicholas tossed him the collar. No need for instructions. Cobra knew the routine. He clasped it around his neck, felt it tighten around his Adam's apple.

"That's a good snake." The blind man fed the leash through the small window of the kennel. "Put that on."

The snake obeyed, clipping the carabiner to the metal loop of his collar. ***Click!*** "Happy now?"

"Always, with Desyre." Her goon selected the right key to his kennel. He unlocked and opened the door cautiously, holding the electric prod in one hand while keeping the boy to heel with the other. With a snap, Cobra stumbled out of the cage.

"Take off your clothes and grab the rings."

The boy's spine popped into alignment when he stood tall, and his quads flexed. Felt like heaven standing up again after all that time spent balled up in a shoebox.

"Hurry now," Nicholas warned.

Cobra undressed, revealing a body that was a mural of Desyre's appetites for torture, bondage, and violence. His hands slipped through the metal rings bolted to the concrete wall. He dropped his head, waiting for the high-pressure blast of the hose to bite into his body. The artic water stung, but Cobra didn't care. *Everything is so numb anyway.* He listened to instructions. Raised his arms when told. Soaped his body when told. Said nothing and spun in place for a spritz when told. After he rinsed off, he dropped the bar of soap. Nicholas tossed him a zip tie for his wrists.

"Nice and snug now," he said, secret eyes twitching behind his inked eyelids. His prisoner threaded his hands through the thick loop. He raised them for inspection.

"Little help?"

"Use your teeth. When it's tight enough, I'll pull it the rest of the way."

Cobra bit into the cord and tugged it along his cheek until the tie cinched around his wrists. He showed his work. When he was satisfied the desert boy was contained, Nicholas took a step closer and grabbed the loose end of the tie.

"Good enough," he said, testing it with a savage yank

The boy flinched. "Seems so, man. *Real tight.*"

Naked, clean, and ready for dinner, Nicholas gathered Cobra's leash. Before he opened the hidden door to the emerald gardens, he stopped and faced his young associate. He offered the tiniest of smiles. "You weren't terrible to work with, Cobra. I should say that. I enjoyed your company for the most part."

"Thanks, buddy. I tried to please her, you know?"

"We do our best because she is worth it."

"She sure is *something*, Nick. *Jharizhuul.*"

The blind man lifted his eyebrow but then nodded with approval. He tugged Cobra's leash toward the shimmering rip to Desyre's sanctum. The young man lowered his head, followed behind, step by step, watching intently as the squirmy, black tentacle slithered across the floor and wriggled around Nicholas' shin. By the time he sensed it, it was too late. Completely off guard, the slender man tripped, and his cattle prod swung and sparked in the air until he let it go. He did not let go of Cobra's leash, however, and when he crashed into the wall of rusty kennels and slid down to the floor, Cobra jumped on top of him, using his knees to pin his shoulders to the ground. Nicholas howled in horror as more tentacles slithered around his arms and legs and held him frozen on the piss-stained concrete. Cobra smiled.

"*No, wait! Stop!*"

It was too late. The boy hooked his thumbs into Nicholas' soft eye sockets, finally peeling open those goddamned cat eyes. What was hidden behind them turned out to be little more than black irises floating in twin seas of lumpy clam chowder. The henchman's yogurt eyes gazed at the snakeshine that cut down into his sacred mind space like a diamond laser.

Cobra was inside of him, eels snapping along the way. Alone in the most sorrowful man's windswept consciousness. He could feel Nicholas' devotion to Desyre and nothing more. No past regrets. No present worries. No future to want. It was the saddest and emptiest feeling Cobra had ever experienced: resignation of self. There was no Nicholas at all to find.

The oily tentacles kept the blind man still.

"After you release me, you're going to find Desyre," Cobra said, slowly and carefully. "You hate Desyre more than you hate yourself, and you hate yourself more than anybody. You will find her, and you will kill her, or you will die trying."

Cobra snap-tilted Nicholas' head forward. His eyeballs spilled down his alabaster cheeks like spoiled milk. No way for the salamander to bedazzle him again. When he pulled back his thumbs, the cat eyes dropped like curtain calls. Nicholas said nothing as the inky tentacles unbound him. He quickly freed Cobra from his chains, tie, and collar. Anger burnt on his gaunt face, and the snaked devotee picked up the cattle prod. He faced the rip to Desyre's garden. "My All, you've been naughty," he whispered. Sparks crackled as he dashed through the rift.

The young man quickly dressed, turned to leave the Aegis Tower, and faced the buggy eyes of the fuck-squid demon. Its fragile look was despondent as always.

"Are you leaving us?" it asked.

Cobra nodded. "Can't stay here no more."

"I serve the name. You spoke my name."

"Sorry," he said with a blush. "When I was a kid, I peeked at it before she took it from my mind. Couldn't help myself, I guess. Never told nobody. Even while she used you to hurt me. I don't like making people or fuck devils or anything else do things for me unless they want to. I don't like using slaves."

"Will you forgive me for hurting you? I serve the name. She speaks the name and is cruel to you."

"Not anymore, she ain't." The boy reached out and touched its squiggling fingers. "Thank you for helping me."

The creature stared blankly. "I am bound to serve the name. Will you take me with you?"

Cobra shook his head. "I'm sorry. Won't ever say it again. When she's gone, you deserve to be free too."

The sex demon said nothing else and disappeared into a pool of ink. Cobra sprinted in the opposite direction. He ran from the portal, out of the penthouse in the Aegis Tower, down the private elevator, and away from Kilgore City for good.

From the bus window, he watched the twinkling skyline fade away like the end credits of a sci-fi flick.

Finally, he thought, *I'm running again.*

Three trucks sped down the old road to Solemn Cave. Esther led the pack in the Blazer. She hoped these biker boys could handle themselves on the loose rock. They needed to move fast today. No mistakes. The shotgun bounced on the passenger seat next to a box of old shells. If there was trouble ahead, nobody was turning around. Sometimes it takes guns to take guns.

"The turn's coming up," she yipped into the walkie-talkie.

"*Ten-four, Coyote.*"

They wound up the serpentine road leading to the summit of the mountain across the river. Esther kept her eyes peeled for trouble near the entrance to the riverfolk's secret facility. She scoffed at seeing a newer, taller fence in place of the one she tore down years back, but surprisingly, no vehicles parked in the driveway this time. Things looked dull. Could they be so lucky?

"*Shit!*" She slammed her feet on the brakes just in time to avoid the one-way spikes installed on the road. The Blazer arched forward, and so did she until whiplash punched her back into her seat. "Close as we're getting," she told the boys on the radio. "Fence up ahead. We need a hole."

Shotgun in hand, her boots hit the dust. She walked the perimeter, looking for trouble. One of the snaked Saints used heavy bolt cutters to snip a square in the fence large enough for them to walk through carrying crates of munitions.

The gravity of what they were doing tried to poke holes in Esther's bravery. Stealing weapons from the skyreaders was an act of war. Once the Council discovered their betrayal, there'd be no way to come back from it. Decades of relations would be tossed into the fire. Not to mention, any last bit of respect Wallace had for her would burn off in the embers. That was the worst part, really. She didn't care much about the rest of it. But Macho? That was the part that still pinched her heart when she thought about their relations. He was a tender man with a good heart.

Then she thought about Minister, a husband who hadn't shared her bed since he returned a holy man from The Dark. Never *slept*. Just floated around, a spook covered in flies. He was a ghost, but real enough to her to make her feel some guilt for sharing herself with another man even while she thought him dead. A bit of anger made her tremble. *Think of all the times Minister stepped out on you! Why don't you think he'd forgive you for finding your*

*own piece of happiness? You deserve it too. Men and women ain't
so different that way. At least they shouldn't be.*

She'd be a fucking liar if she said she weren't lonely. Sure,
Minister tuned in an out like an AM radio station on the highway,
but it wasn't like it used to be. They lived in the past when he came
around, rarely spoke on the future anymore. And ever since he got
his new heart, The Pig never had his turn. That was a good fucking
thing, but…she was still lonely. Missed feeling somebody warm
next to her. Try as she might to keep her mind from it, there was
always that heavy space in her heart she carried where she
pretended to be stronger than she really was.

We all carry our burdens here.

…in the loneliest of places.

"Coyote!" a Saint called out.

She blinked away the perfect sunny afternoons in Macho's
bed. Those sacred hours spent together when The Pig's mark on
her wrist never itched. They were perfect. "What?"

"We're in."

"All right then. Let's go." Stone-faced, she led the way
into the compound. The Sturgis Fall Saints closed ranks behind
her, carrying knives and a baseball bat. "Make sure there ain't no
Injuns hiding in the bushes. Then grab everything you can." Esther
pointed back down the road toward the Ghost River Valley. "Keep
your eyes open for any company. *Got it?*"

The crowd of Other Siders—women, children,
enfeebled—fell back, surrounding the Silver Tree. Above them, a
broken rose window. Beyond that, the door where the King of Pigs
escaped through his secret keyhole out of this gray universe.

"*What is it?*" a child screamed, pointing at the shifting
creature with the molten eyes: part human, part blade, part bull
and golem and feathered eagle.

The crowd hushed and parted for her. Vengeant did not

feel the urge to hurt them. They weren't like Pilgrim and his men. She felt kindness here—tranquility in children.

A lone woman stood at the trunk of the Silver Tree. She did not step away to let Vengeant pass. Her luminous eyes locked on the shifting creature with a familiar, comfortable expression…

Home?

Something remembered.

We're not in Oklahoma anymore, are we, Toto?

The electric ripple of memory spread from the core of Vengeant's chest. All her shapes felt the tremor. The little girl inside cried **Momma!** and Stacy's ghost smiled to hear it.

"I can see you, baby."

The woman reached for the bull's skull and tried to peek at the featureless, smoky face beneath. Her eyes watered with joy. "*I can see you! I can see you, baby!*"

Vengeant did not rush to embrace her. The child in her felt love, truly, but Vengeant was not that child. Vengeant was nothing that felt sentimental at all.

"I seek the door," it said, pushing Stacy aside.

The crowd watched the creature climb the Silver Tree. Vengeant's claws gripped the bark, stripping it off as she pulled herself up branch by branch to reach the top.

Gray sun shone through the rose window. She could feel the heat on her forms. Try as she might, Vengeant could not see the door—no shimmers, no holes, or horseflies.

Had Father Pig destroyed it?

Then, there it was.

A tiny crack in the sky.

A hairline fracture too high to reach.

Why would Mother Dirt shape her without wings?

Vengeant sensed confusion in her forms and climbed down. She would return to Mother Dirt for more guidance. Her instructions were clear but also incomplete.

Go to the chapel and discover your final boon.

What boon?

Vengeant turned away from the grassy Hill and traveled back toward the door. Before she reached the pile of pews they stacked for a barricade, she felt a tug on the beaded feathers that swung on her hips. When she turned around, the mother's ghost was on her knees. She clasped her hands.

"Please, take me with you." Blue vapor spewed from her open mouth. The mist encircled Vengeant. Momma's energy flowed into her, cool and refreshing and kind. A convergence of two rivers. Her many shapes welcomed another experience to join her in their common purpose: vengeance.

The death doll opened her eyes, invigorated.

"Orphans who wish to join us in the quest for justice flow into us here. We can be the river. We can be the flood. We can be the grand destroyer. *Together we can fight The Pig!*"

Other Siders floated around her—captivated by the offer. They dropped their tools, their dresses, their false selves. They became luminous fog, too, and then they became a roaring channel of rage that surged and crashed into Vengeant, wrapping her in a growing phantasmal chrysalis that shimmered with souldust.

"I'll be patient and wait for you to be a gentleman," Shelby said, tapping her prized Doc Marten on the dirt. Jake snapped to attention and pulled back the tent flap.

"Sorry, *Excellence.*"

"Eminence."

"Right. *Fuck.* Won't happen again."

Courtney Philbin sat in a director's chair under the canopy. The make-up girl was a husk, just like the wild-eyed reporter she spread the chalky foundation on. Shelby crossed her arms over a red flannel shirt. She eyed Courtney's smeared lipstick with a frown. Her fresh lip ring protruded from her mask. "Are we going to be able to pull this bullshit off?"

"Grace and Durbin are all about it," Courtney replied, gnawing on a bloody hunk of someone. She pulled a juicy strip of flesh off the bone and held it out for the make-up girl to have a snap. ***Clink!*** Teeth retrieved the meat out of her fingers. Courtney leaned in and kissed her bloody lips. Soon they made out without consideration for their company. Shelby growled with disdain. Courtney giggled, blushed a little. "Sorry. Anytime we want to go live from Ghost River, Channel 10's in. Don't fucking worry."

"Then what?"

"What do you mean?"

"What are you going to talk about on TV?"

Courtney picked something out of her teeth with a chipped, pink fingernail. She shrugged. "Listen. *I'm a professional.* Don't you worry about it. Durbin and Grace will hand it over to me, and I'll do the news, babe. It's what I fucking do. *The news.*" She bit the make-up girl's hand, pulled off a chunk, and the make-up girl only moaned and rubbed her breasts in delight.

"Get it out of your system now, freaks!" Dark Bird snapped. "You can't act like this on camera! They'll drop a bomb on us. Then, I'll be really pissed off. You don't want that."

"No, you really don't," Jake added meekly.

Courtney grabbed the make-up girl by the waist and tugged her onto her lap. The news reporter licked a trickle of blood off her collarbone. "Who cares? I'm empty, kid. *Fuck it.*"

Dark Bird's frown deepened.

Her claws hardened.

"Bitch, *you best behave.*"

Minister really did it this time.

Took off his boots and socks and let the black whiskers crack open his scaly heels to shepherd the deluge of pain into The Dark soil. Gravity and urgency emptied his Vile Heart. Gentle tugging when the Grim Seed suckled him. A baby's lips yanking on a nipple. Except his fucking milk was foul and rancid, the liquid scum of shame, infidelity, and in one strange case, murder in the first degree. The Mound loved to drink him, and so did the Dead Tree. The more he fed it, the greedier the soil grew. Now, his feet sunk into the Mound, down past the ankles, and try as he might to pull them out, the ancient dirt would not release him.

Eugene laughed from the front row. "Ain't you a sight, boy! When you was born, I knew you'd make us proud." He reached his arm out and snaked it around Clara's bare shoulders. Her throat wound glistened like a cut melon. Her legs marred with scratches, cuts, and bite marks from a swarm of hungry pigs.

"Don't look at me, Momma," the holy man begged.

Clara's eyes hemorrhaged. Whites blood red.

"Please, Momma. Put on some clothes."

Bruisy blotches blossomed up and down her thighs.

"I didn't want to do that to you. I didn't." The holy man's lips trembled. Sweat dripped from his chin. "The voice in the mask. You had to hear it. It made you wild as a mongrel. Pushed all the wrong buttons in your mind. You couldn't say no. He'd make you feel like shit for living. Be a man. Be a god. She weren't good enough for you, dirt boy? That bitch done fucked the Pig Father. Don't you look away. Don't you fucking look away from that snatch. From where you came from. We don't get to choose who we are, but we gotta be those people anyway. Oh fuck, Momma. *Fuck, I'm so sorry.* I had to be those people anyway."

"I nabbed the guns."

Minister looked away from the empty pews, eyes dribbling mustard-colored blood. He blinked, tried to breathe. The pad of paper fell out of his shaky hands.

When she bent over to pick it up, Esther's pride melted into confusion. Minister didn't write many words. Only M+E = MISERY, over and over, until his penmanship devolved into scribbles. "Esther, I can't feel my feet..."

"*Jesus Christ.*" She covered her mouth in dread to see the

sorry state of his legs. The Mound swallowed him. He had no pupils anymore—just balls of rotten, reddish-brown cottage cheese wrapped in thin plastic. "Does it hurt?"

Minister smiled. Maggots crawled on his gums.

"So much so it feels like Heaven on Earth, baby."

The producer raised his hand.

Had a couple of fingers left for the countdown.

Courtney understood the fist.

She smiled into the camera. Dark Bird watched her from across the chapel. Her belligerent stare was accompanied by the severed head of the make-up girl. She held it up so Courtney could see her future if she wanted to be a fuck-up on live television.

"Thanks, Durbin and Grace," Courtney chimed in, composed for the camera. "We're live at the Ghost River Revival in Ghost River, Arizona. As you can see, we have unprecedented access to the phenomenon that's sweeping across…well…the globe! We're in the *actual* chapel where the faithful come from far and near for a special blessing from the Jesus Man.

"I've met folks from every corner of the country who've dropped *everything* for the chance to meet Minister Northamm. His message of freedom from pain certainly resonates in a weary nation that struggles with depression, abuse, and PTSD. In fact, it's resonated so much, the roads leading to Orphan Rock have been shut down due to traffic concerns.

"Earlier today, The Ghost River Tribal Police (with additional support from the Sandoval Mayor's office) issued an eviction notice for all non-residents of Orphan Rock by tomorrow morning. According to law enforcement, there's concern that the living conditions in Orphan Rock don't meet the standards for public safety and gathering that state health statutes require. But members of the Ghost River Revival, including Minister Northamm, believe a more nefarious purpose is at play. Religious freedom itself is at stake. Minister Northamm is the spiritual leader of Ghost River Revival, and we're grateful for his time. The Jesus Man, as the locals call him, wanted to share his perspective on the controversy. Thanks for joining our broadcast."

They propped him up with a tree stake and draped a rainbow-striped parka over his rooted body. He wore sunglasses, of course. Horseflies buzzed into the camera lens.

"Thank you for having me tonight."

"Certainly. Minister, folks want to know what you are. They call you the Jesus Man. Are you, in fact, related to Jesus Christ? Or do you share some of his faith?"

"Only in my deep love for people."

"I'd say so. You saved a woman from a psychopath. You put your hands on strangers all day long, and they report a miraculous conversion to joy. If not a messiah, what are you?"

"Just a simple man. Just want to be something you love and understand."

"Wise words indeed." Courtney put her knuckle on her chin, nodding with carefully staged contemplation. "Minister, we have reports of entire families leaving their lives to come out here to congregate and camp. Folks are concerned by that behavior. They say you're brainwashing people. Are you?"

"Me?" Minister laughed so hard he coughed up a moth. "You're the people making television. If you're looking for something that brainwashes people, I'd look in the mirror."

"So, what calls people out here, Mr. Northamm?"

"I'd say we all want to be closer to God one way or the other." He shrugged. "There's really no secret to it. Have you ever felt trapped? Full of sadness because you can't change anything in your life? Ever felt like you're living inside a snow globe that never stops shaking? Well, you aren't alone. Look at all them people who came here to meet God. They're right outside that door, waiting for their turn to be saved from themselves."

"And what does that mean exactly?"

"Well, that's the ***bleep***in' question, ain't it? It means that God isn't some fuzzy concept floating around in a skyspace made of marshmallows invented just to make you feel good for dyin'. He's in the dirt beneath our feet. We feel him bite our knees when we kneel. Ask any person in Orphan Rock if they can feel his almighty presence, and they'll all say the same damned thing: *yes, sir*. There ain't another holy place on Earth that you can come to and feel God inside of you. It's a *mystical situation here*."

"Not everybody sees it that way, Minister. The tribal council and the Sandoval Mayor's Office have issued statements condemning the living conditions in Orphan Rock. They claim there's not enough food, water, or medical capabilities to cater to this many people. What do you say to those charges? Are you at all concerned by their concerns?"

"Oh, ***bleep***ck." He waved the question off. "I say we have a bountiful river to drink from, hands to heal, and more meat than we can eat. It's all hoaxes and bull***bleep***. They play politics because scaring folks is easier than facing the truth. The good we do in Ghost River is going to change the world."

"So, you don't intend to vacate by dawn?"

"Absolutely not. This is my home."

"Minister, if things continue to escalate out here, the government of the United States may intervene. Doesn't that concern you? There are kids here. Old folks. Families."

"Listen, I welcome them to come as I welcome *all wanderers* who seek release from their bonds of suffering. I shall provide them safe harbor here."

"Thank you very much, Minister Northamm—"

"I'm not finished yet. I want to say something important to the people who are being turned away from their right to eternal salvation by scumbags with badges."

"Go ahead. Thirty seconds."

Minister looked straight into the camera.

"Don't give up, seekers! Heed your calling. Come to

Orphan Rock. Don't let them oppressors turn you away. If they take your car, walk. If they take your legs, crawl. If they take your freedom, resist. *Just come here.* Whatever way you can, come to Orphan Rock and bear witness to our *greatest miracle.*"

16.

Cobra couldn't believe how things had changed around Ghost River in just seven years. Outlet malls. Mormon temples. A shiny hospital. Middle schools and movie theaters. Best fucking Buy? The city looked like a concrete picnic blanket spread across a brown skid mark. And right at the edge of it all, Orphan Rock, just a few miles in between Sandoval and Ghost River proper.

"Pull over," he told the driver he'd snaked at the bus station. The Datsun edged off the gridlocked freeway. It idled under the blistering Sonoran sun while Cobra stepped out to survey the dire situation at hand.

Traffic backed up for miles. Both sides of the highway choked off at this point. A string of police lights stretching across the distant exit ramp spelled trouble. A team of local cops attempted to move commuters past the clot at the Ghost River Casino, but nobody was moving anywhere. A helicopter circled overhead, low enough to whip up some dust.

Worse than he thought. The situation was dissolving faster than law enforcement could handle. He knew that time was running out before the National Reserves shut down the area. State of Emergency was on the horizon.

Locals wouldn't last long in this mess.

Abandoned and forgotten, other vehicles parked at the fringes of the desert. He watched a hippie couple run across the freeway carrying backpacks, heading to Orphan Rock on foot. They left their VW bug in the middle of the road, its engine still running. All the orphaned cars and pickups created a dangerous game of *Frogger*. No wonder traffic flow stalled.

People honked. Cussed out of their windows. Middle fingers raised in rude salute. The heat intensified tempers. Behind him, a trucker jumped out of his cab and bounded over to a man in a Toyota Corolla, opened his door, and then pulled him out and began punching his face repeatedly on the concrete. His blood looked like fresh paint on the asphalt and didn't take long to boil in the heat. His wife screamed for help from the passenger seat. Help wouldn't come, however. The people were bewitched.

Cobra jogged back to the car. He reached in the backseat and grabbed his backpack and skateboard. The driver, a pretty college girl with long braids under a beanie cap, looked at him dreamily. *He was an earthborn angel with the prettiest eyes she'd ever seen.* Before he pulled his nibbling eels from her mind, he told her to turn around and drive back to Las Vegas. She said OK and merged back into the shitshow on the highway.

He tossed his pack over his scarred shoulder. It was going to be a trek to Orphan Rock for sure, but there was no other way to get there except through the desert. Unlike the rest of these tenderfeet, he was desertfolk. Never afraid to get a little sun on his scales. In fact, he'd been waiting years to feel it again.

His deck hit the pavement, and after a few hard kicks, Cobra weaved in and out of frozen traffic. He hadn't seen the news program, but he listened to the interview on the radio. Minister didn't sound very well. His voice was *unstable*. He wondered if his mother was faring any better. Probably not. The last time he saw Esther on television, she appeared much older than he remembered. Hardened, maybe. Cobra wasn't surprised. Delora never made it easy for the Orphans of Ghost River.

He wanted to get home to help them. But how?

Orphan Rock had hundreds—if not thousands—of doors that Delora and Father Pig built over the years. Finding a way in without the Crooked Woman knowing would be a challenge, if not impossible. Then, a hopeful thought, like a shooting star, streaked across his mind. Maybe with the commotion, she would be distracted enough that he could slip in without being detected.

But what if he *was* detected?

Cobra was no fool. He'd spent seventeen years living under the heel of monsters. Moreover, these monsters survived for centuries because they never got distracted from their purpose. The second he stepped foot on that property, Delora would know.

How would she respond?

Impossible to tell.

Yet, he was a snake.

She might still value *that*.

Esther leaned against a splintery fencepost waiting for Officer Machado to show up with more of his bullshit speeches and fancy legal documents. Neither of which meant a damn to her. When the police wagon pulled up, she stubbed her cigarette and told her Sturgis Saint roughnecks to stand down.

Keep the stolen rifles out of fucking sight.

Predictably, Machado greeted her with a stack of paperwork and a weary frown. "As promised, Mrs. Northamm. Eviction notice. No more warnings. Everybody needs to leave Orphan Rock *immediately*, which I know you aren't going to do, but it's real and certified now. The National Guard's been called in. Once those rough boys show up, this whole situation gets kicked up the food chain. Not even TV will save you then."

Esther smacked her lips. "You don't say?"

"Secondly, a tribal judge issued a search warrant for Orphan Rock. There's reason to believe your religious group has come into possession of unregistered firearms and munitions. This is prohibited on Ghost River lands, as you *may already know.* Firearms are not under our jurisdiction, so ATF will be handling that warrant once the crowds clear off."

Esther looked straight ahead. "Ain't that convenient. Don't get your feet dirty that way. Anything else, Officer?"

Macho's granite jaw clenched tight as a fist. He exhaled through his nose. "I want to talk to you in private," he said, casting a frustrated look at Esther's henchmen. "You and me."

"Why? Dark Bird handles negotiations."

"I'm not negotiating. I'm asking you *as a friend.*"

Esther considered it, then rolled her eyes with a sigh. She pressed the stack of papers into the barrel chest of one of her snaked Saints, then threw her leg over the cattle gate. She met Macho in the center of the dirt road in a sea of abandoned cars.

"Well? Spit it out so we can both get on."

Macho took off his hat. He ran his hands over his scalp, searching for the right words to say. Finally, he spoke, "You've always been above the law with me, Esther Northamm."

"That's on you, *chief.*"

"You're not wrong, but you're not right, either."

"So?" Esther looked up, saw that helicopter flying above again. "What do you want to say, Macho? There's a camp full of needy people who need my tending to."

"*I warned you, goddammit.* Told you to keep that Dark Bird on a leash. Now that Lazarus man of a husband of yours kicked the hornet nest this time. Gave permission to disregard law enforcement, and now I got a desertful of belligerent assholes screaming about religious freedom. I know that isn't him, Esther, and you do too. How can you let him keep on like that?"

"My marriage ain't none of your concern."

"He's supposed to be dead, Esther. I don't know what kind of witchcraft you're playing with back there, but it isn't right. Minister was dead and gone, and you clinging to a corpse don't make it the other way. What's he doing to people?"

"That ain't your jurisdiction, either."

"He was my best friend. That ghoul sitting in that church isn't him."

"No? Then who the fuck is it?"

"Just another reason to leave Orphan Rock, that's who. *Come with me.* Turn yourself over. You're a victim of a cult. I can help you get away from all of this *death*."

"So kind of you to offer, but I ate the dirt." Esther lifted her arm, showing him The Pig's mark branded on her wrist. "I'm a monster too. I was never meant to be anywhere else than here with the rest of them monsters. What the fuck comes from dirt? I do. That's what fuckin' comes from dirt, Macho. Me."

"Just because you live with monsters, doesn't mean you have to become one. You're better than this, Esther. I've heard you talk about your dreams. They're hopeful."

"Dreaming is fucking dangerous."

"So is never dreaming at all."

Esther's gaze connected with his chestnut eyes. For a second, she wanted to say yes to his offer. To run into his arms, to kiss his lips one more time. He'd put her in that car of his, and they'd drive away from Ghost River. Far away. In the passenger seat, she'd burn to ash, free and smiling.

"Go home, Wallace. This ain't your war to fight."

She turned away.

"This will be my last appeal to you," he called after her, voice desperate and shaky. "I don't think you realize what's going to happen next. You're about to find out what the United States of Fuck You Very Much can do when it wants a piece of your homeland. Trust me, it isn't a gentle process."

Esther paused to offer him a tragic smile over her tan shoulder blade. "You've got a decent fucking heart, Macho. I hope you'll find somebody worthy of it someday."

He watched her spider over the gate, take the stack of legal documents from her goon's hand, and tossed it over her shoulder. A flock of papers flew away in the hot summer wind.

"Holy shit! Look at them all!" Shelby's bright brown eyes examined the horizon. People hiked across the open desert from Sandoval to Orphan Rock. Hundreds more, maybe even a thousand since the newscast aired. They crossed the canals. Hopped fences. Rode dirt bikes. Crawled if they needed to. They didn't carry much. Just heeded the call and came to the desert to be saved. Best of all, the frantic cops struggled to contain the influx. The rest broke through and created a metastasizing distraction that would slow their enemies down.

Dark Bird felt pride in her plan. If Minister could hold it together, they would have this Grim Seed watered in no time. Then? Then she would take Jake and get the hell out of this dusty fucking desert. Away from this sandbox. Forever. The End.

"Do they know?" the intern asked.

"Know what?"

"Why they're coming here?"

Shelby laughed. "They watch TV and they do what they're told. The brighter the fire, the more moths slip into the flame." Speaking of, she turned to let Jake light her cigarette. At least he had improved in that department. Her eyes caught unwanted movement in the distance. *"What the hell?"*

A Broken Kid on all fours scampered around the workshop. They weren't supposed to be out. Delora promised her that they would operate in secret to avoid *disruptions*.

"Excuse me," Shelby said, rolling her eyes.

She jogged after the dead child.

Jake scrambled to keep up with her.

The back of the workshop in the scrapyard was a jumble of wooden pallets and old spools of rusty chain-link fence. Dark Bird sniffed and caught the scent of muddy death nearby. She pulled aside a wooden pallet, revealing a hole that led into the open desert. Finally, a secret door hidden in plain sight.

"Wait for me in the visitor's center," she commanded Jake, who said OK, holding the pallet as Dark Bird crawled underneath it and through the fence. She kept her nose on the scent and raced along a crude pathway that led to the Old Sinkhole.

What are you up to, Mother?

Didn't take long for Dark Bird to find out. Gathered around the bottomless pit, a handful of Broken Kids led by Potato Sack heaved large piles of corpses into the gorge. One by one, butchered men, women, and children fell into the dark hole in the ground without a peep. Another couple of Broken Kids deposited more bodies from a wheelbarrow into the growing fly pile. The air smelled rotten, like old meat. For the first time, Dark Bird was too nauseous to think about eating. That mattered.

What were they doing?

Why kill and not eat the food?

The husks were supposed to be kept in The Dark.

Nothing made sense. This was a breach of the plan. Shelby felt like an asshole believing that Mother would keep her word. History proved that Mother only ever did what Mother wanted. She should have known better than to trust that old hag.

"*Errgghhh,*" a Broken Kid hissed. It gurgled and watched her with oily eyes near the bush she crouched in.

Her claws wrapped around its stitched neck, and she pulled its gagging face close to hers. She burrowed into its shallow eyes. "*What are you hiding from me, Mother?*"

The Broken Kid gasped as Delora retreated from his cracked mind with any answers. Caught red-handed.

Onyx wings lifted from Dark Bird's shoulders when she transformed into the harpy. She broke the dead child's neck and threw him into the Old Sinkhole from her cover in the bushes. The rest of Delora's minions stopped working when they saw one of their own tossed into oblivion. A great black bird rose from the brush, and Dark Bird swooped overhead.

She shot into the air like a rocket—up, up, up—then looped over the Old Sinkhole like the Red Baron.

The darkness of the pit gaped below her. There was only one way to see what that old crone hid beneath the surface of things. So, Shelby plunged headlong into the Deepest Door.

Cobra kicked up his skateboard near the barricade at the Ghost River exit. He counted no less than seven police cruisers parked on the off-ramp. They turned away people who tried to get off the freeway and searched vehicles at an official checkpoint.

Guess I'll have to go on foot from here.

He climbed over the cement partition of the highway and shuffled down a steep hill into a ravine. The crunchy gravel under his feet felt like an old friend. He could take the riverbed for a mile or two to the Orphan Rock Casino. Then he'd have to find a way to cross over into Delora's country. After that, he'd be *home*.

He looked at his skateboard. The gift Desyre gave to him when he was a child. The painted cobra was faded, but the young man had kept the rest of it in tip-top shape. Wheels. Oiled bearings. It seemed like a childish thing to cling to in the desert. Just like the name Cobra. It wasn't who he was anymore. Maybe he never was anything more than Little Snake after all.

Markus spun in place and tossed the skateboard down the riverbed with a howl—it cracked and splintered on jagged stone. He would leave them behind—his board, his false name—just more layers of dead skin he needed to free himself from.

Suddenly, Markus wanted to take off his shoes to let his feet remember the kiss of the rock without barriers. He'd been bruised, broken, and cut up by Desyre for years. He remembered extraordinarily little of that suffering. But his feet—they never forgot the desert. His arches ached for dry stone and brittle brush. They cried for release, and Markus stopped to abide them.

He left his expensive skater kicks behind on a flat rock. "*Whoohoo!*"

His toes curled into the dirt, the balls of his feet springing off river rocks and ancient, cracked mud. Markus gained speed, parkouring from rock to rock. He felt freer than he had in years. Finally, he could feel his heart again. Others hiked near him, slogging to Ghost River with blank, sun-flushed faces.

At the road near the casino, he slowed down and exhaled deeply, careful to mind his position and not be seen. Spotlights, palm trees, and glittering digital signs that read: BIG WINNERS DAILY, PROGRESSIVE JACKPOTS, POKER MACHINES.

Across the street, a parking lot bustled with a bevy of black SUVs, ATF wagons, and agents wearing ballistic armor. Both cops and sheriffs came to play. Tribal police and Sandoval PD stood shoulder to shoulder at the porta-potties. On the other side of the lot in a roped-off area: television trucks, a briefing tent, and politicians standing on podiums screeching about domestic terrorists. Markus recognized a scorpions' nest of trouble when he saw one. And this nest was about ready to drop right on top of Orphan Rock and whatever remained of his family there.

This is what Desyre warned him about, wasn't it?

You can't undo exposure.

Not without a fight.

The roads leading to Orphan Rock crawled with lawmen rounding up folks. It was going to be risky as hell trying to run home in broad daylight. They'd probably shoot him.

Markus considered snaking a ride, forcing some cop or FBI agent to drive him right up to the property line. He scanned the lot, looking for a lone wolf or somebody with a passenger seat to share. But, man, there were so many of them! Talking. Waving in their cars. Smoking. Milling about, armed, and dangerous. He'd have to hide in a trunk, wouldn't he?

He didn't like the idea, but there was no other way.

Markus stood to make his move.

Then, a helicopter landed in the back lot of the casino. His plan changed in a heartbeat.

Dark Bird was nearly convinced the local legends about the old Sinkhole were true—there was no bottom—and she nearly turned back to the surface when the vibration of dimensional transition ruffled her feathers. Then, the harpy dropped into the expanse of the Heart of the Desert. A drumbeat rumbled in the massive cavern miles under the Mound, deep in the earth below Orphan Rock. The air was hot here, blowing through the cistern in waves like exhaling lungs, and steam rose from metal vents and tangles of pipe that slithered through the stone walls like serpents.

That drumbeat somewhere...

Thump. Thump. Thump.

"*You've got to be kidding me.*" Shelby drifted in circles in disbelief. More thrown away bodies fell past her, abruptly ending their long descent in the gaping metal mouth of a mechanism that hummed with sinister energy. When corpses overflowed the bin, iron jaws closed, and whatever meat was inside was chewed up and sucked away in clear tubes. Above, black tendrils squiggled from the ceiling, connecting to valves like slimy spark plugs. *It must be Minister*, she thought, feeding suffering into this grand network of corruption. A very Grim Engine indeed.

Dedicated bloodroots sorted cadavers and body parts and placed them into strange pods. There was no telling where the machine started or stopped. Organic, necrotic, and metal forces worked in unison to feed whatever rumbled around them.

Dark Bird touched down on a metal platform. She folded her wings to inspect the giant, inflamed heart that pumped Minister's black suffering through a network of arteries and flumes connected to its glass chamber. The dermis protecting the organ was translucent and thick. She put her face close to it, trying to see deeper within the balmy liquid. Floating in the quiet malaise, she could see the faint shadow of an unusual fetus—a butterfly child trapped in amber—sucking its tiny thumb in space. Shelby backed away from it, not sure if she was dreaming or not.

How does such a place exist?

Why didn't Mother tell me about this box?

Everything was patchwork—stitched together by her hand—and corrupted by the Grim Seed. A bizarre temple built from flesh and bone and summoned metal and sentient root.

But it was more than that…it was a living machine.

For what purpose, though?

The ground tremored when the large vessel moved. It rotated above her—a massive, floating disc—decorated by thousands of shimmering cocoons. Shelby flew up to observe one that swung by on an unseen conveyor system. She felt the wintry chrysalis wall and watched the strange creature within stir. Faintly glowing blue eyes peered behind folded mantis sickles.

Dizzy with questions, Shelby dropped to the platform again. Fury boiled. Her chest felt tight as a brick. The whole while Shelby had busted her ass to help Mother water her Grim Seed, Mother was busy running her own schemes.

What the fuck do I do now?

"It stitches and screws…"

Something tore into her wing. Abrupt pain made her scream out. Dark Bird tried to flap away from her assailant, but it brought her back to the ground with ease. A twig of a man, blue-skinned with a rat-like disposition, held the other end of the metal wire connected to a large suturing needle that pierced her skin. He wore a belt full of fishhooks and spools of thread spun from braided metal. Over his shoulder, a rucksack brimming with spare body parts. The Cowboy Lizard's eyes sparkled behind a cracked pair of aviators. *"Ain't you precious,"* the Stitcher hissed with wet, black lips, threading more wire into fresh holes in her skin.

"Are you fucking listening to me?"

Minister blinked, mostly blind now. He could barely see his wife standing right in front of him. She came to him like an angel fading-in through static on a dying television. Behind her, colorful shapes undulated in the sanctuary. Moans, the smell of semen and salty blood mixed with dirt. People bent over pews wearing antlers spun from twigs while they fornicated like pigs and bit into each other's backs. All so blissfully empty. Teeth marks. Salty skin. Souls saved from feeling any pain.

"Esther…that you?" he asked dreamily. "I can't see so well today." A brown scorpion ran out of what was left of his nostril and perched on his cheek. Esther sighed and brushed it off with her fingers. The swarm of horseflies cycloned around his body, buzzing so loud she could hardly think.

"I said the feds are coming, but you ain't listening to me," she repeated. "They're locking us in. Shut down the roads too. Just like you said they would. What the hell happens next?"

Minister had few teeth left, and his long hair was patchy at best. He'd sunken past his waist into the Mound in less than twenty-four hours. Squiggling black roots sliced through his skin, and his Vile Heart pumped the potent fertilizer of misery deep into his desecrated garden. Behind the Jesus Man, the Dead Tree sprouted a single silver leaf. Hundreds of Luminarchs glowed on the branches, eager to be near a world on the cusp of a great change. "What happens next?" He laughed. "You know what happens next. You talk to Macho?"

"He's done. I told him to go home."

"Good. For the best. Macho don't need to be a part of what happens *next*. What happens next is *our* happy fucking ending." He reached out blindly for her hand, craning his neck to see over her shoulder. "Where's my boy?" The holy man investigated the milky darkness and almost thought he could see Little Snake sitting in the front pew just like he used to do.

Bony little critter, isn't he?

Esther stroked his frigid hand. As he filled with the burdens of others, her husband fractured more. He slipped in and out of lucidity, realities, and times.

"He's here," she lied. "He loves his daddy, always."

A muddy tear ran down Minister's cheek. "That's nice to hear, baby. I never did know how to teach him much of value beyond how to run away. Eugene was a hard nail. Never tried to be a father to me. My daddy was an *awful pig and a coward*. Then, I became a pig too." Minister fell backward in time. "I remember seeing The Pig standing outside our window. Waiting for his turn. *All snakes are born with a hole in their heart. That hole is a door.*" The frail man shivered; his gunky eyes trained on the dark rafters. "I never wanted to hurt you. But he'd show me the after sometimes. You, curled up, bruised and bleeding…just a little thing on the floor to proud to cry. Eugene told me that was the worst part of it—seeing the after—and he weren't lying."

Esther shook her head, not wanting to think about it. "We don't need to fucking talk about that right now."

"No, it's time you hear me." Minister's sickly face was stone cold. His dying eyes filled with watery regret and pain. *The look* she feared. The one she asked him to give her when the pain was too much to bear. "I know you don't want to say goodbye, and I won't say them words aloud. But you need to hear me say something important. You need to hear me say *I'm sorry*."

"Sorry? Baby, you ain't done nothing *wrong*—"

"I did plenty wrong, Esther. To you. Markus. Myself. I made my choice. I opened the cage. I became The Pig…"

"*Shut up!* You tried to fuckin' help me is all!" Esther wiped an angry tear from her eye in one quick motion, trying not to draw any attention to it. "And nobody else in my sick-sad life ever did more for me! Eugene never tried to make anything better for anybody but himself. Your daddy hid behind a pig mask until the day he died. You chose to be kind instead. You may be what he is, Minister Northamm, but you ain't one single thing like him.

It weren't you opening the cage that saved me. No. It was having a real friend, somebody I could pretend to live well with."

Minister winced. "Esther, you've suffered so much…"

"Well, you used to tell me *we don't get to choose who we are, but we gotta be those people anyway.* You made me want to keep on pretending that everything was going to be perfect one day. What else is life?" Esther still held his hand, gazed at her dusty boots for a moment. Then, she lifted her blue eyes. "I need to tell you something too. Got to get it off my chest…"

"Go on."

She took a deep breath.

"All right then. After you died, I spent a few years hating you. Mostly for getting yourself killed and leaving me here by myself with Delora. That was a promise broken. I wouldn't forgive you. *I couldn't.* Not after Markus was stolen from me. Losing you in the same breath turned my heart into fucking ash. I didn't care anymore, so I let situations evolve.

"I turned to Wallace for love. Then, Shelby, our little girl that was never ours to begin with, for companionship. I turned to whoever could make me feel like fuckin' something other than a nameless ghost. Like the way you always could. Even in that filthy fucking cage out in a shit-filled pasture, you kept me hopeful and laughing. Even if all of this is *bullshit* and there ain't no escaping for either of us, pretending we were living for something was a precious gift." She squeezed his weak fingers, lip quivering. "I do fucking love you, Minister. *I'm sorry if I hurt you.*"

"You can't hurt me, Esther. I've been dead a long time." The holy man smiled, unable to lift his arms to hold her. "And I don't hold grudges from the grave. If it made you happy, I'm happy too." She nuzzled against his chest. She could feel his Vile Heart struggling to beat. "Help me light one more cigarette?"

"All right then." Esther fished a bent smoke from his pack and put it between his bleeding lips. She leaned close to him to light it. He inhaled and coughed a little.

"Fuckin' pansy," she said, smiling through tears.

"You smell like a flower. I love that smell."

"You ill-timed romantic." She laughed. "You sure do know when to set the mood, don't you?"

"If I still had legs, I'd dance with you, Esther Northamm. You are and have always been my better angel." He disliked seeing her cry, and she wasn't trying to hide it anymore. "No. Not one more tear for me, you hear? We all carry our burdens."

"Yes, we fucking do," she replied, interlocking his weak pinkie around hers. Minister's soupy eyes glimmered in the dark, only the faintest of snakeshine left to give.

"Well, it's time to lay yours down."

She felt him slip inside of her mind.

"Minister, what are you doing?"

"Keeping a promise," he whispered. They sat quietly while the snake searched her precious soul for all the poison she carried. She kept everything locked up tight, a scrappy little girl with clenched fists pressed up against a chain-link cage, guarding her broken dreams. He'd wondered if his Vile Heart could remove the deepest of scars. Could he swallow the purest pain he knew that the lost girl kept in her belly? He kept just a little space left in his engorged burden. A sacred hole in his heart. A door just for her. She spat at him when he approached.

"It's time to run away now." Minister unlatched her cage and swung the door open. "Time to see something pretty."

The little girl's eyes watered. "But you always said we would run away together. That's the deal!"

"I'm a known liar and scourge, Mrs. Northamm." He offered her that Burt Reynolds smile she loved so much. "But when I lied to you, I lied with all my heart. Go, Esther. *Run.*"

When he pulled out of her mind, his wife bent over, looking at the pile of wet dirt on her hand.

"What did you do?" she asked, eyes wide with disbelief. *"Minister, what the fuck did you do?"*

He said nothing.

Her husband was somewhere else.

Dissolving into time. Long ago. Where two orphans trapped in a cage named the distant stars until daylight.

At her workbench, the Crooked Woman pounded a mallet into a dead child's chest, pulverizing innards into jam so she could scoop it all out into a dented feed bucket. Potato Sack dropped Dark Bird on the bone pile beneath the nest she grew up in.

"You've been lying to me," Shelby groaned, the fresh stitches in her skin bleeding at the edges. "I found the Deepest Door. I've seen your little secret!"

Delora didn't move. Her stooped spine loomed over her work. Shelby thrashed and tried to break free, but that Stitcher sewed her arms to her sides and her thighs together.

Dark Bird grit her sharp teeth. "You said once we sacrificed enough people, we could leave! We agreed to work together to make that happen. I put together a goddamn plan. You're not following it. *What the fuck is that machine making down there?*" Delora said nothing. "Mother, *answer me!*"

The Crooked Woman finally stopped hammering and slammed the mallet down. ***Boom!*** She turned to Shelby, her vicious expression leering at her behind a shit-covered veil. When her hand extended, Snarl scampered out of the shadows to take it. "Mother says you've been naughty today," the boy wrapped in barbed wire said. "Been exploring dark corners, haven't we?"

Shelby flexed her sewn muscles, but that Stitcher's metal yarn was too thick, even for a strong harpy to tear through. "Tell me, Mother, what is that machine?"

"The Grim Seed. *Enhanced.* Mother has long been a tinkerer. A builder, a shaper of worlds. *A lover of children.* The Grim Seed whispers to her of a grand design, guiding her shaper's hand to build the perfect reaper. It was Sister Death's boon that created it. Mother's boon that inspired it. Sister Salamander's boon that fertilized it. And Sister Worm, whose boon carves out space for its roots to grow. All the Sisters of Sorrow have contributed—even you. Your boon—raw determination—shaped a much better box than we could have ever hoped for. All of this belongs to you too. You should be enormously proud."

Dark Bird shook her head. Mother had gone rogue. Used her dream of leaving against her. "I saw the pods," she announced. "I saw the creatures within. You're building an army of savage freaks down there. What are you planning now?"

"Aren't you lucky, Baby Bird?" Snarl grinned. "You're blessed to be on the right side of our rebellion."

"*Rebellion*? Against fucking who? The Pig's dead!"

"Modernity. Progress. The death knell of our traditions. Those who seek to be like the Pig Father. Humans who would gladly drown us all in a river to protect their false idols."

"Whatever you're scheming isn't the plan," Dark Bird growled, pulling against wire to no avail. A sinister thought planted a seed of rage in her. "Can we even break the goddamn curse? Or have you been lying all these years, Mother? 'Cus I'll fucking kill you if you have. We're supposed to bleed out this crowd, water that bullshit Grim Seed like you've been telling us to and break the dirt curse so we can all go our separate fucking ways. Just like we agreed. *Wham. Bam. Thank you, ma'am. That is the goddamn plan, and you have no right to fuck it up!*"

"Yes, the curse is real, and the curse will be broken when *all* of the people are dead. It's a big, blasphemous world." Snarl's good eye glittered. "Orphan Rock is just the beginning."

Markus gazed down at the Ghost River Valley from the cockpit of the helicopter. He'd never flown before, and it was doing a number on his stomach. He couldn't tell if it was the wild ride or the belly-wringing anxiety of coming home to the Land

Where Pigs Squeal that made him want to puke more. Whatever it was, it made him sweat, and his legs bounced uncontrollably. Even enthralled by Desyre's darkest fantasies, he never felt so far away from the ground. Next to him, the snaked pilot ignored pleas on the radio. Air control begged him to return to home base.

From high, they searched for the right spot to touch down. An open field, if possible. Cars and tents littered most of the flat ground near the ghost town, limiting their options. Markus didn't mind the distance. He could always run into Orphan Rock.

"It just has to be close," he spoke into his headset.

The pilot pointed, eager to please the boy with the eyes that made him feel so good he couldn't stop smiling. "Think I can get her down in that clearing by the river."

The young man knew the spot well.

That's where the roadkills go to die.

"Let's do it," he said.

The pilot adjusted his pitch, reduced speed, and the whirlybird descended toward the grassy patch by the river. Soon, the skids rested on the parched ground. When he felt the landing, Markus took a relieved breath and unfastened his safety harness. There was no time to dawdle. Delora knew he was home. She was everywhere. She saw everything. Heard it all.

The pilot waited for instruction.

"Thanks, bud. Fly back to base now."

Markus reeled in his golden eels.

The man in the bulky headset gave a thumbs-up. In a blink, his door popped open. Little stitched hands stuck him with rusty shivs and shears. *"Ow! Help!"* The pilot convulsed as his blood hit the windshield in goopy streaks. He clawed at his seat but had to let go. The Broken Kids tore him out of the helicopter. **Crack**! His head hit the stone. He spasmed, foaming at the maw, while the harpy's minions climbed all over him like hungry fire ants.

Welcome home, Markus thought gloomily.

A shadow passed behind him.

"This is private property," the bearded man in the biker chaps said. He pointed a rifle at Markus' nose.

"No, man. I'm from here."

"Says who?"

"Me." The snake's golden eels slithered into the Sturgis Saint's eyes. He burrowed deep into his brain goo until he felt the presence of another inside him. The energy was distinct.

"Minister?"

"Little Snake?"

"I'm home, Daddy."

"Come to the chapel, boy. Come see *a miracle.*"

The biker dropped his weapon and teetered on his boots.

"Come with me," is all he said. "I'll drive."

On the motorcycle, Markus wrapped his arms around the Saint's tree-trunk waist and surveyed a vastly different Orphan Rock than he remembered leaving years ago. The desert mutated. Giant red bloodroots strangled the trunks of mesquite trees and burrowed through cracks in rocks with wormy sucker mouths. Desyre's ruby lips materialized in his mind. *Death throes are happening at Orphan Rock! What you just witnessed wasn't the start of something. It's the end of everything.*

They drove past people wandering in the desert, hypnotized but focused on their destination. They moved toward the source of some considerable energy like it was a powerful magnet, and they had bellies full of buckshot. Some folks carried backpacks and used hiking sticks, others dressed in bathrobes and shuffled through cactus patches in pink slippers and flip flops. Partially eaten corpses polluted the road, rotting in the heat. Those nasty red roots burst through arid soil, slowly tugging the carrion underground into the depths of The Dark.

Cadavers. Bloodroots. Broken Kids. Zombies.

Good Lord, this box was a goddamn circus.

A few miles away, a parade of emergency vehicles drove along the road toward the casino. Black SWAT vans parked around the outskirts of the property line. Agents with rifles settled into position. They had no idea what they were dealing with out here, did they? *Fuck*, neither did Markus anymore.

Wallace hiked up to The Needle, the highest point on Orphan Rock a person could climb to without needing special equipment. At the base of the red chimney rock, he set down his backpack and the long rifle case slung over his shoulder. It'd been years since he did the climb, but as a child, he and Minister Northamm explored every cranny of the cathedral spire.

"There is no other way?"

"No, Chief Machado," the councilwoman said, placing her hand on his shoulder. *"We've discussed the risks, and this is our best chance to end this. The Northamms exploit history, hold us hostage in our own country, and our allegiance to them cannot withstand the tide of progress."* The councilwoman nodded to a young man, who then handed Macho a long case. He didn't need to open it to know what was inside. *"When the war starts, and it will start soon, remember our stories and be brave. The Dark One must die, so we can live free again. Without her, they are powerless. If you have a shot, you must take it, Chief Machado. Kill that crow before she feasts on our people."*

"All right," Macho said. *"I'll take the shot."*

Outfitted in his fatigues, camouflage bandana, and his old dog tags around his neck, Macho lay on his belly. Been a long time since he aimed a sniper rifle, but he never forgot how. Vietnam was always inside of him, no matter how hard he tried to forget it. It was there—a gremlin smelling of fire and charred children.

He peered through his military-grade binoculars. From this vantage point, he could see the entire Ghost River Valley. He caught feds rolling into position, setting up along the perimeters. Lot of choppers in the sky now. Soldiers would arrive soon.

When she saw her stolen boy, her Little Snake, the walkie-talkie Esther held to her mouth fell out of her fingers. It broke on the fire pit, batteries and plastic pieces hit the ash, but she didn't care about that. She clutched her chest, couldn't breathe for a second or two. When she balanced herself, confirming the goddamn miracle her eyes showed her to be true, Esther sprinted across the front yard. An older Markus, her baby boy, beamed to see her. He wrapped his quivering mother up in his scarred arms, and they both cried out tears of sweet reunion.

"Oh, my fucking god!" Esther dug her fingernails into his back. She pressed so hard the skin broke. She didn't let up at all. "I knew you were out there. *I just fucking knew it.*"

"I'm home, Momma. I've missed you."

After they hugged a while and cried a bit longer, Esther stepped back from his arms and looked at her boy, top to toes, now a grown man. Her hand trembled as she felt the puffy scars that ran along his neck, the strange symbols Desyre burnt and bit into his skin. She shook with the anger of a mother grizzly bear.

"What did she do to you? *Your skin...*"

"Doesn't matter," the boy said, pushing Desyre away for the moment. "What counts is I got away." He looked around, savoring the rigid mountains, the stringy ocotillos, and the tumbleweeds rolling by on dusty galls. "This is where I belong. I wanted to come home. Rather be here than anywhere."

"Yes, baby, you're home now." Esther clung to his waist, pulled him in tighter. "*I ain't ever losing you again.*"

"Momma?"

"Yes, Little Snake?"

"I need to see Minister."

She considered it, her joyful smile fading. "I don't know if that's a good idea right now. He's not well."

"There's an army coming for us. I've seen it. Daddy needs

to know and probably Delora too. There are a lot of cops. More than we can handle if things get wild."

"Markus, there are situations you don't understand—

"He told me to come to him. I spoke to him in the place where snakes hide. He's in the chapel, right?"

The boy tried to walk down the river rock path, but Esther held his arm tight. He paused, confused by her resistance.

"What's wrong?" he asked.

"Your Daddy ain't the same man you remember. The years here have been unkind to him. Just..." she paused, visibly struggling to find the right way to phrase the worst truth. "Just don't expect too much from him, alright?"

"What do you mean?"

She hesitated, again searching for the right words to capture the dismal situation. "Markus, I don't sugarcoat shit very well, so I'll just come out with it. Your daddy died years ago. The very same day you left. I don't know what happened to him, but just like that both of you were gone. Few years later, Delora brought him back, but he wasn't the same man."

"What?" Markus laughed. "Brought him back? You mean like a Broken Kid? You're joking? You gotta be."

Esther gazed at the ground.

"I wish that were the case—"

Markus pulled away from his mother. He followed the crowd down the river rock path, jogging past the long line of miracle seekers until he stood in the crowded town square of Orphan Rock. Esther tried to slow him down, but he marched up the stairs of the Chapel on the Mound, halting only when a heavy hand pushed his chest. Markus made a fist when the biker blocked his way. Esther shot the Sturgis Saint a nasty look.

"It's all right. Let the boy in," she said.

Dying sunlight coated the filthy sanctuary in hues of marmalade. Beneath the Dead Tree, the atrophying holy man sunk into the soil. Markus elbowed past the heathenistic crowd lost in guiltless rapture and made his way up to his father, a gaunt scarecrow wrapped in wet, black root. Minister glanced around the room aimlessly, teeth missing and gums bloody as an open wound. His sunglasses sat crookedly on his face, and one of his eyes looked like a dried plum behind them. No color. *No shine.*

"*Dad?*"

The holy man twitched, couldn't lift his head from his chest. His dry lips mumbled, lost in broken prayers whispered from the darkest maws of the Age of Filth. Fresh wounds opened on his cheeks, and whipping tendrils lashed at the air like exposed nightcrawlers at first daylight. At the foot of the pulpit, naked, mud-covered bodies crawled across the dusty floor, reaching for the Jesus Man's Luminarch halo with empty eyes. "Dad, can you hear me? It's me. I came to see you like you told me to."

When Minister didn't answer, the young man looked over his shoulder for help. His momma stood there, looking partly ashamed and mostly devastated.

"What's wrong with him?"

"He's a holy man now," Esther said sadly.

"Delora did this, didn't she?"

His Momma stayed silent.

There was a woman
who lived by the
river beneath the
finger that pointed
to the sky.

Macho recalled the old legend of Sister Dirt. His grandmother used to tell it to him at bedtime when he couldn't sleep. All the Sisters of Sorrow had a legend, except for Dark Bird, who would not live long enough to earn one.

*She was a creator,
an old spirit—a
weaver of mischief
who made clay
children from the
mud.*

Wallace had seen the Crooked Woman once back when she was alive, and he hadn't stepped foot on the haunted lands of Orphan Rock since. Never had the balls to try again.

*She wanted nothing
more than children
of her own, so she
bargained with the
King of Pigs and
agreed to become
his slave in
exchange for his
children.*

He held his beaded bracelet and muttered a prayer of protection. Even thinking about the Father Pig was unlucky. So many fools came to the desert to make a bargain with the Swine King to live in his world. All of them dead now.

Well, most of them.

Yet, his abandoned sanctuaries still littered the dark corners of these sacred hills.

*But The Pig would
not honor his
agreement, so the
woman who lived in
the river turned
bitter and angry*

369

*and stole his
children from him.*

Just a boy, Macho stood on the other side of the river. He hid in the sage bushes and watched the desertbilly child stand in the water. The dirty boy held a small clay doll under the current until it dissolved into wavy tendrils of brown river flow.

Minister looked too lean to be healthy, but little Wally knew otherwise. He'd seen the boy run faster than a spooked lizard before—lots of times. The boy had speed like a roadrunner.

*She angered the
King of Pigs, and he
stole her from the
riverbank and kept
her in a magical
birdcage.*

Macho always hid from Minister. Was told to stay away from Orphan Rock and its people. But something told him that he needed to be brave that day. So, the boy waded across the Ghost River, his feet walking on the haunted land for the first time.

Minister didn't run away from him.

"What are you doing?" Macho asked.

The dirty white boy looked up from his knees. He'd been crying. Dirt streaked his cheeks. "Saying goodbye."

"To who?"

"My momma."

*But Sister Dirt was
a cunning bird, and
she escaped from
captivity that made
her crooked and
cruel and vengeful.*

"Your Mother? Did she die?"

"Yeah." Minister kicked a rock.

"I'm sorry. What killed her?"

"What didn't?" the scrawny boy asked, jaw trembling. "She told me that once the worst thing happens to you, it can only get better from there. You think she's right?"

"I don't know." Wally shrugged, skipping a stone on the river. "It's never gotten any better for me, no matter what."

> *And she begged*
> *Sister Death to help*
> *her curse the King*
> *of Pigs for his vile*
> *nature.*

The boy cheered up a little. "You and me ain't so different then, Injun. It never gets any better for me, neither."

"Guess we're alike, white boy." Little Macho shrugged. Then, he had an idea. "Hey! You wanna race? I've seen you run before. You're fast, but I think I'm faster."

Minister beamed, scrambling into his boots.

"*You're on!*"

The wind rustled.

Minister stiffened. The boy panicked.

"Run," he whispered, shoving Macho back into the water. "Get across that river right now. *Now!*"

Little Macho stumbled into the water, landing on his bony ass. Claws reached for the scruff of his neck. The River Woman's black eyes shimmered in the sunlight. Her mouth yawned open like a trap door to hell itself. Luckily, Wallace slipped on a river rock and fell underwater. The boy kicked, kicked, and kicked some more until he found the far side of Ghost River.

> *And Sister Death*

371

granted her wish,
but the price would
be an eternity and
the cost too
impossible and
horrible to imagine.

Officer Machado squinted his eye and peered into the rifle's scope. When the chapel doors opened, and he felt the tension of the trigger, he could taste the warm bubbles of cola on his tongue and could see the scrawny shape of Minister Northamm, always a little ahead of him in the race. Always first to tell a dirty joke. A brother he loved, who dashed toward the sunshine and never looked back to let the shadows get him.

Her son paced angrily in front of the Chapel on the Mound. Near dusk, the sky darkened above the town square. Husks frolicked, chewing on each other, cutting each other open with knives and saws. ***Thwack!*** A woman embedded a hatchet into the back of a man's head. Soon as his body hit the ground, a couple of Broken Kids snatched it up like hungry plague rats. Esther lit up a smoke, grinned nervously. "I'm sure glad you're home."

"He's a goddamn corpse, Momma!"

"I know." Esther scanned the ground. "Delora brought him back, but he's never been the same since. It's been a slow and steady decline to our present fuckin' situation."

"Situation? Fuck me." Markus rubbed his exhausted eyes. Nothing made any sense here. Orphan Rock was weird before, but now? Suddenly sitting in that red dungeon didn't seem so shitty. "If it's about food, you don't need this many people. Trust me, I know what it takes to keep Delora fed…this scale of operation is going to get everybody killed. This is overkill, Momma."

"It's not about food."

"Bullshit! It's always about food with these things." The boy made fists and shook them at nothing but his dark memories. "That's no life for him. Hell, it's not even him anymore."

"But you saw how he responded to your voice? He shook a little. I seen it with my own eyes."

Markus frowned. "Barely."

"But its something! There's enough left I recognize inside of him that's still Minister. At least, there was. You probably think I'm a horrible person letting my own husband wither in the dirt like that. Well, I made a promise to him, you know? We'd never let each other go unless things were too fucking grim. That man, your father, is still there. But the pieces are tinier now and disappearing fast. I told you, Markus. I warned you that he was not well. *He don't have much time left.*"

"They twist things," the boy whispered, still living in his prison. "They're good at making you deceive yourself, thinking there's some grand purpose when there isn't. It's about slavery, Momma! Look around us. Orphan Rock is the grandest con of them all! These people are leaving their lives behind to come here and do what? Die? Suffer? *Become food?* Yet, they think they're going to be saved. It's a fucking scam. And it needs to stop."

"It's not a scam, Little Snake. It's faith."

"And we're the ones who've been duped!" Markus spat. "We're the real marks here. We're the ones helping them do all of this! Our family. Us. All this blood is ours too."

Esther sensed the wicked gazes of Broken Kids congregating in the shadows. Circling. Spying. Broken teeth chattering. They listened with deep interest. So did Delora.

"Markus," she said calmly, dropping her voice. "Let's not get upset now." She flashed her eyes, and her cub caught the signal. He saw the dead ones lingering too.

"You're right," he said.

"Come on. Let's go home."

Mother and son walked toward the river rock path leading

to the stone-stacked visitor's center, but a line of Broken Kids blocked the way—twisted faces, oily eyes, sutures that glued together mismatched patches of skin. Sharp scissors and rusty sickles clutched in tiny fists moved through a cloud of horseflies.

Delora was coming.

Markus grabbed Esther's hand and pulled her in circles. More Broken Kids flanked them from the cottages, chains, and rusty hooks in hand. They growled, ready for a fight.

"C'mon! There're guns in the chapel," Esther said urgently, leading her boy up the small flight of stairs. "Don't be afraid to use 'em. Crate's hidden behind the—"

Markus couldn't hear her voice anymore. Cold, bony fingers slipped around his throat from behind. Esther threw open the chapel doors and turned back to see Delora snatch her firstborn child away from her. She screamed no. *Goddammit no!*

Her voice broke in the night. A thousand miseries spewed from her sweet lips. In the sanctuary, Minister raised his sweaty gaze from the dirt. A glowing smile stretched his chapped lips.

"For these things, I weep. My eyes runneth down with water because the comforter that should relieve my soul is so very far from me now." The holy man swelled, preaching, black roots bursting from his chest and arms, snaking into the soil like a man who finally learned how to live his best life in one spot. He lurched forward, shrieking as worms poured over his lips, splattering on the tangle of devotees that reached for his light. "*My children are desolate because my enemy has prevailed!*"

Crack!

His skull shattered.

The echo of a gunshot sung out from the dark hills.

Thunk! Thunk! Hiss…

Tear gas.

Delora screeched for war, and horseflies flooded the town square with crimson eyes that reflected their last sunset.

VI
Delora

1973

17.

Sister Dirt lined up the children on the riverbank and told them to hold hands. Three boys and two girls, each one less than ten years of age. Dirty and hungry, Gilbert led them from their beds last night, away from the hay piles and pig troughs they dreamed in. The motherless boy had done well in gathering the willing for her. He was such a useful child.

"There will be some brief pain," she told the children while laying a unique effigy in front of each of their toes. "Then, you will find another door to a better forever."

The children said nothing. The beautiful woman who lived in the river had charmed them with her magical eyes once they arrived at the river's edge. They were so deep—her eyes.

"You will serve a better god, in a better place," she told them, standing ankle-deep in the river flow. "I am not cruel. I am a lover of children and life that never ends." Her long finger stroked a girl's muddy cheek. "But I must take my toll. Meat is life. Creation is life. Creation is freedom."

The little girl flinched when the Woman's sharp finger opened her throat. Blood spilled down her tattered dress, and Sister Dirt held the child gently as she died, watching crimson droplets patter onto the little clay doll at her feet.

The boy next to them shivered watching his sister bleed out on the riverbank. The River Woman's cinnamon eyes, rich as muddy milk, absorbed the sunshine. She smiled at him.

"Are you afraid?"

The boy remained silent.

"What is your name?"

"Norman."

"Norman," she repeated. "I am a lover of children. Of life. There are no pigs on the other side of this door. Do you wish to escape the pigs? Do you wish to live forever with your sister?"

The boy considered it.

She watched the scale in his mind tip as the horrors of living with the King of Pigs was equal to no other hell. He took one last look at his beloved sister, Maggie, and said yes. The River Woman was pleased and raked her blade finger across his neck too. He gasped, feeling her cool, wet arms wrap around him. Before it went dark, Norman felt invisible hands gently pluck himself from himself, and he was put inside a tiny doll.

"You have my attention, child," a raspy voice said, usurping the holy man's mouth to speak on its behalf. "But you won't have it for long. What do you want?"

The River Woman scowled.

"*Give me all of your children.*"

The possessed man laughed. "*No.* You take too many already. They grow to serve me. Every time one of my blessed piglets is lost, I feel a new crack in my lovin' heart."

"*You're cruel to them, demon!*" The woman tore her comely mask off her skull in protest, and the rubbery skin hit the water. Her egg-shaped face was marked by two black eyes anchored with golden pins. Thin lips peeled apart, bearing serrated teeth. "I have seen your pigs burn them in fires and toss them into holes in the ground. You waste precious life."

"What I do with my burden is my business." The shadows around the holy man's face darkened. "Speak not to me about holes, Sister Dirt. I've been to the very bottom of things."

"How many dead children will it take for your Age of Filth to begin? Tell me your number. Shall we fill that Old Sinkhole with bones? What then? Nothing will change for you, Father Pig. You are in the ground. *With the worms.*"

"I'd mind your salty manners, chickling. You exist at my pleasure." The holy man kicked a tiny dead arm on the riverbank. "Everything dies in the desert. Thing is, does it stay dead?"

Sister Dirt scowled. "If you will not give me more children to love, then I will take what I want from you. You are cruel and your mission for a second life is fruitless."

"Love?" Father Pig chuckled. "Is that what you call this?" The holy man gestured to the corpses on the clay.

"Yes." The harpy licked her crimson lips, her claws stiffening. "I have great love and gratitude for the meat that fills my belly. It makes me forget I am *just as cruel as you.*"

"Pride is your undoing, Sister Dirt." Flies landed on the holy man's scruffy cheeks. He laughed. "You're nothing but a pathetic bird nesting in *my* big, beautiful belfry. *I've* given you grand accommodation here. Yet you continue to spite me. This is my land, and *you know who's king here.*"

The River Woman frowned. *"King of Pigs!"*

"Well, it seems like you're just another dumb cunt who forgets how to put dirt on her knees when I say bow." The holy man raised his fist, and smoky sickles fanned out in the sunlight. "Looks like I need to teach you a lesson in love."

When Pig Men stormed the riverbank, bristles popped through the harpy's skin. Toenails curled into razor-edged hooks. Links of bone and feather knitted together strong wings. The swarm of charging pigs swung large clubs and threw nets and prodded her with bent pitchforks. They flanked her from all sides of the river—so many filthy little pigs to slaughter—and dozens more hid behind boulders, waiting for their chance to strike.

Sister Dirt howled, weakened by every blow to her half-transformed body. There were too many of them. She crawled across the warm mud toward the safety of her sacred river.

Crack!

The hard butt of a rifle smashed the back of her head.

She hit the clay, then looked over her shoulder.

A rifle barrel tapped her brow.

A filthy pig grinned under a mask.

BOOM!

Sweaty Pig Men built the wooden frame for the new chapel in the distance. Even from afar, she could smell the stink on their skin. Hammers struck wood while men raised crossbeams over The Pig's gravesite near the dry riverbed, a small hill they called the Mound. On top of it, grew the Dead Tree. The Pig's crown. Its roots dug deep into the dark vents below. Sister Dirt had never been to the bottom of that hole. Some places were too deep and dark to snoop around in. Some places reeked of forbidden pacts and forsaken children who never knew love.

The Dead Tree, the epicenter of their chapel, was her cradle. She was born in the branches from a nameless mother who pleased The Pig and carried his burden to term. Her mother was long dead, but she served her purpose. She delivered a boonchild. A builder. A shaper of worlds. *A lover of children.*

The harpy's vision was limited to a finger-sized hole in the thick, black blanket that draped over her rusty cage. The quilt held power over Sister Dirt. Runic symbols glowed faintly in the stitchwork. *Pigspeak.* Everything beneath it felt heavy and kept her mute. She couldn't open doors or speak sacred names. Her hands bound in wire, and her cries absorbed by patchwork. The cage was too compact for her long body, and when her bones healed, they healed crooked. She could no longer wear her beautiful mask. The point-blank rifle blast destroyed it.

The horrible Pig Men kept her in a crude yard stacked with other cages and livestock pens. Some held chickens. A spindly goat and a couple of cows grazed the pasture nearby. Then, there were the girls. They also slept in the mud with the chickens and the goats. At night, Sister Dirt watched the Pig Men come for them. They would open the cages after dark and yank on their arms to come along. After some time, a few would be brought back—a little deader and dirtier than before. The rest would never be seen again. But not *the one*. A blonde-haired girl. The runt of the litter had her own cage. She was marked by the King of Pigs.

The other pack girls did not treat her well. They took offense at her luxuries. Called her names. Threw rocks at her from their pen. Under the moonlight, they would whisper and taunt her and make her cry until she couldn't cry about anything anymore. She would absorb their abuse like she was immune. There was a power in her defiance that Sister Dirt admired.

Hammering from the chapel. Hammering nearby.

The wounded creature shifted her position, looked through the hole in the blanket, and watched the slithery lizard with the cowboy hat build a strange wooden box. He set down the hammer, wiped his greasy nose, and then picked up an awl to keep scratching pigspeak symbols into the wood.

Even though he was the zookeeper here, the Cowboy Lizard never fed her. He dropped table scraps in the pig troughs for the coyote girls and whipped up a nicer meal for the marked one, but he never offered Sister Dirt any meat to eat.

No life. No creation. No energy.

"How's it coming, Wrangler?" The holy man loomed over the sleazy carpenter, drinking from his canteen. His skin was browned from dirt and sun. He was a builder too.

"Amazing what a little hard work can accomplish, eh, Eugene? So long as we can get her inside it without her ripping our goddamn heads off, she'll never be a bother again. Least not until the termites eat her out." The Cowboy Lizard lit a cigarette. "By then, she'll be skinny as a twig. Brittle as one too. But we'll worry about that in four hundred fucking years."

Eugene clapped his bony shoulder. "Father Pig wants it so." Footsteps approached in the gravel. Although Sister Dirt couldn't see him, she knew the holy man stood by her cage.

"I bet you're hungry," he said, striking a match. The hot air smelled acrid with tobacco smoke. "How long can your kind live without food, I wonder?" He chuckled, and it sounded like stones rattling in a tin can. "Too bad we can't put you in a pretty dress and give you a nice American name—like *Delora*—to heel your savage nature. Worked on the goddamn Injuns, didn't it?"

She spotted his dusty boots through the small hole in the blanket. He walked over to the marked girl in the cage, who tried to ignore his presence. Didn't look up at all. He blew cigarette smoke in her face. "Been talking to Minister again, haven't you?"

The marked girl shook her head.

"You're a bad liar, Coyote. My boy's taken a liking to you. Now he's looking at me like I'm the enemy. Likely to cut his daddy's throat in the middle of the night because you keep filling his head with fantasies. Am I your enemy, Esther? Because I *can be* your enemy, if'n you want me to be." The girl shivered. Kept her eyes downcast. "Next time he comes 'round you send him packing, you understand me? Father Pig doesn't want you consorting with any other men until you're a proper woman. You bear his mark, sunshine. You'll bear his sacred children next."

The holy man smacked her cage.

She flinched. He turned back to the Cowboy Lizard.

"These girls ready for the big run tonight?" he asked, rattling the chain-link of the coyote pen. Three battered teenagers cowered in the corner near a pile of goat shit.

"I'll have them gussied up by then, boss."

"No. He likes it better when they're covered in filth."

"Don't we fucking all?" the zookeeper said with a toothy,

tobacco-stained grin.

Sister Dirt's empty belly quaked. Hungry. Creation burns life, and food is life. She hadn't had any meat for weeks.

The old Billy goat knocked around her cage, chewing dry grass in its dumb mouth. Sister Dirt hated the beast. In fact, she hated the smell of all living creatures these days. The smell of life only made her suffer more in starvation.

She thought of the river and the Other Side. Her comfortable, colorless box. The world she shaped from clay, root, and bone. She built it for the children she loved, and for the Sisters she freed. This world of pigs, snakes, and coyotes was only good for spare parts. And meat.

Not long after dark, coyotes howled from the mountains when the Pig Men kicked open their cages and led them into the desert to their secret caves and crackling bonfires. But not the Runt. She sat in her kennel, protected as always, looking at the stars in the sky with endless fascination.

Snap! A branch broke. Fear flashed in her blue eyes.

"*You can't fucking come here!*" the marked one whispered. "Not tonight! You're gonna get us in trouble! He's coming soon! I know he is. We can't talk no more."

A lanky teenager crept over to her cage. He had shaggy hair and some stubble on his chin. Sister Dirt knew this boy. He smelled like the holy man. They were snakes. Boonchildren. She remembered sending his mother to the Other Side years ago.

"I don't care what he says." The boy threaded his fingers through the chain-link of her pen. "I'll kill him. Just tell me to, Esther. I'll do it. *Tonight.*"

She rubbed her cheek on his hand.

"I know you would, but that won't help nobody. I'm marked. I'm *fucking* marked." She held up her arm so he could see the brand on her wrist. "It's going to happen tonight. The Pig wants more snakes. And he knows I've had my first blood. He's coming for me, Minister. He told me so."

"Don't talk about that."

"About what?"

"Him on top of you."

"I'll just fucking disappear when it happens," the Runt said, letting him stroke her hair gently. "I'll go to this place I know inside my head. It's so bright and loud there. I can't think of anything else. It's like walking into a secret sun. You just keep pretending until the hurting stops."

She grinned as if she had already gone there.

"I'm going to run away with you someday," Minister said, wrapping his pinkie around hers. "To a real-life place that's beautiful. I want you to see something pretty."

She grinned. "Where will we go?"

"Anywhere you want."

"I*'ve never been nowhere!*" the Runt confessed. "I don't even know where I'm from I been here so long!"

"Guess that makes you from here then."

"Where the fuck is here?"

Minister looked around the desert. He shrugged. "No fucking idea?"

"Well, that's a stupid name for a place to be from."

Sister Dirt watched them laugh and enjoy themselves with dark fascination. Spittle dripped from her mouth. If they were dolls, she'd place them together on the riverbank.

Delicious companions.

Something spooked him.

The boy looked over his shoulder. The Runt told him to run—*fast!* —and he did. The teenaged snake vanished into the bushes. Then came the heavy steps, the harpy saw those dark boots again, and the holy man soon stood outside little Runt's cage.

"Evening, Esther," he said, sucking air into his nose.

The Runt said nothing, but her silence didn't deter him.

The holy man whistled while unlocking the padlocks that kept her prisoner. She yowled when he grabbed her by her hair and stumbled across the yard when he tossed her. She landed on her cheek near the cage draped in the black, mystical blanket. Sister Dirt could see in her eyes. Could smell her strength.

The Runt smiled at her.

"Come on now!" the holy man said, peeling her bruised body off the ground like a rag doll. She yelped and tripped, getting shoved out into the desert by a stiff hand. "We've been waiting a lot of years for tonight. Hope you're in the mood for love. Romance is in the air, Sweet Pea."

Sister Dirt couldn't see them anymore.

Soon, she would hear the screams, painful shrieking, and a wild pig that squealed and fucked and planted its seed one more time in the saddest of soils.

Later, the holy man walked her back. The Runt trembled—nose bleeding. She crawled into her cage without a fuss. There, she shook in the mud, still walking on that secret sun.

Sister Dirt was asleep but never dreaming, lost under the runic quilt with the air so thick it tasted like sawdust. Her large eyes blinked, shocked by a sudden flash of sunshine. It was so fast she thought she was mad with hunger. Then, it happened again. The rip in the blanket was moving! Sister Dirt crawled over to get a good look, her muscles soft and aching.

The stubby tail of a goat that discovered the frayed edge of the blanket greeted her. The dumb critter chewed and pulled, inching the cover off the cage. The goat nosed the dirt. The hunter waited patiently. Didn't make a peep.

When she saw the white of its beard, the jagged hooks shot from her eyes and pierced the soft jelly in the goat's skull. It was a simple beast—a few doors and no locks to break open. She waded through shallow waters, dug deeper in clay while the goat stood still, a bit of blanket in its mouth.

There it was—the beast's intention.

Sister Dirt laid her bomb.

Self-Destruct.

Baaahhhh!

The Billy goat cracked in half. Its body flip-flopped across the grassy pasture. The blanket snapped off the cage, locked in its jaw, like a magician's pulled tablecloth. Sunshine drenched the pale, starved harpy. Thirsty, hungry, and weak. Skin like rough leather. Spine crooked from months spent in a cage. Flies laid eggs in the creases of her skin. She could feel the maggots squirming beneath her in the mud that her urine kept moist.

The dirty Runt looked at the miraculous creature from her cage. She was on her feet then, legs covered in purple bruises.

"Hello?"

Sister Dirt tried to rip the wire binding her claws, but she was too weak. At least she could see the lay of the land now. Break the minds of the feeble, if needed.

But where were they?

The Pig Men camp was dead quiet this morning. Even the roosters hadn't bothered showing up to crow yet. The Cowboy Lizard, who slept in the van near the cages, hadn't stumbled out of his den yet to feed the livestock either—probably drunk.

Very well. She would change and use her talons and wings to tear this cage apart. Sister Dirt's empty belly cried a refusal. Try as she might, she could not summon the energy.

Meat. I need meat.

"Hello?" the Runt said again.

Sister Dirt scanned the other cages in the yard. Empty. The girls had not returned. Surely, their bones would litter the Old Sinkhole soon. She scraped her face against the ground in frustration. She wanted to lick the blood from the eyeholes of the dead goat. *Meat. I need meat.*

"Can you *fucking* hear me?"

Sister Dirt hissed in annoyance. "I can, *you runt.*"

"I saw you yesterday. I felt you...*inside of me.*"

"I was not the only one inside of you. The Pig had you."

"I lived, didn't I?" Esther's face tightened; her eyes fixated on the cage. "What are you? Why're they so afraid of you?"

"Because I am all they should fear."

"Is he building that for you?" The dirty girl pointed at the wooden box the Cowboy Lizard hobbled together.

"I will break it." Sister Dirt again tried to summon her wings but could not. "I will shatter any cage."

"No." The Runt shook her head. "You won't. There's fucking magic in that box right there. Makes you forget you even exist. You just float until you're gone like a breeze, and you never fuckin' come back." The girl lowered her voice, then said, "The man in the cowboy hat—Wrangler—he makes them with spells. The Pig taught him how. He stitches the quilts and finds the lost girls too." Esther looked at the dead goat. "Holy shit! You're like they are, ain't' you? You can get inside of people."

"You are too far away," Sister Dirt moaned. She glowered at the goat's hind legs bleeding out in the dirt. Inches away from her drooling mouth. *Meat. I need meat.*

"Why are they starving you?"

"Keep me weak. Meat is life. *Creation eats life.*" Sister Dirt shuffled uncomfortably. Her neck cracked when she stretched. "Where are the Pig Men?"

"Fuck if I know. Sleeping it off. There was a...*Coyote Run* last night. That's when they kill the girls."

"I heard the screams. The Pig—"

Bam! The door of the cargo van kicked open. The Cowboy Lizard stepped into the morning sunshine, shirtless, stretching his arms, wearing his trademark black hat and blue jeans. He scratched his ass while he pissed on the dirt. When he finished tucking his junk away, he turned around and saw the black blanket and the dead goat on the ground. *"What in the holy fuck?"*

He ran over to the van and fished out his sunglasses.

The harpy spat and kicked, but nothing stopped the Cowboy Lizard from spreading the quieting quilt over her cage again. Sister Dirt screamed, but the sound dissolved.

She floated in the dark.

The Dark was a prison.

So empty.

Meatless ribs.

It rained quite a bit in the last few days, a strange phenomenon in the desert.

Sister Dirt was lying in the mud. Earthworms worked the soil underneath her knees. Her eyes watered, sockets hollow. Barely a shimmer of gold left. She coughed, choking on rainwater. Her insides rumbled, and she defecated into the puddle underneath her. Her lipless mouth gaped open, and she stared at the rune-stitched blanket feeling only sleepy. There would be no more creation. No more worlds or doors.

She was a shaper—

She coughed again. Blood in her spit.

—a builder of worlds. The King of Pigs was no fool. He knew she would starve, would get so delirious from eating herself alive, she would become weak enough to bury in a magic box.

A bird in a cage! *Her!*

She spat. Her tongue dangled in the fetid water.

But that is how a King of Pigs works, isn't it? Atrophy and submission. Starvation. Control through extended and measured torture. *Patient pig. Greedy pig.* All the Pig Men who hurt the children and tried to kill her Sisters would suffer. She would find a way to kill them all before the Age of Filth came to be. In her mind, she had done so a thousand times already.

Clack!

Something rattled her cage. She could hardly crane her

sore neck to look. The black curtain cracked apart, revealing a pie slice of gray sky. Sister Dirt gasped, looking up at the young boy. Rain matted Minister's hair like a cur and dribbled from his scruffy chin. "Can you understand me?" he asked.

He was so close. So fresh and full of muscle and tendon.

"*Yes,*" she croaked.

The boy blinked off the rain. "They're going to put you in the Old Sinkhole soon."

"*Tell...them...to do it now.*" Sister Dirt tremored in the shitty water. The boy shuffled nervously.

"Can you kill them?" he asked, looking over his shoulder. "If you wanted to? If you were free?"

Bubbles from her mouth. "I am...*so empty.*"

"Here." Minister caught a chicken from the nearby coop. **Crack!** He snapped its neck and threaded the body through the bars of her cage. It landed in the water. So close but too far to taste. The boy pushed the fowl corpse into her visceral jaws with a stick. Still warm. She chewed. Feather and bones. Meat between her teeth. Blood down her throat, delicious ambrosia.

"You can eat them all too," the boy said. "Even...my father. *Especially my father. He has to die.*" The boy's eyes darkened, and the volume of his voice lowered. "I'll let you out. *You gotta kill them all.* Not me, though. Not Esther either. *We live, we leave.* That's the deal if you want it."

"You can't kill...a dead Pig," Sister Dirt said, licking her lips. "He haunts the land—a demon from a very dark river that flows underneath the surface of things."

"Oh boy, that's the wrong fucking answer." Minister shook his head. The boy looked pained and started to close the curtain. "Sorry, you have to die."

"Stop!" she bellowed. The boy held the blanket open. His eyes sparkled like balls of molten sunshine. "He haunts the land. The soil is his grave. The Dead Tree is his broken crown. The part of him we can still see. The rest is beneath us in the dirt, in the

Heart of the Desert. And what comes from dirt must be cleansed." The harpy studied him, looking for any sign of fear. Any weakness she could exploit and bend to her will. He did not waiver. "To do such a thing would be pure destruction."

"I'd give my fuckin' life to make amends here."

"Careful what you say," the balled-up harpy warned. "Promises are powerful. Some you cannot ever escape."

The boy took a deep breath to consider her warning. Then, he nodded. "So, how do we cleanse the dirt?"

"All things created…can be destroyed. That is not debatable. You must answer a more important question."

"What is it?"

"*How* and *how many* other things get destroyed too." Sister Dirt lay in the sewage with eerie indifference. "*I truly do not care anymore.* What do you choose, snake?"

"I choose freedom."

The boy dug into his pocket. **Swick!** The glint of a silver blade. He sawed through the wire around her wrists. "You're probably thinking I'm just a stupid kid for giving you a chance, but I think you know I'm right about this: long as that Pig has the run of the land, you'll never be welcome here. You'll lose every pretty thing you built in that goddamn river. All of the people you snuck away too." The boy folded up his blade after her claws were freed. "He'll fucking take it from you. All of it. He always takes what he wants when he wants to take it. The Way of the Pig."

"You would betray your own father?"

"*He killed my mother.* I watched them cut her open under the Dead Tree. They fucked her body afterward. He made all the men have a turn with her. *Even me.*"

"They are cruel to children here."

"You have no fucking idea, lady," the boy said, shaking his head in disgust. "Next, they're going to kill Esther, the girl over there. I heard my daddy talking about it. They ain't too pleased she don't have a baby in her belly yet. She's marked, you know, so she'll have to die for another to be chosen. Long as she lives, The Pig can't fuck another coyote and the Pig is impatient. Please, *I promise with all my fucking heart*, I'll give you anything you need to make sure she lives at the end of this."

Minister pulled off the blanket completely.

Sister Dirt stared at the cage across the yard.

Stringy hair. Wild blue eyes.

Delicious companions.

"You will not be free, snake, but it will be better than this."

The boy considered her words for a moment. Then he nodded his shaggy head. "OK. You just tell me what you need."

Dogs barked. Men screamed. Rifles cracked. A Pig squealed in rage. Sister Dirt's roadrunner legs zipped her across the desert rocks. Her talons coated in the blood from the brute's neck she had torn out, his eyes wide as oranges when the foul harpy broke free from her bindings. Her wings folded against her back. Still too weak to fly but not to run.

How many had she killed? *All that food left behind!* She could not think of it now. She needed to hide. Not in the river either. She couldn't go there. The King of Pigs would be watching it, knowing her box lay beneath and she'd want it back. Worse still, he was in the dirt. He felt every step she made. He would know where she hid. In his box, The Pig's snout would smell her from miles away. She turned her bald head over her emaciated shoulder. Shadows crept everywhere in the desert at night.

She needed shelter. Clay.

A place to shape.

Sage bushes concealed the cave. The putrid scent of rotting flesh within. A dead animal, maybe? Didn't matter to her. She entered it and could see well enough in the dark to—

Rawr! The mountain lion pawed the stone floor, guarding its den against the grimdark invader.

Whomp! Sister Dirt thrust her finger blades into its lean body and felt the warm squish of intestines. The cat mewled but bled out quickly. Too hungry for tenderness, the harpy ripped his belly open and scooped fresh guts into her froggy mouth. After months of starvation, she was finally eating a halfway decent meal! Starlight shined through a crack in the cave's ceiling. She chewed and missed her nest on the Other Side.

Would she ever go home again?

She thought of the Runt and the Holy Boy. Why did they want to live at all in this horrible world? Did suffering please them so? Why not die and be free to wander into the river? She could shepherd them there. Let them have a new life in a safer world.

But the boy had made a compelling argument to the River Woman, hadn't he? Now that the King of Pigs had declared war, he would never let her live in peace. Never let her have her box in the river back. Freed, she was a threat to him and his flock.

The Holy Boy was right. The Pig needed to go.

But how to rid the world of a shadow?

Sister Dirt was in no condition to fight. Even if she killed the holy man and all his kindred, Father Pig would still be in every shadow under the mountain forever. The age of Filth had begun. This world already marked like that Runt's wrist. He was the stain in the dirt. He would return and grow like a weed again.

She needed to rot him out.

What had she told the boy?

All things created…can be destroyed.

Sister Dirt stood up from the lion carcass—its warm heart in her gnarled claw. She took a bite for flavor and vigor, and then knelt on the cavern floor. There, on the rock, she drew a sacred symbol in blood. When finished, she walked into the center of it and looked to the dark sky. The harpy opened her claws and called out the true name of Death and waited for her Sister to come.

Dirt looked at Death, eyes steady and sure.

"Will Father Pig suffer?"

The bone buzzard grinned with black beetle carapace teeth. "Eventually, it will destroy him."

"Then, yes, I am sure. My life for a Grim Seed."

The buzzard studied her Sister's wounded daffodil eyes with deep sorrow. She inhaled loudly, then nodded. "I understand. I do. He was cruel to me too. And even worse to our other Sisters who never learned to fly from this nest. Salamander. Worm. I remember their tears as children. You showed them kindness." Death held her claw. "You are an angel to the damned, Sister Dirt. Losing you in this war is a terrible price to pay."

"He must suffer too."

The Sisters of Sorrow embraced for a moment in the cave dedicated to their foul Father. Then, Sister Death let her go, offering a confident look. "I shall create a Grim Seed using your life to make it so. However, you must understand the consequences. You will be bound to serve it always, and it will corrupt you more than the Father Pig. But it will also weaken him. He will be a withering stalk of grass in a barren valley. The more you water the Grim Seed, the more it will grow, and his hold on this place will wither and die. In time, he will be forgotten."

"That is what I wish." Sister Dirt could still taste the fetid water in her mouth from her time in the cage.

"For you as well?"

"For some part of me, *yes*. That which I will leave behind to haunt him. *My shadow*."

"You would shatter yourself into pieces?"

"Sister, I have had many days alone in a cage to shape my future from the clay." Sister Dirt unfurled her claw, revealing an exquisite doll she crafted from lion pelt, twigs, and soil. "The part of me I wish to keep will go into the river, hidden inside this sacred vessel. I will leave my hatred behind for Father Pig. It will serve the Seed in my stead. It will embrace its madness. My enemies have already given it a name. Delora will *bleed* them all."

Sister Death accepted the effigy. She eyed it with curiosity. "This tiny doll will hold the rest of you?"

"Yes. For a time. You will bathe it in the river when I am gone. Let the current take me home."

Sister Death frowned. "I'm not sure whether to be glad or sad for you. Perhaps, I can be both."

The Harpy of Ghost River lifted her weary eyes. Her scarred face mustered a brave look. "I am a shaper. A builder of worlds. If there is a sadness to be found at this moment, it is because I cannot *destroy his* fast enough."

"I suppose the rest of the Sisters will owe you thanks a second time. I shall always wonder how you became kind." Sister Death took Dirt's bony hand in hers and led her to the circle. There, Death pointed at the full moon through the crack in the cavern. "Do you see that? The beautiful moon?"

"I do."

"Very good. Savor the beauty..."

Thwock!

Dirt arched toward Death. Her long mouth fell open. The Buzzard's claw yanked out a softly glowing, blue-veined heart from a hole in Sister Dirt's punctured chest. Filled by a freed spirit, her Sister's golem warmed. To make the Seed, Death curled her talons around the shaper's heart, squeezing it with all her strength. Blue blood cascaded over her strong claws until the organ became minuscule, black, and filled with wrath.

When Sister Dirt's corpse hit the floor of the cave, what was left behind loomed over it: A visage of the battered harpy— forever crooked, forever stained by shit water. Baldheaded. No mask. Empty eyes. Fly eggs on her neck.

"Wherever you plant this Grim Seed, that place will become a valley of bones and lost children. I have aided you all that I can." Sister Death placed the Seed in the wraith's soulless claw. "Seek the rest of our Sisters, ask them to bleed for you too.

Together we can slaughter the Swine that made us slaves."

Delora led her flock of Orphans to the riverside. She had an American name now, wore the prettiest dress she could find, and her stained veil would be her beautiful new mask.

Beneath the tall shadow of The Needle, Runt and Holy Boy held her gnarled claws and watched the black-winged buzzard woman dissolve a clay doll in the Ghost River current. Delora said nothing. Her words floated in the river now, along with her spirit. All that was left was hunger, rage, and hatred. She was a shaper. A builder of worlds. She would change this one. Make it better. *The children would finally be loved here.*

VII
The Grim Seed

1993

18.

The Crooked Woman's spidery arms wrapped around his waist. Her claws scratched into his skin. He smelled the fragrances of mildew and black mold—the musk of cemeteries—that wafted wherever Delora roamed. Markus had spent years in the arms of a Sister, and they were never gentle. Fighting back was for fools. She would do with him as she pleased. So, he let go. Prepared to be taken away. The world was cruel to snakes.

Esther's scream diminished under the crack of a rifle. He watched his Daddy's head pop open in the back of the Chapel on the Mound. It all happened so fast. *That's when you know there's no control anymore,* he thought. Events start a chain reaction, dominos fall, and waves of shit hit. Tear gas. Screaming people. Chaos, monsters, bullets, and no time left to think about it. There weren't any moves to make. Once you're whipped up into the funnel of a tornado, the only thing you can do is wait to land.

Markus closed his eyes. Felt the harpy sweep him off his feet. No discussion, only the promise of death to come. He'd been silly to think she'd have some grand negotiation with him, a homecoming worthy of his boon, but the harpy embraced her boon of cruelty instead. Maybe she was just as broken as the rest of them now. Incapable of changing a goddamn thing. Unable to reverse any course taken long ago. The years hadn't been gentle to anybody in Orphan Rock. Didn't take Little Snake long to see that. Desyre warned him, hadn't she? Death throes.

Not the start of something, it's the end of everything.

Fuck. She was right.

Suddenly, Delora's icy fingers let go, and he tumbled through the air, hitting the hard ground near the steps to the Chapel on the Mound. She'd discarded him like a sack of beets. Instead of murdering the runaway, the reaper glided into the chapel, claws reaching for her assassinated orphan's corpse. She screeched, a sound like iron nails scratching across metal.

Wham! The chapel doors slammed shut behind her. The warped wood croaked when bloodroots slithered over the old doors like serpents, and thorns pushed through their rubbery tendrils to ward away any creature with skin they wanted to keep. From inside, a choir of pleas for help. Trapped husks beat on the door to escape, but there would be no mercy tonight.

Rat-tat-tat! More gunfire.

Esther pulled him off the dirt. "*They fucking shot him!*"

Markus wobbled, still feeling Delora's icy fingers on his skin—so cold it burned. "Who did, Momma? What's happening?" Around them, miracle-seekers panicked. The line that stretched down the river rock path dissolved in every direction as people ran for cover wherever they could get it. **Thunk! Thunk! Hissss.** Metal gas cannisters hit the dirt and spewed toxic vapor.

"Guns!" Esther held her t-shirt over her mouth and nose. "The feds, Markus! They're making their move! We need the fucking guns in the workshop."

"What difference does it make?" the boy said, shaking. "Can't fight the army. We're fucked."

"Well, we can't just fuckin stand here and wait to die!"

Markus coughed. "Maybe we should."

Esther grabbed her oldest by the shoulders, turning him to look straight into her blown-out eyes. "I ain't ever been good at sitting still waiting to die, you hear me? Even when I had jack shit and a shoelace, I kept on. Know what? I'm still here. So are you. We're Northamms, baby, and Northamms are some rude sons of bitches when it comes to not dying."

"Alright, Momma." Markus nodded, offering a look of reassurance. "I'm with you. Let's go get some firepower."

Under the choking fog of bromoacetone gas, they followed the river rock path toward the stone-stacked house. It was dark at dusk, easy to disappear in the bushes and boulders. Madness riled up the desert like a dust devil. Sinister shapes moved in the hills. Friend? Foe? Husk? Soldier? Couldn't tell with all the smoke in the air. *Even the Broken Kids weren't ready,* Markus thought, watching a pack scamper for a door to The Dark somewhere in the desert. *This wasn't supposed to happen yet.*

What the hell caused the feds to escalate?

A large shadow soared in the sky above them, covering the rising moon. He must be high. Looked like a giant butterfly.

"Look!" Esther shouted.

Harboring a small army of ATF agents, a wall of black SUVs lined the road along the property line. ***Crack! Crack! Tah-tah-tah!*** A pair of Sturgis Falls Saints ducked behind their makeshift barricades. While bullets soared above them, they reloaded their rifles. One poked his head up to return fire, and his lower jaw blew clean off his head. He kept firing anyway, tongue hanging out of his mouth hole like an overheated hound dog.

Thack! Thack! Thack!

Stray bullets kicked up sand geysers near the Northamms' feet. Some sparked off the foundation of the stone-stacked house before ricocheting into the dark hills.

"Come on!" Esther dragged Markus toward the front door when a massive searchlight passed over the front yard. Helicopter, flying in circles. "Need the keys to the shop."

In the living room of the visitor's center, a swarm of born-again husks huddled together and cried for help and salvation. They writhed and moaned and clawed at the new wallpaper Shelby picked out. When they saw him, they reached for Markus. They called him holy man with wet eyes. They stained the brand-new carpet with blood, shit, and empty tears.

"*Let go of me!*" The boy used his elbows to keep them away. One held up a dead infant by the leg, waving it like a plucked chicken. Courtney Philbin, Action 10 News Reporter.

"*I found a baby,*" she squeaked, biting its ear off.

Esther retrieved Minister's keys from the hook in the kitchen. She peeked out of the window over the sink. She kept as low to the floor as possible. No lights on. The helicopter's searchlight traveled across the yard. A husk tried to stumble away from it, but they shot him. Markus joined her by the window, trying to catch a glimpse of the hellscape outside.

"We need a *fucking* diversion!" Esther said, ducking down before—***clink!*** —a bullet pierced the windowpane and exploded through the cabinet near her head.

Markus looked around the gutted house. Not much to work with. No back door. Tiny windows. A water cooler. A crowd of fools without a brain between them…

He raised his pointer finger. "*I got it!*"

Little Snake gathered the thoughtless husks around him in the living room. "I am the Minister," he said, eyes golden and bright with beams of twisting snakeshine. "To please me, you must walk into the light, My Children. Find me in the light!" The holy man opened the front door and pressed against the wall while his flock squeezed by, eager to obey their holy man. They cried their devotion while chasing the helicopter's searchlight like a cat after a laser beam. "*Go on! Meet your maker in the light!*"

Rat-tat-tat! Rat-tat-tat!

"Now!" Markus yelled to Esther.

They rushed into the yard together, ducking behind their blathering meat shield. The searchlight blinded them from above. ***Crack! Crack! Crack! Rat-tat-tat!*** One by one, the husks fell over into a stinking heap. Courtney Philbin absorbed more than a dozen rounds before she finally let go of her dead baby. Blood lapping out from holes in her chest, she gazed at the moon and smiled one more time for the camera. "Back to you, Grace…"

In Minister's workshop, Esther started the generator while Markus barricaded the door with scrap metal. Crates of guns and ammunition stolen from the Solemn Cave stockpile lined the wall. They pried lids open and rummaged for supply. Markus threw a rifle over his shoulder. Esther stuffed a duffel bag with clips and whatever else went boom. While they suited up for battle, Snarl stepped through a rip in the shadows. His normally apathetic face contorted with rage. His barbs dripped with pus. *"What have you done, Little Snake?* You brought a war with you!"

"Step off." Markus turned around, rifle aimed and steady.

"No. I'm not the enemy here, *you fool.*"

"The fuck you ain't." The scarred boy's finger brushed against the trigger. "I don't know what friends look like, but I sure as shit know who my enemies are."

"Little Snake, this is not the time for settling old scores."

"I say it is."

"We've got a bigger problem."

Esther stopped packing bullets. "Bigger than the goddamn military?"

"Unfortunately, we do. We're not alone out here."

"No shit?" Markus laughed bitterly. "There's a fuckton of people out there with guns."

"Mother is not worried about the people."

"No? Well, considerin' I still have a pulse, *I sure am.*"

"There's been a breach, boy! Mother's contingency has failed. The King of Pigs has…*returned.*"

Esther let out a pained cry. In a blink, all the color drained from her cheeks. Markus caught her before she crumbled to the floor. "Momma!" Esther clutched to his chest, a terrified and vacant look in her sweet eyes that he'd never seen before. She was gone away. Somewhere so far away. Little Snake turned back to the boy wrapped in barbed wire for answers.

"How is that possible?" he asked, holding his quaking Momma tight to his breast. "The King of Pigs died. Just the shadow's left. The rest of him? Dead."

"No, you're wrong." Snarl shook his head. "The Pig Father was never dead. Disassembled is all. But we don't have any time to talk about that now. *He is back.* We've seen him in the sky wearing the skin of an Other Sider." A flicker of worry made the lapdog seem even smaller than he was. "He'll ruin all of this."

"Ain't nothing we can do about that." Markus waved him off. Maybe it was because Little Snake was bigger now, but he wasn't scared of Snarl anymore. He was just another scared kid.

"Open your eyes!" Snarl pleaded. "We're on the cusp of a miracle. Everything we've ever done to get here is on the line. He'll take it from us! *That's what pigs do!* They take what don't belong to them. We need more time to water the—"

Boom!

Snarl's one eye popped open when the bullet tore through his neck. He grabbed at his tattered throat, stumbled backward into a stack of crates, and they toppled on top of him.

The pistol trembled in Esther's hand.

"I don't want to hear about it," she said. "I don't fucking care anymore. No more plans or schemes for me. They can all rot in hell far as I'm concerned." She tossed Little Snake the duffel bag. "Now, let's get the *fuck* out of Orphan Rock."

Gunfire.

Screaming.

The shrill sobs of the almost dead.

The scrape of teeth against bone.

The Harpy of Ghost River eyed the singed hole in Minister's greasy forehead. Arms limp, he leaned backward, still buried in the Mound like a dingy tombstone. Skull pointing at the widow webs in the rafters. Toothless mouth open. Black ooze dripping from the fist-sized hole in the back of his head.

Delora coated the tip of her finger in the stream of his accursed blood. She lifted her veil and dripped some into her froggy mouth. She tasted the crying of children—the purest of suffering. If this weren't enough to water the Grim Seed, nothing would ever be, and she would have been a fool all along.

Something remembered.

"I'd give my fuckin' life to make amends here."

"Careful what you say," the balled-up harpy warned. *"Promises are powerful."*

The Holy Boy made his pact, hadn't he? He opened the cage. In return, the harpy opened Minister's lifeless chest again. She tore the Vile Heart from its rotting ribcage. The organ was worm-riddled, blackened, and swollen with sorrow.

Such a delicious apple it was. She rolled her lips back and took a small bite. Black tar dribbled down her chin, and her dead eyes ignited with renewed fire. *Exquisite.*

Delora held the Vile Heart over the Mound. The same way Sister Death once gripped her own. Her fingers curled into a fist, and she crushed it until all the oil of tragedy dripped from the muscle and splattered onto the soil. The Luminarchs flapped from the gnarled branches of the Dead Tree in a maelstrom of disarray.

The ground rumbled with the sounds of artillery.

The air smelled bitter with smoke.

The moonlight flickered as a shadow passed through the hole in the roof of the Chapel on the Mound. Delora did not lose focus. She wrenched every drop of sorrow from Minister's vault, expecting the monster that buzzed overhead with a triangle-tipped tail to make its entrance at any given moment.

When it did come, the accursed boy with butterfly wings landed before the pulpit, and sickles crossed over an obsidian midriff that pulsed with befouled, demonic energy.

"Let it all out, child," the Lumenswine said, bitter pig eyes glinting behind an old pigskin mask. "Nothing is going to save you now. Not one more goddamn trick, Sister Dirt."

Delora finished twisting the heart and let it fall from her hand. She turned to the abomination, the fugitive King of Pigs, grinning like a mischievous child, defiling a creation from her better self and from her perfect world. He desecrated what did not belong to him yet again. An echo reached her from a long time past, the ***crack!*** of the holy man's rifle on the riverbank.

Her claws curled into sabers.

This Pig would squeal.

Strung up like a piece of cured beef in a butcher's freezer, Shelby swung from the bottom of Delora's nest. Her arms stitched to her sides. She couldn't move more than her fingers. Her ankles bled from the tight noose of barbed wire that bit into her skin. Around her, Broken Kids slept, dangling like windchimes.

Little footsteps appeared in the dust below when the ghost children played hide and seek and sang the Dirt Hymn, waiting for the Crooked Woman to come and break them apart on her gnarled workbench. A ghost serpent lay in the moonlight, soaking in the energy of the forgotten gods it once served. Dark Bird struggled and growled, sick of ancient histories and lingering souls.

Potato Sack lumbered about kicking bones. She could hear the strained breathing through his mask. When he looked up to her, she tried entering his mind. But try as she might, she could find nothing in those burlap eyeholes to grab hold of.

Boom! Boom! Boom!

Explosions. The young harpy could hear the echoes of war through the crack in the cavern's ceiling. Gunfire. The popping of semi-automatic rifles. Flashbangs. Fuck knows what else. Packs of Broken Kids fled through doors in The Dark like spooked crickets. Agitated. Off Delora's leash and…panicking?

Shelby wriggled her body so she could get a better look at

the slumbering Broken Kids hanging nearby. Freshly assembled doll parts and twitching eyes beneath blue lids. Tiny seeds sprouted from the dirt in their bellies, spreading undeath like cancer in their sleep. *But what about Mother's secret creations beneath the Mound? They're not children at all.*

What are they?

"I need to get the fuck out of here," she whispered to herself, sick of questions, mysteries, and riddles. Her eyes slid around the cathedral cavern. *There!* A nearby Broken Kid—a blond boy with shears for fingers. The blades softly clicked against one another as he slept. They appeared sharp enough.

Worth a try, at least.

"Wakey wakey, asshole."

Dark Bird rocked her body to gain momentum and swung toward him. After a few misses, they knocked together. The boy twitched a bit. Awake now, his newborn eyes blinked.

"Have we sung the dirt song yet?"

Shelby seized his mind.

"Show me your fingers."

The obedient boy opened his bladed hand. He was wrapped in barbed wire like the rest of his kindred and could only flick out his fingers a small amount. It'd have to do.

"Hold still, freakshow." Dark Bird swung toward him once more, trying to line up the stitchwork on her arms to scissor blades. Every time she missed, he carved into her skin. Shelby grimaced but kept trying despite the pain. Harpy blood dripped on the shoulders of his burlap gown, and Potato Sack observed her trapeze act with great interest from the bone chamber below.

Markus led Esther along the side trails he remembered as a child. They kept low and concealed in the brush, trekking from the scrapyard, past the Old Sinkhole, wrapping around the base of Orphan Rock toward the cave he knew up on the ridge toward The

Needle. In Orphan Rock proper, a fire broke out in the wooden cottages, making the air smoky and visibility low. A blessing and a curse, considering they couldn't be spotted too well, but neither could their enemies. Husks danced in flames, some racing along the river rock path while burning alive without any sorrow or regret in their eyes. This was God's country now.

"If we can make it to the canal, we can cross over to Sandoval. I remember an access bridge."

"Feds will be all over the Sandoval side," Esther replied, fading back as some feral husks twitched by, chasing after a limping girl in a shredded dress with tent spikes.

"OK, what about the river? We can cross over on the Ghost River side. Maybe head up to Solemn Cave?" Markus hesitated. "Wait. The curse. It'll kill you. We need another plan."

"I...spit it out. The dirt."

Markus turned to her. "What? *How?*"

A look of grief passed over her stoic face. "Your daddy helped me. Had some room left in his heart to spare for a bit of sorrow. *Mine.* He carved it out of me, Markus. Your daddy was a healer to me. Loved me enough to carry my burdens too." She rubbed her eyes. Kept the tears back for now. "But you're right, baby. Delora will kill us if we try to leave this land."

"Momma, she's trying to kill us right now!" Markus glanced over his shoulder. "There's no loyalty with these things. When you're done being useful, *you're food.* That's it."

Tat! Tat! Tat!

More bullets tore into the earth ahead. Markus pushed his mother's head down as a few more stray shots stripped the green bark off a Palo Verde tree just behind her. "We need to get away from town." He looked at Orphan Rock and The Needle above. "I know a cave. It's not far from here. Let's at least take cover?"

Ester nodded, and she followed her brave boy as he navigated the sharp rocks and prickly fauna patches.

"Well, holy shit. That can't be fuckin' good." She pointed

at the sky. The moon looked distended and yellower than normal—fat, sick, and red at the edges. "Things are changing faster than I thought. She's going for it, Markus! This is it. Delora'll have enough sorrow collected, or she fucking won't."

He nodded. "She built a better box."

"*She* didn't build nothing. Your sister did. Shelby."

Markus paused. He hadn't thought of the dark-eyed girl on television since he fled Kilgore City. Wasn't hard to forget about somebody you never knew. Besides, it's not like he's had a second to spare for family reunions and friendly get-togethers since returning to the Land Where Pigs Squeal. "Where is she, Momma? Why isn't she helping us right now?"

"Wish I knew," Esther's tone sunk. "Haven't seen her in a while. Not sure what her state is, but I do know she's strong and won't go down without a fight. Shelby's a special boonchild. A daughter. A Sister. She's like Delora and…"

"Desyre?"

Esther gave him a confident nod.

"Fuck it then," Markus growled, a twang of hatred in his angry voice. "Better I don't know her then."

The young man picked up the pace, leaving his Momma behind. Now wasn't the time to soften him up about Shelby. The boy's mind had been made up already. Maybe when they had a second to breathe, Esther would tell him about Dark Bird's complicated nature. He might listen when the bullets stopped.

Higher up the steps, they watched at least three cabins burn in the town square. Husks laid over the dirt, dying, eating their own fingers in protest, and fucking every spider hole they could find under the rocks with their bloody dicks. Law enforcement practically drowned them in tear gas, and soon the entire Ghost River Valley was blanketed in a white, choking haze.

Esther hadn't been on a hike like this in a while. The climbing made her light-headed—*too many cigarettes.* Markus pointed to a large boulder, and they hid behind it to catch a breath.

She huffed. *"Fuck.* I'm getting' old."

"How old are you, Momma?"

"I think I'm thirty-fucking-four."

"Wow, you're a goddamn dinosaur."

"Wiseass." Esther punched his arm, and they hugged again. It felt good to laugh in the tense moment. Esther stroked his hair while Markus buried his face into her neck. It was the second hug they'd both dreamed about for years: a joyous hug, one of the rarest creatures in all of Orphan Rock.

"I'm sorry I went with her." Little Snake let her go. "Sorry I left you here by yourself. I was young, you know? The idea of spending my life here was too much. Sometimes a kid needs to be a kid. From the second I was born, I only ever thought I'd be a pig one day. I know you and Daddy tried to tell me that things would be different for me, but I knew better. When Desyre offered me an exit, I took it. I guess I wanted to believe in something else for myself. But trading one leash for another only made it worse."

Esther wiped a tear from Markus' scruffy chin. "You said it earlier. They like to twist things. She twisted you is all." She felt the scars on his back. "Tell me what happened to you, baby. I want to understand what you went through. *Please.*"

"Alright, Momma." Markus sniffled, wiped his nose on his sleeve. "Desyre was a cruel monster. She got off mixing pain and pleasure to see how much you could take. Worst of all, the more you tried to please her, the more she expected until you just couldn't be yourself unless you gave yourself away.

"She taught me how to feel nothing until nothing is all I felt. It's a scary place – *nothing.* Fuck, that was the worst part of it. Not the pain or the hurt that comes from the empty feeling of being treated less than you are. That's easy. The real scary, depressin' shit is when you actually believe it's true."

"I know the feeling well." Esther laughed sadly, looking at the rising blood moon. "I'm scarred too. Just like you. Mostly on the inside, though. It's just as ugly, believe me."

"Ugly?" Markus brushed the strands of blonde hair away from her eyes. "I always thought you were the prettiest woman in the world." He kissed her dirty forehead. "Still do."

Something remembered.

Shaped years ago, on the muddy riverbank to be a god, the boy with butterfly wings was not for this world. He was to be the visage of faith in a much kinder realm than this one. She spent years shaping him from the clay for her children, her precious orphans. Twisting perfect braids from desert grass, etched all the right symbols on his body, and she breathed air into his clay lungs. He would be the exact opposite of the King of Pigs. Beautiful and compassionate. A lover of children.

Now, the bony child wore a filthy pig's mask to protect its mind, and a hardened beetle shell breastplate protected its foul heart. Its devil tail pounded the dirt with glee.

"You've made quite a mess of things, Sister Dirt," the Lumenswine said, stepping toward the pulpit. He eyed the harpy with hatred while his sickles scratched along wooden pews. "I've not been myself lately. Felt a bit scattered in the wind, to be honest. But I'm home now. Came back to church. Pleased to see what you've done to the old place."

Swick! He lunged for her, his blades casting sparks from the rock wall around the Mound. Delora landed in the aisle behind him, her wings folding against her shoulders. The rest of her changed into harpy—scaled skin, sharp talons, and hedgehog bristles that burst in blooms of feather. She let her wedding veil fall away, revealing her dented face, exposing the wound where the bullet had destroyed the space between her eyes all those years ago. The scars that never healed. The flies that followed her shit-smell. The spine that went crooked in a cage that cracked when she tried to stand. Her filthy dress dissolved. She savored the sounds of ripping corset. The Harpy of Ghost River cawed, and the dying bodies dropped around her chicken feet.

She was a shaper, a builder of worlds.

A killer of pigs.

Father Pig looked at the Dead Tree. He chuckled a little. "I don't remember every piglet born from my potent seed, but I do remember the day *you* were born, Sister Dirt. You and your filthy, fucking Sisters. What good is another daughter when they're so disobedient?" He faced the harpy with milky eyes. "No good at all. That's why I drowned them all in the river."

Sister Dirt's talons clicked on stone.

The Lumenswine scowled, snout dripping. "You had no fucking right to let them go. Just like you had no fucking right to butcher my flock. And just like you had no fucking right to defile my grave." Spit sprayed from The Pig's rotten mask. "The Age of Filth is mine again, and *you're done stealing from me.*"

The boy with butterfly wings raised his arms to the swelling moon. ***Crash!*** A shadow thick as tar burst through the dingy rose window. It dripped down the stone walls like living tar and pooled around the Dead Tree's roots. It slithered across the cursed dirt of the Mound and vined up the Lumenswine's lanky legs to enter the hole in its godling heart. When he unified with his darkest part, his demonic eyes glowed bright white with completion. Father Pig screamed in triumph. "And now it's time for a miracle. I give you *a prelude* to my greatest *resurrection.*"

The corpses around Sister Dirt stirred, climbing onto their bloody knees, broken jaws snapping.

Way below the chapel—far into The Dark—a wild heartbeat echoed like a timpani drum.

Gears clanked. Vines shifted. Planes cracked.

The world began changing shapes again.

Plink! Plink! Plink!

The Stitcher's wire popped like cut violin strings.

The half-awake Broken Kid hummed the Dirt Hymn, scissor fingers covered in Dark Bird's bluish blood. She used her free claw to slash the leftover wire from the rest of her body.

Felt good to be loose again.

With both arms liberated, Shelby squeezed her belly, flapped her wings, and swiped madly at the barbed wire noose that cut into the scale of her ankles. Sparks rained into the bone chamber. Rusty iron groaned, then weakened. When it finally snapped, Dark Bird's wings stretched and provided the right amount of lift for a graceful flip. She landed safely on her feet.

Her black and orange eyes dared Potato Sack to make his move. At first, they both kept their distance. Dark Bird flexed her razor toe hooks while the Broken Kid tore open his belly mouth. A fat, wormy tongue rolled onto the bone-riddled floor.

"Have we sung the song yet?" a Broken Kid whispered somewhere in The Dark, breaking the tension of silence. Potato Sack thundered toward her, arm lifted, fat fingers reaching for her throat. At the same time, his black tongue swept at her legs. Dark Bird beat her wings to lift above it.

Crack! Crack! Crack! She pounced three times, toe hooks just missing the throbbing muscle and sparking off stone.

Whomp! Potato Sack crashed into her with his beefy shoulder stump. The harpy flew backward, hit the rock wall, and she couldn't suck in enough air to make the rainbow spots in her vision vanish. Her razor feet skidded across bone, seeking something to grab hold of to help her off the floor. Potato Sack roared through his gaping belly mouth. Square teeth glistened with frothy spit in a bottomless pit of stink and swirling shadow. Again, its bristly tongue whipped across the floor for another strike.

Thwack! This time Dark Bird's toe hook pierced deep into the moist muscle. White pus squirted from the wound. The brute howled until fetid breath stunk up the air. Dark Bird kicked away and tried to shred the tongue open, but it was strong like hardened leather and gripped her talon tightly when it flexed. She couldn't unhook herself no matter how hard she tried to wiggle away.

"Let me go, *motherfucker!*"

Potato Sack's giant mouth twisted into a grin that said no. Shelby groaned and hit the floor when his serpentine tongue reeled her in like a fish on a hook. He had momentum now, and Dark Bird's sharp fingers dug into the ground with desperate futility as he pulled her closer to the dark abyss of his throat.

Panic set in when she felt the glacial meat of Potato Sack's mammoth lips, and she pressed her hands against the spongy gums of his gaping maw to keep away. The cadaver fumes on his breath made her eyes water. His jaw cracked open wider, tongue pulled harder, and the black expanse behind his teeth held an infinity that was not of this world. Dark Bird shrieked to see the truth.

The Broken Kid had a rip in The Dark inside of his own fucking body! Not a tongue at all, but a tentacle from something lurking on the other side of a *very* secret door.

That crafty bitch.

"*Raaaackkkk!*" Dark Bird slashed her claws into his meat repeatedly. His flesh split like pork in a sausage casing, and white blood dribbled out from gray meat. Nothing phased him, however. The tentacle tugged in defiance, and one of her feet slipped into The Dark. **Slurp!** He sucked her in like a hot noodle.

"*Grrrr!*" She pushed against his rotten, square teeth to counter the galaxy-sucking vacuum of a black hole. In response, his massive hand snatched her by the throat and strangled her. His impressive weight pressed her against the floor, a mountain of decades-old blubber, drowning her in a gown of stinky burlap.

"*Get the fuck off of me!*"

Dark Bird's lips peeled away from her dagger teeth. With a mad glint in her eye, she snapped a large chunk of Potato Sack's forearm off the bone. The ogre reeled, let up just a little in surprise, and Shelby took her best and only shot.

Before it chewed off her leg, Dark Bird thought about all those years as a chickling. A Baby Bird who wanted to be free.

Potato Sack leashed her, yanked her along like a dog from cage to cage. Never gentle. Never kind. He was just a dumb fucking brute with too much strength and no fucking sense of decency. Dark Bird was sick of being disrespected. Sick of being used and treated like a pile of lizard shit by goons and creeps. This Broken Kid made her cry a few times, and she never forgot how he and the rest liked to hurt Esther. Treated her like trash. Well, Dark Bird made a promise to make them suffer one day. Today might as well be that fucking day. With a snarl, she twisted her free hip far as it would go before kicking her foot at those empty eyes behind the sack with all the hatred in the world behind her talon.

Swaaathh!

The boy's shredded mask fell around his neck. Mewling behind the burlap, the deformed head of a piglet. Newborn in size, its eyes shut above toothless jowls. It squealed for milk.

"*Here piggy piggy!*" Dark Bird's talon raked its thin-string neck and its brittle spine severed like a piece of stale licorice. Potato Sack's body jolted in its second death, and everything let go. When his baby piglet head rolled across the floor, his sausage fingers loosened, and his crushing weight fell off her body.

Dark Bird could breathe again, so she laughed at the pathetic truth of things. Sometimes the biggest and scariest monsters in the world were just small-headed, baby pigs hiding behind their scary masks. She leaned against the wall, took a breath, and tried to pull the slimy tongue from her talon.

Let go of me, you dead—

"Shit!" It twitched back to life, wriggled around her bird leg, and yanked her across the bone chamber with a hearty pull. Even though the monster was dead, the other hidden inside of it still craved its meal! She slapped against the boy's corpse, the rubber band tongue cinching tighter around her calf muscle. Dark Bird howled when those teeth scraped against her knee.

"I don't fucking think so," she hissed, head full of boiling anger. A kettle on the stove that screeched.

Her claws slipped inside The Dark of Potato Sack's mouth, taking firm hold of the wild tongue. Unbridled energy fueled every muscle in her body to reverse course. Legs. Talons. Wings. Without the heft of Potato Sack to counter her rage-fueled strength, Dark Bird reveled in the transfer of power.

When momentum shifted, the demonic worm quickly let go, trying to retreat into the safety of the hidden rip in The Dark, but Dark Bird dug in and tightened her grip. No way she was letting this freak slip away from her. She pulled it like a fire hose, coiling it on the floor around her roadrunner feet. Her wings flapped to give her a bit of extra oomph.

"Come on! Come on!"

Wham! She felt something larger hit the wall of Potato Sack's teeth—a bigger piece—that didn't want to come out to play with her. Shelby's mad grin deepened, smelling certain death for her enemy, while her foot pried open the belly maw just enough to force a dimensional ejaculation from The Dark.

One more solid yank…

Splooosh!

The Dark dweller spilled onto the cavern floor in a puddle of black ooze. It was a spindly thing. The tongue grew from its head above a baby's toothless mouth. Its legs hooked and bent like a grasshopper, desperate to scurry away. A single eye blinked, small, and silver against the black metal of its beetle shell.

Thwack!

Dark Bird ripped its eye from its meat socket.

It tasted like liquid mercury.

The blind creature wept blood and shit itself, while the harpy tore open its cosmic thorax and picked through its white pile of devil guts for more meaty treats to eat.

Under the reddish light of Delora's blood moon, the ghost town burned. Shadows lurked in the outlands while a helicopter chased them with a spotlight through a tear gas fog.

"Cave's this way. Watch your step."

Markus parted the purple sages for his mother. When he was a kid, he rarely climbed up here to play. Something about *this* cave made him nervous. Used to believe monsters lived inside. The dark crack in the rocks looked foreboding tonight, but it'd have to do for a hideout while bullets and husks ripped the desert to pieces. Hard to shoot through a boulder. Better to be inside of a cave—even a haunted one—when bombs dropped.

"Whoa!" Esther nearly lost her footing when the ground rumbled beneath her boots. The tremor shook Orphan Rock and the Ghost River Valley. "Jesus! What the fuck was that?"

Rat-tat-tat! Rat-tat-tat!

"Don't know, don't care," Markus said, pushing her along. "Come on. Let's get inside and regroup."

Esther spent most of her life in Ghost River and she never *ever* wanted to come to a cave like this. Father Pig had sacred places in dark corners across the desert like this one. No good ever happened in these cracks in the mountains. A lot of coyotes were brought here by Pig Men. Few ever left.

"How'd you find this place?" she asked, hand gliding over ancient cave paintings of men, owls, pigs, and rivers that wound like snakes. She didn't say anything aloud about it, but Esther swore to Christ the petroglyphs glowed in the darkness.

"When you're a kid, you get into shit, I guess."

"Don't have to tell me." Esther snickered sadly. "I ended up in fuckin' Ghost River when I was nine."

At the back of the cavern near a broken wooden cross, Markus used a silver lighter to start a small fire for light. They laid down their rifles and the ammo-stuffed duffel bag.

"We best wait this out right here," Esther told her son. "If I didn't know this cave existed, the feds sure as shit ain't gonna find it." She patted her pockets. "Oh, Lord. *Fuck!*"

"What is it?"

She looked pale as a ghost. "I ain't got no smokes."

"Here." He handed over one of his.

She sighed in relief. What a good fucking boy. Mindful of others. Somehow, he'd turned out kind despite all the bullshit he endured in his life. Made her happy to think about.

While she smoked, Little Snake walked along the painted walls. His expression turned grave as if he could see something dangerous hiding in the shadows. "We're not safe here."

"Safer here than out there." Esther exhaled fumes through her nose, relishing the burn in her lungs. "I say we let Delora and the U.S. Army duke it out for a while. Let one fuck the other over. Then, when we have a chance, we make our run for the river."

Click!

"Listen to your mother," a deep voice said from the darkness. Neither Markus nor Esther had time to snatch up their rifles when the handgun appeared from the din.

Wallace Machado stepped into the firelight.

Their lifeless fingers scratched at her scaly skin. Bloody bodies held her wings down, piling on top of her like stinking sandbags. Broken teeth bit into her arms and chewed on her legs. The Harpy of Ghost River roared, claws swinging at reanimated husks. She sliced meat that didn't feel a lick of pain. From the pulpit, The Lumenswine cheered his ghouls on.

Something remembered.

The riverbank in the summertime.

The holy man with a rifle and a hoard of Pig Men hitting her with clubs and bats while she was tangled in a net. She killed so many that day while he watched, laughed, and baited them on. That Wretched Pig, the ghost of the cruelest god. And now they piled on her again. Just more Pig Men with cruddy nails, greasy fingers, and gnashing teeth looking for a cheap bite.

Delora remembered the cage. The metal links that ruined

her spine. She could smell the shit and hear the horseflies cry
Hallelujah! Her bony wings fanned out, throwing the husks from
her body like unwanted grubs. She rose from the chapel floor, a
grisly owl. The zombies fell under her bicycling talons, and she
walked on a cloud of bloodmist toward The Pig.

The Lumenswine squatted over the Mound, busy hooking
his arms around a dead Minister. The demon boy in the pig's mask
flapped his own wings, wresting the holy man's sunken body from
the cursed ground like a rotten potato. Everything lower than his
waist was but a tangle of black soggy root and veins. The Mound
was sinking, all the soil around the Dead Tree's roots collapsing
into the deep hole where Dark Minister held the world together.

The King of Pigs squealed with glee while the wounded
harpy soared over him. She exited through the shattered window
into the smoky sky. He laughed heartily to see her flee.

"Where you running off to, child?" the Lumenswine
shouted after her. *"You're going to miss the best part!"*

Macho did not wear his usual police uniform. He wore
desert camouflage. Army fatigues. Dog tags. His hair was swept
up in a tight ponytail underneath a brown bandanna.

Esther shook her head. *"Macho, what the fuck?"*

The riverfolk man eyed Markus with keen interest. "If I
lower this gun, we going to have a problem?"

The boy said no.

He glanced at Esther. "How 'bout you?"

"No, sir."

The cop dropped his weapon and crouched near the fire.
There was another tremor in the ground. Some dust shook loose
from the ceiling and settled around them.

"As long as there isn't a cave-in, this is the best place to
wait this out," Wallace began, staring at the small flames. "I have
a truck hidden a few miles away around the other side of Orphan

416

Rock. After the feds secure the town, they'll have their hands full with cleanup and the media. That's when we sneak around the mountain, grab the truck, and leave through the back door." He poked the fire with a nearby stick. "That's my plan. You are welcome to live or die with your own."

"It's not safe here," Markus said again. He stood at the back of the cave. "There's a door here."

"What?" Macho walked behind him but couldn't see anything except normal shadows flickering along the wall and some old Pig Men heresy scrawled on the rock.

"There's a door here."

"Are you high, son?"

"He can see the doors, you dumb galoot," Esther said, joining them. "He's got a boon."

Macho ignored her. "Doors to what exactly?"

"The Spaces Between," the young man said, cupping his hand around a cigarette before lighting it. "Delora can build doors to new worlds. But there's space between those worlds. Padding. That's where the Sisters walk. It's...*complicated.*"

"The Sisters of Sorrow?"

"Yes. Delora," Esther said. "And things like her."

Macho frowned. "Things like *Shelby.*"

"Shelby ain't like Delora."

"Tell that to the family and cop she killed."

"For the last time, *fucker*, she was just a child! Why can't you understand that? You can't blame children for being what they are! They don't know shit. She couldn't help herself."

Macho laughed. "So, she hasn't been eating all of the casino trash the tribe's been sending your way the last three years?" He folded his arms. "That'd be a newsflash to us."

"*Of course, she's been eating them!*" Esther yelled, face turning red. "She has to eat like fucking everybody else! Better to have it controlled than not! *Are you fucking dumb?*"

"Half as dumb as you..."

"Quiet, both of you!" Markus interjected, he looked at the hidden door with his snake eyes. "This might be the best way for us to go. There are doors all over Ghost River. Maybe to other places too. Won't know until I check. I'm going to scout."

"Let's all go then," Esther said, looking for her rifle.

"No," Markus rejected the idea. "I'll move quicker without having to worry about you two behind me. I think you should follow Wallace's plan for now. I know how to get around these places. I'll be fine." He looked at Macho and pointed at the wall. "You'll need to watch this area right here. If it's not me that comes through, shoot it. They'll come at you in a pack. If they see you, so does she. You understand what I'm telling you?"

Wallace nodded.

"No! I'm not losing you again!" Esther ran over and wrapped her arms around him. "*Not fucking again.* I won't be able to live with it, and she'll fucking make me!" Esther tried not to cry but failed. "Please, Little Snake, *let's stay together just this once.*"

"All right," he said, gently pulling her in for a hug. Over her shoulder, Markus gave Wallace a nod. He returned the gesture. And with that, Little Snake shoved his mother into Macho's arms and slipped into the shimmering door in the shadows.

Delora circled above the bullets and the smoke. She flew high enough to feel the warm glow of the blood moon. She wanted to be in the quiet, surrounded by silent stars, to watch the ignition. Cracks formed around the edges of the Ghost River Valley—collapsing trenches widened into canyons—and mountain ranges shattered in two like brittle clods of dirt.

The Grim Seed broke free from the spoiled earth.

Finally, *misery was a machine.*

19.

Sleepy-eyed suburbanites watched from the culs-de-sac of Sandoval as Orphan Rock broke free from the Earth and rose from the ground into the yellowing pre-dawn sky.

When the Grim Seed disengaged from its crater, a thundering tremor shook the Ghost River Valley. Power lines snapped. Sewer pipes broke in half, spewing water like blood from cut veins. A growing tidal wave of dirt and rock rolled over the freeway, burying the casino and all the federal agents and first responders who had set up camp in the parking lot.

A mass-casualty event, but only the beginning.

Massive boulders and sharp crags long buried in the forgotten sands cracked away from the underside of the floating desert. They dropped like spearheads toward the ground, crushing SWAT vans and police cruisers trying to escape the reservation before the sinkhole swallowed them. Soil shook free from the eldritch roots on the bottom of the Grim Seed, and gigantic skull worms squiggled through metal holes underneath the juggernaut. Blind, hungry tendrils. Toothy and vicious earth-eaters.

The Grim Seed hovered over the painted desert, a monolith of perfect destruction drifting toward Sandoval for massacre. The Worms of Colossus tugged it along, their noses sniffing out life wherever it could be found. More suffering. *More salvation. More. The Grim Seed wanted more.*

The phantom lioness, Vengeant, burst through The Pig's hidden door from the Other Side to the shallowing Ghost River. Unaware of the landscape collapsing, she flew over the edge of the cliff into the dark chasm. Her golden claws cut into the mossy rocks. She dangled over a deep crater, the socket where a mountain had once sat. The flowing side of the river poured into the black gorge in the ground, draining the tributary. She clawed up the hot, split stone and stood in the mud. Dying fish flopped around her, gasping for air. The desert crumbled.

After all these years, Mother Dirt's shadow had shattered her shackles. Now, she was bound to the land, but the land was bound to nothing. Vengeant was too late.

Wrapped in the armor of a thousand scorned spirits, Vengeant bounded up the riverbank. Her golden leg braces carried her shifting forms—now a ghostmetal lioness big as a house—and her velocity uprooted ancient mesquite trees from the scorched earth when she blasted past. Her claws tilled the arid dirtscape, and her pads crushed boulders beneath them to pebbles.

In the distance, a dread jellyfish, some corrupted replica of the creatures that swallowed the sand on the Other Side, spewed steam and smog and howled in the warming dawn.

Even from far below, Vengeant smelled The Pig.

Surely, he sat above devastation in the Grim Seed now, hovering over the cities of mankind and raining down misery like tincture drops of acid. With a new body, the afflictions of the Grim Seed would not hinder his intention to destroy all the children.

The Age of Filth.

Had it already begun?

"*Jesus fucking Christ!*" Esther rocked her hips back and forth, standing at the mouth of Father Pig's hidden cave watching the world fall apart. They caused this, didn't they? All of them? Should she feel guilty for wanting this? This was Minister's promise. The way out for her. The Grim Seed watered. Delora avenged. The curse lifted. *Or just getting started, Coyote?*

"Get your guns." Macho grabbed her arm. His tone was remarkably unsteady. For as long as Esther knew him, Macho could be many different things but always steady. Now he watched Orphan Rock soar like an eagle, and he had no more sobriety to share. "*Hurry.* We can't stay here."

"Are you fucking nuts? There's nowhere to go!" She followed him into the cave again. "You think we're gonna get that truck and then what? Drive off the side of the goddamn cliff? Markus said stay put. That's what we should do."

"Well, that was before the desert decided it wanted to learn how to fly. The boy is fully grown and can manage on his own. Hell, he's probably safer than we are being in a different dimension right now." Macho checked his pistols in the firelight. "Christ, I can't believe I just said that. Everything is wrong and upside down. What the fuck have we done?"

Esther didn't bother with guns. Instead, she studied the wall Markus had disappeared through. She squinted at the cave paintings, unfocused her eyes, and felt for a draft.

"Can you see the door? Maybe we can go after him."

"Esther, we're not like them."

"I've been in The Dark before." Her search turned frantic as her desperation mounted. "Them Broken Kids know how, and they're dumb as rocks. We can figure it out! Help me look…"

Wallace reached for her. "Esther—"

She quickly slapped his hand away. "*Don't you touch me! You don't get that right.*" She snatched a pistol from his holster.

Macho raised his hands, backing away. "You almost shot my daughter. She was just a baby, and you tried to fuckin' kill her. I ain't ever forgiven you for that. Never will."

"She's killed a lot of innocent people. Futures stolen. Family's shattered." Macho watched the gun shake in her hand. "Don't their lives matter just as much?"

"*Not to me!*" Esther spat. "They don't mean shit to me." She pointed at the exit. "Go on and look out of that cave again. You'll see nothing but Orphan Rock, this fucking desert, and the goddamn sun. Well, that's all I've ever seen. My view don't change much. *My children are all that I have left.* I'm surrounded by ghosts, and they're all I've ever had to love."

"Esther..." He approached slowly. She didn't fight back when he wrapped his arms around her. Felt like home, those strong arms, a place she missed more than she'd ever say. "I loved you," he said. "Still do, I suppose. That's why I'm here. I did what I swore I'd never do again, and that's step foot on Sister Dirt's land. But for you? I'd step into Hell and shoot the Devil himself."

Esther looked up from his chest.

"Macho," she whispered. "All my life men made me promises. Tried to save me from what I am." She kissed his cheek. "But nobody ever was brave enough to do what I wanted them to do. There's only one way to save me." *Click!* The pistol pressed against his forehead. "Make me a promise."

Macho nodded calmly. "OK, Esther. I'm listening."

"If they come for us, if they find us here...the Broken Kids, Delora, Father Pig, or whoever the fuck else crawls out of whatever hole is left...I want you to promise to shoot me in the head." Esther's voice cracked under the weight of her request. Macho had never seen her scared before. Not once.

"Esther..."

"I'm fucking serious. I don't want to be one of them. I don't want to be here anymore. I'm done letting Delora hurt me. Please, Macho. Promise. *They'll never let me go.*"

"Only if you do the same for me."

Esther lowered the gun and raised her other hand. He looked at her uplifted finger, not sure what to do with it.

"Pinkie swear me," she said, her tone serious as a graveyard. "That's a sacred promise. You can't ever break it, or else it's a hundred years of bad luck."

Wallace wrapped his around hers.

"All right, I swear. We go, we go together."

"Come what may?"

"Come what fucking may."

Quakes. Explosions. Gas fires. Broken glass. Severed limbs. Crushed corpses leaking hot guts on concrete. Giant earthworms swallowing homes, cars, people, pets, and potted plants without discrimination. They devoured everything, erasing an entire neighborhood in minutes. The Grim Seed hummed above, a flying sleigh of devastation pulled by the Worms of Colossus. The juggernaut drifted toward Phoenix. Sirens wailed in protest. Jet planes screamed across the sky. The city greeted the new morning dominated by chaos and teeth.

Vengeant kept her molten eyes locked on the smoky horizon, chasing after the croaking dreadnaught that slithered over gas stations and strip malls. Her ghostmetal form stomped over cars, fleeing people, and whatever else was unlucky enough to be between her and killing the King of Pigs.

Whomp! A peculiar pod hit the street before her, nearly striking the lioness down when it dropped from the underbelly of the Grim Seed. She veered away just in time, slamming into a house, buckling its aluminum garage door. Whatever fell from the sky hid beneath a fog of dried clay dust.

What was that?

Vengeant eyed the hazy street. Then she roared when a spindly marionette leaped from the bloom of dust onto the

423

pavement, its scythe-shaped arms raised by strings of dirt magic. It had the face of a mantis—two black eyes set on a horse-like skull—and it skittered on four legs. The bony creature, stitched together by unearthly means, spread its blue wings, and screeched like a detuned violin. Vengeant jumped for it, ready to strike it down, but it flew into the sky with newborn vigor.

Whomp! Whomp! Whomp!

She spun on her golden braces as more pods hit the burning cityscape. Hundreds of them descended from the bottom of the Grim Seed, dropping into Sandoval like bombs from a fighter jet. Soon the streets swarmed with the mantis reapers. They sliced through homes, snatched crying people from their hiding places, and delivered warm bodies to the worms to devour.

Vengeant could not stay down here. There was nothing she could do from below. To murder the Pig Father, she needed to ascend to the floating chunk of desertscape. There, the King of Pigs would be watching the world smolder with milky eyes.

But how? Without wings on her form, she could not fly. Without ghosts to absorb, she could not grow tall enough to reach it as she had done with the sky door on the Other Side.

Whoosh! An entire row of two-story homes disintegrated into wood chips and bits of Spanish tile as a worm swept down the street. Vengeant made her decision, ran, and leaped after it, and buried her cat claws into the fleshy, brown tube of the dirt eater. The colossal worm zigged and zagged, but she held on. Around her, grim marionettes gathered in the air for battle.

Dark Bird soared over the living nightmare that was Orphan Rock. *What a sight!* A floating mountain that touched the clouds, a zit on the face of Earth that had plucked itself from the planet and tossed itself away in the sky.

How did Mother build such a machine?
How did this box hold together?

Is Jake safe?

So many questions, but who cared anymore? She'd been betrayed her entire life, and Shelby wanted off this fucking ride. The Grim Seed was watered, and the garden had bloomed. She was going to take Esther and Jake and Pink and blow this pop stand. Fuck the dirt curse, the Broken Kids, and a special fuck you very much to Mother Dearest, Delora.

A pulse of blue in the smoggy din, then a shadow emerged from the plume of smoke. A creature that Dark Bird recognized buzzed past by carrying a dead woman. A stitched-up mantis built from the meat of the dead and fueled by the suffering of fools in that factory below. She gnashed her teeth, ready to rip the bug apart, but it flew past the harpy toward the Old Sinkhole.

It doesn't care, she thought. *More slaves.*

Dark Bird folded her wings to gain speed in her descent. Her talons touched ground in front of the stone-stacked house. Piles of corpses littered the yard. Tents and bloody coolers, smashed windshields, and wailing alarms. Where were the Broken Kids? Clearly, Mother no longer cherished her Baby Bird. They would come for her, just like Potato Sack had.

Let them fucking come.

Inside the remodeled visitor's center, Dark Bird transformed into Shelby again and marched into the nursery. Two women straddled a naked husk in the corner. One of them studied Shelby's naked body and called her pretty before cutting open her own throat with a broken bottle. The teenager rolled her eyes—*I hate this place*—tore open the fly door and stepped into her sandbox oasis. Pink met her at the top of the dune, gurgling happily to see her. Shelby ran down the sand to her atrium.

"Jake!" she yelled. "Where are you? Jake? Answer me!"

She couldn't smell her servant nearby. The scents of him faded. She knelt and put her hand on the ground, trying to shape an answer from the sand. But he was not here.

"*Jake!*"

425

Shelby chewed her knuckle, unsure of what to do next. She thought of the corpses bleeding in the sand. Was Jake among them? She had not smelled him there either. But if he and Esther weren't here, where would they be? Jake was told to wait in the visitor's center, and he would not disobey her commands. Jake was a wonderfully obedient slave with cool hair.

Shelby rounded one of the ancient columns and met the only good eye of Snarl. The Broken Kid sat on the sand, his barbed arms wrapped around his bony kneecaps. There was a nasty wound on his neck. He raised swollen purple hands when he saw Dark Bird. "I come in peace," he said weakly.

"Where's Jake? *He's mine.*" Shelby lunged toward him with a ferocious grin, but the boy didn't move.

"I don't know," he said.

"You're a liar. She tells you *everything.*"

"Not anymore. It's over, Baby Bird. We won."

"And you're crying about it?"

"I am a little." His face looked more childlike than she'd ever seen. "I only ever wanted a mother. She was that to me. For a long time. Now I sit in your sandbox, an orphan once again."

"What? She break up with you or something?"

Air bubbles popped from his bloody throat gash when he laughed. "I'm no longer needed to speak for her. No one will ever speak to Mother again, in fact. *Misery is a machine.*"

Leg on the pedestal, Shelby laced up her favorite oxblood Doc Martens with a frown. How could anyone, living or dead, love Delora? "She is a cruel and terrible mother."

Snarl shook his head, eye heavy with sorrow. "She was the opposite of that. Suffering was her love language. The more Mother hurt you, the more she loved you."

"You're talking in the past tense."

"That's what we are, Baby Bird."

Shelby pulled a black Nine Inch Nails t-shirt over her bruised shoulders. Potato Sack's teeth marks still fresh on her skin.

"If you're free from Delora, you should be fucking celebrating," she said. "All your little cockroach friends seem to be off the leash right now." Shelby tucked an extra pack of smokes in her flannel pocket. "I killed the fat one, by the way. Pulled a fucking demon out of his already-a-demon mouth. Thought you should know."

"Such is life for a forsaken child."

The teenager folded her arms and tapped her steel toe against travertine. "You're a sad fucking sack, Snarl. I planned on killing you, but you're almost too pathetic to hurt. Definitely too pathetic to eat." She paused to think. Then, she had an idea. Her lips curled. "Where's Jake and Coyote? Tell me, and I might be nice to you. Maybe you'll have a happier ending."

"Happy? I doubt it." Snarl coughed up more blood, cursed dirt dribbling from his chin. "But it doesn't matter anymore. All of the meat is one of two places: the chapel or in The Dark."

Shelby said nothing else and marched up the white dunes. The Broken Kid returned his head to his knees and sniffled in the sandy expanse. When the fifteen-year-old returned, she held the hand of Pink. Snarl looked confused to see the little one in the filthy dress. Pink grinned a little to see the motherless boy.

"This is Pink," Shelby said. "You're going to take care of her, you understand me? *She is mine.*" Dark Bird's black eyes glimmered beneath her mask. "And now, *so are you.*"

Vengeant's claws sunk deeper into the rubbery flesh of the towering worm she clung to. Its body rippled as rolling waves of food squeezed through its system, pumping flesh, bone, and debris upward and into the bowels of Orphan Rock. She examined the wormholes in the belly of the floating juggernaut. Still so far away from the top. But the holes might provide a way to slip into The Dark after the Lumenswine if she could make it inside of one.

Buzz! She swiped at an approaching mantis, her claws shredding through its satin wings. The creature shrieked as it fell toward the burning city below. Others tried to peel her away, too, but she batted the invaders away like mosquitoes.

She kept climbing.

Up.

Eyes up.

No other direction but up.

The ghostmetal lioness gripped the ridges of the worm's skin with her golden braces, brown meat dripping from the holes her claws left behind. Luckily, the worm was too busy eating to feel her pinpricks. And if the puppets remained captivated by the carnage below, she might have a chance at making—

Thwack! A black barb pierced her unarmored paw, pumping fire into her ghostly veins. Vengeant yelped and held on with her other claw. Moth wings beat against the sky, and multifaceted fly eyes watched the lioness climb without emotion. Below its human waist, the fiend only had a long black scorpion tail. She howled when it pulled its stinger away to strike again. Vengeant dodged another blow, narrowly avoiding a second dose of venom. The stinger pierced the flesh of the worm instead. Above, the rubbery tube moaned, annoyed by the prick.

Then, two strange scorpion-beasts fluttering around her, flicking their whiplash tails. Vengeant was dragged into a game of whack-a-mole, except she was the mole, and the whackers were deadly. She absorbed several stings but resisted the poison, so they switched tactics, trying to pull her off the worm instead. She swung her claws whenever they came close. She cut the tail off one, and the monster simply drifted away on the wind.

Meanwhile, the worm underneath her grew agitated. It wriggled out of rhythm. The defenders paralyzed it with every missed sting, injecting more numbing poison into their giant ally. When she glanced up, Vengeant noticed her worm slipping out of its hole. "*Hold on,*" Vengeant urged her living ladder.

But it was already too late. Poison made it convulse, and the mighty worm fell from the belly of the Grim Seed. Vengeant roared and leaped off the falling coil, burying her claws into the tails of two more scorpion men that swooped down from the misery machine. Their moth wings flapped helplessly under her weight. Before they could shimmy free, the lioness tore their tails from their bodies and propelled her phantasmal mass toward another passing Worm of Colossus. When her claws sunk into the slimy rubber, guts and grease leaked out all over her. She slid down the skin, slicing it open like a cat on curtains.

Yet she held on.

Didn't lose too much ground.

This time, she kept her eyes open for the flying sentinels. Coast turned clearer, the higher she ascended. Seemed like the worker bees had their hands full with razing suburbia. Soon she was under the umbrella of the floating mountain.

I need an entrance.

Her worm wriggled in a tight hole it did not want to share. Across the squiggling landscape, she eyed the empty socket from where the other worm had fallen. She could see the dead behemoth below, stretching a mile across the inflamed ruins of the city.

Rocks and exposed roots helped her monkey bar across the jagged bottom of the Grim Seed. When she was close enough, she heaved herself into the cavernous hole left behind by the poisoned worm. Glad to have a footing, she faced The Dark ahead.

Markus tracked the sounds of sobbing. At least there was *something* to guide him in The Dark.

This place was unlike any box he'd seen before. Desyre always said that Delora was mad as a mongrel, a deranged architect of the highest order. Maybe she was, but Markus couldn't help questioning the sheer volume of doors built in the Spaces Between Things. Haphazard, manic, twisted, yet somehow ordered into a black labyrinth designed over decades that only led deeper into the core of whatever made reality. But the sobbing.

That was something to follow, wasn't it? It grew louder, and so did the light as Markus stepped through another door.

A cliffside framed the nightmare below. A city swallowed by meat-sucking serpents. Rubble and smoke. Neighborhood blocks and gridded roads ground to sand and bone.

Lying on the open ledge, a freakishly large girl watched the living catastrophe like it was on television. A film of ruddy silt covered her skin. Her violet eye—her only eye—blinked at the destruction with indifference. Around her, glistening worm heads squirmed, dying, severed from their bodies when part of the mountain broke off over Sandoval.

"I can smell you," she said, clutching an old teddy bear against her chest. "You are not dead. How have you come through my tunnels?" She sniffed the air. "Ah, boonchild."

Markus nodded. "Born a snake."

"Then you are Pigborn."

"And you're one of them. Sister…?" Markus approached the hulking child's body. The rifle on his shoulder warned him to be ready to use it.

"Worm," she said. "I eat the dirt. I shape the tunnels between things. But there are no more things to shape now. They've destroyed so many boxes. Those who serve the Filth."

"Is this really happening?" He gestured to the madness unfolding beneath them. When he'd stepped into The Dark, Orphan Rock was just a dumb, dirty mountain and not a mayhem machine. "I know not all places and times are real here. Your kind shapes illusions, but I've never seen anything like this." He inched toward the dangerous ledge. Below, a state of emergency. Helicopters whizzed by, blades slicing through the smoky air.

Markus felt the seedling of an idea take root.

A fucking long shot.

The girl sighed, exhaling a poof of dust from between her dirt-caked lips. "The Grim Seed is real, Snake Boy. All this is real. To catch a pig, she needed a cage."

"You mean, Delora?"

"She's not the one to blame. Sister Dirt. She's the sneaky one. She reached too far into the dirt, trying to poison what dwells in the oldest cracks. Now the Grim Seed will eat the world to feed its growing roots. I will watch from here, tell little Reuben all of my secrets, and wait to be eaten by the Filth too."

"The Filth?"

Sister Worm's eye sparkled with grim knowledge. "There are very deep doors, so old and scary, you'll never want to find one. One door leads to a place that is full of things like me. Like Delora. Like The Pig. That's how all of this began. The Pig was first to slither through, but he won't be the last to stain the dirt." Sister Worm smiled darkly. "More are coming, and I fear my Sister did more to help them than she knows."

Markus thought of Esther. Nothing he could do about forbidden doors, dire prophecies, and worlds filled with monsters waiting to break through the crust. Those were problems for heroes to handle. He had real people that needed his help now. He could focus on that shit. Fuck the rest.

"Sister, can you show me a way out of this box?"

Her violet eye looked away. "There is no way out. Nowhere to go. No ancient earth to eat." The Grim Seed rumbled, and more debris fell around them. "There is only filth now."

"I need to get to the river." Markus knelt beside her. The outline of his body reflected in her quivering eyeball. "Is there a way to the river here somewhere?"

"To the river above? Yes. Below? Not anymore." One of the wounded worms nearby curled up, shit out its organs, and died. "Can't you see what's happening?" Sister Worm's large bony fist punched the ledge in anger. "Doors and tunnels crumbling. Everything is changing! Everything is dying. *I hate it!*"

Markus pointed upward. "The river above. *Please.*"

"Why? It is dry and cracked and boring."

"I left something there. Will you help me find it?"

"I think I'm finally dying," Sister Worm replied. "I have so few lovelies left to love. What can I do to help you if we're all dying and without love?"

"You're a builder. You can make doors."

"No. Sister Worm digs the tunnels between doors."

Markus grinned. Sister Worm's cheeks turned rosy to see his charming affections. "So, can you...dig a tunnel *for me*? Would you do that and show me your power?"

"Just you?"

"And my mother and her friend."

"I could *maybe* do that..."

"But?"

"If I do, you have to be my boyfriend. You must stay with me forever. I am tired of spending years alone in the dark holes of my box. *We can be married in the mud.*"

Sister Worm found strength and lifted her head. Her sharp, metal teeth were capped by the ancient dirt she ate. Markus used a nearby rock to steady himself when the cavern shook once more. It would not be safe in The Dark for long. It, too, was changing. And fast.

"So, if I agree to be your...*boyfriend*—"

"*Forever.*"

"*Forever.* You'll help us get to the river?"

"I could *maybe* do that..."

Shelby slashed through the horsefly door into the nursery. As she passed through the static of dimensions, the harpy tore down the portal behind her. She folded the entrance to her oasis like an origami flower. Inside was her sandbox, her childhood, and Pink and Snarl. She folded it tight enough to slip into a cellophane wrapper from an empty pack of Marlboros. She slid it into her combat boot for safekeeping. Moving day was bittersweet, but she wouldn't leave Orphan Rock without a souvenir to remember it by. Now she needed to find Esther and Jake.

She emerged from the stone-stacked house, a smoke dangling out of her wide mouth, her black eyes circled by shadow. She would not hide her true face anymore. Her razor-sharp plume stood on edge. Her long fingers sharpened to blades. She would not fully transform yet, but she would be ready to fight.

Broken Kids reveled in the corpse-scatter down the river rock path. As she suspected, they were feral now. Carrion pickers. A few dared to look at her, but the rest scampered away.

In Orphan Rock proper, the cabin fires raged, but that was just the beginning of the wildfire. The desert was a tinderbox, even during monsoon season, and flames spread in all directions. It crept up the mountain, leaving a trail of black ash behind.

At the Chapel on the Mound, bloodroots grew all over the stone structure, even wrapped around one of Esther's biker servants. His body hung from the chapel porch while squiggling roots slithered down his throat and burst through his belly with purple blooms. She stomped up the stairs, took a puff, and pressed her cigarette ember against the thorny bramble. Roots squirmed away from the fire, clearing away from the brittle doors.

Bam! They exploded off their rusty hinges and landed somewhere in the dim of the ghastly nave.

Dark Bird marched over corpses piled at the entrance, freshly slaughtered by Mother. She walked down the desecrated isle between the scratched pews. Her boots splashed in puddles of bloody filth. She stood before the shadow at the altar—a crooked figure kneeling next to the Dead Tree that had sprouted new silver leaves that jingled like church bells in the dry wind.

"*Mother*. Give me Jake and Esther."

The figure did not stir.

"I did my part. I'm leaving like I said."

The figure rose from the dirt bed and turned to face her. It was a child covered in centipedes, wearing a hideous mask sewn from skin, sitting in the darkest hole where the Minister funneled sorrow into the Heart of the Desert. It had Luminarch wings, a greasy pig's nose, and its eyes curdled like cream.

"There you are," the figure said, voice twangy and low. "*My youngest.* Come to watch her daddy be reborn?"

"Who are you?" Shelby took a step back, feeling a shiver rattle her spine. "Where's Delora?"

"She's relinquished command of this operation," the stranger said. Sickles motioned for her to approach the Mound. "I've never seen your real face before." His expression turned wicked. "You're a pretty little thing, aren't you? You like to misbehave? It's OK. So do I." He winked over a wet snout. "Why don't you come a bit closer? Let's get to know each other."

"Father Pig," Dark Bird said, smoke drifting from her lips. "That right?"

"In the flesh." The swine king bowed.

"You're not supposed to be here."

"Oh yeah? Well, here I am, chickling."

"How?" Shelby abandoned her smoke and crossed her arms. "Tell me. We watered the seed. You're supposed to be smoke in the wind. Some dead history by now."

The Lumenswine snickered. "Sister Dirt forgot where I came from. Where she did too. Our home is a world filled with grimmer seeds and ghastlier gardens than this one. Her seed ain't the only special crop in this soil that needed a little love to grow. I spent years cutting throats after throats after throats here, trying to grow myself again. Then Sister Dirt came along to tend to my garden. Her green thumb was blood red, and I couldn't be happier. Only thing you've been pumping into this dirt is the blood into *my* fucking veins. She led her sheep astray. Shocking, isn't it?"

His shrill laughter cut into her mind.

He mocked her—all of them.

Her claws tempered. "This can't be right…"

"Oh, it's more than right." The Pig beamed. "It's what was meant to be. I am the prophet, you see. And holy men must always die before the *big* resurrection happens. I had to spend a little time in the wilderness, finding my faith again in The Dark. Meanwhile, my flock built a church to welcome me home. The Grim Seed was the architect, and you and your kin were my hands."

"That's not what we were trying to do."

Putrid eyes sparkled with glee. "But it's what you did." He paused to savor her discontent, watching her face fill with anger and confusion. "That's the sweet poison pill about prophecy and destiny," he continued. "It makes you think you have a choice. That you're not just some dumb pawn playing a rigged game. But guess what? You are, and you did. *Sucker.*"

Shelby's stomach roiled with fury. Her long lips bent into the bitterest frown she could muster, a frown so deep, it looked like her face was melting off her oval skull. Her voice flattened. "I want Jake and Esther, and then I want to leave. Whatever hippy-dippy Jonestown bullshit you're running here isn't my concern. I want out. And I want the dirt out of my fucking belly too."

"No. Esther's mine until she's dead."

"So, she's alive then?"

"Until she ain't no more."

"She deserves to live. She's been kind to me."

The Pig laughed. "Why torture yourself with empathy? You're not some little pretend human living in a dollhouse. There's no happy family in your future. Embrace your pigginess." The Lumenswine's eyes grew brighter and beadier. "Besides, this world don't want you anyway. If they knew what you are, they'd toss you into a dirty hole without thinking twice about it."

Shelby smirked. "Like the one you're sitting in?"

The Pig's eyes sparked up like flint. Cold fingers slipped under her skin, ran down her mouth, and even though he was across the chapel, she felt him touching every part of her body, groping, and squeezing her in ways that made her sick. Suddenly, he was a parasite inside of her, stabbing and scratching and biting at her walls of self until they gave way to him. Dark Bird grabbed her head, dropped to her knees, and cried out in terror.

"Get out of me!"

But he refused. Greedy sickles flicked through her memories—relived conversations, re-created moments, and smashed her lockboxes. Shelby howled while the King of Pigs chased her in the metal halls of her mind, cornering her in a dead-end. The desert demon snorted, gummy jowls dripping with thick mucus. Inside, Shelby screamed for help. Outside, her nose bled.

The Lumenswine cackled in delight. "My, my, I was right! You are prone to misbehaving. *Delicious sin.*" The Pig's greasy snout pressed against her lips. She felt him crawl on top of her. "So delicious, my little princess. *I could just kiss you—*"

Boom! Boom! Crash!

Bramble, brick, and plank shotgunned across the sanctuary. The Lumenswine withdrew, and Shelby fell to the floor, gasping for breath, unable to smell the shit-covered fur grinding against her skin anymore. Sunshine poured into the giant hole behind her, and Dark Bird rolled over, covering her eyes against the dazzling desert sun. There in the nave, a giant phantasmal lioness roared, wrapped in wisps of spirits, and trimmed with gold metal. Beneath a broken bull's skull, two crimson eyes burned brighter than dying coals. When it leaped for The Pig, Dark Bird scrambled to her feet and eyed the exit. Freedom, Esther, and Jake were somewhere through it.

And then, so was she.

Drone ants and worker bees.

That's all they were.

Carrying food. Back to the hive? To the queen?

Somewhere.

Macho lowered his binoculars.

"Fuck if I know, Esther," he said, answering her question before she could even ask. "I've seen some messed up things in my life. Some left deep scars. You own a few. 'Nam owns a handful. My upbringing in a stolen world owns the rest. I've always had a way to see the answers and lessons in tragedy...but I don't know what to say this time. Whatever rules there are never applied here in Orphan Rock. Why should any of it make sense now?" Esther took his hand, but he didn't blink. "They're fucking monsters. They're everywhere. What can we do but pray?"

"Macho, there's a simple rule in Orphan Rock that never changes. Never has. Never will. *Give up hope, and you have no value.* You're food is all." She felt his fist tighten, loosen, unsure. "'Sides, monsters are easy. They have rules. People? Fucked up people like you and me? We're something they'll never put down because we know it will *always* get worse unless we fight back."

He placed his hands on her shoulders and let his face settle into resignation. "We're probably going to die," he said sadly. "I want you to be clear-eyed on that—no sugarcoating. I guarantee you there's a super-secret situation room in progress in Washington DC right now. They're looking at fancy charts about collateral damage and picking the shortest bar on the graph. We're that bar. We're going to be the choice they pick."

"What choice?"

"Bombs away."

Esther chuckled. "It's really for the best."

He cracked a tiny grin—solemn but playful. "I cannot argue that point, Mrs. Northamm. It would be better for all of mankind if Orphan Rock were vaporized this afternoon."

"Miss Northamm," Esther said distantly. "I guess I'm officially a fuckin' widow now."

"You've been one for a long time."

Esther looked to the ground.

"What's wrong?"

She dropped her voice to a murmur. "I need you to hear me say something. I don't want to, but it needs to be said. I won't ever speak on it again afterward so don't ask me to."

"What is it?"

Her watering gaze met Macho's tender eyes. She squeezed his hands so hard they hurt. "Thank you for doing it. *Minister.* I know it was you. The one who put him down."

"Esther—

"I dreamed of it, promised I would be the one to pull the trigger, but...he wanted to hang on. See it through. You won't understand, but it was our promise, our secret thing we both needed to believe in to be OK. I couldn't snuff that out. I—"

"He was my best friend," Wallace interrupted. "The day I met him in the river, I knew..."

"Knew what?"

"He'd already signed his life away to this place. After I met my first ghost, we ran together."

Rumble! Stone crumbled in the cavern. A puff of dust blew down the throat of the Father Pig's abandoned cave. Macho snapped down his rifle, forgetting all about the reapers in the glum sky, and Esther followed him, forgetting her tears. There, by the fire, a freshly dug hole in the wall where the Pig Men's mural used to be. When the particles settled, Markus appeared.

Esther hugged him. *"Thank Christ, you're safe!"*

The boy looked in no mood for sentimental reunions. Sweat dampened his brow. "It's bad. Real fucking bad." He looked at Macho. "Can you still fly a helicopter?"

"A helicopter?"

"I came here in one. We left it near the river by the old shed where Daddy took the roadkills. Might still be there if that part of the valley ain't been destroyed."

Wallace straightened his spine. "If it's there, I'll fly it."

Esther poked her head into the tunnel. She felt like she wasn't alone. Felt like eyes were on her. Beady-fucking-eyes. Then she saw one blink in a flash of lavender. "Holy shit!"

A pulsating tube quickly covered it up.

Esther raised her rifle, eyes wide with fear.

Rat-Tat-Tat! The muzzle flash illuminated the rounds piercing the giant worm's rubbery dermis.

"*Stop!*" Markus pushed her smoking barrel down.

"*There's a goddamn Medusa back there!*"

"No! Momma, no!" He looked helplessly in The Dark but could only see a worm leaking meat and soil from bullet holes. The girl hid in the shadows beyond. "*There's an ally back there. Sister Worm is her name. She's nice and...pretty.* She has the loveliest worms who are going to carve us a special tunnel."

"A Sister of Sorrow?" Macho joined Esther in raising his pistols. "That what you mean?"

"Yes, but she's cool." Markus winked, giving them the signal to play along. "She's going to help us dig a tunnel to the helicopter. They're killing everybody in the open."

Esther cocked her head. "An ally? What the fuck is in that hole, Markus?"

"Sister Worm. She's going to—"

"*I'm furious at you!*" a childish voice yelled.

"Everything is fine, darling! Little mistake is all! Folks are a bit scared!" Markus laughed nervously over his shoulder. Then, he turned back to his companions and lowered his voice. "Listen, if we want out of here, we have to trust Sister Worm, and we have to run. We gotta stay close. No matter what, we have to keep up and stick together. The tunnels aren't lasting. The Grim Seed's changing reality in ways I can't reckon with. It's a goddamn Rubik's cube in the Spaces Between Things right now."

Esther peered into The Dark again. "How are we going to see down there?"

"I've got some flares." Macho unzipped his backpack. "They'll last a while."

"Remember, we need to run like the desertfolk we are. Pretend the whole goddamn mountain's coming down on top of us, 'cause it is. *Don't stop for nothing.*"

Vengeant's heavy paws pinned the Lumenswine to the Mound. The possessed boy with butterfly wings struggled beneath the lioness. Her fangs dripped with liquid excitement, sensing her betrayer inside a frail, little vessel. The Pig, who tricked the little girl and left her for dead in a world without color or love, tried to slip inside of Sister Dirt's warrior to dominate her, but there was a legion of minds in between him and the true soul of Vengeant. He could not pry his way through them fast enough.

"*What are you?*" he asked, squirming in the mud.

"You do not remember us?" Vengeant spoke with a thousand strong voices. "Beneath you, burned by you, beaten by you…we are the orphans who will haunt you forever."

The King of Pigs squinted. The demon behind the mask smiled upon recognizing a tiny ghost in the maelstrom of Vengeant. "I know you, don't I?" he whispered pensively. The ghostmetal lioness said nothing. "Yes, I surely do. In a room with windows, Mary caught a Little Lamb…"

"One of the many shapes that *hate you*."

Vengeant shifted into the form of a golem, a creature made from claw, bone, clay, and straw. Her rocky fingers curled around the Lumenswine's throat. She squeezed it with all her strength. His sickles sparked off her stony wrists in panic. He gasped and choked and spit until his white eyes rolled back into his boyish skull and his head fell limp. No more kicks. No more struggle. No snorts. No more squeals. She didn't let go. Not yet. His mouth lolled open. His pig mask fell from his black-veined cheeks.

"You are just another dead child."

When spoiled earth tugged for his lifeless body, she finally released him. The dead Lumenswine sunk into the crumbling Mound, pulled under by greedy roots until he was gone.

I have avenged you, Mother Dirt.

The wildfire spread to the rafters of the chapel. Old wood

crackled with flame. Bloodroots squiggled in horror, twisting, and shrieking in fiery disarray. *This unholy place will fall soon.*

Vengeant stood from the Dead Tree. Her quest had ended with the Pig's death, and now he slept in the same dirt he long stained. The phantasmal warrior looked around the filthy chapel— quiet now, except for the snap of fire kissing wood. The beast wondered *what next?* Mother Dirt never told her what to expect once justice ended in blood. Would she disappear? Would the spirits inside of her flicker into memory? Would she burst into white light and then be gone? Surely, Mother Dirt would not leave her to haunt this accursed ground for eternity.

Or would she?

Crack! Crack! Craaaacccck!

Vengeant leaped away from the spreading chasm when the gore-soaked ground shuddered, and the wooden floor bowed and cracked apart around her in a storm of splinters. The collapsing chapel tremored as the ground swelled beneath her claws like a boil. The Dead Tree shook free from the dirt, and Father Pig's greatest miracle rose from the Mound: A King of Pigs, reborn.

Dark Bird landed softly in the bone chamber beneath Delora's wretched nest. Little ghostlings giggled and scampered around like flickering crickets. A spectral snake with red eyes could not catch them. In death he struck with smoky fangs. No poison. No dislocated jaw. Just echoes.

In her mission to find Jake, Esther, or Delora, Dark Bird tried to shake the memory of The Pig from her mind, but he had left too many wounds inside of her to forget so quickly. She could feel herself bleeding internally. Vicious, greedy pig. Powerful. More than she was. Dark Bird was no fool. Fighting against a desert demon was a losing proposition. Besides, she had other plans. Whatever is happening at that church had nothing to do with escaping Orphan Rock. The desert was a jail cell. Fuck Ghost

River. Fuck pigs. Dark Bird *was busting out.*

"Jake?" she called out, her Doc Martens toeing over dry femurs and skulls from old meals. "Esther?" Shelby spun in the dim cavern. "Anybody home?" Only the breeze of the high skies whistling through Orphan Rock made any noise.

She paused to admire an old mural on the wall painted from blood and cactus juice by long-dead hands. The eater of men. A shaper, a builder of worlds. An owl who lived in the river next to a pig. *Delora.* Where had Mother run off to? Too ashamed to learn that all of her work was for nothing? Too embarrassed that The Pig tricked them all into doing exactly what it wanted?

"Mother! Show yourself!"

Dark Bird walked near the harpy's prized workbench. It smelled like skin. Potato Sack lay where she left him. He decomposed without the Grim Seed's false life. A figure hunched over the boy, stuffing her grinning face with graying flesh.

Clink!

The rusty hook just missed Dark Bird's face, and she flapped to the far side of the room. Spider Girl shuffled back and forth on the floor, intent on protecting her prize. Juicy lips stretched between pigtails in a mad clown's snarl. Her four bent legs scrambled, moving her across the floor in a hypnotic widow's dance. She raised her arms in a strange rhythm, her movements a beautiful warning. She hissed at Shelby, who only watched with darkening, rage-fueled eyes.

"Bitch, you picked the wrong day to fuck with me." Dark Bird retracted her talons and shot like a bullet toward the arachnid, puncturing the Broken Kid's waifish chest. The Spider Girl slammed against the wall, kicking desperately. Dark Bird seized her lanky arm by the wrist just before a hook struck her ear. With a twist of the elbow, Spider Girl's cheek hit the floor.

Whomp! Shelby's heel smashed the freak's face into the ground. Spider Girl's jagged grin collapsed, her jaws crushed against stone. ***Swink!*** A curved talon pierced the steel toe of her boot, splitting Spider Girl's lower lip to her chin. The monster howled, hooked like a fish, while Dark Bird beamed, twisting her brittle arm with such force that it broke off her shoulder.

The battered Broken Kid squirmed and choked on rusty screw teeth, but Dark Bird was in no mood for mercy. She used her arm as a bludgeon and repeatedly bashed the rusty hook into Spider Girl's face. *Clink! Clink! Clink!* Pieces of meat soared from the curvature of the hook and graying muscle stripped from grinning cheekbones. Over and over and over again, Dark Bird beat her, laughing with unrivaled joy with every blow until the Spider Girl was dead again. Her bendy legs curled up into the air as her final, stinking breath released her from the world.

Dark Bird kicked over her corpse and tossed the arm away. She wiped blood across her cheek like warpaint. Her oily eyes burned with the glow of after-death.

"*Mother!*"

Her voice ricocheted off the cave walls.

"Have we sung the song yet?"

Her bloody smile drowned in deepening waters when a perfect rock star played the encore of his unlife. Jake drifted down from the dark womb above her where the eldest widows' webs were woven, his body held in place by a noose of barbed wire. A few Luminarchs lit his skeletal smile. He was dead and made broken—one more thing taken from her by Mother.

Dark Bird screeched so loud the hollow mountain shook.

The Dead Tree was not a tree.

A rack of antlers atop the god's head burst from the dirt, striking the rafters in the sanctuary. Hairy shoulders rose from the spreading sinkhole that sucked under all the splintery pews. The Chapel on the Mound collapsed around the reborn deity in a pile of tinder and stone and thorny vine. Huge pig eyes, white as pearl bowling balls, rose above a furry frame.

The Gloom Boar, the first Prophet of the Age of Filth, stood on two hooves, a monstrosity wrapped in bloodroot and covered in football-sized grubs. Desiccated flesh stretched over the desert demon's bony ribs. Metal tusks glinted in the midmorning light. His face was wooly and his snout long. When his dusty jowls peeled open, it flashed rotten pig teeth.

Beneath the Dead Tree, a usurped boy-god with butterfly wings sunk into the Gloom Boar's forehead. The Lumenswine drove the giant wretch like a crane operator. His alabaster eyes shimmered beneath an impious halo of a thousand shining Luminarchs. *"Good news!"* the Pig cried jubilantly. *"I am risen!"*

Vengeant fled from the chapel as it fell apart around her. She did not know where to go, but she wanted to put distance between her and the Harbinger of Filth. She sensed fear in her form, a sea of spirits who had never seen such an impressive monster before. They wanted to retreat, doubted their own mission, and she could feel her bond to them weakening.

The Gloom Boar's hooves kicked through the old stone-stacked house, knocking down two walls, and collapsing the roof. The TV antenna skipped behind the rocks, pulled along by the towering god that lumbered after a ghostmetal lioness. Luckily, Vengeant was faster, but she was running out of land. Soon, the edge of the world would provide limited options.

Jump or fight.

She mustered her energies, told them to be brave, and Vengeant changed course, turned back, and ran straight underneath the Gloom Boar's hind fast as she could. As she passed underneath him, her claws split the ligament of his hoof.

The behemoth toppled, its rump smashing into dozens of occupied tents. *Splurt!* A ketchup-like liquid squeezed out of rippling rain flaps. While the Gloom Boar regained his footing, Vengeant took her opportunity to strike. She clawed up his hammy hock, cutting deep as she could into his undead muscle. The desert devil answered by plucking the lioness from its body like a wood

444

tick between two sickles. Even her large, shifting ghostmetal form couldn't pry itself loose from the Gloom Boar's iron pinch. The Lumenswine cackled with joy from its perch.

"Poor kitty-kitty," he said. "Big as you are, you're still too small." He held her up by the scruff, and she gazed into its cruel, creamy stare. This creature had come from Another Side before it died in Orphan Rock, and Vengeant could see that Other Side clearly in the reflection of his piggy eyes. A world of broken bones. Bloody seas filled with corpses. Devils clawing at the door framed in teeth. Their snouts wet, eager for it to open. The Age of Filth had so many grand delights in store for the world of humans, and Vengeant saw every monster look eager to feed, fuck, and fury on the other side of that crumbling bone-tooth doorway.

Ghost River was only the beginning.

Sister Worm's lovely punched through the desert crust near the old shed by the clearing. Hissing in the heat of the sun, the sightless worm burrowed back into The Dark. Markus, Esther, and Macho stood at the maw of the fresh hole. "It's still here!" The young man pointed at the helicopter in the clearing.

"Weird not hearing the river at all," Esther noted.

Markus turned to Macho. "Can you fly that?"

"UH-60. Looks intact. *Absolutely.*"

"Works for me." Markus turned to Esther. "You ready, Momma? We're getting out of here now. A long time comin'."

She squeezed both his hands. "As I'll ever fuckin be."

"All right then." Markus checked his rifle one last time. "Just like I told you: keep running. Don't stop for nothing. Got it?" They nodded in unison. "Straight for the helicopter. Get in. Take off. And fucking pray to whatever asshole god you think is listenin' that we make it out of Ghost River alive."

Esther hugged her brave boy.

Macho gave him a firm handshake. "You're the first Northamm I've met with any sense," he said, placing his heavy hand on the boy's shoulder. "Your daddy would be proud. You're a better man than he was, by a fair bit. That's the sort of progress Minister wanted for you. For all of us."

Markus let that sink in. His daddy was a good man who had to do bad stuff because he was born a boonchild. There was never a choice for him. Desyre and Nicholas tried to teach him that same hard lesson, but he never listened. Never believed in it enough to make it true. Not trying is what cowards do. Even if you aren't special or have any destiny that brings any good to the world, you had a life. *That was something.* It wasn't what you had to do to survive that mattered; it was how you lived. Loved. Tried to be better, even if you failed and sunk into the shit anyway.

Markus wiped a tear away.

The world was cruel to snakes.

"On the count of three," he said. "*One...two...three—*"

20.

The Gloom Boar's mouth was a black hole. Its musty breath smelled like a sun-drenched sea of corpses abandoned in a shallow tide. Held over the gaping maw, pinched between two corroded sickles, Vengeant couldn't wriggle free. She peered down a throat lined with ebon roots with sucker-maws that snapped, reaching for a morsel to pull into The Dark.

"I'm going to eat you!" the Lumenswine screeched from his perch in the titan's forehead. *"I'm going to put all of your bones in my mouth and chew them into mud!"*

Vengeant sensed the descent, the drop in temperature inside the gargantuan swine's maw. Tentacles tugged on her golden braces, licked down her phantasmal fur, and chomped off ghostly bits of her panicking soulstorm. She sliced and swatted them away, but there were so many devilish whiskers to fend off. When the Boar's grubby lips closed around her, she couldn't see any of the snakes that ate her in the icy, wet dark.

Vengeant howled, extending a claw for something to scratch open to let the light in again. Dark was a prison, and this was the darkest hole of them all. All the ghosts inside of her wailed in despair, and she could feel them letting go, dissolving away in fright. They resisted her commands in a mutinous panic.

Then, a small light pierced the damp, vast emptiness. The Vengeant symbol Mother Dirt carved in her skull burst to life and a fiery, crimson beam sliced through the snakes in the Gloom Boar's throat. The energy blade cut away the hissing vipers from her body until they were little more than twitching, leaking, headless tubes that quickly retreated into the black sea of nothingness below. Vengeant held on when the Gloom Boar wailed in rage, and its mouth dropped opened to cough out the poisoned light. It spat her into his palm, and Vengeant was happy to feel the sun again. The Lumenswine was not pleased. It commanded the Gloom Boar crush her like an insect. She felt the muscles of his giant palm flex in preparation to make a fist.

"Playtime's over, Little Lamb!"

A flowing, loosening vibration rippled her form. A babbling stream of heat. Vengeant's ghostmetal liquified and softened. Before he closed his sickled fist around her, she fell apart into a thousand crystal droplets of luminous energy that rivered down the giant swine's hairy wrist. He couldn't grasp her, for she was now a mercurial ghostling dripping from his elbow and pooling on the desert floor. The Gloom Boar snorted in furious awe and looked down into the mysterious pool of silver.

"Come out, come out, wherever you are," the Lumenswine sang teasingly. The Gloom Boar knelt beside the shimmering mirror to investigate. It winced to see its own reflection in the sheen—a rotten, worm-eaten Pig whose silver tusks had tarnished from decades in the dirt. For but a moment, even the Lumenswine pitied his own visage and had to look away.

Whoosh!

Two metal-plated hands burst through the radiant surface of the pond, unzipping a jagged line of silver across the desert floor. White light raced toward the Harbinger of Filth and burned the darkness of his purulent eyes. The Gloom Boar fell backward again, stumbling over a smoldering ash pile that used to be Wrangler Vandersloan's coyote pen.

The rip became a flood of light that spread in all directions, and soon the knifelike hands pulled the rest of Broken Girl's body from the light. All the ghosts flowed back into her as she rose, and the Broken Girl grew as tall as the dreary devil she faced. Each spirit injected their rage into her, fueling her with a crystalline fury that rebuked every part of The Pig.

Markus welcomed the sunshine on his face. Being in caves, wormy tunnels, and the infinite black ho-hum of The Dark didn't warm up his snake blood at all. But outside, in the open desert of Ghost River, he felt that sunburn that ignited his veins. It made him feel alive. Made him want to run somewhere fast. Good fucking thing there was a helicopter left to aim for.

The ground rumbled, making it hard not to lose footing. *Just get them to the chopper,* he thought. *Nothing else matters right now.* A far cry from his old life of putting kids in cages, wasn't it? Left to make his own choices now, Markus wanted to free a few souls and help them escape slaughter. Wouldn't make up for a fraction of the lost kids he fed to Desyre, but it was a start. Felt better anyway. Might be some hope for his snake heart yet.

Bam! Another quake from the mountain. Markus broke his own rules—don't stop, don't look back—and gazed over his shoulder to Orphan Rock. Something large thundered around in the smoke. Didn't matter what that was, though. Godzilla battling King Kong for all he cared. The copter. *That* mattered.

Even though he was faster than most folks, Little Snake kept to the rear to provide cover for Esther and Macho. They followed instructions, keeping their heads down, and used the bushes best they could to keep out of sight. The boy had his eyes on the sky. Those blue-winged reapers seemed busy doing their work and hadn't noticed the fresh meat on the run yet.

They were finally catching a break!

"You promised! Forever!"

Something slithered around Markus' leg, and he tripped over it. **Wham!** His kneecap smashed against a sharp rock. He felt bone shatter beneath his skin. The blow was sudden and knocked the rifle out of his hands. He tried to crawl back to it, but the worm wrapped around his ankle had other plans.

"*Help!*" he screamed loud as he could, but Esther and Macho were too far ahead to hear him. He struggled to escape, while gravel crunched and rolled beneath him. Worm Girl's lovely tugged him back to the tunnel by his fractured leg.

When Broken Girl sprint across the barrens, a trail of ghostly wrappings followed behind her. A cape of bloodthirsty echoes. **Thwack!** When the slobbering heathen bucked her advances, finger swords hacked through a tangle of antlers. She pruned through arms of the Dead Tree, and it bled with every lopped off bough and branch. The Harbinger of Filth grew agitated, ripped sickles across her belly with crushing swipes. Broken Girl tried to ignore the attacks, right and left, but pieces of her ghost armor shredded away with screams fading on the wind. With every lost soul, she felt herself tighten. Diminish a little.

Shrink.

Worst of all, the more she fought against it, the angrier the Gloom Boar became. It fed off her struggle. Grew with fury, veins popping on its goat thighs and wormy-veined biceps.

Broken Girl pulled back. Her strategy wasn't working. Attacking and resisting The Pig made it stronger. Angrier, and more powerful. Moreover, the physical strain of losing parts of her form begged for a hasty retreat. She bled ghosts from silver wounds and limped away from the towering cretin.

The Lumenswine laughed. *"Don't go yet! I like you better in pieces. Just like I was before you put me back together again!"*

The behemoth snatched up a boulder and pitched it. **Bam!** Broken Girl's shoulder shattered like glass. Vengeant tried to staunch her wound, but the Harbinger of Filth pressed his advantage. Rock after rock struck her body, cracking off shards infused by souls. Ghosts soared over the edge of the Grim Seed, wailing with regret as they rained down on Sandoval.

She was losing with distance. Needed to press him back. Eyes burning, she dashed toward him, feigned weakness, and waited for him to gain confidence in his next move. When the Gloom Boar took a clumsy swipe, she rammed her metal mohawk into his tight gut. Her spikes punched holes in his belly, and writhing snakes poured out of the wounds on spills of ancient dust.

The impact shook the entire floating island. When he collapsed into it, another large chunk of Orphan Rock broke away from the mountain. Cracks and fractures deepened, and a landslide gathered momentum and ripped the sickle fingers off one of his piggy hands. *"You're gonna get it now, Little Lamb!"*

Stumbling, the Gloom Boar found his hooves and raised his bloody stump. A whipping mass of ashen tendrils and cursed roots spurted through the corrupt wound. Something was happening, but Vengeant lost sight of it. A cloud of those blue-winged demons descended upon her, slashing, and stinging her ghosts faster than she could react. They yanked her apart spirit by spirit, and the reapers tossed crying ghosts over the lip of the misery machine like sacks of trash.

Razorblades and pinpricks.

Ranks vanishing from her army.

She was shrinking, becoming smaller and smaller.

She needed to find a place to hide.

Away, away, away...

The Gloom Boar raised his hairy arm, and the necrotic mass that wriggled from his wrist hardened into a black scythe. *"Reaper's coming for you, Little Lamb!"*

In pursuit of the last ghost standing, The King of Pigs dragged his doomblade along the charred landscape. A little girl in bright white Keds jumped over the edge of the world.

Rat-tat-tat-tat! Rat-tat-tat!

Bullets whistled over the scrub brush, aimed for the violet eye in the back of the crumbling tunnel. Macho and Esther loaded more clips as fast as they could.

"No!" Markus pointed at the copter. "*Keep running!*"

The worm around his ankle pulled harder, reeling him back into the lightless hole that Sister Worm dug in the Spaces Between Things. There, she waited to snatch him away *forever.*

Rat-tat!

These Sisters of Sorrow sure liked to keep Little Snake around, didn't they? He laughed a little, as the shards of flagstone grated the skin off his back. It was just his luck the only girls that fought over him happened to be undead avengers, deranged masochists, or goddamned cyclopes with only child issues. Sucked being so popular with the ladies of Ghost River.

Rat-tat-tat-tat!

Bullets popped through rubber and dirty goop leaked from fresh holes. The worm, determined to deliver her prize to the furious Sister of Sorrow in The Dark, tightened around his leg and wrenched harder. Soon tugs turned into a steady pull, and Markus slid on his back through the crispy desert grass.

When he lifted his head, he could see her crouching in the entrance of her tunnel. Sister Worm. Her long mouth curled into a selfish smile, lips rolled back from dirty metal teeth. She clung to a teddy bear that was dirtier than she was.

Whomp! Larger rocks battered his body. Markus cast his arms out for one. After a few desperate tries, he finally caught a boulder. Suddenly, he wasn't moving anymore, arms wrapped around reddish and silver ore. But the asshole worm didn't give up and flexed itself to unsnag its catch from the rough patch. It lifted his broken leg, tried shaking him free, but Little Snake held on tight. "*You get back here, Mister!*" Worm Girl shrieked.

Markus grimaced, his fingers tiring. The more the worm tugged, the more it leaked greasy shit from its wounds. *Just keep hugging that rock. Hug it like your Momma.*
      Rat-tat-tat!
      Wormskin absorbed more rounds, and the dumb beast writhed in pain. Little Snake hugged the rock tighter. *"Come on, let go!"* he growled as his nails ripped off his fingertips. His gamble was simple: either the worm would let him go to save itself, or it'd die trying to catch a slippery snake that had nothing left to lose. Either way, Markus wasn't fucking letting go.
      Rat-tat-tat-tat! Bam!
      The worm chose self-preservation, and Sister Worm's lovely uncoiled from Markus' shattered leg. Shredded by hot rounds, it flopped and slithered back into the depths of the tunnel, chasing after the sobs of a terribly angry child. When it whipped and rolled back into the Dark, what was left of the tunnel in the clearing crumbled under a pitfall of boulders.
      Markus attempted to walk but couldn't put any weight on his knee. Even crawling on it was painful. He used nearby rocks to help him climb up to one leg. With hope in his eyes, he tried to find Esther and Macho in the clearing. There they were! He waved for help. With a little teamwork, he might just make it.
      "Little Snake!" his Momma yelled back, pointing at the sky above him. Macho wrapped his arms around her waist, pulling her in the opposite direction. The horrified expression on Esther's face told him that Macho tugged her back against her will.
      Something's wrong.
      The color drained from Markus' tan cheeks when the shadow enveloped him in feather and razorblade claws. He looked up at those ancient eyes, unforgettable as comets in space.
      Those eyes. Those goddamn eyes.
      When Delora ripped into his chest with her ichor talons, Markus thought of running along the painted hills with Minister, and he was happy to be just a Little Snake again.

They were gone.

All the ghosts.

She was only the little girl again.

No superpowers.

Just the one who remembered a room with windows.

You are not Liz. Liz is dead. Her story is over.

Should I just let go now?

Why do you cling to yourself?

The tiny ghost held onto a tangle of roots, dangling over the cliff above the city under siege by the Grim Seed. Dizzy at first, she glanced at smoldering ruins below. The rest of Vengeant—the pieces of her armor—pooled on the ground until a giant mass of phantasmal energy flooded the streets of Sandoval. Each drip of lost souls splashed against the ashen earth below.

Screeeeeeechhh!

Dirt fell on her face when the curved blade of a giant black scythe scraped along the rim, grating away tenuous rock and soil from the edge of the world. Before it knocked her loose, Liz scrambled into a small rut carved into the side of the floating valley. There she huddled, a frightened kitten in a Care Bears t-shirt who didn't know where to turn next.

Screeeeeeechhh!

The scythe ripped out more stone and root. Her little hole was no bigger or brighter than it was under her Strawberry Shortcake comforter back in Oklahoma. There, too, she trembled and listened to a Father Pig fury in the dark. She wanted to hug Reuben, but he was long gone. She wanted to cry out to Stacy, but she was long gone too. It wasn't fair, was it? Children aren't supposed to be so lonely. Why did everything in the world have to make her feel so small?

Screeeeeeechhh!

The Gloom Boar's blade grated away more earth, and she

could feel the rock beneath her body loosen. Soon she would fall like the rest of the ghosts. Maybe that was for the best. Trying to exist in a world that clearly hated orphans was a sad state of being for anybody unlucky enough to try. Best to become a silver raindrop and dry up under the hot, unforgiving sun.

Just gone. Liz liked the sound of that.

Above, she could hear the Lumenswine laughing. That same pleased and self-amused chuckle that Paul offered after beating Stacy into submission. She'd cry and curl up on the floor beneath his torn knuckles while he snickered at her tears. And what did Liz ever do to help? She hid under blankets or sat in the corner, hugging her teddy bear with quivering eyes. She was always too afraid to say anything. Too afraid to fight back in a home that was never a safe place for her to stand up and feel tall.

Just a kid. A small, frightened child in The Dark.

And the dark is a prison.

"Nooooo!" Esther unloaded her rifle. Bullets pierced the back and shoulders of the Harpy of Ghost River until her clip emptied and clicked. Delora screeched in agony, beat her punctured wings, and abandoned her fresh kill. She soared into the sky, vanishing inside plumes of heavy smoke. Desperate to find Little Snake, Esther dropped her gun, ran toward the tall grass. Her only boy was dying somewhere in the desert. Surely, he needed his momma more than ever. A strong hand hooked her arm, and then Macho was holding her back again.

"Let me go!" she screamed, eyes wild and wet.

"We need to go."

"No! She's healing. Let's get him now! *While we have the chance!"* Esther pulled at Macho's arm, trying to wriggle out of his iron grip.

"He told us to run!"

"No, goddammit! We're not leaving him!" She finally

wrested out of his arms and ran back into the clearing. Although she could see blood smears on the flagstone, try as she might, she couldn't find her boy's body in the shrubbery. "Markus! *Say something, baby!*"

Macho ran after her. "Esther! Get back here!"

"*Raaackkk!*" Delora descended from the smog like a hungry hawk. Onyx claws outstretched, slitty mouth parting to snap up some fresh meat in sharky jaws. Instead of running for cover, Esther opened her arms in acceptance. Angry tears rolled down her cheeks.

"*Do it,*" she said, closing her eyes to welcome death. "*Please.*"

Whoosh! A black bullet punched Delora out of the sky. The harpy's wings went crooked when she lost control, spun out, and crashed into a grove of yucca plants in the distance.

Bloodhungry, Dark Bird pounced on top of her.

"*He was mine!*" she bellowed, stripping Mother's undead flesh from her bones.

Screeeeeeechhh!

The doomblade scraped by again, and Liz couldn't move or think clearly. Petrified by everything. Frozen in a hole. Why would Sister Dirt send her on this fool's errand? She was never strong enough to kill a monster like the Gloom Boar. Why pick her? Out of all of the ghosts in the world, why pick the smallest?

Liz felt a warm crack of light on her forehead. She looked up and saw a fissure in the earth as her shelf prepared to crumble away from the Grim Seed. He stood in the sunlight, fingers held up in the shape of a heart. Blindfolded Boy! Still a ghost!

Still trying to lead her into the light.

"Find me!" he said urgently. Then he faded away as the shadow of the Harbinger of Filth covered the sunshine from which he came. Milky eyes glimmering with malice instead.

No. This Father Pig wouldn't be satisfied until all of the children suffered and cried in The Dark. It would never be enough violence and tragedy for him—greedy, hurtful, selfish piggy. Liz made tight fists. She would not baptize him in her cowardice. He'd spent decades making innocent children cry, stealing away their lives. She wasn't going to give him one more damn tear. The last ghostling used her twiggy legs to shimmy up the crack.

Macho tackled her in the nick of time. A flying mantis nearly lopped off her head when it buzzed by, carrying a half-dead man toward the hungry Old Sinkhole. They collapsed together and lay staring at the hazy, blue sky. When she made her move to get away from him, Macho rolled over and pinned her to the dirt. Esther squirmed and kicked beneath him, cussed and spit in his face, yet he hugged her even tighter, refusing to let go until she listened to reason. "We have to go," he said again, looking overhead as a squadron of fighter jets screamed by. "Esther, can you hear me? We're running out of time."

"No," she said, shaking. "*My children.* I won't leave them. You go. Take the fucking helicopter and leave me behind. I want you to go, but I ain't leaving my babies here."

Nearby, Dark Bird and Delora rolled in the bushes.

Macho bore into her blue eyes. "Esther, listen to me. They were never your kids to begin with. *Not one thing here is yours.* You don't get that right in Orphan Rock. Your children are Ghost River orphans just like you. Like Minister. Like me. Doesn't matter where they came from. Here is where they were always going to die!" He wrapped his hand around hers when more blue-winged monsters circled above. "If you want to stay, we'll stay. I'll die too. Like I promised."

"No!" Esther cried. "Don't you fucking dare do that."

"I know a promise don't mean shit to a dirtbag Northamm, but to a Machado, it's everything." He held up his pinkie. "Come on. Let's leave the monsters to their Armageddon. Let's you and me do something else with the day. Let's fly around the sun."

Esther noticed his handsome, kind face for what felt like the first time. She wrapped her pinkie around his.

Mother was strong. Dark Bird's upper hand didn't last long. They tucked their bony wings on their backs and wrestled on the ground. A family of jackrabbits ran for cover as they rolled over their burrow. Delora swiped at Dark Bird's eyes but cut Shelby's cheek open instead. When Dark Bird kicked her off, the elder harpy skipped across the desert floor, landing in a grove of eldritch saguaros, and jumping cholla.

Shelby flapped back to her feet. "You went too far, bitch," she said with a bitter stare, chicken legs scratching on the flagstone shards. "He was mine. You killed him. Now, it's your turn."

Delora emerged from the cactus patch, and barbed cholla pods fell from her scaly skin. The Crooked Woman spread her speckled wings, one of which was struggling to heal. Dark Bird paused for a moment, sensing something wrong with Mother. Her movements were off. She was not regenerating as fast as she should, nor did her eyes carry the fire Shelby expected.

Had the curse abandoned her?

Didn't matter. No pity. No mercy.

Destruction is my boon.

Dark Bird swooped in, teeth glinting like knife tips. She pedaled her talons in the air like a windmill. To counter, the Crooked Woman beat her wings and snagged her protege midair. Two predators knotted in a tangle of porcelain swords. After a dominant twist, Delora tossed the younger harpy from the sky. All the air escaped her lungs when Dark Bird struck the ground.

Whoosh!

Mother's weight crushed her into the cursed earth. Shelby couldn't breathe when she placed her raptor's foot on her neck and pressed down. The death twinkles came too fast, the sound of her own heartbeat faded, and the fleeting attempts of her claws trying to rip her foul foot away grew ever weaker. Dark Bird gasped and looked into the dead grin of a spook watching her legacy choke out and die without a flicker of emotion. There was never another look from Delora. It was always indifference, even when she was just a dirty little bird in a big nest alone, crying for meat and love. A mad shaper lost in her work. That's all this pathetic creature was. There was no love in her. There was no Mother.

Boom!

The bullet tore a hole in Delora's face near the scar that never healed. The elder harpy whimpered when one of her black eyes popped. White pus poured over her thin lips. Air raced back into Shelby's lungs when she stumbled off of Dark Bird.

The Crooked Woman croaked and hissed, struggling to stand. Wounded. Bad. Instead of finishing the fight, the Harpy of Ghost River took to the air in retreat. Dark Bird rolled onto her side, coughing, and saw a boy propped up against a rock some distance across the clearing. A rifle slid from his bloody hands.

At the chopper, Wallace Machado threw open the cockpit door. The boy had been right, and the Huey was in fine flying condition. He hadn't logged many flight hours in a decade or two, but some things stuck with you. Flying over the dense jungle canopies of South Vietnam was one of them. Trying to stay calm while you escorted an infantry of scared, shaking young boys to war. Heavy mortars. Explosions in the sky and on the ground. *Not so different than Orphan Rock*, Macho thought. Would take a few minutes to complete the cold start procedure. He'd need to prime the gas pump. Engage the generator and warm up the blades. He turned to Esther. "Climb in. I've got you."

He took her hand and pulled her toward the—

A violent snap. Ripped from his fingers.

The Harpy of Ghost River snatched Esther into the sky.

The dying boy sat against a boulder.

His wounds: fatal. His white shirt torn and stained black with blood spill. He struggled to breathe. Coughed in fits.

Dark Bird was bold in her advance. Didn't wear a mask to cover her true face, nor did she hide her feathery figure from him. Her body healed, but her clothes were beyond repair. Little more than a tattered NIN flag around her neck, a bit of flannel and a pocket around her left shoulder, and her hooked talons poked through the toe boxes of her favorite boots.

The young man had scars on his arms, and Dark Bird sensed sorrow from them. He looked like Minister in frame, skinny with stubble. But he had Esther's gentle face.

"You're a snake," she said, kneeling in front of him. The young man's golden eyes pulsed, fading in and out with snakeshine. "You are…my brother. A boonchild."

"Big brother," he said, hacking up blood.

"You are dying."

He nodded, looked to the sky.

"Why? Why did you come here to die?" Her tone was angry and scornful. "You were *free*, weren't you?"

The snake scoffed. "I wasn't free. None of us are."

"I am."

"Keep telling yourself that."

"What happened to your arms?"

He laughed a little. "Women problems." His heart pumped more blood through the lacerations on his chest. He winced through the pain, years of practice. "You're the one I saw on television with Esther. She told me a long time ago that I had a sister. A little sister that would need my help one day. Had no intention of helping your kind, though. No intention at all."

"My kind?"

"A Sister of Sorrow."

"Is that what I'm called?"

"Sorry to say."

Dark Bird blinked, unsure of how she felt to hear such a grim nomenclature bound to her. There was power in a name. She watched the life leave her brother's body, and she could feel his disdain for her in his last remaining moments. She did not like feeling hated. But what could she do?

Sister of Sorrow, she was.

"Markus," she said after a tick. He looked up. "Is it really so bad to care for something like me? I have always been cared for by others. Served. Protected. Worshipped. But I think never loved. What is it like to be loved by something?"

"Momma definitely loves you, *Shelby*. That's why I shot Delora. You saved her, and Esther's the only one worth saving in all of Orphan Rock. It'd break her heart to lose you."

"She is kind."

"She is. So was our daddy."

"The Pig?"

"Jesus Christ!" He rolled his eyes and let out a long hiss in frustration. "You're something else, aren't you? *Minister!* That's who I consider *my* father."

Dark Bird paused to think about it. "I hardly knew him. Delora kept me in a nest and then in a birdcage. He died when I was young, and what came back was…*not the same*."

"Too bad for that," Markus said. "He weren't perfect, but he loved his family. He taught me all sorts of things like how to run. I wanted to say goodbye, but…"

Markus' gaze drifted into sorrow. His words did too.

"He spoke of you often. He would relive dreams. Slip into other times. See false realities. During those episodes he often spoke to you as if you were still a baby on his knee. So did Esther." Shelby offered a tiny smile. "Can I tell you something? It might bring you some…comfort."

"Go on. Clearly, I ain't running away."

Dark Bird placed her claw on Markus' knee. The boy shivered under her touch but didn't fight it. "Esther and Minister loved each other in a way only humans in a cage can. They took care of one another. The emotional part. Talked about their dreams. About the after…"

"After what?"

"Orphan Rock." Dark Bird watched the mantis-infested sky float by as they rode a demonic lawnmower over humanity. "All this Grim Seed and dirt curse bullshit. They'd spend hours talking about make-believe situations, make outlandish plans, and resort to the kind of mad thinking you learn in a jail cell with nothing else to look at but walls. I used to make fun of them. Never understood why they would be so delusional. Thought it was a waste of time to dream."

"*Dreaming is dangerous,*" Markus coughed.

His little sister nodded, her dead-dark eyes trying to catch some of his fleeting snakeshine. "Yes. I can see why you'd say that when you've grown up here. But the more I learned from them, the more I understood something about humans. *Hope is a skeleton key.* No matter how many chains and padlocks Mother kept wrapped around her orphans, Esther and Minister had their secret escape plan. Their dreams were all that they needed to get through their horrible days…"

Markus listened to Shelby recount the years he was gone with captivated intrigue. It did bring him some comfort to hear that his family had found a way to transcend the shackles of their box. Didn't matter if it was putting too much stock in fantastical thinking. There was no other way to think in Ghost River. It hurt to laugh, but he did. Hurt to smile, but he did that too.

His freak sister shared stories and tried to ease his passing. Maybe she had enough Northamm in her to be better than her kind. No, Northamms weren't particularly good people by and large, but they got on the best they could without having any freedom to choose a better life. This Shelby creature carried that burden too. She understood the core truth that all Northamms swallowed at birth: suffering is salvation. It was the dirt on their tongues.

Dark Bird could sense his apprehension and hatred for her dissolve under the ashy sky while she stroked his knee and told him about the love of their parents. Snakes were more human than harpy, that much she knew, but Markus was a strange sort of snake. She felt a pang of sadness hit her heart space thinking about the time they never had. Maybe Jake was always a poor replacement for the brother she never knew. She imagined Markus coming to see her in the oasis. They would've shaped her sandbox together and built a better world. Had some fucking fun. That's all Shelby ever wanted. A friend. A companion. Somebody to help her dream. Her own Minister. A dreamcatcher.

When snakeshine fizzled from his eyes, Dark Bird held his hand for a moment longer. It was strange to think about somebody out there like Markus, who thought about her all of these years while she mostly thought about herself. Family mattered to him. Dark Bird never really felt love before, but this strange feeling worming its way through her body seemed close. This Little Snake spent his days thinking of ways to make life better for his lost loved ones. *Fantastical thinking*, she thought, placing his hand down on his bloody lap—*a true Northamm*.

Click!

Shelby bounced up from her brother's corpse. Wallace Machado pointed a pistol at her heart. "Killing you would be the greatest gift I could give to my people," he said.

"Then shoot," the harpy growled, feathers bristling. "See what happens next."

Macho's lips tightened. His finger danced on the trigger.

"You've killed innocent people. Where is the justice for them?" Sweat beaded on his forehead. "You took the future from a child. You swallowed it with her head."

"A girl's gotta eat, you know."

Macho snickered and took a step closer. The barrel of his pistol aimed at her head. For a resolute cop, his visible hesitancy spiked her interest. Something was wrong. After a moment, he lowered the gun. "If you are as decent as she says you are, you'll help her," he said, voice shaky with fear. "The Crooked Woman took Esther. Snatched her at the copter and flew—"

Whoosh!

Wallace held his hand up to block out the sun. Dark Bird was just another monstrous speck invading the sky.

Liz from Oklahoma sprint through the bushes, her scuffed-up Keds skating over loose gravel the best they could manage. A tower loomed behind her, a savage monster worse than she ever could have imagined hiding in her closet or under her bed. Despite every odd stacked against her, Liz dodged the Gloom Boar's crushing blows, but not without great effort and expense to her energy. Her ghost was disappearing, flickering from reality. Her energy fading, letting go of the world.

Should I just let go?

Why do you cling to yourself?

Then, she tripped on a stump.

Thud!

Her head hit the ground.

Something remembered.

"*Paul, please*, not in front of her. Take me to the bedroom. Do it there, OK? Not here! Not in front of—"

Smack!

Momma landed on her cheek. She looked into her scared daughter's eyes; blood ran from her nostril to the tan carpet.

"We can be strong," she said. "*We can fight back.*"

Momma faded away from the room with windows, and Liz was alone on the gravel. She turned her head to see the Blindfolded Boy across the smoldering desert landscape.

When you're feeling too small and ready to quit, find me.
He waited between a pair of broken telephone poles.
His fingers made the shape of a heart.

Before she could open her mouth to call to him, the Gloom Boar plucked her from the ground with his good claw and held her up to the Lumenswine. The boy-god was mostly roots now, his body tangled in oozing bramble. His cloudy eyes glittered with piggy delight, and he smiled like an old friend to see her.

"I knew it was you," he said. *"Troublemaker."*

The little spirit couldn't flicker away. No more ghost energy left to help her. She kicked in the air, trying to slip out of her Care Bears t-shirt, but those greasy pig teeth crept ever closer.

"I can be strong," she whispered. *"I can fight back."*

"Oh, please do!" The Lumenswine hollered with laughter. "I like it better that way. There ain't no better feeling than the moment when you break her down. When she stops fighting and lets you win because you're too strong. Are we there now, Little Lamb? You ready to let me win?" He laughed again. "I only mark the scrappy ones because they're worthy. I don't think you're one of them. *The fighters.* You're too small. Too scared. Besides, what can a pathetic little thing like you do to a big old thing like me anyway? It ain't no fun for a Pig when it's easy."

From within her chest, Liz felt herself collapse.
Her body crumbled to blue dust.
One last form—a hidden vessel.
The smallest of things. Like her.
Something forged from souldust.
She became a Luminarch butterfly.

Esther was above it all.
Macho.
The helicopter.
Orphan Rock shrinking away.

She had never flown in her life.

This is what freedom is, isn't it?

To be above the dirt for once.

Delora's talons pierced her shoulders. Esther's blood felt cool in the windrush. The harpy was wounded too, her face disfigured and falling apart. They soared high above Sandoval, the land of cityfolk. Fast food, faster churches, and mega malls. She watched monsters of mayhem tear suburbia to pieces, and heavy-bellied worms devoured a world she never knew. Esther recalled that smooth-talking city councilman who visited Orphan Rock years back. How had he described the impending expansion of civilization into their sacred land? *All good developments for progress, modernity, and invention.*

Esther snorted. Problem for him and everybody else in that burning city below was that progress and modernity and invention weren't welcomed currency where the oldest things lived.

In fact, they were grave fucking insults.

"*Ki-yo-tee*," came a hoarse voice from sun-cracked lips. Esther's gaze snapped up to the one-eyed witch. The claw-clutched woman thought her mind had finally gone to mush and played terrible tricks on her. The Harpy of Ghost River never fucking spoke! Only Snarl could hear her. That's just the way it was. Ridiculous to think otherwise. Esther shook off the batshit-crazy notion and watched Sandoval burn instead, enraptured by the flames and the queasy feeling that grew in her tummy. The feeling she could only imagine at the apex of a roller coaster.

Flying like a bird. Me.

"*Ki–yo–tee.*" This time Esther was sure she heard it. While Delora beat her tattered wings against lifting ashes, her one black eye looked down at her last orphan. Esther could barely see the flickering gold flame that was always inside of Delora's vicious stare. It faded fast.

"What?" she asked, suddenly shaking.

"You...*live.* You...*leave.*"

Then, the harpy let her prisoner go.

Esther's scream was mute against the roar of the wind. She reached for The Crooked Woman, who never looked back. Was this act of murder Delora's first act of...*kindness*? Love? Did some fractured part of her remember the pact that she and Minister made in the coyote pen that rainy day years back? Did she kill Markus and attack Shelby to save them from some worse thing to come? Thoughts raced with her heart. None of which mattered anymore. It was over. Finally, Delora had given Esther what she'd always wanted. Release. Her shackles were broken.

Inside of her, a little girl with skinned knees stood at the edge of her chain-link pen, twiggy fingers threading through the holes in the fence. Minister had opened the door to her cage, but the child refused to leave it behind. She guarded it, even the ratty lawn chair. Didn't even bother her that a wildfire consumed the pastures around the pens, creeping closer.

"I don't wanna leave! I ain't known no other place."

Esther knelt in front of the sandy-haired runt.

The child backed away.

"But you can't stay here. Everybody's a ghost now."

Little Esther shook her head in defiance. "Please, I'm not supposed to ever dream about nothing else. It breaks my heart when I do. I'm broken. That's why they hurt me."

"Even here people loved you, you know," Esther told herself gently. "Especially the ones that hurt you the most. You could feel them, right? The ones that mattered. You're not so broken as you think you are. *Minister. Markus. Macho. Shelby.*" Esther coaxed the little one closer. "Love," she whispered. "The *only* pain I ever felt in my fucking life. The best kind." The dirty-cheeked coyote touched the tips of Esther's fingers, moving a little closer to the door of the cage. "*Father Pig. Delora. Eugene. Wrangler.* We didn't ever let the bad ones see us cry, did we? Never gave them the pleasure. We're brave, Esther Northamm. You're fuckin' brave, and you deserve to be free."

The little coyote smiled. Her tearful eyes that once shone with fear blossomed into bright pools of liberation. Esther held out her hand, and her little self stepped out of her rusty box. She hugged her, stroking her trembling, bruised body. When she peered up, the cageless sunlight dried all of her tears.

"Hold on!" Dark Bird's feathery arms slid under her body. The young harpy cradled the human who bore her in the branches of the Dead Tree. Her black wings beat against the smoky air until they straightened, and they glided toward Sandoval. "I'm going to take you below, so you can run."

Esther shook her head. "Macho. I promised I wouldn't leave him." Wild desperation settled in her eyes. "Please, take me back! A promise is a sacred fucking thing to me."

"Back to him is back to danger."

"I don't want him to be alone in that place. It's one more wrong thing, Shelby! I ain't got any more room left in my heart for wrong things. It's time to live the other way."

Dark Bird stopped her descent and considered Esther's mad request. Her expression shifted from one of confusion to reluctant acceptance. "Fucking humans," she said.

"Fuckin' humans," Esther agreed.

"Promise me you'll leave with him."

"We'll all go. You're coming with us too."

"Esther, I'm not—"

"Shelby, please. The curse is broken. We can leave here! You, me, Macho, Markus—we can go somewhere else! We can start over as a family. Do it right this time."

"Markus is dead. I watched him die."

"Don't say that," Esther said weakly. "Even if it's true. I just can't—"

"He died saving you, by saving me. He was a *good brother*." Her caretaker's bottom lip trembled, but Dark Bird's disposition remained stoic. "Don't honor him with despair. He knew what he was. A snake never expects to be free. My brother came home to die with his family. In the end, he wanted to make a difference for you. He's laid down his heavy burdens now. Be proud of him. He's no longer a slave to any Pig or Sister." The woman held herself against Shelby's downy breast, her heart drowning in a mother's quiet despair. The harpy embraced her a little tighter. When Esther returned from the murky swamp of loss she knew so well, Dark Bird continued, "The skyreader loves you. Go with him. He's kind for an asshole."

"I'll talk to Macho," Esther said softly. "Get him to see past his hatred. I think he'll grow to love you too."

"Doesn't matter, Coyote. I won't be going with you."

"*Goddammit, Shelby!* Why are you so cruel to me? I've been a loving mother to you—"

"But I am not your child, Esther," she replied, tone grim and firm. "You know I never was your baby. You just made me is all. *I am the child of pain.* Where orphans are bled and desecrated, you'll find my kind eating our fill of the carnage. I'm not a safe bet for you or any human. It's my very nature to destroy life. One day, when you're free from death and bones and dead children, you'll thank me for leaving you behind. I'm not saying goodbye to be cruel. No, Esther, I'm saying goodbye *to be kind.*"

"*You're breaking my heart.*"

"You need to fucking hear it." They drifted through foggy clouds toward the menacing Grim Seed. Dark Bird's scowl softened, noticing Esther's tears. "You've been tender to me. You've shown me compassion, empathy, and courage. And if that is what being a mother is, then you are the only one I've ever had." Esther's arms tightened around Dark Bird's neck. "I'll be grateful to you for that for the rest of my life. Long after you're dead and dust, I'll still love you. But I'm a predator, and destruction is my boon. *Call me Sister Crow now.*"

Esther's tears paused, basking in the absolute strength and sense of self Shelby had now. Gone was that fumbling, scraggy little meat fiend. The Baby Bird that couldn't say no to her darkest impulses. She could not see Delora in her anymore. This harpy had changed for the better. She knew what she was and embraced it. Embraced herself. Even gave herself a name.

Esther's little girl, all grown the fuck up.

"Did you pick that yourself?"

Dark Bird smirked. "Yes. Pretty fuckin' metal, isn't it?"

"Sounds perfectly metal to me." Esther stroked her downy cheek. "Just like you are, *Sister Crow*."

Shelby smiled proudly to hear her new name. They circled the rumbling Grim Seed, passing by hordes of blue-winged drones stripping the flesh from the world below. When they touched down on the clearing beneath Orphan Rock, Macho waved from the cockpit of the helicopter. The blades whirled, ready for liftoff. She turned to Sister Crow, a powerful and beautiful young huntress. A little bit of herself, she'd leave behind.

Esther hugged her one more time. Sister Crow squeezed her and gently pushed her away. "Go," she said. "Never think of this place again. You're free, Coyote. Spend the rest of your years serving the seeds of your happiness now." She spread her onyx wings and rose into the mad sky. She circled above, taking one last look at her true mother, who waved wildly below. Then, *cawing!*, she swooped toward the apex of Orphan Rock. To Delora's Cave. She wasn't finished reaping yet.

Macho held the helicopter's door open for her, and Esther scrambled into the co-pilot's seat. He reached over and secured her safety belt and handed her a headset. She fumbled with it, fingers shaking, and he helped her adjust the microphone in front of her mouth. "Why the hell did you come back?"

Esther smiled, hooked his pinkie, and gave him a little wink. "I know a promise don't mean shit to a dirtbag Machado, but to a Northamm, it's everything."

"Sacred." Wallace grinned, pulled back on the cyclic control, and the helicopter ascended.

The little Luminarch surfed on gusts of soot and ember toward Blindfolded Boy standing between the two crooked telephone poles near the base of Orphan Rock. Try as it might, the mighty Gloom Boar couldn't lay a sickle on the tiniest creature made from souldust. She crossed a wicked desert that ended so many stories. She glided over the bloodroots that spread across the ground stealing corpses, danced over the fires that burned down mesquite trees and old cabins, and swooped above metal basins and steaming vents that cracked open in The Dark under the artificial crust of things. She was small but strong. Her energy burned brightly in the form of the Luminarch. No, she could not turn into a giant ghostmetal lioness or a rock-fisted golem anymore, but not all battles were meant to be won by big things. Not every fighter was the size of a mountain. Some were small yet brave. Tiny yet cunning. Fragile, yet determined. Some were Father Pigs, and others were Little Lambs.

"You get back here!" the boy with blackened butterfly wings cried. The Lumenswine shuddered in his dirty hole, trying to control a body that was meant to kill big things.

The butterfly landed on stitched fingers making the shape of a heart. "The boy always chose love," the Blindfolded Boy told her, lifting his eyeless brow to his slobbering, cruel father above him. "He always wanted love to win in the end."

The Luminarch crumbled on his wrist, and Liz spun in the room with windows while warm sunshine hit her face. She laughed and leaped and twirled in the afternoon light.

When Liz fell on the carpet and looked up, she could see the bright sun above. She punched two fists in the sky, pretending to pull the telephone wire across her face like a tight, red jump rope. A tall shadow fell over her, starved for violence, but Liz did not flinch beneath him. She could be strong now.

She could fight back by being a hopeful child.

Her perfect form.

Clumsy and ferocious in his avaricious frenzy, the Gloom Boar charged over the Little Ghost. His metal hooves snagged the telephone wire. *Crack! Crack!* Wooden poles unsheathed from the dirt and whipped around his gnarled ankles. Legs bound by wire, the Harbinger of Filth tripped, and Father Pig wailed when his chariot collided yet again with Orphan Rock.

Screeeecccchhhh! The Grim Seed tremored when his scythe arm drilled into the side of the mountain. The behemoth squirmed and oinked and struggled to pull free from the spoiled earth. His fury made him blind to anything else but hurting the weak one beneath him. Father Pig had spent decades terrorizing the meek here, and he did not like such a little critter disobeying his will. The Way of the Pig made him rabid for her suffering. The Age of Filth had begun, and the Lumenswine cried out for pig justice. When sheets of ancient stone cracked, and the quaking mountain fell to pieces, its milky eyes looked up in prayer.

Above him, The Needle—the chimney of Orphan Rock—broke free. It toppled onto its side and slid down the mountain on a conveyer of boulders. When it fell over the cliffside, it dropped like a spear tip, impaling the Gloom Boar's desiccated chest. Waves of shadow splashed from his wound, and pure darkness, like tar, painted its necrotic flesh the color of coal. The desert demon squealed like a scared piglet, struggling to yank the shard from its rancid breast, but it was too late. The Needle sunk further, pushed down by gravity, and punctured his hairy back. More shadows and lashing tentacles spilled from the deadly wound— The Dark itself—as the Harbinger of Filth buckled, yet again chained to the sacred desert it could never escape.

Elizabeth from Oklahoma stood up from the ground and dusted off her dirty Keds. She watched the monster, the fallen pig god, die a second time. The silver leaves on the Dead Tree turned brown and brittle, and the Gloom Boar's reverberating breaths turned shallow until it made no sound at all.

Sister Crow soared through the doors in The Dark, following Delora's dead scent as deep into The Pig's box as she could go. The Deepest Door. There, in the Heart of the Desert, the Crooked Woman waited beneath the beating heart of the Grim Seed. The space around her was a macabre cathedral. Puppets flew in and out, dumping flesh and bones into bins with metal teeth.

Shelby landed behind her, eyes glowing with hatred in the shadows. "No more running, Mother. I'm going to kill you. I'm not your fucking slave anymore."

Flies covered Delora's wizened body, but she did not move. Sister Crow's claws turned rigid.

Her grin hungry for death.

In the shifting cistern, giant gears clanked in the vacuous shadows. Somebody somewhere screamed for help. Blood oozed from a mysterious boil on the wall. A thrumming heartbeat intensified as a legion of mantises delivered more misery to feed the machine. And then came the echoing *Thwack!* when Sister Crow's talons pierced the skin of the Crooked Woman's brittle back, punching through and out of her ancient chest. Crow's sharky smile, one of triumph and dominance, shifted when the Harpy of Ghost River crumbled like a sandcastle.

"What the fuck?" When the cave breeze picked up, Delora blew away on warm gusts.

"Sister," an unfamiliar voice said.

Sister Crow spun around, claws at the ready to strike. The tawny eyes of an unfamiliar woman greeted her. Tall, elegant, and dressed in a meticulously beaded frontier dress. Shelby spread her wings, ready for a fight. *"Who the hell are you?"*

"I am a builder, a shaper of worlds, and a lover of children," the stranger replied, walking past the young harpy to the dust pile. She watched Delora blow away with some fascination, perhaps a hint of sorrow in her honeyed eyes. "This was my shadow, what was left behind to serve the Grim Seed. Now, it has been watered, and her service ends."

"Your shadow? You're Delora?"

"No. That name does not belong to me. I am Sister Dirt."

Shelby recalled the name from Snarl's lessons when she was a child. Sister Dirt lived in the river and stole children from Father Pig until one day, he put her in a magical birdcage. A punishment for saving souls and the lives of some of her kindred sisters. "You're the one that planted the Grim Seed, aren't you?"

"No. I did not plant it. That was my shadow's choice. I gave my life to make amends. Now, *vengeance is mine.*" Sister Dirt looked around the Heart of the Desert with pride. "We have won. This day is for celebration. Justice is served."

"*Justice?*" Sister Crow backed away from Sister Dirt. Around her, guts spewed from pipes while a mad Stitcher threaded his rusty needle in the darkness. "How is this justice? I've spent my entire life in a cage, and it's all your fucking fault!"

"Now you're talking like a pig!" the alpha harpy snapped. "He was cruel to children. Cruel to me. Cruel to our Sisters. Cruel to you. Now, The Pig will spend eternity chained to this hungry leviathan, and when the world of men come to destroy it with their toys of war, he will become dust too."

"You're insane," Sister Crow replied, eyes aflame. "Your little revenge plot is going to destroy the world."

"You may think my actions are driven by revenge, and yes, that was part of this creation, but not all of it." Sister Dirt's face softened. "Come. Let me show you something."

Shelby followed her to the Chapel of the Vile Hibiscus, the purple-petaled blossom that grew from the chest of a strange body in a sanctuary of twisting bloodroot. Sister Crow studied the petrified creature—larger than a man—with twin, tarnished tusks sprouting from its stone jaw set beneath a granite pig snout.

"Here is where the real curse began," Sister Dirt said, watching the young harpy investigate the primeval corpse. "Many ages ago, this was the first Prophet to come through the Deeper than the Deepest Door. Yes, child, there are places even darker and lower than this Heart of the Desert. Those places are filled with pigs and other foul beasts who want to be free. They yearn to hurt children, torture for pleasure, and abuse all the life in the world without regard for conservation. Below this shell, this ancient corpse is that door. This Pig came here as the first Prophet of the Age of Filth, but he would not be the last. Many wait to travel here. Many worse than Father Pig."

Sister Crow stroked the soft petals of the Vile Hibiscus. It vibrated at her touch. It whispered to her, and she leaned in. Suddenly, she saw black roots cracking into a world wrapped in chains and bathed in blood. It burrowed through the Heart of the Desert into the Deeper Door to what could only be described as Hell. There, she witnessed shadows and bleeding monsters writhing in bramble. They cried in agony as Sister Dirt's Grim Seed spoiled the desecrated sludge around their hooves.

"The Grim Seed was meant to weaken The Pig, yes, but even more it was meant to poison the dark well from which he came. From this world, it reaches into the next, and from there, the realms even deeper than that. It will never end."

Sister Crow stood from the flower. "The King of Pigs tricked you. He said the Grim Seed was from the very same place you claim it now attacks. That the suffering we fed it only made The Pig stronger, not weaker. He said it would resurrect him."

"My Grim Seed is special."

"Special how?"

"It is a vessel for a potent weapon," Sister Dirt replied. "Filled with not only rage and hatred but with all of the burdens of my *love*. The demons cannot spurn it so easily. Love is a poison to them, and they have no understanding of it. It will not end the Age of Filth, but it will stem the Tide of Shadows." Sister Dirt smiled. "Fear not, chickling. The boon it gave to The Pig is only temporary, and I have already shaped a contingency to strip all that he has left away from this land."

Shelby turned back to the flower, back to the hellish world hidden beneath the surface of things. "So…we're *demons?*" A small grin appeared on Sister Crow's face. "Cool."

"We are many things." Sister Dirt folded her long arms and offered a delicious smirk. "Now that you are free, you'll have a lifetime to shape what they are. Tell your own story."

"Free?" Sister Crow scoffed. "Newsflash, lady, but I ate the dirt. There's no free for me."

The elder harpy pointed a curved finger at the Vile Hibiscus. "Ask it to release you. The Grim Seed favors you now. It knows you are not the enemy."

"*What?* Just ask? That's all I had to do?"

"No." Sister Dirt laughed. "It would not have listened before. Now watered, it listens intently."

Sister Crow knelt next to the lavender bloom. She felt the cool filaments and ghostly fingers tickle the skin of her palm. It waited for her words and shimmied with expectation.

"*Let me go, you fucking Grim Seed.*"

The petals ruffled, chimes twinkled in jubilation, and Luminarchs circled above as the young harpy sniffed the open bloom. She inhaled, and purifying pollen dusted her nostrils. A great shudder started from her belly and rose to her head. She bowled over and coughed up a pile of unholy dirt. When she was empty, the Vile Hibiscus dimmed, and its petals closed again. When Sister Crow rose to her feet, unshackled from the burdens of the dirt curse, Sister Dirt waited by a shimmering door.

"You are free," she said. "As am I. You may leave this land and find your own way, or you may come with me and learn. Either way, you will shape, create, and feed to live. Be warned, however, that this world is not safe from what is coming. The Age of Filth has begun, and some fates cannot be escaped from."

"I want to learn how to open and shape doors," Crow said eagerly. "Your shadow and her minions wouldn't teach me."

"Of course, they would not!" Sister Dirt laughed, eyes twinkling with wisdom. "My shadow was no fool. If you had the key to open your own cage you'd fly away, wouldn't you?"

"In a fucking heartbeat."

"That is the easy part. *Opening doors.* But it does require practice. When you are a true builder, you can do so much more than you've ever dreamed of. Your boon is—"

"Destruction," Shelby interjected. "*I'm really good at breaking shit in style.*"

Sister Dirt smiled, noting a little bit of herself in the eager child who wanted to shape worlds. "Well, from destruction comes creation, and I am quite adept at that." The alpha harpy pulled open the portal, revealing a fantastic realm—a vast jungle with golden temples on hills and two suns shining in the sky. "I can show you some ways if you'd like. The choice is yours."

Sister Crow liked the sound of that. Choice. "All right," she said. "We'll hang out for a while. I could use a change of scenery anyway." She retrieved her sandbox oasis from her tattered boot. "Hope you don't mind, but I brought some company. They're annoying, but they're my kind of annoying."

"As you wish, chickling." Sister Dirt offered the young harpy her slender hand.

"Sister Crow."

"As you wish, *Sister Crow.*"

Shelby took the elder harpy's claw, pleased to meet her new Mother. They walked into the portal together, two godlings ready to cut and shape the curvatures of every universe. "Hope you get MTV in there," Shelby said, perfectly serious.

"When this body dies, I'll steal me a fuckin' new one!" The Lumenswine tried to tug himself out of the dead Gloom Boar's skull. Liz stood nearby, watching the piglet thrash. His blue wings had been torn apart like weathered sails, his arm didn't move, and his legs had become oily black roots. "I am the stain in the dirt, the filth that cannot be washed from the hills! I am the King of Pigs. The first Prophet of the Age of Filth come to claim your world. *Do not underestimate me!*"

Slurp!

The Lumenswine dribbled from the little dirty hole. He slithered down the cheek of the dead Gloom Boar and spilled onto the ground. The King of Pigs lit up to see Liz standing over him. "Little Lamb! You are just in time to help me out. I'll forgive you for this mess. I know you didn't *mean it.* Mistakes happen."

Liz crossed her arms.

"Come on! Don't be like that. *Delora was no saint either!* Not a fucking saint to be seen out here in Ghost River." He craned his neck to see her better. "Let's you and I cut a deal: I'll put you back in that pretty room with the windows. Would you like that?"

Liz tapped her foot.

"*Don't be a dumb bitch! Together we can make miracles happen.*" The Pig looked around nervously when the bushes rustled. Nailed kneecaps. Stilts wrapped in wire. Shaved, stitched-up heads. Eyeballs replaced by bottlecaps. Toes stapled together like sutures. Busted teeth captured in bloody smiles. The Broken Kids gathered behind Liz, and she still said nothing. A few of them pulled a wooden box up the hill on chains.

"What are you doing, my little piglets? *You get away from me.*" The Lumenswine rolled over and tried to crawl away. He would find a hole and slip back into The Dark.

Liz didn't budge.

Clink! Clink! Clink!

Broken Kids dropped their spikes, knives, hatchets, hammers, chains, and sickles. Their stitches burst, and blood, dirt, and maggots spilled from their twisting faces as they released their spirits. Purple cactus flowers bloomed from their dead eyes, and green hummingbirds zipped around their crumbling bodies to drink the nectar from their sockets. A haunting army of

Luminarchs rose from their abandoned shapes—beautiful creatures formed from souldust and ghost parts. Liz opened her arms to welcome them, and they wrapped around her, melding into her form. She made space for all the liberated orphans. In return, she grew into Vengeant one more time.

"Get away!" the Father Pig squealed again as the giant Broken Girl picked him up from the ground. He was so small, this pig who wanted to be a king. In the end, he was only able to become a tiny boy with broken butterfly wings. Fragile and important. He squirmed, a baby against her breast.

While hundreds of children cheered inside of her, Vengeant placed the Lumenswine inside of the Quiet Box. The Pig tried to claw out, visible fear stretching across its black-veined face. "No! *Fuck you!* I am the filth! I am the stain in the dirt—"

Slam!

Vengeant closed the Quiet Box—

I am floating.

I am nowhere.

I am no one.

—and The Pig was gone.

The children cheered when The Broken Girl heaved the casket over her shoulder and traveled down the river rock path. Around her, more Broken Kids became souldust and joined her procession. She led them to the edge of the Old Sinkhole. Not one more tear was shed when he fell into the Deepest Door, locked in a prison of darkness that would never let him be free again. A god without a flock. A king with no crown. A pig with no name that would never be prayed to again. The orphans were free!

You are not Liz. Liz is dead. Her story is over.

But Liz had one more part of her story left to tell.

The End.

The Luminarchs congregated in celebration, each one flaring and igniting in sparks of powerful energy. A crackle of last life, igniting a blue fire that burned beneath her paws as the ghostmetal lioness ran for the edge of Orphan Rock.

Nothing would stop her.

She would tear it all down.

Whomp!

Magnificent butterfly wings sprouted from her back, and the angelic manticore soared over the edge of the Grim Seed. Her paws flexed when silver claws burst through her soft pads.

Insectoid marionettes tried to stop her, but crumbled to ash, incinerated by a sizzle of blue energy—the rage of the lost and taken—which wrapped her form in a protective aura.

Vengeant roared when she hooked one of the Worms of Colossus that lumbered along in its dredging of Sandoval. Powerless against her strength, she yanked it behind her, pulling the Misery Machine itself along for the ride.

The flying mountain bellowed in protest, gears stripping, steam blowing out of vents at the bottom of the unholy machination that only had one protocol: devour.

On the ground was a mirror of purifying light. Pieces of Vengeant lost in the fight with the Gloom Boar. She aimed for it, pulled with all her vigor, and plunged headlong into the shimmering silver lake that flooded the besieged city.

When she struck the surface, it broke like glass, and Vengeant felt the souls of the scorned take her under. Thousands of dead hands pulled the worm she carried into the undertow.

Soon, waves of blue energy splashed down the streets of Sandoval, washing more fiends away into the ether. Falling, the Grim Seed drowned in a river of ghosts.

From the helicopter above the shattered city, Esther and Macho watched the Grim Seed sink into the spirit lake beneath them. The dread jellyfish drifted slowly into the radiant waters that vanished like a mirage in the high desert sun.

All of it was over. Dying before Esther's eyes.

It was the prettiest goddamn thing she'd ever seen.

Minister promised her exactly this, hadn't he?

When she glanced over at Wallace Machado, who loved her and wanted her to have more than either one of them ever thought possible, she decided watching Orphan Rock disappear was a pretty fucking decent way to end a Monday morning. She gave Delora and the King of Pigs the fucking bird one last time.

Macho chuckled. "Feel better?"

She nodded and grabbed his hand.

Really felt it this time.

No more pretending.

Acknowledgments

Thank you for reading my book! Ghost River is a story that came to me like shards of broken glass: in pieces and connected to a different novel I intended to write. After separating the Siamese twins, Orphan Rock and its residents were born.

It took eight months to write this piece, and I owe my family a thousand thanks for letting me slip into the desert during that time. They kept me together, especially when I felt like I couldn't unravel this ball of yarn, which, by the way, was often! Without their love and support, and their willingness to sacrifice their time with me, I wouldn't have made it. They are my heart.

Secondly, I would like to thank my dear friend, editor, and business partner Ashley Hutchison for her contributions to this piece. She spent a lot of time in Ghost River, and her brilliant contributions are everywhere in this tale, left behind like petroglyphs on a cave wall. With her support and professional expertise, Ghost River flourished like a cactus bloom.

I would also like to thank Micah Chaim Thomas for his enduring support of the project. Not only did he beta-read the work, but he also supplied the cover art and marketing pieces. Micah is a great friend, an old soul, and a supremely talented artist and writer. Check out his work: micahchaimthomas.com.

Next, I owe a debt of gratitude to Perry Wolfecastle (perrywolfecastle.com), who beta read Ghost River in its early stage and provided critical feedback on the project. Perry's been a fantastic supporter and friend, and he's one to watch as he begins his own writing journey across the pond.

Lastly, I would like to thank all of my friends (in real life and online) who have helped through this process. Without your support and love, Dark would have been a prison.

About the Author

Chad Ryan lives in the Arizona badlands. He grew up running in the arid mountains, catching lizards and scorpions in a burgeoning suburb next to an Indian Reservation.

He is a managing partner of Lost Boys Press, an independent publisher of daring fiction (lostboyspress.com). He also runs the substack *Broken Window*, and his blog: writingiswar.com

When not writing dark, spooky, or fantastical tales, he enjoys fitness, craft beer, rock music, and video games.

Find him on Twitter: @writingiswar

Printed in Great Britain
by Amazon